ALL·RISKS MORTALITY

ALL · RISKS
MORTALITY

A
NOVEL
BY

Peter Cunningham

LITTLE, BROWN AND COMPANY • BOSTON

FIRST U.S. EDITION ·

Library of Congress Cataloging-in-Publication Data

All risks mortality.

I. Title.
PR6062.A778A79   1988   823'.914   87-36158
ISBN 0-316-16460-7

*The characters and events in this book are fictitious.
Any similarity to real persons, living or dead, is
coincidental and not intended by the author.*

RRD VA

Designed by Jeanne Abboud

PRINTED IN THE UNITED STATES OF AMERICA

For
NICKY AND REDMOND

"We shall . . . vanish into the atmosphere, dissolved into atoms, one of these days."

— Albert Einstein writing to
President Roosevelt, 1939

PROLOGUE

"LES CHEVAUX SONT SOUS LES ORDRES"

The vast crowd turned their binoculars on the green, steel starting-stalls, to the left of Longchamps' famous windmill. The loading-up process was well under way: over half of the twenty-six runners were in stalls.

To those jockeys who had time to look, the stands to their right were a huge block of humming noise, towering up from one of the widest straights in racing. They had come from all over the world to ride in this race, which numbered in its field the winners of five individual Derbys as well as the champions of no less than eleven other races in the Group One category. The collective worth of these horses was inestimable; it had been suggested that morning by *Paris Turf* that their total value exceeded the current trade deficit of France.

The winner here on this sunny October afternoon would gallop into the stud book a great champion. No one ever forgot a horse that won the Prix de l'Arc de Triomphe.

Sitting perfectly still, four berths from the inside rail, Gus Trilby patted the moist neck of the horse beneath him. Cornucopia! Despite the fact that he was forty-two and had done it a million times before, Gus still could feel his heart hammering away beneath his bright silks. This time the stakes were so high. It was bad enough for Cornucopia to start the money-on favorite in a race with six or seven other potential champions; it was bad enough for your face to be beamed live to places as far away as Hong Kong and Venezuela; but to also have the world's biggest syndication for a stallion depend on your victory was asking a bit much. Gus's eyes darted left and right. Nearly all in. He pulled down his goggles.

"*Partis.*"

High up in the stands, in a large, private *loge* situated exactly opposite the winning-post, a number of dark-suited men turned their attention to the race which had just begun. One of them, seated at the front, concentrated with an intensity even greater than his associates. He was in his middle sixties but with a ramrod figure, pencil-slim. His head was domed and covered in white hair, combed straight back from a high forehead. Spectacles with heavy lenses in tortoiseshell frames shielded eyes of pale, almost diaphanous blue; they dominated his face, which had deep lines down either side of the nose causing the cheeks to sag in sacks of empty flesh. Surprisingly thick, hairy wrists ran down to rock-steady hands holding Zeiss binoculars, which were trained unwaveringly on the scene below him.

"*Avant le Petit Bois.*"

He narrowed his eyes to pick out more clearly the horse that carried his first colors — no less than three participants in the race ran in his name, the most famous by far for its achievements in this racing season: that of Carlo Galatti.

Behind Galatti and slightly to his right sat a woman one-third his age. She was dressed in white, her long, red hair elaborately arranged under a wide-brimmed, black sombrero. Barbara Galatti glanced again in the small compact mirror, turning her classically structured model's face with its full mouth, the high cheekbones and the eyes which with a slight upturn hinted at the exotic. She would look her very best for the *paparazzi* whom she would in all probability meet in about five and a half minutes. Then the moment would be hers as she led in the sweating, snorting animal to the adulation of all Paris and the world. She felt a tingle of anticipation spread through her. The whole world gazing at her face and body, acknowledging her success: that was the stuff of pure excitement.

"*Après le Petit Bois.*"

"Cornucopia, he goes well?"

The question was addressed to Galatti by a swarthy-skinned man of

Middle Eastern appearance, with thick, sensuous lips below a caterpillar of black hair.

"I think so," Galatti replied. Without taking his eyes from the race, he leaned slightly back to a younger man with tight, red curls. "What do you think?" Galatti asked.

The younger man's binoculars were also unwavering. "He's okay."

Carlo Galatti nodded briefly to his original questioner, who then in turn leaned back to a man seated behind him. There was a rapid exchange in Arabic.

"Approchant la ligne droite."

Carlo Galatti's eyes were targeted on the famous blue-and-red colors hugging the rails as the great wall of horses rounded the sweeping bend at the top of the straight. He could see Gus Trilby's bobbing head as he sought to restrain Cornucopia, to hold him up for the final effort which in seconds would be demanded. Luck, thought Galatti, you always had to have luck. Planning got you to the start but luck delivered.

Suddenly there was a crescendo in the noise of the crowd. From the swell of ten thousand throats the name "Cornucopia" was now distinctly audible.

"A trois cents mètres de l'arrivée."

Cornucopia, still running on the far rail, was now fractionally in the lead and making for home as fast as he could; but on his outside a veritable cavalry of his opponents loomed right across the course, held for this moment to make their challenge. This was where Gus Trilby's tactics would pay off or not. The little man increased his momentum on the colt's back and began to show the animal the whip in a stabbing, driving motion. Cornucopia edged ahead, now the leader by a neck, and the crowd's roar rose to a new pitch.

"A cent mètres de l'arrivée."

Inside the final furlong it seemed as if the rapidly closing line of horses must engulf Cornucopia. Carlo Galatti's knuckles showed white on his binoculars.

"Come on Trilby!" he hissed through clenched teeth.

With the ability for which he was famous, Gus Trilby urged the animal to lengthen his stride even more. One moment his supple body drove forward in an extended arch near the horse's head, the next his flailing whip hand was at the beast's quarters, digging in for the very final reserve of speed. Cornucopia's head, his eyes wide, stuck straight out from his body in effort; they might have been a centimeter in front. The entire box rose to its feet. Nothing else could be heard. Nothing else mattered. Gus Trilby punched at exactly the right moment.

"Yes!"

The man behind Galatti leaped in the air. The two Arabs grabbed each other's hands and then Carlo Galatti's. Barbara Galatti stole a side-ways glance at her husband. His tongue darted out iguana-like and licked his upper lip; otherwise he appeared unmoved. Then slowly he rose to his feet, a look of triumph on his face.

"Come, my lovely," he said to his wife.

Her face glowing, she faced him. "Now you are glad you came to Europe," she whispered.

To the hurrahs of the people on either side they made their way out, past the smiling Arabs, the younger man with the red hair, and the final occupant of their box, a huge, silent man, whose eyes resembled armored observation slits, and whose solid, pink head was square at both ends and devoid of any hair. Wordlessly this man closed behind Carlo Galatti as the jubilant party made their way to an elevator and then down and out to the sacred turf of Longchamps.

Gus Trilby stood high in his irons as gradually he allowed Cornucopia to lose speed. It had taken all of Trilby's thirty years of experience and every ounce of his strength to settle the horse during the race and then to deliver it in front at the finish. They were at the far side of the course now, not far from the famous Petit Bois. Gus Trilby turned the colt and began to half-walk, half-jog back down the bottom of the track.

Horse and rider arrived at the top end of the stands and the Parisian crowd started their famous welcome, reserved for the big race winner.

"Treelbee!" they roared, "allez Treelbee!"

Gus Trilby was grinning from ear to ear. This was the part he loved — God, he would be inhuman not to. For one thing he was a hundred grand better off, but this was something else. He sat against the world's most expensive animal, showing the crowd the riding style that was uniquely his. Up ahead he could see the running mass of photographers and TV reporters who had swarmed onto the course. He was at the center of the vast auditorium; to his right the crowds in the cheap enclosure pressed five deep at the restraining fence to get a look at their champion.

"Treelbee!" was the roar, repeated again and again.

A groom came to catch Cornucopia's head. At the exit to the track there was a fresh commotion: Gus could see Carlo Galatti and his wife, pursued by a fresh flock of men with cameras, stride out to greet their victor. The horse jinked, then without warning a section of restraining fence collapsed, spilling several hundred enthusiastic Parisians out onto the turf. They were good-natured and formed a cheering, heaving circle around the Galattis and their wonder horse.

Then something extraordinary happened.

From his elevated position Gus could see an old woman, part of the crowd, approaching the nucleus of everyone's attention. She wore a thick, black woollen jacket with bright, red embroidery down its front. She was quite bent, her hair white, her face yellowish and dominated by an unmistakably Semitic nose. Cornucopia performed a side-stepping dance, causing the crowd to scatter back.

"Watch out!" cried Gus to the woman, who was perilously close. But his warning went unheeded. Instead, she stood as if riveted to the greensward, her mouth hanging open and gasping for the breath which had deserted her body. At that moment Galatti turned and saw her.

Although it was the moment of his greatest triumph, it was the look on Carlo Galatti's face that Gus would never forget.

PART ONE

1　THE WIND WHIPPED UP SCHOTTEN RING CAUSING THE BUSI-
nessmen hurrying to lunch from the Börse to turn their collars
up and curse the first flurries of the snow that would certainly
follow.

In the second-story office of Franz Josefs Kai the bulky man shifted
in his chair and stared again at the photographs arranged in front of
him. He was in his mid-sixties and very wide, nearly a yard across; his
head was also large with thinning gray hair. He had a thin, graying
mustache that ran irregularly over his curving mouth. He sat in his
shirtsleeves, his suspenders for the moment off his shoulders, his big
hands holding a blown-up print. In the office around him were twenty
steel cabinets, each containing hundreds of files meticulously annotated
and cross-referenced; there was a photocopier and a paper shredder, and
two big windows fitted with venetian blinds. He put down the photograph and picked up a one-page typed report, scanning through it for
the third time. It was enough. He picked up the telephone.

An hour later in the back of a tiny coffee-shop near Stephansplatz he
was joined by a man roughly thirty years his junior. This man looked
fit to competition level. He had hair between dark brown and black;
his very clear, deep brown eyes were of unwavering intensity. His skin
was sallow, the skin of the Levant.

"There's no doubt?" he asked.

"No doubt, Yanni," answered the older man. His Hebrew was heavily accented. "Apart from the original woman in Paris, we now have

three other witnesses who, from the photographs, swear it is he. This report of Dr. Anton's confirms it. Although he is obviously much older, the circumference of the head is the same." He fumbled in a worn leather briefcase and took out prints which he spread on the table. "The glasses are a disguise," he said. "The thick lenses suggest poor eyesight and distort the shape of the actual eyes themselves. But using new American techniques, Dr. Anton has been able to remove the spectacles and show us the eyes without them." He pointed to a photograph. "See the small scar over the left eyebrow?" he said. "That was always there."

Yanni's mouth was grim. "We have been monitoring him, as you know," he said. "Since his visit to France — and that was over two years ago — he has been extremely careful. No further trips to Europe and just one last October to the Middle East."

"The Lord has strange ways," said his companion.

The two men drank their coffee. Yanni collected the photographs and put them in their brown envelope.

"Any further progress on the background?" he asked. He wore the collar of his white shirt open. There was a physical quality about even his simplest movements which suggested competence.

"It's gradually coming together," answered his companion. "It's a huge jigsaw; shortly I hope to have all the pieces. We now know that in 1946 the Papal Nuncio in Buenos Aires gave him a temporary visa — that was when he assumed his present name. It seems he jumped ship in New York Harbor, perhaps in 1948, married a U. S. citizen, and later became naturalized. Soon after, he divorced her and remarried. He has lived in New York incognito ever since."

Yanni put the envelope into an inside pocket.

"This is way beyond my authority," he said.

The older man nodded.

"The time is gone," said Yanni, "when the blood ran warm in all our veins — the spirit of the *aliyas*." He looked at the shrewd old eyes. "Now it is different. Now everything in Jerusalem is talk: talk about money, about inflation, about how the world perceives us. Once we fought, now we talk. The Arabs have done their job well. Today in the eyes of the West it is we who are the aggressors."

"And what is their talk of history?"

There was no mistaking the depth of feeling in the question.

"Maybe," the younger man said, "that too is a problem — too much history. The world grows deaf from a surfeit of righteous insistence. The human mind is a fickle palate: too much sweet, then it demands sour. Cairo has recently begun to publish learned articles that suggest the Holocaust was a myth."

"That is why," said the older man leaning forward urgently, "that is why something like this cannot be allowed to slip. The trial of such a beast in Jerusalem will demonstrate beyond doubt the hideous reality."

"The thing has become very complex," said Yanni. "Our commercial section in Washington may have unwittingly complicated matters for us."

The old face frowned puzzlement.

"It is true," Yanni nodded. "For years they have been pressuring the U.S. Justice Department to investigate his company for anti-Semitic discrimination. Now just when we don't need it, it seems that something may be about to happen."

The other man shook his head in exasperation.

"Anything that could upset the Americans," Yanni continued, "is anathema in Jerusalem. Everything has changed, each move must be cleared, each target sanctioned." His brown eyes bored into the old head. "It is possible that in this case they will insist we go the extradition route."

"That, as you know, is hopeless," said the old man in despair. "An extradition request could go all the way to the Supreme Court in Washington — there is no guarantee it would succeed. And who's to say he would live that long?" He wiped the straggling line of his mustache with a paper napkin, which he then balled tightly in frustration. "The things he did," he said in a whisper, "a beast would never."

They sat in silence. Then the Israeli spoke:

"They lived in dread of botching up something like this," he said quietly. "Of taking the wrong person."

The older man leaned slowly forward, his mouth quivering. For a moment the Israeli thought that he was going to catch his hands in his. The large face was shining in supplication.

"At the right time," he promised fervently, "you will have all the information you need: the size of his shoes, birthmarks, a dental chart from 1932, even his blood type which is tattooed underneath his left armpit." He smiled grimly at the Israeli. "Oh yes," he said, "it was standard procedure."

A clock ticked somewhere in the back of the wood-paneled *Kaffehaus*. It was busier in the mornings and later on, when people came out for an evening aperitif. Outside, the honking of horns and the roar of traffic signaled the start of Vienna's rush hour.

"I am going to Jerusalem tonight," said Yanni slowly. He saw the other's anxious face. "I'll recommend that a plan is put into action."

The big face broke into a smile.

"Thank you," he said. "Justice will be done."

"The Americans won't like it," said the younger man.

The older man shrugged.

"People have short memories," he replied. "Justice is frequently unpalatable."

The younger man rose and with a brief nod made his way out through the door of the coffee shop, turning left on Wollzeile.

Ten minutes later the older man followed. His step was lighter than when he had arrived.

2 THE BEAUTIFUL WOMAN AT THE CENTER OF THE CROWD HAD reached the stage of welcome isolation.

The work over, she had politely refused the sparkling wine, the canapes of pâtés and smoked fish.

Everything that should have been said to her had been said.

She stood with her hands before her, her face composed in its usual serenity. With a slight movement she shook out her long, red hair and glanced at the wall clock of the college's great hall. In another ten minutes she could decently leave.

The chattering men and women around her had the relaxed air of academics freeloading in their natural habitat. They had almost forgotten her. A slightly bemused man, tall, with a fussy bow-tie, steered another, smaller, bespectacled man in her direction.

"My dear, this is Professor Dunstan, our visiting professor of architecture."

She took the hand, smiled politely at the beaming face with its incandescent network of ruptured veins, then cocked her head into its listening mode.

"This is a wonderful privilege," she heard him say. "Your husband must be a wonderful man. . . ." She blanked him out.

She had seen the eyes about five minutes before. Now, startlingly, they reappeared over the soundless mouth of her current penance; start-lingly, because of their cool clarity, their deep brown, unwavering in-tensity, their . . . vibrancy. She allowed her own eyes to leave the red face in front of her and to explore casually what surrounded these new orbs. She saw dark, tanned skin, hair not quite black, an open-necked shirt — a body in condition.

There was something else, something suddenly familiar. Then it hit. She saw like her, in the teeming blare of crowded noise, an island.

She was amazed to feel a sudden heat, a glow at her core. As if an anesthetic was retreating, her senses began to reawaken.

". . . make these endowments of such importance."

She looked at the silly little man as if she had just seen him. Then she saw lips, full, yet firm, smiling mockingly.

"Riveting."

A smile tugged her mouth; her tongue ran out minutely.

"I see your hair as a great, red cloak, something to wrap in when I'm cold, something to hide in when I am afraid."

The voice was even, cool.

The sound of the great hall was now a great, crashing sea, somewhere far-off.

"Or the frame around a priceless masterpiece."

He was a head taller than she. He radiated an energy, a physical competence that she thought she had forgotten.

She wanted to touch. He must have sensed it, for he allowed the fingers of his lowered hand to brush the back of hers. The glow became a brush-fire. She felt claustrophobic.

"What is your name?" he asked as they left the crowded hall behind.

"Barbara," she said, her voice strange, thick.

She scarcely noticed the chill blast of night air as he opened the door.

"My name is Simon," he said.

She linked arms with him as they walked across the cold quadrangle, over grass that crinkled underfoot, past rows of cars, all empty, except for one, whose lone occupant had denied himself the comfort of the heater for fear of making noise and who surveyed the departing couple through eyes that were fissures in a pink, solid head.

PART TWO

FEBRUARY
3–8

MONDAY: P.M.

3
"FORTY, THIRTY."
Matt Blaney walked to the net and bent for the ball. Although it was nearly freezing he was sweating lightly. High above them, in the darkness beyond the arc lights, he could hear the buzz of traffic on Riverside Drive. To his left was the quiet of the Hudson and, far beyond, the lights of New Jersey. He walked back to the base-line and filled his chest with cold air. He was in his late thirties, over six feet tall, broad across the shoulders. His face was strong, ending in a square, cleft chin. His black hair fell across his forehead and licked over the tops of his ears, its blackness emphasized by his eyebrows, two elongated sweeps above deep, gray eyes. The eyes were constantly changing: one moment the gray was soft, gentle; now, under the artificial lights of the tennis court, Matt Blaney's eyes were steel-gray and hard.

He could see his opponent weave in anticipation. He was a stocky man, bald, a bachelor, a successful architect, a left-hander with a powerful return. Matt watched him edging minutely toward the center of the advantage court, pretending not to have moved, but maneuvering to protect his backhand. Matt bounced the ball twice, steadied, then floated it up high over his head. As the adrenaline juiced into him, Matt arched after the ball, as high as he could go, so that at the very limit of his extension the racket in his right hand blurred forward, connected, and sent the yellow ball over the net and skidding down the line. The architect ran to the net, his hand out. "Well done, Matt." Matt shook the outstretched hand. "Thanks, Paul."

The two men hurried from the cold night toward the small, cement-block changing room. Jets of scalding water filled the shower room with steam.

"I think this is the only reason I play tennis," Matt Blaney said with a laugh.

There was a contrast in their bodies: the architect's was pear-shaped, now glowing red, a physique that he had to work hard on; Matt's body was that of the natural athlete, long and hard, his chest covered in a sheen of hair that ran like a black river to his loins. Muscles rippled down his back, to a white scar, the length of a man's finger and the shape of a crescent.

"I think the only reason you play tennis is so that you can beat me." Paul smiled. "Hey, how about a beer?"

"Sorry, Paul," Matt said. "I've got a dinner date, I'll have to rush."

"Sounds promising. Anyone I know?"

Matt stepped from the shower and began to towel himself. "I'm seeing Delis," he said quietly.

"I see," Paul said.

They got dressed and walked to the parking lot together. They both wore heavy coats; Matt's coat collar was turned up around his neck against the cold. Paul squeezed Matt's arm as the taller man bent to open the door of a low, red car.

"See you Thursday, usual time," Paul said.

"See you," said Matt Blaney.

There had been a time when just the sight of Delis would have been enough to make Matt smile. Small, vibrant Delis with the perfect face. Matt looked across the restaurant and saw her distantly, not a stranger — a stranger would create mystery, even excitement — but distantly. All feeling was long gone. Their conversation of the past hour had been formal and vapid, no punch line, although Matt knew that the punch line would soon come. Still classically photogenic, in a floral-patterned dress, its downward sweep from her throat emphasizing her breasts, she strode toward him; he saw the people on either side looking up as she passed. Delis had blond shoulder-length hair, perfectly coiffured, framing her face. Great face, perfect hair. A waiter hurried to pull out her chair.

"Will there be anything further?" the waiter inquired.

Matt looked at Delis and she shook her head. "Just some more coffee," Matt said.

Delis allowed Matt to light her cigarette, then blowing smoke from the corner of her mouth, she put her elbows on the table.

"I assume since you haven't mentioned it," she said, sweetly, "there's no change in your . . . status at Insurance Fidelity."

Matt brushed hair back from his forehead.

"No change," he said. "Why do you ask?"

"I just wondered," Delis replied. "I read a lot these days. Companies are forever gobbling each other up. When that happens often people get thrown overboard. I was just wondering if someone had gobbled up Fidelity and I haven't heard."

Matt smiled, a smile of genuine amusement.

"No, Delis," he said, "we're still there, same old office, still halfway down Park Avenue. Call in any time. And be assured that you'll be the first to know if there's any change in our status." He leaned back as the waiter refilled his coffee cup.

"I think you should know I'm seeing an analyst," Delis said apropos of nothing.

Matt blinked. "An analyst? For what?"

Delis stubbed out her cigarette. "I have bad dreams," she said. "The analyst calls them anxiety dreams. They started about six months after we split up. They're horrible, the kind that don't go away when you wake up. The analyst says they're my subconscious fears spilling over. He worries about me."

Matt sighed. "What kind of dreams?"

Delis checked the nearby tables. "Take the most common one," she said. "I call it my cancer dream. In it I'm told that I have cancer — it's always me, no one else gets it — I'm told that I have only a month to live."

Delis gripped the white tablecloth. "The cancer has made me thin. I'm half my usual weight, my face is gone. I'm in some hospital, everyone's being very nice to me, they're trying to get me to come to terms with death. One moment I slip into a kind of peace, I think that death may not be too bad after all, then the next moment I think that it's all so damn . . . unfair." Tears had brimmed into Delis's eyes. Matt took a deep breath.

"Delis, for Jesus sake, you don't have cancer," he said.

"Then there's my murder dream," she said.

Matt closed his eyes. "Delis, I don't want to hear any more," he said.

"Don't you want to know what the analyst says?"

Matt shook his head. "What does he say?"

"That I'm suffering from rejection. That all my life I've been rejected. That when I married you and when you finally rejected me it was too much for me to cope with."

"Delis," said Matt, "you left me to live with another man."

Delis looked at Matt wide-eyed. "Yes, but why?"

Matt sighed. "We've been through —"

"I know we've been through it," she said. "That's why we got divorced. But you survived. Look at me."

"Delis . . ."

"I thought when we got married that I was the only person in your life, Matt. I didn't realize that I wasn't a bride but a widow — I didn't know that my new husband was going to spend more time in a plane than in our bed."

"That is untrue and absurdly unfair," Matt replied quietly. "Unfair because we've been over this ground so often that we both know the facts by heart — and they're not as you tell them."

"Okay, dismiss my condition as something we've been through," Delis said. "File closed. Next please." She lit another cigarette.

Matt closed his eyes for ten seconds, then summoned the waiter.

"Would you like a drink?" he asked.

"A vodka on the rocks," Delis said.

"A vodka on the rocks and an Armagnac," Matt said.

"You abandoned me," Delis said. "You abandoned me for Insurance Fidelity and a little creep named Jim Crabbe."

Matt shook his head.

"You and he have some father-son fixation going," Delis persisted. "It's unnatural."

Matt laughed shortly. "Delis," he said, "you have the smoothest approach of anyone I know." He held up both hands. "Listen, I worked my butt off to fulfill the position of trust that Jim Crabbe gave me in Insurance Fidelity. I started out as a junior claims adjuster and now I'm a partner. All I ever wanted was a good life for us, decent vacations, a nice home. I came home one afternoon when you thought I was in Denver and found you in bed with the guy from upstairs. Why don't

you hassle him about your anxiety dreams — or has he maybe bowed out of the picture?"

They fell silent as the waiter arrived with the drinks. Matt swirled the Armagnac around in the glass and inhaled its aroma.

"Delis," he said quietly, "let's at least retain some mutual respect. Why don't you tell me what it is you want."

Delis looked at him. She had large blue eyes and for a millisecond the fleeting hope presented by his question softened them. Then she straightened. "The analyst says I need a change of environment," she said shortly, "a vacation. There are two girls I've met on Staten Island, they're going to Venezuela for two weeks. I want to join them. The analyst says I should. I need three thousand dollars."

Matt nodded.

"Okay," he said slowly, "okay. You'll have the money in two days." Matt finished his drink and called for the bill.

Delis's smile was almost warm. She tilted her head. "By the way, you shouldn't take it too seriously when I say things about Jim Crabbe. I actually think I kind of like him."

"I don't take anything you say about him seriously," Matt said as he signed the bill, "because I know that anything you ever knew about him, you have almost certainly forgotten."

It was almost midnight when Matt got out of the red Porsche and locked it. He said goodnight to the parking lot's uniformed guard and walked east, the fur collar of his coat warm against his face. He carried an armful of files which he would attend to early the next morning before going to the office. There was a very bright moon, a freezing moon, shining down on the stark, empty street. As after all encounters with Delis, Matt felt exhausted. He reached for his keys as he approached the steps of the building. Lights suddenly flashed. Matt stopped. The lights flashed again, from the curb, then there was the hum of an electric window being lowered. "Good evening."

Matt saw the small face behind the steering wheel of the Rolls.

"Jim," Matt said. "What the hell are you doing here?"

"Listening to Chopin and wondering if this is where you really stay or if it's just a mail drop."

"I was out to dinner," Matt said.

"I've been trying to reach you since five."

"Before that I was playing tennis."

"I need to be able to reach you. I really wish you'd put a telephone in that fifty-grand toy of yours," Jim said. "I'll pay — I'm serious."

"I know you're serious," Matt said. "And I'm freezing standing out here. Come on up."

Matt led the way in and to the elevator. "I spend all of my waking hours and many of my sleeping ones on the problems of Insurance Fidelity," Matt said. "Driving is about the only chance I have to get away from them. I've got Chopin cassettes as well, and Mozart."

"You think you're busy?" said Jim Crabbe. "You should see my schedule."

"You own the company," said Matt, unable to suppress a smile.

"You're a partner," retorted Crabbe sharply.

Matt's smile was undiminished. "I'm a partner, but you own the company," he said.

"So I own the company," Jim Crabbe said. He thrust his chin upward, relieving his neck from the strain of its collar. "So who was the lucky date?" he asked.

"Delis," Matt answered as the elevator doors opened on the third floor.

"How is Delis?" asked Jim as Matt unlocked the apartment door.

"Same as ever," Matt replied.

Jim Crabbe was a short, wiry man with hair cut to the bristle. He had the sharp, quick movements of a sparrow. As his host was large, so everything about him was small — his hands, his feet, the tiny, shining diamonds that linked the french cuffs, and the round, steel spectacles that clung to his weathered chestnut of a face.

Jim threw his coat on a sofa and sat in a chair as Matt went to the kitchen and returned with two beers.

"Cheers," Matt said.

"Cheers," replied Jim. He took a small sip, then put the beer down and leaned back, his hands across his waistcoat. "So what's been happening?" he asked. "I've been tied up with auditors."

"I'm overseeing about half a dozen major claims investigations," Matt replied. "All in the million-plus category." He pointed to the files on the floor. "Including these, which came in over the last couple of days."

"Are they all reinsured?" Jim asked.

"Sure," Matt replied, "but we have to maintain faith with our underwriters. The dirty work is up to us."

Jim nodded and smiled cautiously. "Ever regret having taken all this on?" he asked.

Matt looked at Jim for a long moment. "Nope," he said.

Jim looked at the younger man. "For what it's worth," he said, "I'm kind of pleased with the job you're doing, okay?"

"Okay," Matt said, smiling. "No car phone?"

"Goddammit, even if I insisted you'd disconnect the damn thing," Jim said.

They both laughed. Matt sat back and raised his eyebrows. "Well, let me think of the reason for this late-night visit," he said, looking to the ceiling. "You've gone and underwritten the first private expedition to Mars, they've run out of gas on the far side of the moon and now you want to declare fraud, right?"

Jim Crabbe cocked his head to one side.

"What makes you think of fraud?" he said. "Get up there and bring the mothers back!"

Jim Crabbe's expensive gold bridgework flashed as he drank some beer. He put the can down, then sat forward in the attitude he reserved for business.

"Look," he said, "I am sorry about the time, but I do have a problem."

Matt nodded. He looked at the small eyes with their surrounding web of crow's feet.

"It's like this," said Crabbe joining his hands together. "Two and a half years ago I was in London. We'd had a good year." He sighed and shrugged. "It's always the same story. People are never happy. Most of the trouble you get into is of your own making."

Matt sat back. The sight of the chairman of Insurance Fidelity confessing himself was amusing.

"I was in Lloyd's," continued Crabbe. "I had lunch with Chris Downs of Downs Ashcroft — we do a hell of a lot of business with them, particularly through our agency side, as you know."

Crabbe wet his lips with his beer. "Cast your mind back," he said. "Does the name Cornucopia mean anything to you?"

Matt frowned.

"The horse?" he asked.

Jim Crabbe nodded quickly. "Right first time," he said. "*The* horse. They say the greatest ever. Won everything he ran in. He even made the cover of *Time* magazine."

"Yes, I remember Cornucopia," Matt said.

"Well, like I say, I was lunching with Chris Downs," Crabbe said. "He mentioned something they were placing. It was the insurance on Cornucopia. The horse had just won his last big race and was retiring to stud. It was the biggest all-risks mortality on a racehorse ever placed — two hundred million dollars, absolutely unprecedented."

"I remember reading about it," Matt said.

"Nearly all the insurance was placed, but Downs Ashcroft were running into capacity problems," Jim continued. "They offered me a million, there and then, at four percent. It sounded good, forty grand a year to me without putting my hand in my pocket — if I took it up." Crabbe looked at Matt. "I took it up," he said. "For two years I earned forty grand." He clenched his teeth. "Last night the damn animal died."

"Ouch," said Matt.

"You can say that again," said Jim Crabbe. "And don't ask the obvious question because the answer is no, I didn't reinsure it, and what's more I was greedy and did it in my own name which is why you knew nothing about it and which means I can't write it off against corporate profits. It hurts like hell."

Matt threw his head back.

"What's so damn amusing?" bristled Crabbe.

"I'm sorry, Jim," said Matt. "It's the name: Cornucopia. It could hardly be less appropriate."

Jim Crabbe jinked his cuffs down a millimeter and then nodded.

"You're right," he said, "and it is my own fault. But a million bucks right now is a lot of cash to me."

"What's the time scale?"

Jim shrugged. "The assured have already requested payment in full from Lloyd's." He looked at the gold watch on his wrist. "They could get it within two weeks if they push hard enough."

"It's a regular policy?"

"Sure, a standard Lloyd's livestock policy. Downs Ashcroft do a lot of this kind of business; their attitude to me is, 'Hard luck, old boy, you win some, you lose some.' Lloyd's will have the thing so thinly spread they won't feel a thing. They'll pay as soon as they're happy with the paperwork."

Matt Blaney crossed his legs. "So what's the story?" he asked.

Jim Crabbe leaned forward and steepled his small hands precisely.

"The horse was bred in the purple," he said. "His parents were equine aristocrats, winning nearly everything they ran in. Cornucopia surpassed them. I can't remember precisely, but he smashed every record of every race."

"He won the Derbys in England and Ireland before coming over here to win the Belmont," Matt said. "I went to see him. He made the other horses look ordinary. Then he went back to France where he won the Prix de l'Arc de Triomphe."

Jim nodded slowly. "I remember you were a racing guru," he said. "I'd forgotten how much." Jim reached into his pocket. "Here's a photograph of Cornucopia," he said. "You'll recognize him."

Matt saw a magnificently proportioned animal with a white blaze on his face galloping across a paddock. "That's him," he said. He narrowed his eyes in recall. "I'm trying to remember who owned him."

"A guy called Carlo Galatti — he's big in construction."

"Carlo Galatti," Matt said nodding. "Carlo Galatti and Cornucopia, the unbeatable combination. Didn't I read something a couple of months back, something about Galatti and construction in the Middle East?"

"Probably," Jim said. "Galatti's one of these superrich guys into megaconstruction. He built a whole city for the Saudis a couple of years back."

"That's right," Matt said. "He's really big with the Arabs."

"Well, when Cornucopia retired to stud," said Jim, "some of Galatti's Arab friends took a stake in him. The syndication valued the animal at two hundred million dollars, but Mr. Galatti still hung on to eighty percent."

"So Galatti got forty million bucks cash when the horse retired?"

"Exactly. The horse went to a stud in France owned by Galatti and that's where he's been ever since."

"Until yesterday."

"Evidently a month ago the animal began to be sick. They flew in veterinarians to see him, but they couldn't do a damn thing."

Matt opened two more beers.

"Five days ago things began to go really wrong," said Crabbe. "Lloyd's sent their own vet to France. His brief was to do everything possible to keep the animal alive, but even he had to agree it was hopeless. The horse's guts were twisted like spaghetti — he was rolling around in agony. Last night they all concurred there was only one humane thing to do. They put him down."

Matt shook his head. "Tough," he said.

"I know," Crabbe said. He gritted his teeth and pocketed the photograph. "And the mother's now going to cost me one big one." He ground his jaw in self-admonishment.

"From what you say they seem to have brought a lot of independent experts in," said Matt. "I'm sure they're covered way up beyond their ass in medical documentation."

"Not only that," said Crabbe, "but they've done a postmortem that says the horse had cancerous tumors which caused the whole thing."

Matt Blaney looked at his boss. For the six years that he had been in Insurance Fidelity, no one had ever accused Jim Crabbe of being an easy pay.

"What do you want me to do?" Matt asked gently.

"I don't know," said Crabbe, scratching his white head. "Its hard to judge from over here — but I just have no *feel* for this thing."

Matt smiled. Jim Crabbe's "feel" was famous in Insurance Fidelity.

"What are the outs?" Matt asked.

"Okay," said Crabbe splaying out the small fingers of his left hand and using the index finger of his right to enumerate. "One, value. The horse's insured value was two hundred million bucks. Now this was established exclusively by the syndication arrangements two and a half years ago — I mean a stallion's value is determined by the quality of his offspring and Cornucopia's are still only a year old — so, even if they are all damn useless, that won't be known for another year. That means that when he died his value was still what people paid for him — and that was two hundred million."

"This syndicate — the people who paid forty million for twenty percent and established the horse's value. How do we know they're for real?" Matt asked.

"We don't. They're a combination of Arabs and off-shore companies: Panama, the Bahamas. These could be Galatti in disguise. But money did change hands, so for the moment we're stuck with the valuation. But it's a possibility."

Matt nodded.

"Two." Crabbe hit his second finger. "A horse has got to be in good health when he's insured and when the insurance is renewed. I presume he was. Renewal was sometime last November.

"Three. Under the policy, as soon as a horse shows the slightest sign of illness — I mean if he even sneezes — Lloyd's have got to be informed immediately so they can appoint their own veterinarian to go look at the animal."

"And were they?"

"They say they were," said Jim. "But here's another thing I don't like. Downs naturally appointed a French insurance adjuster to look after their interests there, but the guy they picked, whose name is Laurens, is also the French representative for Hawkshaw Zimmerman, the big insurance agency in New York. And Hawkshaw Zimmerman," said Jim Crabbe, "handle most if not all of Carlo Galatti's insurances."

"What are you suggesting?" asked Matt gently.

"I don't know," Jim replied. "Carlo Galatti's a really big wheel, a very wealthy man whose insurance commissions run into millions of dollars every year. He must swing a lot of influence."

Matt looked skeptical.

"The look on your face reads 'conspiracy theory,' " Jim said dryly. "The condition precedent to schizophrenia — I know, you've told me."

He stabbed his hand. "All right, forget it, let's go on. Four. I scarcely need to tell you this, but unless Galatti has played it completely by the book, unless everything he has said, every statement and claim he has made about this horse is one hundred percent factual, then the insurance could be null and void."

Matt Blaney looked at his boss.

"That's it?" he asked eventually.

"Those are the possible outs," said Crabbe lamely.

"If the horse died of cancer, Jim . . ."

"They *say* he died of cancer," Crabbe said, "but how the hell do I know?"

"Lloyd's are happy?"

"No one's happy on a claim this big, but Downs tells me it's in the bag — in other words we'll have to pay out. They've got a pathologist's report, they say they were notified all along the way about everything that was happening. But I just don't know — I mean, there could be an angle to this that we don't know about. Galatti is a powerful man, now he's turning the screws. This thing is all happening out of our control."

"This Galatti," said Matt, "is he mob?"

"I don't know," answered Crabbe. "I'm trying to find out more. He lives in New York City but is rarely seen — something of a Howard Hughes. It seems he's originally from Argentina."

"Why don't you ask our clipping service in Manhattan what they've got?" suggested Matt.

"I already have," said Jim. He sighed. "It's most unlikely that a guy like Galatti's going around pulling insurance scams on his own race-horses," he said. "Still things are rarely as they seem." He stood up and put his hands in his pockets. Even with the wizened face he still looked like a schoolboy in his first long pants. "Look," he said, "I need this thing like a detached retina. It couldn't have come at a worse time." He looked away. "I've a lot of commitments."

"Okay," Matt said slowly. "A horse is dead and as it stands it's going to cost you one big one. We know nothing except what you've been told. On the face of things, everything is fine, and Carlo Galatti is a big guy who buys an awful lot of insurance, worldwide, so nobody's going to pay much attention to little guys like us making noise."

"Precisely," Jim said.

"In the morning," Matt said, "I'll call up Galatti Incorporated here in Manhattan and try and get to talk with whoever handles that side of things for Galatti himself. A guy like that always had minions in charge of everything — his villas, his jets, his horses. I'll just try to float in there, innocent as a baby, and see if I get any bad smells."

Jim Crabbe's face had brightened. "That's what I was hoping you'd suggest," he said. "I'd do it myself, only I don't think it would look good to go in personally. It might suggest . . ."

"Don't worry," Matt said. "I'm the person to do it. I'll let you know as soon as I've been there."

"I'm in Miami tomorrow," Jim said. "There's been a nibble for that condominium development I'm trying to unload. I'll be back around seven."

They walked toward the door.

"I'll call you," Matt said. "Besides, I kind of owe it to Cornucopia."

Jim frowned. "Owe it? How?"

"Well, out at Belmont that day, my hundred on him got me three." Matt laughed as he opened the door.

"Goddammit," Jim cried, "in that case don't you dare come back without getting me off the hook!"

Slowly Matt walked back into the room. Jim used expensive after-shave and now its smell lingered in the room. Matt took another beer out of the refrigerator. Outside he could faintly hear the perfect sound of a Rolls Royce engine coming to life. He closed his eyes.

It had been typical jungle daybreak: already cloyingly, drenchingly humid with bright sunlight dappling intermittently through the foliage fifty feet overhead. It was a measure of their clandestine success that the shrill bird and insect chorus continued unabated around them, the echoing chorus of the tropical dawn reverberating in its natural acoustics like a choir in a great cathedral.

Sweat poured down Matt Blaney's face, chest, and back as he slapped at a bullet-shaped insect that had alighted on his hand. They were lying side by side in deep foliage, their faces blackened, their M-16s cradled at their elbows. Matt Blaney consulted his watch. He fancied he could feel his heart thump against the warm earth beneath him. He turned his head and looked at the man next to him — anywhere else in the world he would have been called a boy but in the jungle anyone over twelve who could fire a gun was a man.

Private James Crabbe Junior's index finger was on the trigger of his M-16; his left hand gripped the forward stock so tightly that his knuckles were showing white. He caught Matt's look and smiled briefly, his teeth flashing white. Matt winked encouragement at him; he had felt the same on his first assault mission, which seemed a lifetime ago.

On either side of Blaney and Crabbe lay twenty-five men in similar positions, all concentrating fixedly on the wisps of smoke two hundred yards ahead, the domestic morning fires rising from the huts of the Vietcong village.

On a given signal, the entire company rose to a crouch and then peeled off left and right in their planned encircling maneuver. As in the lengthy briefings, hammered home in the days before, Blaney was anchorman on the left-hand thrust, Crabbe in the same position on the right. The gap between them widened as the company split; there was a wide, green glade which might have been in a New England wood if it was not for the call of the cockatoos. Matt saw Crabbe walking backwards like himself, then disappear.

It was meant to be all over before lunch. The village had been used as a base by the Cong, but not for some weeks. The object was to destroy it, disperse the villagers, and get the hell out. That was the objective, and it was repeated as such at the inquiry. Matt's group effected their encirclement without problem. Now they were on the very edge of the village; they could see old women cooking and small children being washed. A dog barked, suddenly alert. There was a violent overhead clatter as a hundred thousand birds made for the sky. Matt Blaney looked at the man in front of him: his mouth had fallen open in undisguised fear.

There was confusion in the inquiry evidence as to which had come first — the shouting or the shots. In Matt's recollection they had occurred together, but what he remembered best was that he had felt relief: the shooting was from M-16s and that meant U.S. firepower. The captain commanding the left-hand flank had done the only thing open to him: they had hit the village immediately, screaming at the terrified villagers to flatten face down. A suspicious movement in a peripheral hut had merited a hand-grenade, and three generations of one family had been put out of their misery.

Cautiously the bulk of the unit crossed the village and probed the perimeter on the other side. There was eerie silence. Matt Blaney was one of the first to reach the scene. The soldiers in their battle fatigues and netted helmets lay like broken dolls around a fifty-foot area — broken dolls with bright, crimson decorations spattering their bodies.

In the hysteria of the next hour as the peaceful jungle was once more disturbed, this time by the roar of shuttling Sikorskys, two things were discovered: one, nearly all the ambushed men's rifles were missing, and two, of the thirteen men in the right-hand flank only ten bodies were recovered, absent among them that of Private James Crabbe Junior, nineteen next birthday.

Matt Blaney blinked his eyes.

It was shortly after dawn, in Washington. He stood alone at the deepest part of the black granite memorial, surrounded by the thousands of names. He was there, partly because it was the tenth anniversary, partly because he had some friends in Washington and, as he had forgotten what it was like to have a job, there did not seem to be much point hanging around for the weekend in New York.

At this early hour the sun was creeping up over the nearby stands of beech. He had passed makeshift platforms at the roadside with their colorful awnings: the top brass would review the next day's veterans' parade in style.

The sun glinted bright on the sea of inscriptions as Matt turned. He had not noticed the small man arrive. He was walking slowly down the plunging wall with a wreath almost as big as himself, his bespectacled eyes searching the columns and columns of names. As he passed, Matt could not help glancing down at the wreath. He stared.

"So hard to find the name," said the small man, peering.

"James Crabbe?" Matt asked.

"How did . . . ?" Then the small face smiled slightly. "Oh, the wreath."

Matt Blaney nodded silently.

"He's down here," he said, leading the older man back down. He pointed high on the wall. He could see water glint behind the wire-rimmed spectacles as the man placed the wreath and turned around.

"They never found . . ." The man looked pleadingly. Matt put his hand on the slight shoulder.

"He was my buddy, sir," he said.

Matt slowly came awake. He reached down for his beer; although it was warm he drained it.

Yawning, he made his way to bed.

TUESDAY

By SEVEN THE SUN HAD CLIMBED OUT OF JORDAN. ITS RAYS, not yet warm, filtered out across the desert of Ha Negev, caressing in their path the arid wilderness of rock and scrub, a land arid and scored, of drought and darkness, where no man passes and no man lives.

By seven fifteen it was a blinding ball of fire, clear of the highest peaks of Jebel El Hasa and pouring out across the great flat plain to

Beersheva, where wide sprays of water fanned out from revolving sprinklers set in patches of greenery clawed back from the desert, one agonizing yard at a time.

In the center of the plain two miles from the dusty road and surrounded by squat buildings and some trees, a silver-plated dome twinkled in the morning light. To the Bedouin tribes who traversed the barren landscape it was further proof of the perversity of the Yehudi who had come to possess their land: a magnificent mosque built by the aggressors, yet totally inaccessible to the true sons and daughters of Muhammad.

Deep beneath the earth of the compound which housed this magnificent dome, a man rode a slowly ascending elevator, its open sides and metal gate allowing him a view of each of the floors as he passed them. A loud ping-pong sound, echoing like a TV game only much louder, reverberated in the brightly lit, subterranean *machon*. He passed level after level of self-contained production units, hissing and throbbing as endless miles of stainless-steel pipes quivered with the pressure of manmade product racing through them fathoms beneath the desert floor.

The man was five and a half feet tall and slightly built. His head was larger than one would expect for a man of his size, large and long with an extra bump at the crown, which, although nearly bald and covered by a small, embroidered *kipa,* nonetheless conveyed the impression that nature in this case had concentrated on the head and left everything else to follow. The face was kindly, if sad, an Eastern European face with a curving, Semitic nose, close brown eyes, and a wide mouth that seemed always to be on the point of smiling. He turned slightly and the light struck his left cheek: from the lower rim of the eye to the line of the jaw it was uniformly the color of port wine, a hemangioma, the genetic abnormality of the blood vessels for which no known cure exists. He was no more than forty-two or -three.

The elevator shuddered to a stop and its sole passenger slid back the gate. He walked down a pipe-lined corridor, his white coat flapping about his knees, his plastic lunch box under one arm, a large tartan Thermos under the other.

His heartbeat increased a notch as he halted before a door. He listened intently for any sound; as on the previous five mornings everything was quiet. Using a key he opened the door and entered a small room where a knee-high counter halted his progress. He placed the plastic box and flask on the counter before sitting on it himself and easing off the yellow regulation boots. Then ensuring that his stockinged feet kept clear of the floor, he swung over into the outward part of the room, picked up his lunch things, and proceeded to the next obstacle.

On the left was a hip-high, stainless-steel turnstile through which he had come in eight hours before. To the right was a six-foot-high steel cubicle with two similar turnstiles, one on either side of it. The blood began to pound in his ears. He listened again. He could hear nothing. With a deep breath he bent down below the first turnstile; then, placing his plastic lunch box on the floor, he slid it out along the tiled surface to the other end of the room.

The Thermos, because of its rounded shape, was more difficult. He shoved and it immediately veered off to the left, rolling crazily until it came to a noisy stop at a steel locker. He stood up shakily, realizing that he had almost punctured his tongue with the force of his biting teeth. He went through the turnstile on the right and stepped into the booth, the sweat now pouring down his face. He placed his two hands deep into the recessed grooves of the wall and closed his eyes as the unseen radiation sensors scanned the length of his body.

The all-clear bell sounded. Scrambling through the final turnstile he heard it click-record his exit, then he froze. There were voices at the outer door. He half fell, half ran to the plastic box and scooped it up. The door opened. A youngish man entered, his head turned back to his companion. The bulky Thermos lay immediately in his path.

"Oh, *sliha*," he said to the stooping figure, "excuse me, Doctor Shenlavi."

Dr. Yoseph Shenlavi straightened up, his Thermos in his hands.

"*Shalom*," he said, his face in a smile, "good morning."

"*Boker tov, Doktor*," said the second of the two military chemists. Still chatting, they went to their lockers and changed into white coats. They removed their shoes and pulled on large, yellow socks into which they tucked the ends of their trouser-legs. Then they made their way through the entry turnstile and into the active area.

The man they had called doctor sat on a bench in front of his locker and tried to regulate his heartbeat. He slipped off the white coat with its dosimeter clipped to the lapel, hung it in his locker, then, picking up his meal things, he left the building.

He walked in the sweet, cool air, past a line of offices where people had just started work. To the right the gleaming dome came into view. In front of him was a ten-foot-high, wire-mesh gate, a gate-house and a raised, sand-bagged sentry-post housing a competent-looking *sabra* with his finger on the trigger of a machine gun.

"*Shalom, Doktor,*" greeted the uniformed guard as he glanced cursorily at the proffered pass.

"*Shalom.*"

Through the gate-house, he began to relax. He was now in the residential compound, still secure, but in the concentric circles of security employed at the base, only two moves away from the perimeter. He approached a low, narrow building made of wood, the sleeping quarters for the senior operatives and physicists like himself. A few cars were parked outside.

He pushed through the unlocked door and sat on the bed, his box and flask on his lap. He ran his hands over his disfigured face and kneaded it like india rubber, then he shuddered as a spasm passed through him. Out the small window he could see a young soldier with a watering can attending to a bed of yellow roses. He felt the lids of his eyes close; he jerked to his feet. The most crucial part was yet to be implemented.

He opened the plastic box and took out a small, tin-foil-wrapped package. It contained a dosimeter, identical to the one he had left clipped to his white coat in the active area, but in this case the reading was in excess of 200 rads. Taking a sheet of newspaper, he placed it on the floor, then sitting the dosimeter at its center he brought down the full weight of his heel, fragmenting the pocket ionization chamber into a thousand pieces. Balling the newspaper around the wreckage, he consigned it to the waste-paper basket in the corner.

Outside, the green Volvo 340 was already warm. Dr. Shenlavi unlocked the driver's door and placed his overnight bag and Thermos on the passenger seat. His eyes noted the square, cardboard box in the foot well on the passenger side. He closed the car door, then allowed himself a thorough 360-degree inspection of his immediate vicinity. The car was as he had left it the day before, a few dead flies lying under the back window and on the dashboard. Very gradually he bent down, like someone tying his laces, until his fingers touched the canvas webbing of the sleeves he had sewn under his seat. Slowly he worked his way along the rough fabric; abruptly the fingers of each hand stopped as they came into contact with the curves of hard metal. He nodded to himself, then straightened up and repeated the investigation under the passenger seat. Thus satisfied, he snaked his left arm to the back of the car and verified the presence of a further shape, nestling in its canvas sling, sewn horizontally along the very back underside of the passenger seat. He prepared to start up. His left hand adjusted the Thermos so that it was wedged firmly between the seat-back and the bag. Its rounded metal base was no different from the five other shapes he had just felt.

His route took him past buildings such as the one he slept in. A number of people were walking to and fro; many of them saluted the familiar face of the plant's senior physicist, on assignment for two years now from the famed Weizmann Institute at Rehovot.

Dr. Shenlavi slowed down as he saw two men approaching, both dressed in clean, white coats, on their way to work in the active area. One had a small, gray beard, the other was younger with thick spectacles; like the doctor, they both wore *kipot*.

"*Shalom*, Yoseph," said the older, as the Volvo's window was rolled down. "*Le' Yerushalyim?* Off to Jerusalem?"

"For a full two weeks, my friend," replied the doctor, his ready smile in place. "It's been a long time and I have much catching-up to do."

"Of course, Yoseph, of course," said the other kindly. "And with the plant closed for maintenance, what is there to be done here? Off you go and enjoy yourself. *Tevaleh!*"

He squeezed the thin arm affectionately and stood watching as the Volvo made its way to a barricaded checkpoint. He shook his head. "*Misken Yoseph,*" he said to his younger companion. "Poor Yoseph."

"That was Dr. Shenlavi?" asked the other man, a newcomer to the plant.

The bearded man nodded his head. "Dr. Yoseph Shenlavi," he confirmed. "Only the good Lord knows the torture in poor Yoseph's soul."

"Isn't he the one whose family were killed last year?" asked the younger man.

"In the Haifa outrage," said the older, "his wife and daughters. But then at least he had a son."

The younger technician paused. "I seem to remember something," he said.

"He was seventeen, in his second month of service in the army," the bearded man said.

"Near the northern border, at Sasa, wasn't it?" said the younger. "Just last summer."

"That's it," said the older man. "The PLO killed three and took three; Yoseph's Levi was one of those captured."

"And is the boy still alive?" asked the younger technician as they neared the door of the *machon*.

"Who knows?" replied the other, his eyes sad. "He could be somewhere in Beirut; poor Yoseph believes he is." He shrugged. "After all these months, who knows?" They entered their place of work. "*Misken, Yoseph,*" he said as the heavy door closed behind them.

In front of the high gates Dr. Shenlavi sat in the car waiting for the normally automatic exit procedure. In slow-motion horror he saw the two uniformed technicians walk toward him from the guard hut. On other Fridays the regular guard had simply waved him through. Now he saw that one of the two young men was carrying a rectangular, steel machine: it was a portable monitor for measuring radiation.

"*Boker tov, Doktor.*"

"*Boker tov.*"

He could feel the sweat popping out on his queer face.

"Just a random check, doctor," said the technician in charge. He was young and tall with the frank, brown eyes of the *sabras*. "We're carrying out a twenty-four-hour survey of radiation levels."

"*Beseder,*" nodded the doctor. "Of course." He smiled and felt a trickle of sweat course through the dirt of his stubble.

The *sabra* made his way around the car. At the front passenger door he stopped, frowning. He indicated the dial on his machine to his colleague.

"Can you open the door please, Doctor."

Dr. Shenlavi leaned over and opened the door. The *sabra* was now poking the instrument around.

"*Yesh bayot?*" asked the senior physicist frowning, "anything wrong?"

"This machine's reading has leaped, Doctor," replied the young man gravely. "To over ten rads."

"Impossible," said the doctor shaking his head. "Ten?" He smiled at the technician like a patient father. "How could that be?"

But the young Israeli, whose training and upbringing were founded on the principles of suspicion, would not be put off that easily.

"The machine was calibrated perfectly this morning, Doctor," he said firmly. "This reading is accurate."

The senior physicist feigned total puzzlement, then all at once his face split into an even more radiant smile.

"*Aizeh metumtan ani!*" he cried. "How stupid of me!" The young technician was frowning again. The doctor pointed to the lead cylinder on the front floor. "Its the cobalt," he said laughing. He could see the confidence ebb from the *sabra's* eyes. He continued, "There are a hundred curies of it in there. I'm returning it to the metallurgists at the Weizmann. Here, take it out and see for yourself."

The second technician bent into the car and gingerly picked up the cylinder.

"It's a strong gamma ray emitter," said the doctor, chuckling as the first technician monitored the box. The young man smiled and nodded at his colleague, who replaced the cylinder on the car floor.

"Sorry, Doctor, just doing our duty," he said.

"Very good," came the understanding reply. "*Shalom.*"

"*Shalom,*" chorused the two boys and waved the car through the checkpoint.

He gripped the steering wheel with the intensity of a drowning man. His foresight in placing the cobalt in the car had been vindicated. But if the technician had tried to monitor inside the car while his companion held the cylinder outside, then the result would have been quite different.

He drove the Volvo across the mildly undulating terrain of dirt and scrub to the final security point on the perimeter. Here another mounted machine gun guarded the exit. A fit-looking guard with receding hair waved to him. He wore a beretta, cowboy style, low on his hip. The doctor returned the greeting.

"*Shalom.*"

The guard opened one side of the high, wire-mesh gate and waved the car through. The doctor smiled and drove out. He was now on a short spur road that led out to the narrow, desert highway. He reached it and swore under his breath. A group of off-duty soldiers, young men and women, sat on the side of the dusty road, waiting for transportation to Beersheva and Jerusalem. The men all wore laced-up boots and carried their Galils slung casually over their shoulders. The girls were in crisp brown uniforms; some of them smoked cigarettes.

"*Hey, Doktor!*"

The slight doctor smiled at them and then shrugged. He indicated right. The soldiers' faces fell. Normally the doctor turned left for Jerusalem and gave them lifts. He waved as he drove off east and the soldiers waved back as one. Dr. Shenlevi was one of the nicer senior people working at Dimona.

The green Volvo purred along the empty road, climbing into the mountains. It reached the plateau of Har Hamarmar, now bleached a blinding white by the hot sun, and continued across it until the road began to descend. The sweat had dried on his face and the gut-tearing suspense was being replaced by fatigue. He had not eaten for five hours; now he was going home the long way around. The route he was taking, over the mountains, down the valley, and up the west shoreline of Yam Ha-Melah, the Dead Sea, guaranteed that he would be alone. He passed a sign pointing to a phosphates quarry. A huge truck crawled out of the white pit, making for his road. He passed it, continuing his descent. A small buzzing had started in the back of his head. He shook himself, cursing once more. He knew what to expect.

A sign saying "Sea Level" flashed by as he pushed the car faster downwards. The noise was gathering in pitch. An image began to flash into his mind's eye. He blinked to remove it, but it persisted, alternating each second in his vision with the landscape, which was now flat and straight. He blinked and shook his head as the vision came clearly into focus. It was the eye-level picture of a man's left hand covering his naked genitals.

The Volvo was doing seventy, along a road that separated stark mountains to the left and to the right a great plain of salt. The salt stood in a million stalagmites, each its own sculpture, each utterly dead. The noise was now a roar.

Abruptly he pulled the car to the side of the empty road in a cloud of dust. He covered his face. The noise grew louder, and as it did his vision became distorted until everything he saw appeared in miniature, as if viewed through the wrong end of a telescope, miles away. He held his hand out in front of him: it looked no bigger than a postage stamp.

He covered his eyes again as perspiration broke out all over his face. There was nothing he could do to stop it.

To have lost not once or twice, Papa, but three times!

With trembling hands he reached for the tiny, distant catch on the glove compartment, the noise now a roar in his head, every squeak and rustle in the silent car exaggerated a hundredfold. His fingers found the photograph and he withdrew it, bringing it to within an inch of his eyes. The proud young soldier in his new uniform beamed at him. As if the noise in Dr. Shenlavi's head could be given release through his throat, he held the picture tightly and cried out, a cry of guttural abandon and grief that went on until every ounce of breath was expelled from his body.

Dr. Shenlavi sat, his eyes staring. He saw not the arid land outside the car, nor the lake of nearby salt shimmering in the morning heat, but a cold room in Haifa, a room of cold, clinical white where three forms lay unmoving, a towel covering the stump which should have supported his wife's head, the bodies of his daughters so perfect and unblemished that it would always remain a mystery to him why they had died.

After five minutes Dr. Shenlavi got out of the car. Placing his overnight bag on the hood, he opened it and withdrew a folded blue-and-white robe, his *talit,* which he shook out, and in a single flourish wrapped around his slight shoulders. He raised his lined face in prayer to the warm sun. Again he reached into the bag, this time for the *tefillin,* a light harness of leather straps, which he bound first around the biceps of his left arm and then seven times around his forearm, before wrapping it once into his palm. He had begun to sway slightly back and forth as the verses spilled from his racing lips.

Next from the bag was the *shel rosh,* another harness of straps, which this time he fitted around his head so that the front of the device rested firmly on his forehead. Adjusting the palm strap so that it wound thrice about his middle finger, he intoned the words from Hosea: "*I will betroth myself to you in righteousness and in justice.*"

A car full of Arabs going to their jobs in the Dead Sea works passed the Jew with the marked face at the roadside as he swayed back and forth at his *tephillot.* The dust from their passing covered the frail, rocking figure and clung to his face, which was wet now but not with perspiration.

All the images of his life crowded together in his brain at this moment of supplication; all the objects of his love who had been taken now lived solely inside his head, leaving outside only objects of hate. He wrapped the *talit* tighter about himself as the magnitude of what he was about to do suddenly shook him like a terebinth in a sandstorm. Raising his face again he began to smile upward, radiantly, confidently, his contract with his God completed.

"*Because ye had no cause to weep,*" he cried in his ancient tongue, "*this day will remain a day of weeping for generations to come.*"

TUESDAY: A.M.

5 THE RECEPTIONIST LOOKED UP FROM HER DESK AS A SHADOW fell across her. She saw a well-built man with soft gray eyes, wearing a well-cut, pinstriped suit, carrying a coat on one arm and an umbrella on the other. She smiled.

"My name is Blaney. I have an appointment with Mr. Jaffe."

The receptionist wrote Matt's name into a book, then pressed out a number on her telephone console with her long fingernails.

"Mr. Blaney in reception," she murmured, then smiled again. "Mr. Jaffe will be right with you, sir. Let me take your coat. Please take a seat."

Matt had found Galatti Incorporated between Madison and Fifth. The reception was through doors and up steps to a mezzanine. The building, all fifty stories of it, was what a construction mogul's building should be: outside, rows of indented windows, towering upward in solitary grace, unattached to any other building; inside, an emphasis on space, great curving concrete beams, a floor of blue-veined, white marble covered with rugs of the Middle East.

Matt sank into a chair, genuine leather slung over the cross-members of a gleaming chrome frame, and sat back. The girl at reception raised her head and smiled at him again. Matt returned it. He had called that morning and, after initial hesitation, had been put directly through to Mr. Jaffe.

"I'm Bob Jaffe. J-a-f-f-e. How can I help you?"

Matt explained his interest in Cornucopia.

"We've been over this thing extensively with Lloyd's," Jaffe said. "Essentially the horse was managed from France."

"I'd like some background," Matt said, "just for our own interest." Matt laughed diffidently. "To be quite honest, Mr. Jaffe, this is a first for us."

"Let me take your number," Jaffe had said. "I'll try and get back to you."

"I'm free this afternoon," Matt said.

"I can't promise when," Jaffe replied.

At eleven, Matt's phone had rung. It was Jaffe's secretary, confirming an appointment for three. Matt had smiled as he replaced the phone.

Outside, a biting rain had begun. Looking down from the mezzanine, Matt could see the New York evening traffic build, cars with their lights already on. On the table in front of Matt were newspapers and several magazines, including *The Bloodhorse*. Matt picked it up. On the inside front cover and facing page was a color photograph of Cornucopia, advertising the stallion's services at Haras du Bois, Deauville, France. The picture gave an even more dramatic impression of the athletic conformation, the potency that had propelled Cornucopia to his great victories. Matt looked at the date: the advertisement had been placed the previous month.

"Beautiful, wasn't he?"

Matt looked up. A man had come to stand beside him. He was medium size, fattish, had blond, receding hair, small blue eyes, and wore a double-breasted suit.

"Mr. Blaney? I'm Bob Jaffe. We spoke earlier."

Matt took the offered hand. "Glad to meet you, Bob. And it's Matt."

"Shall we?" Bob Jaffe led the way to elevators recessed in marble-faced walls. They stepped in: the inside of the elevators were leather padded with brass handrails.

"You're an insurance adjuster?" Jaffe asked.

"I'm a partner in Insurance Fidelity," Matt said. He balanced his umbrella on the elevator's rail.

"Insurance Fidelity." Jaffe brought a single finger to scratch the crown of his head. "Do we deal with you? I don't recall the name."

"We're an independent company," Matt said. "Insurance Fidelity was founded by our chairman, Jim Crabbe. We do a lot of agency business as well as direct participation."

"I see." Bob Jaffe nodded wisely. Then he smiled, a jolly, self-depre-cating smile. "It's sometimes difficult to keep up with everyone," he said and laughed. The laugh was a trademark, given at the end of a sentence.

They walked down a corridor, into a corner office, past a secretary and into a further office which had considerable expanses of carpet and glass. Jaffe gestured to armchairs around a table. "Help yourself," he chortled.

"Are you the horse expert?" Matt asked pleasantly.

Jaffe made a face and gave a laugh. "I'm a personal assistant to Mr. Galatti," he said. "I'm a sort of sweeper; I get all the little things that seem to get left over. Still . . ." His hands flew upwards; he gave his laugh.

"Sounds interesting," Matt said.

"It can be," Jaffe said. "It involves one hell of a lot of travel. Take the last three weeks — I've been on four continents." He held up four fingers as if Matt might not have heard. "Still, that's how it is if you want to work for Mr. Galatti."

Matt smiled. He said: "I'm grateful for this opportunity, at short notice, to talk about the Cornucopia case. Can you fill me in?"

Jaffe made a face. "How do you describe a dream?" he said. "The horse won everything he was ever asked to race in, both sides of the Atlantic. When he retired to stud he was hailed by the world press as the greatest hero of all time. He was a phenomenon."

"I read about him in *Time*," Matt said.

Jaffe said: "A rarity, an equine athlete whose like may never be seen again."

"That's the word that sprang to mind when I saw his picture down-stairs," Matt said. "Athletic."

"You know something about horses, Matt?" The face was still jovial but the eyes had changed.

"Not much," Matt said, "but I can empathize with beauty. A beau-tiful sculpture, a woman, a horse. They're all just different facets of beauty." Matt smiled at Jaffe. "Sorry. What happened after Cornucopia retired?"

"He was syndicated for two hundred million dollars and sent to Haras du Bois," Jaffe said. "That's Mr. Galatti's stud in Deauville, France. He had a great career in front of him — until a week ago." Jaffe shook his head. "I'm sorry if I sound somber," he said, "but this was more than just a horse. Everyone in here is pretty cut up about what happened."

"I understand," Matt said, "I understand." He brushed his hair back. "Bob, did Mr. Galatti take a personal interest in Cornucopia or are horses just another investment for him?"

Bob Jaffe's eyes widened. He smiled patiently. "Matt, I've worked for Mr. Galatti for five years. I have never seen him so upset about anything. He loved that horse" — Jaffe laughed — "I don't think that's too strong an expression, no, Mr. Galatti loved Cornucopia."

"I see," Matt said. "You don't mind if I . . . ?" He had taken out a small notebook.

"Not at all," Bob Jaffe said.

"My memory," Matt grinned. "If you could just bring me through it from when the horse first became ill."

Jaffe sat back and crossed his legs.

"Cornucopia," he said carefully, "up to the beginning of last month, had never had a day's illness in his life. The horse was robust. He underwent regular medical checks and examinations. At Haras du Bois there is a resident veterinarian. His name is Cambier." Jaffe paused as he recalled briefly. "At the beginning of January," he said precisely, "Cornucopia began to go off his food. This at first was put down to a colic or temporary digestive upset, but it became progressively worse. Lloyd's were immediately informed. Cambier was really worried that the horse was failing to respond to normal treatment, but ten days ago there was a dramatic deterioration and Cambier then suggested that Cornucopia had what is called a twisted gut — literally a twisting of the intestines."

"This Cambier, is he competent?" Matt asked.

Jaffe laughed. "You don't survive around Mr. Galatti unless you're competent," he said.

"Mr. Galatti was kept informed of Cornucopia's illness?"

"At all times," Jaffe answered.

"By Cambier?"

"No, by the stud manager, his name is Dijon."

Matt nodded. "Dijon," he said, and wrote the name down.

"Mr. Galatti's immediate response," Jaffe continued, "when he heard this appalling news was to send the best American vet there is to try to save Cornucopia. He chose Dr. Colby from Kentucky, probably the world expert in this area."

"When did Dr. Colby travel?" Matt asked.

"At the beginning of last week," Jaffe replied.

"But all to no avail," Matt said.

Jaffe shrugged. "Dr. Colby concluded," he said, "that Cornucopia had a badly, if not fatally, twisted gut. The only answer was surgery. He phoned Mr. Galatti and recommended such a step."

Matt looked out of Jaffe's office window. He saw cloudy Manhattan sky through tinted glass. "And Mr. Galatti gave the go-ahead?" he asked.

Jaffe shook his head. "Mr. Galatti was devastated," he said. "He understood the implications of what Colby was saying. You see, Matt, to operate on the abdomen of a horse is a drastic measure. The horse is a large animal — everything about him is dramatic. His guts, for example, are enormous — the small intestine alone measures over seventy feet. Surgery on such a beast is a gigantic undertaking, following which everything has to be tightly repacked and kept in place by stitches behind an abdominal wall that is at the most a quarter inch thick. Even assuming, Matt, that the operation is a success, how do you keep a patient weighing over half a ton quiet for his convalescence?" Jaffe smiled benignly.

"Yet Dr. Colby recommended surgery," Matt said, writing.

Jaffe nodded. "Correct," he said. He sighed. "Of course, at this stage, as I'm sure you know, there was a Lloyd's veterinarian at the stud as well, who also concurred with Dr. Colby's assessment. But Mr. Galatti . . ." Jaffe shook his head grimly. "Between you and me, here's a man, Matt, who's got an empire worth hundreds of millions, maybe billions. He got where he is because he's tough." Jaffe's laugh. "I work for him, by God, I tell you he's tough." Jaffe shook his head. "And yet, here he was, paralyzed — yes, I don't think that's too strong a word — he loved the horse so much he was paralyzed with concern. He couldn't make up his mind. He asked for time in the hope that somehow Cornucopia's guts might straighten themselves."

"He did this despite the fact that Lloyd's had okayed the operation?"

"Insurance wasn't on his mind, Matt," Jaffe said. "The only thing

Mr. Galatti was concerned about was Cornucopia. I can tell you, I was here with him, right through it." Jaffe's glance went toward the ceiling. "I never want to go through anything like it again."

"But they operated," Matt said.

"Eventually, three days ago, they operated," Jaffe confirmed. "They saw the cancer; they did the only thing they could; they put Cornucopia to sleep." He let out a big sigh. "Now, let's hope, for Mr. Galatti's sake, Matt, that the thing is wound up as quickly and as decently as possible."

Deferentially, Matt nodded. "What can you tell me about Mr. Galatti, Bob?" he asked. "I know he's an Argentinian and worth an awful lot of money. But when did he come here from Argentina, for example?"

Bob Jaffe stiffened. "I just work for Mr. Galatti," he answered.

"You tell me he's extremely tough, has you flying all over the world, doesn't suffer fools, between you and me, probably a mean old son of a bitch," Matt said. "Then you tell me he's devastated over a dead horse?" Matt smiled engagingly. "Is that all for real?"

Jaffe took a deep breath. "I think this conversation has gone far enough," he said. "Now if you have any other pertinent questions . . ."

"Just one, Bob," Matt said, putting away his notebook. "Mr. Galatti strikes me a very hands-on sort of guy. He had a horse that you tell me he dearly loved." Matt spread his hands. "So what's he doing here, four thousand miles away while his beloved horse lies dying?" Matt asked. "Why didn't he go to France, Bob, why didn't he go over and see the situation for himself?"

For a moment Bob Jaffe's mouth remained partly open. Then his eyes changed again. "There are some things," he said coldly, "that mean so much to some people, that to be near in a situation like I've just described would be unbearable." His stare held Matt for several seconds. "Now if that is all . . ." Matt smiled.

A red telephone behind Jaffe, on his desk, rang.

"Excuse me a moment," Jaffe said. He rose and picked up the receiver.

"Jaffe." His eyes stayed on Matt. "Yes, sir." He stood more erect. "Ah . . . yes." Matt could see Jaffe thinking, his eyes, although still on Matt, now not seeing him. "Do you really think . . . ?" Jaffe was saying. Now he turned his back. ". . . just going . . ." Matt heard. Then Jaffe turned again, his jovial demeanor back in place. "It seems, Matt, that you're not about to leave us after all," he said.

Matt Blaney smiled inquiringly.

"That was Mr. Galatti," Jaffe said, his small eyes scanning. "Someone must have told him you were in the house." Jaffe gave his laugh. "He says he'd like to see you himself."

The elevator's floor indicator showed that they had reached the summit. The doors hummed back to admit them directly into a hushed area, almost the width of the building, with floor-to-ceiling expanses of glass and at one end a vast bronze statue that Matt recognized as the god Poseidon. The area was completely empty. Jaffe led the way across deep carpet for a good thirty yards, past Poseidon, until they came to leather-faced double doors. Jaffe pressed a button. There was a minute click overhead and Matt looked up to see a bracket-mounted camera swivel on to them. A green light glowed and Jaffe pushed the door inward. They were in a modernly appointed secretarial office with rows of discreet filing cabinets. Opposite them, to one side of a pair of double doors, was a desk with a computer terminal and a television monitor. A smallish woman rose from behind it. She nodded to Jaffe, glanced at Matt, then preceded them into the inner office.

"Mr. Jaffe, sir, and his guest," she said.

Bob Jaffe cleared his throat as he strode past her. "Mr. Galatti," he said, "this is Mr. Matt Blaney."

Matt felt a tingling sensation. He was in a huge room with amazing views on all sides. He was conscious of a person seated to his left. But his attention was entirely held by the man standing, ramrod straight, in the dead center of the room. It was the eyes: they dominated; they bored into Matt, tiny, pale blue pinpoints behind thick lenses. Matt met the gaze.

"So good of you to come up, Mr. Blaney." The voice was deep, slightly guttural. Galatti was dressed in a black suit, a white shirt, dark blue tie. He turned to Bob Jaffe and nodded once. The personal assistant looked questioningly for a fleeting second, then, along with the secretary, withdrew.

"Please." Galatti was gesturing to chairs around a table, set to one side, beside a tank of tropical fish and a panoramic view. He looked to his watch. "I won't detain you long."

Matt turned. Then he saw one of the most beautiful women he had ever set eyes upon.

"This is my wife, Barbara," Carlo Galatti was saying.

"How do you do." Matt took the firm handshake. He saw a mane of red hair, unwavering eyes, the same color as his own, a generous mouth, and a figure that was full and firm in an expensive suit with a silk blouse buttoned to the throat.

"Jaffe had mentioned you were coming in," Galatti was saying as they sat. The ghost of a smile crossed Galatti's face. "You are the first insurance person to show any direct interest. I felt I should see you."

Matt inclined his head. "Thank you, sir," he said. "May I saw how sorry we were to learn of your tragedy."

Carlo Galatti's head shook slowly from side to side. It seemed out of proportion with his body. "I still cannot believe it," he said. He shook himself, like someone with a chill. "However, we must not burden the rest of the world with our sorrow." The eyes, almost invisible as the window light reflected on the spectacles, turned to Matt. "Did Jaffe answer everything to your satisfaction, Mr. Blaney?"

"Completely," Matt replied. "He was very thorough."

"Your company . . ."

"Insurance Fidelity."

"Ah, yes, Insurance Fidelity, you were involved in the underwriting of the horse?"

"Essentially, yes," Matt replied.

Galatti shrugged and smiled toward his wife. "I don't get personally involved in these things," he said quietly, then frowned slightly. "I had, however, understood that you people had done most of your work. In fact there was an insurance veterinarian present when Cornucopia . . . died."

"That is also my understanding," Matt replied affably. "But as I explained to Mr. Jaffe, we find ourselves in a unique situation: we have never insured a horse before, let alone one for such a huge sum of money." Matt smiled. "I've been sent along to see if we can learn anything."

Carlo Galatti sat back and looked toward the multicolored fish in the tank. "I did all I could," he said in a voice little above a whisper. "I knew when they opened him up that would be the end." He made a large clenched fist. "Goddammit, what a way for him to go!" They sat in silence. Fish, some with huge, telescopic eyes, observed them from the tank.

"Do you know, Mr. Blaney," Galatti suddenly said, "what the statistical chances of owning a horse like Cornucopia are? As an insurance person I am sure that statistics are never far from your heart."

Matt smiled pleasantly. "I have no idea, sir," he said. "Extremely small, I would say."

"In the region of twenty million to one," Galatti said.

Matt nodded. "Almost as low, if you'll forgive me, as the chances of a fit young horse getting cancer," he said.

Carlo Galatti never moved, but he looked at Matt balefully, like a large old dog who has been disturbed. "I suppose," he said eventually, "I suppose."

Matt turned to Barbara Galatti. "Were you as involved with Cornucopia, Mrs. Galatti?" he asked.

Her eyes held Matt's with interest. "Of course," she said, "I was there to see him win in Europe when my husband had too many business commitments to travel."

Matt turned to Carlo Galatti. "You never saw Cornucopia win any of his big European races, sir?" he asked.

There was brief eye contact between Galatti and his wife. "I could get there for just one," he replied to Matt. "Cornucopia's last race. The Prix de l'Arc de Triomphe in Paris."

"Ah yes," Matt said, "the Prix de l'Arc de Triomphe."

Barbara Galatti's eyebrows had arched. "You have seen the race, Mr. Blaney?"

Matt shrugged. "Unfortunately not," he said and smiled.

"You should," Barbara Galatti said. "Longchamps is the most beautiful racecourse in the world." She smiled. "There is an elegance in France between horse and setting that is hard to describe," she said.

"Is that why Mr. Galatti's stud farm is in Normandy?" Matt asked her.

"Probably," Barbara answered. Her lips had minutely parted and the tip of her tongue showed between them for an instant. "You should go there too, Mr. Blaney," she said, "as part of your ongoing education."

Matt looked at her and then to Carlo Galatti. Impulsively he said: "I think that's an amazing idea. Do you know, you're absolutely right! That's what I'm going to do. How else can I learn something about a case like this unless I go to the place where it all happened?"

Barbara Galatti reddened. "It was simply a suggestion . . ." she began.

"But a brilliant one," Matt responded. He turned to Carlo Galatti. "That's if you have no objection, sir," he said.

Carlo Galatti looked once at his wife, then stiffly got to his feet. "You do whatever you feel you must, Mr. Blaney," he said. "Now, if you'll excuse me, I've got a very busy schedule." He extended his hand. "It was good of you to come up. Thank you very much again."

Matt rose to his feet and shook Galatti's hand. He turned to the seated woman. "Very glad to have met you, Mrs. Galatti," he said. Again she met his eyes, but where before there had been interest and warmth, now there was apprehension.

"My pleasure," Barbara Galatti said.

Galatti opened the doors, showed Matt out, and bowed to him as the secretary rose to escort Matt to the outer doors.

"Mr. Jaffe isn't here?" Matt asked the woman as she opened the outer doors with a hand-held remote-control.

"Mr. Jaffe returned to his own office," the woman said. "Do you wish to see him?"

"No, I just wondered where he'd got to." Matt smiled.

They walked side by side, past Poseidon, across the enormous, empty foyer, toward the elevator thirty yards away. Ten yards short of it, Matt stopped and turned. The woman had gone four further strides before she realized he wasn't there.

"Sir!" she shouted. "Where are you going? Stop!" But Matt was already around Poseidon. The woman pointed the remote-control and there was an immediate hum. Matt saw the doors begin to close and dived. One of the doors shuddered as he struck it on his way through; he landed rolling on the soft carpet. He could hear the cries of the secretary out in the foyer. Matt scrambled to his feet, brushed himself off, and grasping both knobs of the inner doors, flung them open. Matt stopped and stared. A frozen tableau greeted his eyes. Seated in the chair where he had left her, Matt saw Barbara Galatti, her face, which had been memorably smooth and unblemished, now bright crimson down its left cheek, her eyes red with tears. Matt saw Carlo Galatti standing over her, his eyes, without his glasses, much bigger and blazing, his features warped in a fixed mask of hate. And for the barest instant, at the jamb of a far door that Matt had previously noticed, at the very other end of the enormous office, Matt saw the top of a pink head and the eyes below it, drilling into him for the millisecond before they disappeared.

"I am sorry," Matt smiled awkwardly. He stepped forward and bent. "I forgot this," he said, withdrawing his umbrella from beneath a chair. Barbara Galatti had turned her marked face away. Behind them the out-of-breath, flustered secretary appeared.

"I'm very sorry, Mr. Galatti," she gasped, "I tried to stop —"

Galatti silenced her with a gesture. "It's all right," he said icily, his eyes on Matt. "I think Mr. Blaney now has what he wants."

Feeling his neck hairs stand on end, Matt turned his back and walked from the room.

"I don't know, Matt, I just don't know."

Jim Crabbe sat at the boardroom table of Insurance Fidelity and fidgeted with a paper clip. Matt sat opposite in a white track-suit, his feet in white jogging shoes with luminous strips on the chair beside him.

"I tell you, Jim, the old bastard hit her. Right across the face." Matt put his feet down and sat up. "And who was the guy leaving the room? My money says he'd been listening and observing the whole time I was there."

"So what?" Jim said. "Guys like Galatti have goons." He threw the misshapen paper clip away. "I had second thoughts about this whole thing on my way back from Miami. We can't afford to screw around with Lloyd's. They're too big. I'd about made my mind up to arrange the money, pay up, and learn my lesson."

"It's your money," Matt said. "You asked me to go and look at something that you had no feel for. I did and now I think that whatever it is, there's something going on there. That woman was terrified, Jim. As soon as I said I would go to France, everything changed. I had no intention of going near the place when I said it — but now I really think I should. And because of the time frame, I should go right away."

"Barbara Galatti could be terrified for a thousand and one reasons,"

Jim said. He made a face. "She's a good-looking broad and straightaway you have the hots for her. I know you."

Matt smiled. "And I know you too, you old fox," he said. "You're not going to piss away a million bucks if you think there's even a hair's breadth chance of saving it."

Jim Crabbe's face was tight. Then slowly he relaxed.

"I guess I've just talked myself into subsidizing a vacation in Normandy," he said dryly.

WEDNESDAY: A.M.

6 MATT BLANEY GLANCED BACK AND SAW CHARLES DE GAULLE Airport's gray satellites recede behind him like gigantic beehives on the flat, Paris plain. The February morning was clear and cold, yet still held a small promise of better things. His taxi, a Mercedes, gunned down the motorway passing industrial complexes and behind them great tracts of agricultural land already sprinkled with spring green.

Before Matt left Insurance Fidelity, the English pathologist's report had come through by telex. It referred to lymphosarcomas, intestinal blockages, and dead bowel. Three veterinarians had attended the stricken stallion; they all had concurred that death was inevitable. A footnote to the Lloyd's telex read: "Please remit one million U.S. dollars to our bank account below."

Matt had booked himself on Air France's Tuesday night service out of Kennedy. Before leaving, he had hastily written a check and mailed it to Delis. Venezuela, Matt thought, and shook his head. That part he believed, but not with two girlfriends from Staten Island.

Matt folded the pathologist's report and returned it to the inside pocket of his sports jacket. As much as the Mercedes would allow he stretched his gray-flanneled legs and looked out the taxi's window.

They were caught in dense traffic in the narrow rue Saint-Honoré. Shops on either side sold expensive furs, leathers, and colorful children's toys. Matt looked at his watch. They had been sitting outside the same shop-front of tinted glass for three minutes and he was already half an hour late for his appointment with Laurens, the Parisian insurance adjuster whom Lloyd's had appointed.

"Far to go?" Matt asked the driver and tapped his watch.

"*Pouah!*" said the driver and hunched his shoulders in the French way indicating an uncertain outcome. "*C'est dégueulasse. Nous sommes tout près, mais . . .*"

Five minutes later Matt looked up at the blue wall-sign and turned left into an even narrower street. Here the emphasis had moved to food. He searched for the number, passing windows full of preserved meats, chocolates, wines, and vegetables. There had been a time when, away on trips, he would always have taken the time to stop and buy something to bring home: chocolates from Brussels, lace from Amsterdam, a modern painting from Berlin. Now there hardly seemed much point. Matt crossed the road toward a shop stall, overflowing with the carcasses of pheasant and partridge, enormous hares and miniature deer. Almost beside them were further displays, of glistening fish, of pink crustacea, and of dull, round oysters set in deep beds of ice. Between the two shops, in a narrow, rounded arch, was the address he wanted.

Matt pushed the door open. He was in a long, stone-paved corridor leading to a small internal courtyard. To the left behind double glass doors a winding staircase could be seen. The steps were of old, sanded wood, the banisters wrought-iron and cold to the touch. Matt looked again at the address he had scribbled down and kept climbing. The fourth floor was identical to the three below it, three plain wooden doors on a small landing. He looked at the nameplates and pressed the bell to the left. It simply said "J. Laurens."

Matt stood while a girl announced him. The outer office had a high ceiling and no window; despite this it was bright, and home to a flourishing plant that someone had painstakingly trained across two of the four walls.

The door opened and the girl stood back to allow Matt in. The internal office was larger and had one window. Its floor was covered in a large Eastern rug whose reds and yellows blended pleasantly with graceful furniture, either period or good reproduction.

"Mr. Blaney, you are most welcome."

A man as tall as Matt came out from behind his wide desk, hand outstretched. Monsieur Laurens was distinguished. His hair was wavy snow white, his sallow face that of a Florentine professor of the arts. Clear blue eyes twinkled behind rimless glasses. The handshake was firm.

"Your flight was good?" The English was almost flawless, with an Oxbridge accent.

"Sure, no problems." Matt smiled. "But the traffic has really worsened since the last time I was here."

Laurens smiled. "No one in Paris drives a car anymore," he said, his even teeth sparkling. "But we still have the Métro, the best in the world." He indicated a gilt, upright chair.

"Some coffee, Mr. Blaney?" he asked. "I have a weakness for Turkish."

"Please," said Matt, sitting down.

Laurens went to an apparatus on a sideboard. He took two small cups from a tray and began to fill them from a spigot.

"You are here about Cornucopia," he said, matter-of-factly.

"That's right," Matt replied. "Mr. Crabbe asked me to look in on you."

"I see," said Laurens. He placed the cups on saucers and brought them over. Small silver spoons followed, and a bowl containing wrapped lumps of sugar. Despite his age, he moved like someone who kept in shape. He went behind his desk, and Matt could see a small military decoration in the lapel of his double-breasted suit.

"Your Mr. Crabbe," Laurens asked, sitting down again. "He knows horse insurance?"

"This is a first for both of us," Matt replied.

The blue eyes surveyed him.

"He has read the pathologist's report?"

"Yes, he has," Matt said. "So have I."

"You know," Laurens said, "that Lloyd's will shortly agree to pay Galatti his money?"

"I know," Matt replied. He drank some coffee. It was thick and sweet.

Laurens nodded logically.

"Very well," he said. "How can I help you?"

"Perhaps by taking me through exactly what happened," Matt said.

Monsieur Laurens brought his cup up to his lips and studied the man opposite him. Then he nodded again.

"You know Normandy, Mr. Blaney?" he asked.

Matt shook his head.

"Well," said Laurens genially, "I would say, Mr. Blaney, you have missed meeting the equivalent of a beautiful woman." He spread his hands. "Normandy is famous, of course, as the place where the Allies landed to liberate France. It is also famous for its horses and its Calvados. Some of France's most prestigious *haras,* stud farms, are situated in the countryside near Deauville. One of them, Haras du Bois, is owned by one of your countrymen, a Mr. Galatti. Cornucopia was his horse."

"That much I do know," said Matt.

Having finished with his cup, Monsieur Laurens stood up and brought it, plus Matt's, back to the sideboard. He moved with an air of unhurried dignity.

"A week ago I received a telephone call from Downs Ashcroft, the Lloyd's brokers," he continued. "I know the firm well; we have spoken once or twice before." He smiled. "As they say in England, Mr. Blaney, insurance is a big club, and I have been a member of the club nearly all my life."

"As an adjuster?" asked Matt.

Monsieur Laurens nodded and reseated himself. He surveyed Matt and as he did so a shaft of sunlight bounced from a finger ring. "The underwriters had asked Downs Ashcroft to arrange for the immediate examination of the horse by a British veterinarian," Laurens said. "I was asked to meet a Mr. Wilson at the airport and to bring him up to Normandy, to Haras du Bois, where this extremely expensive animal was seriously ill. I was also asked to make my own report." Monsieur Laurens looked distantly out the window. "I did as I was asked," he said. "Mr. Wilson is an English vet of great repute." He shrugged. "At Haras du Bois we met Mr. Galatti's young manager, a Monsieur Dijon, and two further veterinarians, one the local man, Monsieur Cambier, and an American, Dr. Colby from Kentucky, a famous expert in the field, sent over by Mr. Galatti himself." Laurens paused. "They were waiting for Mr. Wilson, so when we arrived they proceeded to an immediate examination of the horse." Laurens removed his glasses and rubbed one eyes with his knuckle. "I am not what they call a horsey man, Mr. Blaney . . ."

Matt gestured that he understood.

". . . Well, then you will understand," Laurens said, "that I am speaking simply as an observer, a layman I think you say, and not as an expert."

"It's often the best," said Matt.

Laurens smiled. "I agree," he said, and popped his glasses back on. "We went to a stable. There, lying on the straw, was this magnificent animal. He was lying quite still, but his stomach, his flanks," — Laurens indicated in front of him — "were swollen out to here, also his back legs." He nodded his head sadly. "He was Cornucopia," he said. "It was incredible to think that this beast was worth two hundred million dollars, however . . ." He shrugged. "Dr. Colby explained that the animal had been sedated due both to his state of agitation and to the fact that they were just about to drain fluid from his stomach. This Dr. Colby then proceeded to do, inserting a rubber tube or pipe through the horse's nose."

Laurens stood up and went to the window. "We returned to the house," he said, "and a conference took place. It was unanimously agreed that Cornucopia had a fatally twisted gut, that his condition was rapidly deteriorating."

Brief sunlight illuminated Laurens's profile. His comfortable office was quiet and overlooked a small courtyard that contained several wooden seats and a tree.

"The decision reached by these eminent men was that surgery was the only chance," he said. "The horse would die if nothing was done; surgery was the only remaining alternative." He made a face. "I could not disagree. Dijon was asked to obtain permission from Mr. Galatti, I proceeded to inform Lloyd's, and Mr. Wilson prepared his report for the underwriters." Monsieur Laurens jingled some coins in his pocket. "Insurance people are interested, as you know, Mr. Blaney, in one thing only," he said. "I suppose that is true of all businesses. But briefed by Mr. Wilson, Lloyd's gave the go-ahead."

"And Mr. Galatti?"

Monsieur Laurens turned at the window, the light behind his patrician head.

"Mr. Galatti was another story," he said. He sat down again. "Monsieur Dijon communicated the bad news to him in New York. Mr. Galatti was" — Laurens searched for the word — "inconsolable. He was very, very upset. Cornucopia had been a champion for him; he could not accept that this champion, still so young, was now in fact near death. He also knew that surgery on such an animal was a drastic step. He asked Dijon that nothing be done for twenty-four hours — he wanted time to think, but he also hoped that by some miracle his beloved Cornucopia's gut would straighten itself if given time."

Matt looked up. "Did Mr. Galatti never consider coming to France to see the situation for himself?" he asked.

Laurens shrugged. "I do not know the man, Mr. Blaney," he said, "but I understand that he runs an empire which straddles nearly all the continents of the world. Appointments are made sometimes a year in advance. Time is rationed in a way that makes men such as you and I look like spendthrifts."

Matt brushed hair back from his forehead. "Still," he said, "I find it oddly cold."

Laurens spread his hands in an almost papal offering. "Millionaires and their playthings, Mr. Blaney. Who can understand them? I have been in this business for a long time and I certainly do not."

Matt smiled. "I guess you're right," he said.

"I asked Monsieur Dijon to keep me in close touch," Laurens resumed. "The next afternoon he called me here at this office."

Laurens turned the page of his diary and looked down his nose at it. "Yes, at four o'clock on Thursday. It was to say that nothing had happened. The animal was in the same condition, Dr. Colby was standing by, but still Mr. Galatti would not concede the required permission. Monsieur Dijon said that he had spent over an hour on the phone to New York and that Mr. Galatti was so upset at times that he could barely make himself understood."

Laurens sighed. "I suppose it is in fact rather sad," he said quietly. "An old man being asked to decide about the thing he loves most." He shrugged, then joined his hands together. "This continued for two further days, Mr. Blaney," he said. "Mr. Galatti would call Normandy every two or three hours, right through the night, to inquire if there was any improvement. Of course there was none. Dijon kept me informed on a daily basis — he also was extremely upset at the stallion's predicament. The poor horse was in excruciating pain and no amount of analgesics could now help him.

"On the morning of the third day — that is last Sunday — Dr. Colby had had enough. He decided on his own initiative to operate. The horse was now clearly dying and surgery was a last, desperate gamble. I was telephoned at home; Lloyd's position had not changed. Mr.

Galatti, it was agreed, would be informed after the operation."

Monsieur Laurens looked sadly across his desk. "At midday," he said, "Monsieur Dijon called me again. The operation had started at ten. Dr. Colby had immediately found the cause of the problem, a massive tumor in the bowel that had caused the obstruction. However, on further probing he discovered at least eight other tumors, densely adhered to Cornucopia's intestines." Mr. Laurens took a deep breath. "It was hopeless," he said. "The horse was rotten with cancer. Under the anesthetic of the operation he was at peace, asleep, feeling no pain. In his day he had scaled the heights, given joy to thousands of people, and earned a great deal of money. Dr. Colby did the only thing he could, Mr. Blaney. He injected a massive overdose of anesthetic into the sleeping horse. He was dead in twenty seconds."

Matt put his pad down on the desk and shook his head. The silence in the small office was broken by the sound from the secretary's typewriter in the outer room.

"What about Galatti?" he asked. "How did he take it?"

"He was heartbroken," Laurens said. "He said the money was irrelevant to him." The eyes twinkled. "However, I expect it will help him to get over it."

Matt nodded. He glanced at his watch.

"Mr. Laurens," he said, "you've been most helpful. I'm sorry for taking up your time . . ."

"Don't apologize," said Laurens, getting to his feet. "We are in the same business. Where there is a lot of money you must be careful." He walked with Matt to the door.

Matt stopped and faced the older man.

"Monsieur Laurens," Matt said, "an off-the-record question?"

Laurens smiled as if nothing would surprise him.

"Do you know of any reason," Matt asked, "why Carlo Galatti might actually want Cornucopia dead?"

Laurens blinked and took a step back. "Want him dead?" He looked at Matt over his glasses. "In insurance the only reason someone wants something dead, Mr. Blaney, as you know, is for the money." The sides of Lauren's mouth went down and he made a gesture with his shoulders. "In the case we are dealing with a man whose wealth is measured in the hundreds of millions and whose horse, had he lived, would have made him many millions more." Laurens shook his head. "Add to that the fact that Cornucopia had cancer . . ." he finished.

Laurens opened the door and Matt walked into the small, outer office.

"Where do you go now, Mr. Blaney?" he asked.

"To Normandy," Matt said, "to Haras du Bois. I might get in some sightseeing as well."

"As I said, Normandy is beautiful," said the cordial Laurens. "Its countryside, its castles, its cooking. Haras du Bois is near Deauville. In the summer it is marvelous — the orchards in the rolling hills, the sea nearby, racing if you like it, every day." He shook Matt's hand. "You must also remember, Mr. Blaney, *le trou Normand,* the Calvados." He smiled and his fingertips flowered for the superlative. "In Normandy, its home, it is the very best."

As he made his way down to the street Matt glanced back up; Monsieur Laurens's aristocratic face still smiled down at him through the winding, circular stairwell.

7 THE ROOM WAS THE LENGTH OF THE NARROW BUILDING; ITS walls were whitewashed and it was sparsely furnished.

On a rug before the gas-log fire, the olive-skinned man lay back and savored the beauty of the woman who sat astride him. Her hair, abundant and red, touched his knees as she rocked back, then forward, moaning for her pleasure. He reached up and crushed the flower of her breasts. She closed her eyes and rocked. Her face was one of perfection, molded with the sureness of beauty, unforgettable. She rocked more intently, then bent so that her perfumed hair covered his head and her breasts brushed his lips. Her tongue darted.

"Oh Jesus! Oh Simon!" she cried.

Effortlessly the man came to his feet, bringing her up with him, still joined. She locked her heels around his deep cleft back. Standing, he steadied himself, catching her buttocks. As if her life depended on it, she thrust wildly against him, her breath coming in high-pitched gasps.

"Oh Jesus! Oh Simon!"

Then, their bodies shimmering like living sculpture, he finished it.

Five minutes later she lay on her flat stomach as he traced his finger down the line of her long back. She cupped the coffee in her two hands and smiled over at him.

"Did they teach you all that in San Francisco?" she asked.

His brown eyes were amused. He had the ability to remain silent for long periods, even when questioned.

"Maybe," he answered eventually.

"What's it like, San Francisco?" she asked. "I've never been there."

"Clean. Cool. Pretty."

"You went to Stanford?"

He nodded.

"And your parents were both teachers?"

He nodded again.

"Where were they from?" She could feel his eyes on her.

"My mother was Italian," he answered. "My father came from Lebanon with his father when he was a small boy."

"Did he speak to you about it, about his country?"

"Very little."

"Have you been there?"

He shook his head silently.

"Don't you yearn to go there, to discover your origins, to find relatives, to find out who you are?"

She never knew if he was mocking her. "I know who I am," he answered softly.

She felt uncomfortable. "Are your parents still alive?"

"No."

"You've got their coloring," she said, stroking him. She stood up and began to walk around the elongated room, touching things, his narrow bed, the wooden table with the arc light, a shelf of well-worn books, many of their spines showing white with age.

In the corner there was a recessed door, leading into a small toilet and shower. On their first evening he had observed her from behind the door as she had examined his wallet, his library pass, his university I.D. card.

Now she touched the worn books, making her way down the short row, occasionally stopping to examine titles.

"Applied engineering," she said. Then: "When do your classes end?"

"In May."

She put the book back and came to be beside him. She cradled her head on her arm. The light of the fire flickered over their bodies.

"Why did you come to New York?" she asked.

He shrugged. "It's one of the best engineering schools in the country. It runs the best postgraduate course."

She smiled. "And you know who funds the main chair?"

His face was unmoved. "You told me. The first time."

"You're extraordinary," she said. She rubbed his leg with her foot. "Don't you want to know about me?"

He turned and stared at the fire. "I know what I see," he said.

"What do you see?" Her voice was small.

"A beautiful woman."

"Is that all?"

He propped on one elbow and looked at her. His examination was so assured that she began to color.

"A beautiful, forgotten woman," he said.

She tried to laugh. "Forgotten?"

Simon nodded his head slowly. His unwavering eyes never left her face. She tried to brave it, tried to control her mouth, but then all at once tears sprang to her eyes, glistening. She crawled toward him and huddled under his arm.

"Forgotten," she wept, shaking. "I am forgotten, and I had forgotten — until you."

Silently he held her, stroked her.

"I am on a pedestal," she said. "Before you, no one dared."

He kissed the sweep of her neck.

She shivered. "Oh God, I'm afraid."

"That he'll find us?"

She nodded, wiping her face with her forearm. "That," she said. Then she looked into his calm, dark face. "There's also more," she said. She began to cry again. "He's used me."

Simon brought his finger to her lips.

"Ssh," he whispered. "Forget the old man. Think about us."

Suddenly, glorious hope soared in her. She clung to him. Nothing else was important. She felt an overpowering peace.

WEDNESDAY: P.M.

8

THE CAR WAS A BLUE BMW 320i WITH A SHIFT STICK. WITH a map on the seat beside him Matt made his way on to the *périphérique* and then out on to the Autoroute de Normandie. Around the turn-off for Versailles traffic thinned out. After fifteen minutes he was enjoying himself, humming along at nearly seventy with a freedom rarely possible in upstate New York.

The autoroute swept through wooded countryside, over hills and into sparkling valleys where rivers made their way to the sea. He climbed uphill past the exit for the inland port of Rouen, then down again, passing signs for Le Havre and Cherbourg. A graphic illustration of a jockey riding a horse flashed by and he turned off the main route, until soon the motorway came to an end.

Ten minutes later he was in second gear, climbing on a narrow road, behind a tractor, its trailer piled high with hay. The apple trees Laurens had spoken of were everywhere, their branches black and stark.

At a crossroads, Matt looked down at his instructions and turned left. A high wall of weathered brick to his right held a cotoneaster, which climbed from the other side to tumble outward. After a hundred yards the wall swept in, revealing graceful entrance gates, brick piers supporting a roofed pediment, and a sign saying "Haras du Bois."

Matt drove between lawns down a short, graveled avenue, and pulled up. The porch of the house was formed by blocks of granite into which a modern door of darkened glass had been incorporated. To the right, over an old wall of cut stone, Matt could see the green roofs of barns.

"*Oui?*"

Matt turned back to the door. A man of about thirty-five stood there. He wore bright yellow cords, a sports jacket of eye-catching checks, and a green shirt and tie. Thinning blond hair combed sideways contrived to conceal premature baldness. His eyebrows and lashes were fair to the point of being almost invisible, and he had the kind of mouth that might easily cry.

"Hello," Matt said producing his card. "Mr. Dijon is expecting me."

The man scrutinized the card.

"You are *les assurances?*" he asked. His mouth remained partly open as he waited for the answer.

"That's right," Matt replied.

"I am Alain Cambier, vet to Haras du Bois," the other man said stiffly. He extended a hand that was thin, white, and moist.

"Ah, I've heard about you," Matt said. "Mr. Laurens, the adjuster, said you might be here."

"Ah, oui, Monsieur Laurens," Cambier said. He shook his head and frowned briefly. Then he asked: "You wish to see Monsieur Dijon?"

Matt nodded. "Please," he said.

"He is in the stallion barn," Cambier said. "I was just going there. Would you care?"

The two men made their way through a gate in a wall and into a yard of cobblestones. The vet walked with nervous, springy steps too long for his height. Rows of stables formed three sides of the yard, which had at its center an empty flowerbed. They walked past it toward a large shed.

"It's been a bad time for you," Matt said.

Cambier nodded firmly. "Very bad," he said. "*Spécialement pour* Monsieur Dijon. Mr. Galatti gave him much responsibility here; Cornucopia was very special to Mr. Galatti — *son favori.*" He shook his head, and the wind caught his hair and blew it upright revealing a bright, pink pate.

"His death was . . . *une catastrophe,*" he said pasting his hair down again.

"Does Mr. Galatti have many other stallions here?" asked Matt.

"*Bien-sûr,*" Cambier said, "Of course. You will in a few moments see one, Man of Reims, covering a mare." He turned. "But Cornucopia," he said, "he was special."

They had stopped outside a steel door which Cambier now rolled open. Inside was a lighted shed with thickly padded walls and a floor overlaid with green Astroturf. Strains of Mozart in stereo reverberated through the high building. A man stood just inside the door. He looked younger than Cambier. He was well built, middle-sized, and carried his head thrust forward on broad shoulders. He had ginger hair which clung in curls to his head, heavily tinted glasses, and a small, tight mouth. He too wore cord trousers and a zip-up jacket into the pockets of which his hands were stuffed.

"Monsieur Dijon," said Monsieur Cambier by way of introduction.

Dijon nodded once to Cambier and then briefly scanned Matt's face before returning his attention to the center of the shed, where a black mare stood sweating and shivering. Two men in blue overalls attended to her head. All at once a door at the other side opened and a tiny pony was led out by a tall girl in blue jeans and knee-high boots. She wore her blond hair halfway down her back in a thick plait. The pony saw the mare and began to squeal and lunge. The girl groom led him to the center of the shed where he reared on his short hind legs in an effort to mount the object of his desire, but his seeking penis could do no more than slap harmlessly at the larger animal's hocks. The mare herself, fully conscious of the erect male member at her tail, splayed her hind legs wide in an effort to receive him. In her disappointment she whinnied, and tossed her head as much as the men holding it would allow. The teaser lunged again, his forelegs groping in increasing rage.

"Ça va suffit!" snapped Dijon.

Matt Blaney watched as the girl led the protesting pony out the way he had arrived.

There was some noise at the rear entrance, then the hero came on stage. He was a magnificent sight. He pranced on faultless legs, his snorting head held tight to his deep, potent chest. He was not a big horse but his size became irrelevant as the eye took in the perfection of his physique. The gleam and polish of his all-bay coat as it swept back and upwards from his belly to the symmetry of his flanks held an elegance that would have delighted Michelangelo.

The horse was being led from left to right. As he passed in front of them, something caught Matt's eye. He looked over the stallion to the very back of the barn; tiny electrodes exploded all over Matt's body: standing in the shadow of a doorway was a large, powerful man, whose head was pink and square at both ends and devoid of any hair.

As quickly as he had appeared, so he vanished.

Matt returned his attention to the horse. He saw that its front legs had been fitted with protective boots. As he approached the mare, he became hugely erect, his bright member quivering the length of a flagpole beneath his muscular body. He shook his head from side to side with impatience. The mare whinnied and splayed once more in anticipation. In a fluid leap the horse found her, his rigid member traveling endlessly into her softness. With his padded forelegs pressing on her back and withers, he thrust deeply and urgently, the wet sounds of his penetration clearly audible in the shed. Then with a bellowing roar that shook the whole building, he delivered himself.

The stallion was guided to the ground by his helper, then led away. Matt wiped his forehead with his sleeve.

"I thought this was a family show," he said as the two men turned to him. Dijon had taken Matt's card from Cambier.

"It's very good of you to see me, Mr. Dijon," Matt said.

"I heard only one hour ago that you were coming," the red-haired man said. He looked at his watch. "We are most busy. I have fifteen minutes," he said, and walked toward the yard.

Matt followed into the sunlight and across the yard to a small office located in a stable block. Dijon sat behind a desk and looked up at Matt. Hostility flowed from his small eyes, just visible behind the sunglasses. Cambier sat to one side.

"I thought," Dijon said, "that everything was finished."

"Mr. Dijon," said Matt, sitting down, "I am very sorry that you have lost your horse. Please understand that my presence here in no way means that there won't be a payment to Mr. Galatti. We simply want to go through the thing ourselves — this is the first time we have had a claim like this."

The small eyes were unwavering.

"So?" said Dijon at last.

"I would like to ask you a few questions," said Matt. "You will forgive me when I tell you that what I know about horses is, for all practical purposes, nothing." He took out a notebook. "I have spoken to Mr. Laurens in Paris," he said. "He has told me what happened. Could you tell me, Mr. Dijon, what you make of it all?"

Dijon looked at Matt, almost through him. Turning down the corners of his mouth he put his hands in his pockets, got up, and went to the window.

"If you spoke to Laurens in Paris, monsieur," he said, looking to the yard, "you will have heard the story. The horse had cancer. In horses it is a rare disease." He turned. The hostile vibrations from the man were palpable. "Cornucopia was just six years old, a young man of twenty-five or thirty. It is our tragedy."

Matt nodded sagely. "Could we go back to the beginning," he asked, "to when Cornucopia first came here?"

Dijon looked at Matt as if he was a madman. "The beginning?" he said, then turned to Cambier and gave him a staccato blast in French. The vet's lower lip gave a small quiver.

"Monsieur Dijon," Matt said, "I must remind you that even though you may find my questions ridiculous, I advise you, in Mr. Galatti's interest, to cooperate."

The mention of Galatti's name seemed to work and Dijon sat down, his fists clenched.

"You worked here as manager when Cornucopia first came to Haras du Bois?" Matt asked.

"I did," Dijon replied.

"What was the procedure for ascertaining that Cornucopia was in good health?"

"He was examined by Monsieur Cambier. He was healthy."

"In the first year here, did he have any sicknesses, any problems?"

"No."

"When was the next medical examination?"

"The horse would have been regularly checked. And of course a full examination would have been made each October when the insurance renewal took place."

"And there was never a problem, the horse was never ill?"

"Never for one day — until two months ago."

"And he performed all his stud duties satisfactorily?"

"Completely satisfactorily, monsieur."

Matt turned to the stud veterinarian. "Mr. Cambier, if cancer is so rare a disease in a young horse, why do you think Cornucopia got it?"

Cambier made a big face and looked at Dijon, then back to Matt.

"The person who understands the cancer, monsieur," he said, "he will change history. Why do we get cancer? It is a disease unique to everyone, it develops within our bodies. It is not . . . contagious, *par ex-*

ample, but it may be environmental, as you see when it attacks people working with *l'atom,* the radioactivity or the nuclear business, or even by people who smoke. But *finalement,* Mr. Blaney, it is the secrets within each of us that provide cancer the means to take over and kill."

Outside the evening shadows crept over the yard. Men led horses across it, their hooves ringing on the cobblestones.

"Other than yourselves and Dr. Colby," Matt said, "has there ever been anyone else involved in Cornucopia's treatment whom I should speak to?"

The two men shook their heads. Somewhere in the distance a church bell had begun to chime. No one spoke.

Matt Blaney returned his notebook and pen to his pockets and cleared his throat. He stood up.

"Gentlemen," he said, "thank you for your time. I apologize if it appears we are being overscrupulous, but . . ."

Dijon stood up. Matt could see the ropes of muscles rippling inside his open shirt collar.

He nodded fractionally as Matt allowed himself to be escorted toward the door by the vet.

"Good-bye, Mr. Blaney," said Dijon from his desk.

Matt turned. "I won't say good-bye just yet, Mr. Dijon," he said. "Not until I have seen the horse."

There was a complete silence.

"You wish to see the horse?"

The incredulity was total.

"Yes, I do."

Slowly Dijon came around the desk. Cambier, the vet, looked extremely uncomfortable.

"We do not normally keep dead horses here," Dijon said in a voice just above a whisper. "This is a place for the living."

"But the postmortem took place here last Sunday," Matt persisted, "after the operation. This is only Wednesday."

Dijon looked at Matt pityingly and then launched into a rapid exchange with the vet. Both of them shrugged their shoulders hopelessly several times, then Cambier turned to Matt, gesticulating.

"After the postmortem, monsieur," he said to Matt, "monsieur" — he indicated Dijon — "sent the 'orse to Madame la Baronne" — he pointed generally to the countryside outside the stud walls.

"Madame who?"

In exasperation Cambier squared himself and tried to encapsulate his explanation in the air between his two readied hands. He looked like someone about to catch a ball.

"The 'orse, monsieur," he said to Matt, " 'e goes to *les chiens,* the dogs."

Matt's heart sank.

"You mean . . ."

"Kennels, Mr. Blaney," Dijon said, his small mouth tight, "kennels. Why don't you go there for yourself?" He turned to Cambier. "*Peut-être qu'il veut examiner les morceaux de merde,*" he said, and walked back to his desk.

"What did he say?" asked Matt as they walked across the yard.

Cambier looked delicately at the ground. "He says for you to look at" — he hesitated and his nose wrinkled in distaste — "*merde,*" he finished. "Shit." He looked apologetically at Matt.

"I am sorry," said Cambier nervously. "He is most upset — he thinks that all the bad luck it falls on him."

"Don't worry, I understand," Matt said gently. He paused. "Listen, I'm sorry as well," he said to the hapless vet. "I'm just doing my job. I've seen very few live horses in my day, not to mention dead ones."

"You are going to Paris?" Cambier asked.

"No," said Matt, "I've been traveling a lot — I'm going to stay around here tonight."

"Ah," said Cambier.

"Can you recommend a good restaurant?" asked Matt.

"Of course," replied Cambier, "Normandy has many."

"So I've heard," said Matt as he watched the vet write on a piece of paper.

"This is particularly good," Cambier said. "La Belle Epoque. It is just twenty minutes from Deauville, in the old port of Honfleur."

They went out under the stone arched gate and turned right at the gable end of a block of stables. Matt put out his hands to protect himself as someone collided straight into his chest.

"Oh God, I'm sorry!"

Matt found himself holding a pair of check-shirted arms and looking into wide, brown eyes.

"I'm sorry," the girl said again as he released her.

"That's all right." Matt smiled. He stepped back. "Are you American?"

"Yes, I am." She was tall, up to Matt's shoulder. She had an open, laughing face, and full eyebrows that were almost black. In an unconscious gesture she put her hand behind her head and brought her thick plait of honey-colored hair over her shoulder so that it rested between the rise of her breasts. Matt found himself staring.

"That was you in the shed back there," he said. "You had one hell of a job with that little horse."

"Poor Timmy," the girl smiled. "It's rough on him. Still it's his job — and he does get to meet horses his own size every once in a while."

Cambier, the vet, was standing dutifully to one side, his hands behind his back.

"I'm Matt Blaney," Matt said, shaking the girl's hand.

"Cathy Vandervater," she said. There was a freshness about her, an almost tangible outdoors scent of horses and leather and sweet meadows of hay.

"I've never seen a . . . performance quite like the one back there," Matt said. "They told me Normandy was the place to go but . . ."

Cathy Vandervater laughed. "Where are you from?" she asked.

"New York," Matt said.

"New York?" she said. "So am I."

"How long have you worked here?"

Cathy shrugged. "Two years. I'm going back home to a job this summer — hopefully in Kentucky."

There was a discreet cough and Matt turned to see Cambier glancing at his watch.

"Look," Matt said, turning back to the girl, "I know this is kind of sudden, but Mr. Cambier here has just been good enough to suggest the best restaurant in the whole of France." Matt looked down at the piece of paper which Cambier had given him. "It's in someplace called Honfleur."

Cathy shook her head. "I really couldn't."

"Oh, I'm sorry," Matt said, "is there a Mr. Vandervater I should have thought of?"

"No, there's not," Cathy replied. "It's just . . ."

"Just what?"

She burst out laughing. "It's just that tonight's my needlework night," she said.

"Needlework?" Matt pretended outrage. "Two fellow Americans, thousands of miles from home, and you talk of needlework?"

Cathy Vandervater was smiling broadly. "I can be ready at six-thirty," she said.

9   THE LETTER WAS CREASED AND DOG-EARED. THE TALL MAN sat at his desk and once more unfolded the blue square of pages.

Papa. Dear Papa.

All these years I had sought you. All the hours of the long, lonely nights with no one but myself for comfort, I begged you to come back. Dear, dear Papa.

I am blessed, or more likely cursed, to be a man whose recall is as simple as opening the pages of a book whose pictures tell the tale from the beginning. It is all there. Not just the images of the huts, the snow, the uniforms, but the noises of the shouts, the shots, and the smells, the cold, your warmth, the color of your beard. Now, this very moment, I can feel the outline of your great, warm body, I can tell its every contour, I know how it rises and falls with your every breath.

The reader adjusted his thick spectacles:

Dear Papa.

I at first could not understand why you left me. I should have known that you had to go so that now, after all these years, you can come back to give. And I never forgot you, that I promise. *Ich versprich es dir!*

He shook his head.

I have had a life, Papa, of both sorrow and of joy. This I have told you. I was born with the wrath of God on my face, but I have tried to atone through love. I have my memories which no one can take of the warm orange groves of Bat Yam, of the kindly folk who reared me, of long, glorious days of God-given labor in the fields, and of picnics with my wife and lovely children on the slopes of Mount Sidon.

But I have been saddened and bereft.

White tablets of Jerusalem stone now mark those whom I have loved, as the never-ending cycle of hope given and hope taken away goes on.

With one exception. Somewhere in the land of the fedayeen, some-where out there beyond the boundaries of our tiny country, is a boy, the first product of my loins. I know he is there, Papa; as I know the sun will rise tomorrow over Jebel El Hasa, I know he is there. He is just a child, a boy, a beautiful, unblemished boy, sent by the madness of man to a jungle of beasts. But he is there. Waiting. He is there.

The reader nodded slowly.

Papa, help me. Help me to get him back. Is it too much to ask? What do they want? A life? Here, here is a life, take it, it is nothing, take it now. But give back my boy.

Can you understand this, Papa? Can you understand that my love for him is of a different kind than my love for you? Perhaps it is how you feel for me? For I know that once you loved me. When the snow was deep and the eyes of the wild beasts circled us at night.

But that was many years ago, dear Papa, and now I need your help. Tell me what to do and I will do it.

At the end, we still have each other, Papa dear.

With a sigh, the reader rose. Carefully he folded the letter; then he made his way across the room to sit at the window in an upright chair.

WEDNESDAY: P.M.

 FIFTY-THREE STORIES BELOW, ICICLES CLUNG TO THE RAIL-ings in Battery Park. Large ice wedges floated down the Hud-son and out to sea under the Verrazano Bridge. From where he stood the man holding the phone could see a ferry from

Staten Island dock and discharge its passengers, tiny specks, on to the freezing cold tip of Manhattan.

"I see," he said slowly. "Thank you — and keep us in touch if you can."

He put down the telephone and then, biting his lip, allowed his mind to sort and analyze the information he had been given. He was bald, but lean and hard with deepset eyes that never rested. In shirtsleeves, his lower forearms were competent and covered with dense mats of black hair. He grabbed the phone again. "Where's Crocker?" he snapped.

"He's just arrived, Mr. Johnson," said the voice of his secretary, two rooms and an acre of carpet away.

Hugh Johnson sank slowly into a leather swivel chair and put his feet up on the mahogany of his desk. From this desk he could survey the area from which for eight years he had conducted the affairs of First Transnational Banking Corporation and its twenty-two thousand employees. The emphasis was on space: large vistas of it were broken up by woodland and a miniature waterfall. As he looked, a blond girl rounded a headland of vegetation followed by a man in his late forties. The girl smiled at them both, then withdrew. Hugh Johnson pointed to a chair, then fixed his visitor with his intense eyes.

"Galatti, Seymour," he said without preamble.

Seymour Crocker held the stare. He was taller than the bank chairman and had more hair. He had a smooth face, which could look smug or benign depending on the situation. Now he cleared his throat and frowned in concern.

"What about him, Hugh?" he asked.

"You remember the rumor we heard last week?"

"Shit, yes," said Crocker.

"I just got a call from Washington," Hugh Johnson said. He nodded grimly. "The Justice Department investigation into Carlo Galatti for violation of the Sherman Act is nearly complete. They will probably move on him inside the next couple of weeks."

"What will the charge be exactly?" Crocker asked.

"Refusal to deal with U.S. suppliers and subcontractors blacklisted by the Arabs in their latest boycott of Israel. Refusal to deal with Jewish suppliers or subcontractors here or abroad, or anyone currently dealing with Israel. The Arabs love him, but now Justice are out to get his ass." The bank chairman got to his feet. He wore a wide leather belt, emphasizing his disciplined regime. "Run the Galatti numbers again," he ordered.

Seymour Crocker pursed his lips. "As of last night," he said, "Galatti Incorporated owed this bank three hundred million dollars. The bank are secured with first charges on all the corporation's assets, last valued at four hundred and fifty million, plus the personal guarantees of Galatti himself, and his own shares in his company, valued at one hundred and fifty million dollars. We're way in the clear, by our last estimate at least two to one. Even if his corporate paper halves, which I think is unlikely, we're still A-okay."

Hugh Johnson bit his lip. When the chairman of First Transnational felt concern, small worry-ridges appeared on his forehead and ran all the way back to the crown of his head. "I don't know," he said. "These construction companies have assets which dissolve like snow under cat piss when things go wrong." He sat down again and looked across at his immediate subordinate, the president of First Transnational Bank. "Five years ago, when you brought it in, this looked like the sweetest account in the bank. But Jesus, now we've got too much exposure."

"I agree, it's time to get tough," said Seymour Crocker. "Now that oil's on the way down, being the biggest builder in Arabia isn't as smart as it used to be."

"And oil's going to continue to go down," Hugh Johnson said.

"You really believe that, Hugh?"

"Why not?" Johnson replied. "It caused us hell all the way up, now it's going to screw us all the way down. Galatti's a classic example. He's owed millions by Arabs who suddenly can't pay."

"I think, however, that we're above high water," Crocker said. "The Arabs' cash flow has got to improve."

"Look," said Johnson, "it's only yesterday that these guys came in after seven centuries in the desert. To them it's funny money — always has been. For Christ's sake, Galatti's built a university down there with more teaching space than Harvard. Most of them can't read or write." He wrinkled his forehead. "I've got this gut feeling, Seymour. It tells me that Galatti's in an awful lot more trouble than anyone knows."

"We're going to get tough," repeated Crocker. "There's a meeting this weekend; we called it, as you know, but Galatti wants it in Barbados. I'm going down there. I'll be demanding an immediate reduction of the loan — like a third — straightaway."

Hugh Johnson kneaded the palm of one hand with the fist of the other. "If the Justice Department action gathers momentum," he said, "Galatti may have trouble getting bonded next year. That will cause all sorts of problems in his servicing ongoing contracts. In a scenario like that, his cash flow could really dry up and then the manure would be all over the carpet." He clenched his fist so that the rigid sinews of his forearm stood out. "We've got to get that debt halved," he said. "The Galatti account is not to rise one nickel above today's level, understood?"

Seymour Crocker nodded as the clear, blue eyes tunneled into him. "Understood," he said.

"I never liked Galatti," said Johnson. "I don't know who he is or where he comes from. Something like this could make shit out of one of our quarters, just when Wall Street is dazzled by our twenty-two quarters of unbroken growth. Don't forget, we're only worth three times what Galatti owes us."

"Don't worry," Crocker said. "I'm comfortable with it. It's under control." He smiled. "Incidentally, I see that our stock broke eighty this morning. Congratulations."

"I know, and I think it will go higher," Johnson said. He brought his fist down quietly on his desk. "It puts the Midwest Star deal in the bag."

"That's a beaut," Seymour Crocker said, shaking his head in admiration. "A real beaut."

"They're as good as ours," Hugh Johnson replied. "If it's the only thing I ever do for this bank I'll be happy. It gives us just the presence in the Midwest we need."

"It's brilliant," agreed Crocker. "And it's got your name written on it for everyone to see."

"Herman has to get some of the credit," Johnson said. The bank's chairman allowed his eyes to flicker over Seymour Crocker. "He called just before you came up. We're on the point of agreeing a rescheduling with the Paraguyans, but it's subject to the final word from the IMF. As that's not going to come in for a week, Herman's coming home." Johnson nodded confidently.

"Some people are in the shit down there," Crocker said. "We've been lucky."

"What about our offshore business?" Johnson asked. "Anything happening there that I should know about?"

"Nothing bad," Crocker said with a smile, referring to a particular area of his responsibility. "Our new branch in Panama City is busting with cash, mostly tax driven; it's very profitable business."

"I still prefer downtown, Stateside," Johnson said, his eyes on the distance. He snapped back. "Anything else?"

Crocker spread his hands and smiled. "When are you off?" he asked.

"Eight-thirty tomorrow morning," Johnson said. He sprang to his feet and also smiled, the first time in their meeting. "God, I feel like a drink," he said, leading the way to leather chairs.

"Look at this weather," said Crocker indicating New York Harbor. "I really envy you." He accepted a glass with two fingers of bourbon and watched as the chairman added water to one for himself. "London first?" he asked.

"Concorde in the morning," Johnson said, sitting down and putting the heels of his highly polished shoes on another chair. "We stay in Claridges, and if Mitzy isn't too tired we'll hit the Connaught for dinner — God, I just adore that Yorkshire pudding. Then, next morning, front cabin all the way to Hong Kong." He spoke in a low, controlled drawl and revolved his glass by its base on the tips of his fingers.

"Will you stay there for long?" Crocker asked.

"A few days. Grayson wants me to meet with some of our big Chinese customers, just for an evening. Mitzy's never been there so we'll take in the sights, the Jockey Club is hosting a lunch for us, we'll go to Canton — that sort of thing."

"And then?"

"And then it's up, up, and away and down to the sun and the sand and the clear blue sea." Johnson made a flying motion with his hand. "You know it's nearly been six years since Mitzy and I got away like this together. She had one hell of a job persuading me to do it, but now that my mind is made up, I'm just rarin' to go."

Seymour Crocker smiled broadly. "Great Barrier Reef, isn't it?" he asked.

"That's it," the bank chairman said. "We're going to this little hotel on a sort of desert island. Eight rooms. We fly in there in a small plane. Seems they've never heard of TV or telephones, and certainly not of the Dow Jones."

Both men laughed.

"Relax and enjoy it," Seymour Crocker said. "You know that everything here's going to be fine."

"I know that," Hugh Johnson said, swinging his legs to the floor and sitting up. He pushed his glass aside. "Our offer doesn't go to the Midwest Star shareholders for two weeks, so there's nothing to worry about there." He looked pensively in the bank president's direction, then he stood up. "Take Herman Katz to Barbados with you on the Galatti trip. There's no harm to have two on something like that. You can do the nice-guy, bad-guy routine."

"No points for guessing who'll play bad guy," Seymour Crocker said dryly.

"Herman's okay," Johnson said. "He's a meticulous asshole at times, but he's a good banker. He won't give other people's money away." He looked at his watch. "I'd better get going," he said. "The kids are home for dinner this evening — sort of a bon-voyage party for us old pair."

Seymour Crocker nodded. Johnson lived in New Jersey and came to work each morning by a combination of limousine and helicopter. Now he walked Crocker out to the lobby. The chairman's secretary smiled up at them. I wonder, does he . . . ? thought Crocker. The uncertainty associated with the question was the only reason he had not tried himself.

"Listen, give my love to Mitzy and have one hell of a time," he said, shaking the chairman's hand. "See you in a few weeks and in the meantime forget about this place. It's under wraps."

"That's my firm intention," said Hugh Johnson as the bank's president stepped into the elevator.

Seymour Crocker leaned back against the mirror and breathed deeply. The coming three weeks would give him a fleeting taste of the power he so coveted. Johnson, a man of huge organizational ability and vision, and a workaholic, had every area of the bank battened down so tight that for the three weeks of his absence Seymour Crocker could play caretaker chairman but no more.

He sighed. The bank's earnings, although good, could be so much better. Hugh Johnson was an arch-conservative. The offshore network that the bank had begun to build was a good example. Crocker had pushed for branches in tax havens like Nassau and Panama, where hundreds of millions of dollars were attracted from the international operators who ceaselessly shifted their cash around the world in their endless quest for tax avoidance and in their desire for investment anonymity. First Transnational's rewards had been handsome, but still, at rock bottom, Hugh Johnson did not trust anything that failed to fall within his particular definition of respectability.

Tagging Katz on to the Barbados trip was typical; Herman Katz, executive vice-president and comptroller of the bank, was widely assumed to be Johnson's choice as successor. Known throughout First Transnational as Catshit and feared accordingly, Katz would report on any move that Crocker made, straight back to the chairman.

As Seymour Crocker stepped into his office, his telephone purred.

"Your wife, sir," said his secretary.

"Hi, Pam, sorry I didn't get back to you, honey, but I've been kind of busy, and Hugh's going away."

"That's all right," said his wife of thirty years. "I just wondered about dinner. It's my bridge night."

"Don't wait dinner for me, pet," Crocker said. "I've got another four hours here minimum." He contrived a sigh. "I'll catch a bite in our cafeteria, but I won't be in Connecticut before midnight."

"Poor Seymour."

"Some things have to be done."

"See you later."

"Bye, have fun."

Crocker pressed for his secretary and instructed her to book a table for two at a new Italian restaurant he had recently discovered on Third Avenue.

Far below and out to sea he could make out the small, red shape of a helicopter, scuttling across the black sky toward New Jersey. Crocker lifted the telephone again and pushed the buttons from memory. A woman's voice answered.

"An hour," said the acting chief executive of First Transnational

Banking Corporation to a lady whom he had first met six months ago in an elevator in the Waldorf Astoria.

Sitting back, Crocker felt a spreading glow, whether of expectation or of fleeting power he was not sure. But it was pleasant. Putting on his coat and scarf, he made his way from his office and the building, his mind firmly on the six hours ahead of him and nothing else.

WEDNESDAY: P.M.

11 OUTSIDE, THE OLD PORT OF HONFLEUR WAS DESERTED. Through an open window Matt could hear boats creaking at their moorings and steel mast-stays rattling in the wind. The restaurant had great beams supporting a low ceiling, wide flagstones, and a blazing fire big enough to roast an ox on. Matt leaned back and felt a warm glow, a combination of Calvados and the sight of the girl sitting opposite him. Somehow he had expected that when he collected her she would still be in the boots and jeans and the checkered shirt. When he saw the stunning woman with glistening, honey-colored hair around her shoulders, wearing a turquoise dress fastened at her slim waist by the thick white belt, Matt for the second time that day had stared. He looked at her now in the light from the fire; her eyes had become an even deeper brown.

A waiter came with two more balloons of Calvados on a silver tray.

"A guy I met in Paris," Matt said, "told me that this stuff and horses are what Normandy is all about." He raised his glass. "He omitted to mention the quality of the grooms. Cheers."

"Cheers." Cathy smiled. "And thank you for a lovely evening."

They were the last in the restaurant. Matt sipped his drink.

"People with such blond hair are meant to have blue eyes," he said.

"And insurance men are meant to be small and weedy and wear thick glasses," Cathy replied.

"I wear glasses for reading — in bed," Matt replied. He saw her put her tongue in her cheek, just for an instant, then smile and look away. Somewhere in Honfleur a church bell chimed ten.

"This is the best time of the year to come here," Cathy said, her head cocked to one side to hear the chimes. "In summer everything gets clogged up — traffic jams, tourists, people from Paris with tiny boats who think they're Christopher Columbus."

"Vandervater," Matt said. "That's Dutch."

"It sure is," Cathy said. "The way Father tells it, we were in New York before Peter Stuyvesant."

"How did you get here, to Deauville, to Haras du Bois?" Matt asked.

"I used to work for a company in the States that specialized in horse transportation," Cathy replied. "One day we were delivering a mare here and I met Dijon. He offered me a job. France was one place I'd always dreamed of coming to, so I said yes."

"So how has it been?" Matt asked. "Two years you said?"

Cathy nodded. "It's been okay," she said. She swept her hair back from her shoulders. "Like everything, it's had its moments."

Matt's antennae caught the change in her tone.

"Tell about this afternoon," he said, switching the subject. "I saw . . . Man of Reims, was it, at work? Although if that's work I'm a Frenchman."

Cathy laughed. "I've never seen anyone look so uncomfortable," she said, her head shaking. "Your eyes were out to here."

Matt spread his hands in innocence. "I'm a babe in the woods," he said. "I need a guide to take me through this horse jungle." He couldn't take his eyes off her. "Any takers?" he asked softly.

"It's not all that mysterious," Cathy said. "It's business, like any other, I guess."

"Take Man of Reims," Matt said. "How much, for example, did the service which I saw today cost?"

"Seventy-five thousand dollars," Cathy said.

Matt whistled. "That's big money," he said.

"But not as big as the reason that you're really here," Cathy said.

Matt looked at her.

"Cambier told me," she said softly. "I asked him before you came to pick me up. He said you were here about Cornucopia."

Matt nodded slowly. "That's right," he said.

Cathy crossed her legs and leaned back, her glass of Calvados between her hands on her lap. "Is it true he was insured for two hundred million?" she asked.

Again Matt nodded.

"Poor Cornucopia," Cathy said quietly. "What a disaster."

Matt shrugged. "Carlo Galatti will collect his money," he said. "He may not agree."

Cathy snorted. "What feeling has a man like Galatti for a horse?" she said. "He's never even been here."

"I understood that he was pretty cut up about Cornucopia," Matt said.

Cathy looked at Matt skeptically. "Cut up as hell, I'm sure," she said. She put her glass on the table. "What are you looking for, anyway?" she asked.

"We try to make sure that no funny stuff went on," Matt said; "that no one is trying to steal our money; that nothing suspicious happened to the horse that died."

"Exciting," Cathy said, her eyes on Matt's face. "But isn't it all a bit high-powered for a sleepy little place like this?"

"The man I work for has a favorite saying," Matt said. "It is that things are rarely as they seem."

"And what do things seem here?" Cathy asked.

"That a two-hundred-million-dollar racehorse died of cancer," Matt replied quietly. "That's what it seems."

The waiter came with the bill.

"You remember back in the barn today?" Matt said. "Just after you left I thought I saw a big man, bald, very strong, standing just for an instant at the very back. Any idea who he is?"

Cathy looked at Matt thoughtfully. "He's called the Kaiser," she said. "Why do you ask?"

"I have the impression I know him from someplace," Matt replied.

Cathy shivered. "He gives me the creeps," she said. "He's Galatti's right-hand man. He always appears when you least expect him. People in the stud are terrified of him."

They sat for some moments in silence. The logs in the fireplace had ceased to flame and now their embers glowed a deep red.

"After duck, Pomerol, and Calvados, I think I need some fresh air," Matt said.

"Let's go for a walk," Cathy said. "I'll show you Honfleur."

Matt helped her into her coat and put on a leather jacket.

They left the restaurant and followed the meandering street upward, away from the harbor, past sleeping shops and houses until they came into a square. In its center was a small, medieval church topped with a clock and the bell which they had earlier heard. Most life, it seemed, had ceased in the ancient houses, their wooden crossbeams running like irregular veins, exposed and weather-beaten by centuries of sea air.

"The entire village has been preserved from fifteen hundred," Cathy said. "It's so peaceful to think that we're in the midst of such antiquity. It's almost like carrying on a tradition."

They crossed the square together, the girl up to Matt's shoulder. They walked down wide, steep steps that brought them back out on the quay. Some lights still shone from a few boats, but otherwise Honfleur had definitely retired. They went the long way around, past shops and restaurants whose windows by day would be teeming with the night's catch. They passed under the shadow of a tree; a high-pitched squeal broke the silence as a haggard cat dashed to safety, a fish-head in its jaws. Instinctively she caught his arm. He held it there on their walk down the dark pier and along the seafront to the car.

For a moment they stood together looking out at the harbor estuary. A crescent moon had come out to beat a path on the dark water.

"Isn't it lovely?" she said. "Beautiful, quiet, unaggressive." A little gust of wind came off the sea to blow her hair. "I come here at night," she said, "just to listen to the curlews. They're such peaceful birds, yet so lonely."

"I like curlews," Matt said.

She linked him a fraction closer.

"I often think that when I die and then come back," she said in a small voice, "I would like to be a curlew."

"You would make a lovely curlew," he said quietly.

She shivered. He turned and traced his hand along the line of her cheek. For an instant she looked at him, her eyes fathomless, then she ran both her hands up and around his neck. Her kiss was long and searching.

"This is disgraceful," she murmured, "we've only just met."

Matt held her tightly, her body suddenly as familiar as his own.

"I think you're nice," she whispered to him.

"I told you," he said. "I like curlews."

Over her neck he could see the outline of lonely seabirds wheeling against the sky.

 REFLEXIVELY THE MAN RETURNED THE SPECTACLES TO HIS face. On the second floor of his house he sat, before a window, staring sightlessly out at the large flakes of snow that had begun to cover Manhattan.

Increasingly he thought of that time, particularly when he was alone. Even now as the nonstop hum of the traffic on Fifth Avenue floated up to him, he could quite clearly visualize the scene.

It was snowing, great fluffy flakes that you could catch in their fall. The explosions like thunderclaps that had gone on all day now lit up the eastern sky and were nearer. It had snowed for over a month. The weather had hampered and finally halted the work: over a thousand dead bodies lay in grotesque, naked piles, the frozen earth ally to the approaching Russians, guardian of the horrific evidence, defying all attempts to dig even shallow graves.

"*Los jetzt!*" he shouted to the driver and jumped into the back of the truck as it lurched into gear. He could see the glowing arc lamps on the other side of the high wall. For an agonizing moment the wheels spun in the snow, but then with a jolt they were on their way. He sat as they drove through the forest, looking back at the receding camp. More thunder rent the blind sky. He looked down beside him to what at first sight appeared to be a bundle of rags.

"*Noch wach?*" he asked and shook the bundle. "Are you awake?"

A small face appeared. It was that of a child, no more than four or five. His cheeks were gaunt, almost hollow, his eyes large from malnutrition and fright. But it was something else which caused recoil: one side of the child's face was a hideous, livid purple. He made himself touch it . . . and tried to say something, but at his touch the child became rigid.

"Ach, mach was du willst," he said in distaste, "have it your way."

The very process of dressing in the clothes had made him want to vomit; the thin pants and jacket, the soiled shirt and cap. But it was essential that he wear nothing that would give him away. Now he reached into the greasy pocket of the coat and withdrew the papers. The likeness was what had given him the idea. The Jew had had an almost Aryan face, a genetic fluke undoubtedly, but nonetheless true. But the real ace was the child, not old enough to be taken seriously by anyone yet old enough to travel. A father fleeing with his little son. With the Eastern Front collapsing, it was almost the only hope. The truck lurched on into the night.

He always marveled at how clear it would remain. It was the night they had gone into hell. His driver of eight years never knew what happened as the bullet from his own Mauser fragmented the back of his head. They had started out on their journey, he as a young, athletically fit man, something he had always been proud of. After three weeks trudging westward with snow often up to his hips, the disfigured child across his shoulders, he had aged ten years. At first his own survival had been the sole reason for keeping the boy alive. He was pathetic, emaciated and in a state of shock. They had eaten, drunk, and slept together like animals, in the barns of farmyards, in ditches, and in disused cow barns. They had lain down side by side on rough earth and on pine needles in vast forests, where only a compass and an iron will stood between them and the salivating jaws of beasts whose eyes flashed from the perimeter of the night. In terror the child had cried out. He had caught the small body closer, making them both part of one mold and then in the great stillness of the winter night he had begun to sing, in a melodious baritone, "Rosamunde, give me a kiss and your heart."

It was the favorite German song of 1944, but to the small Jewish child from eastern Poland it was the song of assurance, of happiness, and of sleep. Would his new papa sing if there was any danger?

When at last on the other side of the frozen lake the church spire of Litomerice came suddenly into view, he jumped in the air for joy and hugged the child to him.

"Wir sind gerettet, mein Söhnchen!" he cried. "We are saved, my little son!"

And the child looked at him strangely, but did not move away. At that moment each had recognized the bond that had been made: he surprisingly and against everything he stood for, the child simply because he needed someone to love.

Carlo Galatti breathed deeply. His survival and success had been breathtakingly daring in their concept. He had refused to hide like a rat in the hills around Buenos Aires — instead, he had struck right back at the heart of his victors, gained a foothold in New York, and then beaten them at their own game. His mouth curled in distaste. Most men were hypocrites. At least he and his kind had had the courage of their convictions, to rid the world of the offal that then and now was poisoning every stratum of life.

For the most part the exercises in which he had been involved were humane — far more humane than the wholesale displacement of an entire race of simple people from the desert land of their birth by marauding Jews, the outcasts and scum of Europe.

Galatti sneered as he remembered. What he had hated most was their arrogance! He remembered once on the platform at Lublin, overseeing the arrival of a train. The disembarking Jews were convinced that they were going to a special resettlement center. One of them, a middle-aged, greasy Pole, actually paused at the carriage steps to tip the train personnel. The arrogant swine! Little did he understand that the very fingers he used to dispense his filthy coins would, within a week, be pulverized fertilizer in a burlap sack on its way back to the Fatherland.

Galatti raised the curtain momentarily and shivered.

Since the Jews had been given Israel, the rules had changed.

Now they could commit acts of terrorism with the full, legal backing of a so-called State. It had not changed his iron conviction — he had never dealt with them and never would. With one exception.

Twenty years ago, he had been looking at a newsreel, one of the new colored kind. The item was about an award to an Israeli prodigy, another Einstein, they said, a young man who had already broken down many barriers of experimental physics.

Galatti's mouth had been set in distaste before he frowned, then stared. At first he thought it was a fault of the Technicolor process. He felt a jolt. The young man on the screen had a vivid discoloration down the left side of his face.

Galatti had made discreet inquiries. The more he inquired, the more profound his feelings became.

The chances of coincidence were too great. It was Yoseph Shenlavi, adopted son of survivors of Theresienstadt, the first convoy to Geneva in '45.

The room was in a modern building, just completed, off a busy Harvard Square. It was November and students were avidly discussing John Kennedy's assassination in Dallas the day before. Galatti knocked on the door.

"Come in."

The quarters were tiny. In one corner, sitting at a long table, was a young man. He had a sallow, sad face which he kept in profile; his head was long, rising at its crown in a small bump and covered there by a circular, Jewish *kipa*.

"Can I help you?" The young man smiled kindly up at his visitor. The left side of his face was disfigured. He saw a tall man, well built and pencil-slim with a full head of blond hair that was just on the point of going white.

"Yoseph Shenlavi?"

The student nodded. Slowly the visitor closed the door and removed the heavy spectacles he was wearing.

"Can I help you?" repeated the student in accented English.

Next his visitor did an extraordinary thing. He walked to the student's table and crouched down beside him. Then in a deep German baritone he began to sing "Rosamunde, give me a kiss and your heart."

The reaction was electrifying. The student made to rise but as the melodious song continued he sat again, staring, his eyes wide. Eventually, the song was over and Galatti stood up. Yoseph Shenlavi did likewise. The two men embraced.

"Papa," cried the youth, "Papa."

Slowly the focus of his vision returned. The snow outside had for the moment ceased and the white street came into view. A lone van pulled around the far corner and gradually approached, its wheel marks vivid black scars on the clean snow.

Carlo Galatti's eyes narrowed as he saw it. His hand went to a pair of binoculars on a sidetable, and, rising so as to hold back one side of the curtain with his shoulder, he brought the vehicle into close-up. Galatti's lips came back in a snarl. The van's markings and registration were the same as on the last three days: it was as if he had been waiting for them all his life, ever since the days when he had, at random, decided which of a family would live and which would die. He had been conscious at that time of what he did: he had been aware that with a simple gesture of his baton he had ordained the fate of musicians, doctors with years of experience, mothers with large families, grown-up daughters, grandchildren. Yet Galatti saw his relationship with the Jews not as that of executioner and victim, but more a type of ongoing contest or battle in which for many years he had managed to keep the upper hand, but which now, with the almost inevitable advent of the closed van, the Jews were beginning to win.

He drew back from the window and turned around. A split second before the telephone rang he knew it would do so. He picked it up.

"Yes?"

As he listened to the transatlantic call, Galatti realized that what he was hearing, like the arrival of the van outside, was just another part of the overall unraveling that was taking place. He set his jaw defiantly.

"So the American has now met the one person who has all along represented the danger?" he rasped.

"I am afraid so," said the person on the other end.

Carlo Galatti said: "You are not to let them out of your sight, is that clear? Time, to me, is now of the essence."

Then he returned the telephone to its cradle and stood there, staring sightlessly into space.

THURSDAY

13 THEY WALKED ARM IN ARM OVER THE SWEEPING BRIDGE, then to the left, following the line of the coast as it curved in to make the head of Deauville beach.

"That meal was wonderful," Cathy said. "You've obviously got a knack for these things. I've been here nearly two years and I never knew that little place existed."

"The trick now is to stay awake," said Matt and drew her nearer to him. A stinging wind whipped in from the sea and pulled loose, long strands of her hair from the scarf that had held it about her neck.

"Tell me about yourself," Cathy said.

"I'm thirty-seven," Matt said, "I'm originally from Saint Louis, Missouri, my parents are both dead, I'm divorced."

"When did you get divorced?"

"Two and a half years ago."

"Was it rough?"

"Very."

Matt felt Cathy pull his arm closer. He looked down at her: she had lovely clear skin, tinged rose now by the wind. He kissed her.

"Some people are takers, others are givers," Cathy said. "You're a giver."

They walked on, past empty, boarded-up shops, past deserted tennis-courts and an outdoor swimming pool.

"Has it always been insurance?" she asked.

"No," Matt replied. "Before insurance there were a few years when I guess I did everything except wrestle in mud before a live audience. Before that there was Vietnam."

Her brown eyes held compassion. "Is that where you got the scar on your back?" she asked gently.

Matt laughed. "That's where that old scar came from," he said and squeezed her closer to him.

They had neared the end of the boardwalk. Through the mist on the sea the squat outlines of the oil storage tanks in Le Havre, the greens and yellows, appeared at the limit of vision like giant toys.

"What does a case like this mean to you?" Cathy asked.

Matt thought. He said: "Normally it's a job. However, in this particular case the guy I work for, who also happens to be a very good friend, his money is personally on the line. He took a million dollars of the Cornucopia insurance personally and never laid it off. It's hit him at a bad time."

"Who is he?" Cathy asked.

"His name is Jim Crabbe," Matt said. He smiled. "He's really a great guy. He gave me a job and a chance when no one else would. People like him are rare."

"That's nice," Cathy said. "You obviously have a very special relationship."

"I've known him now for ten years," Matt said. He looked toward the sea. "Jim's son and I were in Nam together."

"Does his son work for him as well?" Cathy asked.

Matt shook his head. "One day we walked into an ambush," he said. "Jim's son was one of those never found."

Cathy winced. "How sad," she said.

"War is sad," Matt said. He bent for a stone and then, detaching himself, flung it as far as he could. Cathy looked at him fondly and smiled.

They walked out on the empty beach. The tide was full out, and what seemed miles away, clouds of gulls rose and fell on the flat, wet sand. Up on the road behind them, a car pulled slowly away.

"Whereabouts in New York do you come from?" Matt asked.

"Brooklyn," Cathy replied.

"What about the horse bit?" Matt asked. "How did that happen?"

"Dad's a cab driver," Cathy replied. "I'm the eldest of three. During holidays I always went with him when he was working days. Dad knows some of the smaller trainers out at Aqueduct and Belmont, he sometimes does jobs for them." They paused as a flock of gulls in their path rose and moved on. "Some of my happiest moments," Cathy said, "are of summer mornings on the track with Dad, watching the thoroughbreds being put through their paces. It's when I fell in love with horses."

They had come to the wooden poles and sleepers of an old jetty, covered in green slime and seaweed. Matt bent and then came back up holding a small green crab, its legs thrashing. He lowered it back to the sand where it scuttled frantically for the sea.

"What did your father think about you and the horses?" he asked.

"He thought what he always thought," she said wistfully, "he thought it was terrific."

Matt touched her — her face radiated an inner glow. "He sounds like a nice guy," he said.

"He is," she said simply. "Do you know that if any of us ever came home with a badge, a funny rosette, or any of the silly things you get at school, we came home to such acclamation, to such pride and support, that it felt like you'd hit a home run in Yankee Stadium and a hundred thousand people were on their feet."

Some spits of rain had begun to fall. Higher up on the beach were lines of lonely, upright poles, awaiting the summer and the colorful, tented *cabines de bain* which they would support.

Matt stopped and caught both of Cathy's hands in his. "I have a confession to make," he said.

She looked at him, her eyes amused.

"When I first saw you yesterday," Matt said, "and then realized you were an American, I saw not just an amazingly attractive creature in faded blue jeans, but also an opportunity."

Cathy laughed. "Am I meant to be flattered?"

"Look," Matt said, "I'm serious. I'm crazy about you. You're the most beautiful woman I've ever met. I want to go on seeing you, again and again. I want to see you ever single second that I have left over here. When I go home I want to call you, every night of the week. I'm going to write to you. When you come back to the States, I'm going to buy a season ticket to get to Kentucky."

Cathy's eyes sparkled.

"But there's something I want to tell you," Matt said.

Cathy looked into his eyes and saw the deep softness give way to something harder.

"My confession," Matt said seriously, "is that I first saw in you an opportunity to get some easy information. That's all changed." He held her eyes intently with his. "Okay?"

"Okay," Cathy said cautiously.

"But I've met Carlo Galatti," Matt said quietly, "and I don't like him and I don't like Dijon. I don't like the Kaiser with the pink head and the narrow eyes. I don't like or trust any of them. And I get a feeling of danger, Cathy, real danger. I know danger, instinctively I know when it's around, and it's around these men. For example, I'm sure the Kaiser was sent over here to keep an eye on me. I can look after myself. But if I'm in danger, and if you're seen with me, that could mean that you're in danger too."

Cathy let go his arm. She sank down and began to trace circles in the sand with her finger. "Why is there danger?" she asked in a whisper.

"Where there's two hundred million dollars around," Matt said, "men get very greedy. And where you have greed you also have danger."

He hunkered down beside Cathy and took her hand in his. "I don't mean to try to scare you," he said. "I'm just concerned."

She opened her mouth and for a moment he was sure that she was going to say something. Then the spits of rain suddenly turned to a downpour. Cathy jumped to her feet.

"Race you to the car!" she cried.

Later, Matt took the BMW along the road of the darkened coast. He could feel her fingers along the base of his neck.

"When does all this have to end?" she asked.

"Never," he said. "I've decided to stay."

"Seriously."

"I'll have to go back on Saturday," Matt said. "I've a mountain of work waiting to be done. I also want to break the news to Jim that despite all our feelings to the contrary, nothing appears to have shown up to save him a million bucks." Matt adjusted his rearview mirror.

"You haven't called him yet?" Cathy said.

Matt shook his head, then brushed hair from his forehead. "I was hoping something might turn up," he said. "I guess I basically hate giving Jim bad news."

They pulled up at the side of a whitewashed, one-story restaurant, where through warm windows they could see a fire and dark beams crisscrossing a low ceiling. The smell of shellfish on a charcoal spit was tantalizing. They got out and, as Matt locked his door, he looked across the roof of the car and saw Cathy looking at him, her eyes almost sad. Just as earlier on the beach, so Matt was once again sure that she was about to say something. Then the lights of another car caught her, full beam, and she turned away.

Arm in arm they walked around to the front of the building where the sound of the tide on round stones was like the music in a childhood dream.

"I'm falling in love with you," he whispered, his mouth at her neck.

She kissed him gently. "Let's get these poor lobsters," she said.

THURSDAY

14 WITH A SIGH DR. SHENLAVI LOOKED EASTWARD. FOLLOW-
ing his *tephillot* he had taken a stroll in the small garden that
rose on the side of the valley above Mevasseret. He could see
Jerusalem, sprawling golden over the central mountain-massif
of Palestine. He turned. Dr. Shenlavi's garden was neat and ordered.
Careful drills had been laid containing sturdy plants of lettuce and red
cabbage. Beside them were neat rows of onions, tomatoes, and green
peppers. There was a fig tree to one side, spreading over a white seat,
an apple tree, and a pomegranate.

Throughout the year the garden was weeded and thinned, sowed and
reaped, although most of the produce he gave away. It was another
reminder of a time now gone, when everything was eaten the day it was
picked. He had kept it up, never letting a day pass without an hour
being spent in the garden. When he went to the Negev he had let an
Arab youth from the village take his place trading the produce of his
plot and a little money for the boy's labor. Everything was the same as
the day Levi had left. Unseeingly, Dr. Shenlavi turned his eyes on the
valley.

My son, Yoseph, mein Söhnchein.

Dr. Shenlavi smiled happily.

Only you, now a father, can truly know the love I hold for you.

The slight doctor nodded his discolored head.

I have followed your achievements and my heart bursts with pride.

Dr. Shenlavi nodded confidently again, then he turned from the valley, which was charged with birdsong. He followed a winding path,
through a small raspberry plantation and down two steps to the back
terrace of his house. He went inside and made his way through the
kitchen, then down steep wooden stairs to the lower-level garage.
Slowly he made his way to his workbench and picked up a lead-lined
apron, which he knotted at his waist. He sat heavily down on a wooden
bench and sighed again.

Mein Sohn.

*When you called me to tell me of your sorrow, I wept. I wept because I realized
that you, the one I truly love, are once again alone.*

Dr. Shenlavi reached for an industrial dustmask, fitted with an elastic cord. He fitted it over his face before he donned a pair of leaded gloves.

He reached for a large, tartan Thermos flask, one of four, standing to his left. With extreme car he unscrewed its plastic top; a heavy lead stopper was revealed, quite unlike the normal cork used to keep coffee warm. Slowly he unscrewed the threaded metal, reached for a large Pyrex beaker, platinized on the inside, and decanted the contents of the flask. The two quarts plus of plutonium nitrate poured silently out like an oily crème de menthe.

Like me, my child, you now know what it is to lose a son.

But unlike you, I have found my boy.

I weep, because I understand.

You want my help?

I am ready.

The adaptation of the Thermos flasks was something of which Dr. Shenlavi was particularly proud. The most difficult part had been purchasing them. He had needed six, all identical and each with the unusually large capacity of nearly two quarts. Over a six-week period, on weekends, he had picked up four, mostly from hardware stores around Jerusalem, never buying twice from the same place. Then there had been a dead end: it seemed that whoever had the franchise for the tartan, Taiwan-manufactured flasks had not managed to have them stocked in any of the remaining dozen stores that Dr. Shenlavi visited. He had driven to Tel-Aviv and picked them up within half an hour on Dizengoff.

From each flask he had removed the innards. Then, employing the ingenuity with which he had made his name, Dr. Shenlavi had fitted into each one a snug tube, fractionally smaller than the flask itself, and made of an inner and outer wall of borosilicate, separated by three millimeters of mercury. The arrangement had proved not only an ideal method for transporting plutonium nitrate but had also increased the capacity of the flasks to over two quarts.

Filling them had, in the end, been easy. With his unfettered access into the sampling point of the plutonium cell, Dr. Shenlavi had been able to milk the pipe carrying the plutonium nitrate. Normally it dispensed small droplets for laboratory examination; a very sensitive Gallenkamp balance recorded disbursements in units of one fluid gram and displayed them on a digital counter. Removing the outside panel, he had temporarily broken the link between the discriminator and the basic counter: as he milked the plutonium into the flasks, the electronic impulses never reached the external display.

Over a two-month period he had taken it three times, each time six days in a row, finishing in the previous week. The holding-tank deficiency was unlikely to be discovered in time — if at all. Israel was not party to the International Atomic Energy Agency in Vienna, and so Dimona was not subject to its safeguards or inspections. The fact that the reactor was now on a two-week shutdown was an added protection.

I did what you asked.

I went into the lair of the wolf so that the lamb might be spared.

For you, Yoseph, mein Sohn, I went into the lair of the wolf.

Meticulously Dr. Shenlavi added the contents of the remaining three flasks to the beaker. He now had nearly nine quarts of dull, green plutonium nitrate before him. He stood up and from a raised shelf took down an elongated metal rod, eighteen inches high with one of its ends formed in a large, bulbous onion. The tip of the onion was threaded and formed, as was the rest of the device, of pure tantalum. Over the upper fourteen inches of the rod Dr. Shenlavi now slipped a sleeve of tightly fitting glass. Gingerly he inserted the threaded end into an insulated slot incorporated into the floor of the beaker; gently he turned it home. He stood back briefly to admire the slim pillar of metal standing upright in its green sea.

Imagine my joy to be able to tell you, yes! yes! he is there! He is safe!

Dr. Shenlavi's smile was broad behind his dust mask.

But we must stay our hands from the cup of victory. Although he is alive, to those men who hold him, his life is valued less than that of the common earthworm who with his body's waste lubricates the soil.

There is a price.

Farther down the wooden workbench sat a conventional twelve-volt car battery. Two thin copper wires were attached to its positive and negative points, and to one of them a simple ammeter had been wired. The extremity of each wire was fitted with a small spring clip. Dr. Shenlavi now stood up and fitted the positive clip to the lip of the beaker and the negative to the tip of the tantalum rod. He checked the ammeter. The plating-out procedure would take at least two and a half hours. The current would fall off when the plutonium had been driven by the electric current out of its acid solution and onto the onion-shaped tantalum.

Of course there is a price.

There is always a price.

He sat down again. At the level of his knee were a number of drawers. He slid one of them open and lifted out a small wooden box. Its lead lining caused it to be surprisingly heavy. He eased back the lid. Inside was a package, wrapped in polythene. He tipped it out and, resting the package in the palm of his left hand, he prized back the polythene with the thumb and index finger of his right. The onion-shaped lump of crystalline metal, crusted, knobbly, and no bigger than a tennis ball, winked at him in the garage lights. Even through the glove and the polythene, the intense alpha disintegration taking place in the two-pound lump of plutonium caused his hand to feel heat.

Carefully he rewrapped it, returned it to its leaded box and the box to its place in the drawer. In all, five small boxes lay beneath him in five different drawers. Four of them contained a similar package to the one he had just inspected; when the plating-out procedure in the nearby beaker was completed, all five would be full. Such isolation of each chunk of plutonium was basic. To allow any of them to come together and form a critical mass would be to risk vaporizing himself and that area of the Judaean Hills without warning.

Their price is but a symbol, yet something you can do.

You asked me for my help.

Yes, I am saying, yes, I can help.

Your son is safe, he kisses his father, and he begs you, Papa, please bring me home.

My heart is tortured to hear a son crying for his father. Bring him home, my own son, bring him home.

Here is what you must do . . .

Dr. Shenlavi rose again and made his way to the very far end of the bench. Here his Volvo 340 had been reversed in and stood with its trunk open. The trunk floor covering had been stripped away, and in the recess normally reserved for the spare wheel stood a truncated domestic gas cylinder. Five bolts had been drilled into its base and then joined to a steel brace which he had welded to the underside of the car. The result was that the gas cylinder would remain rigidly upright in its new position for the journey.

Four-fifths of the way up, where the cylinder usually sloped, an oxyacetylene torch had sliced its head and shoulders off. Fresh holes had been drilled all around the newly created lip, large enough to take the screws of the right-angled bolts that would unite the cylinder with its new steel lid.

Adjusting the workbench light, Dr. Shenlavi peered into the decapitated cylinder. Its base and sides were lined and packed with the gray putty of plastic explosive. At the center a rounded area remained. Here a honeycomb of five wax nests could be seen, each one fractionally larger than the crystalline onion just replaced in its lead box. When the detonation occurred, the steel cylinder, tightly sealed, would act for the critical millionth of a second as an implosive tamper. The nests of plutonium would be squeezed together in a supercritical mass from which energy would expand at thousands of miles a second. The resulting fireball would be awesome.

Then Levi will come home.

With a long sigh Dr. Shenlavi opened the four doors of the Volvo and continued the complicated wiring circuitry which he had begun earlier that morning.

THURSDAY

 "SOMEWHERE, BARBARA, WITHIN ALL OF US THERE IS A germ of unhappiness. Like cancer we must not let it grow. We must find the antidote. And the antidote to unhappiness is peace."

He finished speaking and picked up his mug of steaming coffee. She looked at him across the wooden table. Their emptied plates were pushed aside. Nearby, the gas-log fire flared, shooting its shadows up the whitewashed walls.

"Define peace," she said.

"The ability to live with yourself," Simon answered.

"Is that always within our control?"

"It can be. With work it can be."

He wore an open-necked shirt of brown and black checks, its sleeves rolled to below the elbow. Her eyes savored him.

"Since I met you two months ago I think I've found a peace," she said softly. "With him I suffocate. He . . ."

He was smiling. Deliberately he shook his head from side to side.

"Okay," she said, "I won't mention him again, I promise." She made a small gesture of exasperation. "He's like a big, black cloud that covers my life," she said.

"Barbara," he said, "it is not up to him, it is up to you. When your time has come, you must decide."

She got up and brought the plates to a sink.

"There was a time," she said, "when if anyone had told me that I would now be Mrs. Barbara Galatti, married to a millionaire tycoon with houses all over the world, I would have said they were mad." She came back and knelt at his feet. He touched her cheek. "I was one of eleven," she said quietly. "We lived in three rooms in New Orleans." She put her hand on his knee and looked into his face, her own suddenly urgent. He saw a beautiful, concerned face, long, red hair tied to one side with a black ribbon. "Simon, I want to tell you something."

He nodded fractionally. She took a deep breath. "I turned tricks," she said, "starting when I was fifteen. I had to. We lived in squalor, I had to get out. I was a whore for four years." Her voice was steady. "I worked in clubs in Louisiana, I've had two abortions."

He covered her hands with his.

"Then I came to New York. I promised myself that I would never do it again — and I never have."

He stroked her face.

"You're the first person I've told."

"Why me?" he asked.

"Because . . . I don't know. Like I say, I'm suffocating. I'm living with a man I've grown to fear. He's watching me. He's . . . he's a monster. I think he's also in trouble, and when a man like that is in trouble, nobody is safe."

She saw his eyes.

"Do you like me?" she asked.

"Today you've achieved a little peace," he said. "Your soul is better for what you've told me. You must work, Barbara, at the health of your soul."

"I want to make love," she said.

"You are so beautiful," he replied.

Later as they lay together at the fire he looked down at the perfect face, almost asleep.

"When will I see you again?" he asked.

"Not until next week," she replied dreamily. "We're going away, to the island. There's some big meeting."

"When next week?" he asked.

"When I get back," she murmured. "Tuesday."

Her eyes were closed, her breathing regular and even against him.

Quietly he detached her, then covered her with a blanket. Glancing at his watch he began to dress.

THURSDAY: P.M.

16 THE HOTEL WAS OUTSIDE THE TOWN OF DEAUVILLE, HIGH on a hill. Reached by a steeply climbing avenue cut into the hill, and surrounded by a golf course, its elegance had been created for a different age. Enormous chandeliers sparkled high in the ceiling of a vast hall, empty except for a bored porter.

The second-floor bedroom was off a corridor wide enough to park a bus in. There was a small fridge, a large, central bed, and a bathroom fitted in white marble.

Matt lay back, the pillows propped behind him. Cathy nestled into him. Her hair was luxurious, gathered over one brown shoulder. There was a chink in the curtain through which they could see the moon, high in the clear Normandy sky.

Cathy leaned her head back on his chest. "I'll miss you," she said. "The next few months will seem like years."

"I don't want to go home," he said. He stroked her hair and felt himself stir. In the perfect stillness of the night it was suddenly hard to visualize life again on his own.

Matt brought his head down and slowly circled the tip of her breast with his tongue. He felt her fingers in his hair. He circled more, and above him heard her breath shorten. He left her breast and went lower, working his way down, tasting the honey of her skin, feeling the firm outline of her physique. He nibbled her in his descent, and licked her. He felt her push upward, against him, striving for firmness, for pressure. Her legs held him.

"Come on!" she gasped. "Come on!"

But he continued to knead her gently as she rocked into him. She kicked the clothes back.

"Come on!"

When it became too much he brought his hands beneath her and pulled her down to where he was. He felt her arch, lifting them both up from the bed. Just at the penultimate instant she brought her hand up between his legs and gripped him. A thousand sensations coursed, all at once, through their bodies.

They both lay back, side by side, their bodies ivory in the moonlight.

"I love you," Matt said simply.

"On the beach this afternoon, you said some pretty serious things, right?"

"Did I scare you?" he asked with concern.

"It's not that," Cathy said. Matt could see her bite her lip. "It's just . . . well, it's just that I think you may well be right," she said.

Matt leaned up on one elbow. "How 'right'?" he asked.

Cathy turned on her side and moved her back into him, molding herself against his body. "I know something about Cornucopia," she said, almost inaudibly. Matt could feel her heartbeat through her naked back.

"What do you know?" he asked, his mouth suddenly dry.

"Will I get into trouble?" she whispered.

"Not through me," he said, running his hand down and around her waist. "I promise."

"I'm not meant to know this," she said, "and if you ever ask me to confirm it I'll deny I ever met you, but one night back at the start of November something happened here."

She moved closer to him.

"Cornucopia had been out in his paddock all day, and I brought him in myself at four. He was a beautiful animal," she said softly, "a lovely horse, big, proud, a real racehorse. It was about midnight, and for some reason I couldn't sleep. I decided to take a walk. I bundled up and went out to the back of the barns, climbed into a paddock, and then walked in a sort of wide arc, across six or seven fields. It was a fabulous evening, very cold but totally bright. Every star in heaven was out that night."

She turned and wrapped an arm around Matt. "The way I went meant that I came back to the yard from the fields," she said. "I thought about it later, but no one could have heard or seen me. There wasn't a sound. Nothing much happens on a stud farm at that time of year, and apart from me the only other person there that night was the night-man, and he was probably asleep. Cambier was on vacation, the secretary used to live in but she's moved to Deauville, and Dijon was in Paris for the night."

She rubbed her cheek on his shoulder.

"I made my way back over the fields, coming toward the stallion barn. When I got closer I could see Cornucopia's box: his top door was closed and there was a light on. That was strange because I had left the door open and I couldn't think of who else might have put the light on."

The breeze ruffled the bedroom curtain.

"I got closer," she whispered. "There was a car parked in shadow. I went up to it — it was Dijon's. That was a big surprise, because as I said Dijon was supposedly in Paris. I looked into the car: on the front seat was a woman's leather handbag, the big expensive kind with lots of side pockets." She shivered and Matt held her close to him.

"I don't know what came over me," she said, "but instead of just going to Cornucopia's door and opening it, I went around the back and let myself into the small groom's room which separates each two stallions' stables. These rooms have small observation windows on either side. I was wearing tennis shoes and didn't make a sound. I guess I wanted to see the lady of the moment who was being shown Cornucopia."

Matt put both arms about her.

"What I saw," she said softly, "was three people. There was Dijon, there was a tall man heavily dressed who looked uncomfortable, and there was a woman in a sheepskin coat and with a fur hat — Dijon changes his ladies pretty regularly, so at the time she meant nothing to me. But it was what he was doing that was so startling."

Cathy shivered again.

"Dijon had the horse tied up to a ring in the wall and was clipping a small patch on his neck with surgical scissors, the type vets use. The horse didn't like it one bit. Dijon hasn't a great way with horses at the best of times and now Cornucopia began to play up on him." She paused. "I was just about to go in to help when Dijon picked up a twitch from the floor — it's a stick and rope device, you twist it around a horse's upper lip and the discomfort distracts him from what you're doing elsewhere. He twitched Cornucopia and the tall man stepped over and held it. The woman stepped to one side. Then Dijon took out a syringe and a small bottle," said Cathy. "The horse was getting fractious. Dijon filled the syringe and the tall man twisted the twitch tighter."

Matt felt goose bumps forming on his arm. Cathy said:

"Twice Dijon tried to inject the needle into the horse's jugular, but each time he missed. He was getting impatient and was looking toward the door. The third time he used the needle on its own and got a direct hit — you know because the vein bleeds through the needle. He attached on the syringe and then slowly injected the contents into Cornucopia."

She snuggled closer in the bed. Matt's mouth was totally dry. There was no other sound except the girl's soft voice.

"When he was finished," Cathy said, "he dabbed the horse's neck with an antiseptic swab. Cornucopia was sweating and trembling. He took off the twitch and untied him. Then he put out the light, opened the top door the way it had been, and the three of them left."

The girl turned to one side and laid her head on the pillow. On the white linen her abundance of hair spread out like a halo which swept down to kiss her shoulders.

"That was in November?" Matt asked.

She nodded her head.

"What do you think they were doing?" he asked.

"I don't know," she said. "Maybe the horse was sick even then and they didn't want it known. Whatever it was, Dijon looked as guilty as hell. He came back from Paris next morning as if nothing had happened."

He stroked her face with his hand.

"Does anyone else know about this?" he asked.

She shook her head from side to side like a little girl. Matt kissed the tip of her nose.

"Is that it?" he asked.

She thought for a moment.

"I suppose after that night you could say that Dijon began to take a greater interest in Cornucopia," she said. "There was a new instruction also: only Dijon was to feed Cornucopia. Other than that, nothing happened. I guess I'd forgotten until I met you."

Matt lay back beside her. He saw her outlined against the sky as she moved toward him. Her head was at his chest. The moon seemed to race at speed through light cloud, and at that moment a sudden gust blew the french window wide open. With a tug Matt pulled the heavy eiderdown up and over both their heads.

"Aren't you going to ask me who the woman was with Cornucopia?" she asked huskily.

"I thought you didn't recognize her."

She was working her way beneath him.

"I didn't at the time, but it came to me later. I'd seen her picture."

Her mouth was sweet. He felt her fingers dig into his back.

"Who was she?"

Her mouth was at his ear.

"That bitch was Barbara Galatti," Cathy murmured.

Outside the lights of a solitary car cut into the night sky as the car wound its way through the golf course and down the steep hill toward Deauville.

17

THE ROOM WAS ON THE GROUND FLOOR AND LOOKED DI-rectly out on Saint Peter's Square. Outside a fine mist of early rain had polished the cobblestones and the statues by Bellini; it drifted over the dozen or so mackintoshed tourists and wet-ted the plumage of the pigeons.

The room was dark. Little light came through its colonnaded window or its heavy, brocaded curtains of dark red satin. A single lamp shone weakly through a yellowing lace shade. On the wall hung a haloed madonna, a crucifix, some faded prints. There was a smell, not unlike that of overripe apples.

The single occupant of the room, a man in advanced middle age, sat on the edge of an uncomfortable leather chair. He was very broad, nearly a yard across, and had a thin, gray mustache that followed the irregular line of his mouth. He was tired: he had arrived in from Vienna late the night before, and had not slept well. With the tips of his fingers he held a worn leather briefcase, which he swung lightly back and forth.

The door to the room opened; a tall man with black robes coming to the floor stood there. He had a thin, sparse face, an inquisitive nose, and wore round, steel glasses. He beckoned once, his hand briefly fluttering, then turned.

The Viennese followed him down a long corridor that was tiled and narrow and cold underfoot. They crossed a hall, climbed steps, passed a statue of the Virgin with Child. The man ahead led the way resolutely, up further stairs and through doors, through a murky book-lined room, then up right-handed curving, almost spiral, steps.

He paused outside a door of heavy oak while the Viennese caught up. Then he knocked once and entered.

The room was quite large and square. A bed stood in a corner against the wall, a washstand, jug, and basin beside it. There was a window giving on to a garden where the rain could be seen to have increased. A handful of coal burned in a tiny, central fireplace, and before it, almost lost in the depths of a chair, sat the hooped figure of a very old man. His head was vein-lined and brown-spotted; his red-rimmed eyes had sunken in his head like small stones in wet, white sand. He turned.

"*Ah, Padre, buon giorno,*" he chirped in a surprisingly strong voice. A coat, arranged on his shoulders, slipped, and the younger Jesuit moved to reposition it. He then dropped to his knees and spoke quietly to the old priest for about a minute. The old eyes took in the blocky visitor standing at his door. He nodded his understanding to his brother priest.

The younger Jesuit rose and went to a table; he lifted a reading light to beside the seated priest and turned it on. Then his fingers fluttered their command.

The Viennese approached. He undid his briefcase, withdrew an envelope, and then the photographs.

The old Jesuit accepted a magnifying glass from the younger priest. Several times he ran it over the face on his knees. He moved to the next picture, repeating the examination, and to the next. He gave a number of high little grunts. Then he put the glass down and looked up at the younger priest and the Jew.

"*Sì,*" he said simply, "*è lui.* It is he."

Sixteen hours later the same Viennese sat facing a younger man in the booth of a crowded restaurant in New York's Greenwich Village. They suspended their conversation as a waitress spread a paper tablecloth and took their order. The younger man had deep, sallow skin and intense brown eyes; black chest hair sprouted from the open collar of his white shirt.

"So the priest was in the Vatican in 'forty-five?" he said.

The big head opposite him seemed to sit directly on the broad shoulders without recourse to a neck.

"In February of 'forty-five," came the reply with a confirming nod, "when His Holiness was playing host to hundreds of helpless, homeless, in-transit Nazis." The eyes flashed in the big head. "He remembers two young Jesuit seminarians, Yanni, who in February of 'forty-five were referred to him on their arrival in Rome."

Yanni raised his eyebrows and the older man nodded.

"They had come by train from Geneva. He doesn't remember what happened to one of them — he may have gone north, perhaps to Paris — but the other, the man in the photograph, was turned around like clockwork; in two weeks he had fresh papers and was on his way to Argentina."

The Israeli was frowning.

"From Geneva?"

"That puzzled me too," said his older companion. "Then I had another look at the date: February nineteen forty-five. That was when the first Jewish convoy arrived in Geneva from Theresienstadt."

Yanni shook his head.

"I'm sorry," he said, "you've lost me."

The older man's face was eager.

"You see, it's always been one of the great mysteries," he said. "Last camp commandant in Majdanek, but the few records available make no mention of him there when the Russians took it in 'forty-four. Now we know that he's alive and living in New York, so he must have escaped. But to where?" He sat forward. "You're a Nazi in Majdanek in 'forty-four. The Red Army is advancing from the east, you decide to get out. Where do you run?"

Yanni shrugged. "West," he said.

"Exactly." The older man leaned forward. "Have a look at the map.

Where is Theresienstadt from Majdanek?" He nodded happily. "That's right," he said, "west."

The Israeli was shaking his head.

"A Nazi labor camp?" he said, "I don't get it. Are you saying he escaped in a Jewish convoy to Geneva? How is that possible?"

The big hands spread wide.

"It's a jigsaw," said the older man pleasantly. "In a jigsaw you must have patience. When a piece does not fit you don't force it in — you wait and search until its true place is found. I have put the word out that I am looking for survivors from Theresienstadt who can help me." He smiled and leaned back. "I've also got other sources that I'm working on. It will all help build the final case against him."

The waitress arrived with steaming plates of veal stew and piped potatoes. "And the man with him, the one who went to Paris," Yanni said. "Do we have a candidate?"

"Perhaps," said the Viennese, "perhaps."

He took a bread roll from a basket and, breaking it in two, began to fork food into his mouth.

"You, Yanni," he asked between munches, "how goes your plan?"

Yanni's eyes flickered. "There is progress," he said. "Little by little we are learning his schedule."

The other nodded. "When will you take him?" he asked bluntly.

"That is a problem," Yanni replied. "We could not push our . . . source any quicker, but now we have learned that Saturday he leaves for the Caribbean. He will not return until after the weekend."

The older man used bread to wipe his plate.

"Unfortunately," Yanni continued, "we also hear that the Justice Department now plans to move on him; the word is Thursday or Friday of next week."

The waitress placed a stein of beer before each man.

"That is bad," said the Viennese taking a sip.

"It is," Yanni agreed. "Once that's been confirmed, Jerusalem will back off like a bunch of frightened rabbits."

The Viennese pushed his beer aside. "He must stand trial in Israel," he said passionately. "If justice exists, then he will."

"You are talking about Jews kidnapping a U.S. citizen off the streets of New York," Yanni said. "Remember, he will be screaming his head off that we've got the wrong person. We must be careful."

"Israel needs this," said the older man urgently. "She needs this boost. When Ben-Gurion announced to the Knesset that Eichmann was in Israel awaiting trial, the nation wept with joy for a week."

"Those were different times," said the Israeli. "And the evidence against Eichmann was overwhelming."

"Yanni, Yanni." The older man leaned forward and caught one of the Israeli's hands in his. "I have spoken to an old woman," he said, "a grandmother, now living in Poland. I have read her deposition." He took a deep breath. "She was shipped from near Lodz to Majdanek in the winter of 'forty-two. She was a young bride, pregnant, in the full bloom of her life." A film of moisture glazed the deep-set pupils. "Her husband was shot in the first three months, one of seven trying to make their escape. She was nearing her term and this brought her on." The Israeli felt his spittle dry. "This man," said his companion hoarsely, "caught her baby," he took another deep breath, "and ripped it apart by the legs." The Israeli closed his eyes. "He liked to wager," said the other almost inaudibly, "on which way the head would go."

Neither man spoke. The muscles in Yanni's normally calm face were working with a savage monotony.

"Next week," he said, "Thursday. We will take the beast on Thursday."

FRIDAY: A.M.

 THEY SAT SIDE BY SIDE, NOT WANTING IT TO END. DAWN had split the Normandy sky and was rushing upward, a soft pink glow on the curving, red-bricked wall of Haras du Bois.

"It's unlikely that you're going to find anything," Cathy said.

"I know," Matt agreed, "but I owe it to Jim to at least try."

Cathy looked at her watch, then put her hand on the door of the BMW. A thick pullover of Matt's covered her dress. Her coat was folded in her lap.

"I'd better go," she said. "I've got to change and be on duty by seven-thirty."

Matt drank in her face, her radiant expression in the early morning. She saw him and stroked his face with the back of her hand.

"I want you to think very carefully about what I've said," Matt urged her. "Don't underestimate these people. They must never suspect what you know."

Cathy smiled. "I'll be careful," she said and kissed him. "You be careful too," she said, catching his chin in her hand.

Matt saw her eyes, the brown flecked with concern.

"I'll be back for you no later than five," he said as she got out.

She looked back in. "I'll be ready," she said.

They held each other's gaze for a long moment. Then Cathy bent into the car and kissed him again. Before Matt could say anything, she had hurried through the gates of Haras du Bois.

The countryside was largely deserted in the early morning. Matt gunned the BMW down the autoroute toward Caen, his head buzzing, both with the image of the beautiful girl and what she had told him. He pulled off the main route, following Cathy's instructions, and eventually came to a tidy house in a quiet Caen suburb. Matt hooted the horn and immediately a small man emerged carrying a briefcase.

"*Bonjour*," said Matt as his passenger climbed in. "Thank you for obliging me at such an early hour — I hope this won't take long."

Matt's passenger frowned skeptically.

They left the residential suburb and were soon on the autoroute.

The smaller man had a smudge of a mustache, which wrinkled each time he frowned, which was often; he wore gloves, an outsize cap with a double peak, and tweed trousers that ended at the knee, where ribbed yellow socks completed his leg down to shining brown brogues. Altogether, Monsieur Petitjean should have been a *fin de siècle* golfer rather than a vet in Caen with a small animal practice.

"Don't use a horse vet," Cathy had said. "The first thing he'll do will be to call the stud."

Matt found Petitjean's name in the yellow pages. "This says he's a small-animal specialist," Matt said. "He should be safe."

"That's if he'll go," Cathy said.

"He's French," Matt had said. "For money he'll go."

They left the autoroute and drove inland for over half an hour on narrow country roads that rose and fell between neat hedges and farmhouses built before Napoleon. Monsieur Petitjean gripped the sides of his seat as Matt flung the BMW around another bend.

"So there is a chance that the horse may still be there — intact?"

Monsieur Petitjean weighed up the question for the fifth time.

"A chance, yes," he said with a sigh. He wished he had brought his own car.

"You were explaining about this Madame whatever her name is," Matt said.

Petitjean had once worked near Deauville. He nodded.

"Madame la Baronne," he said. "A woman, *complètement folle*." He tapped the side of his head. "Crazy. Dogs everywhere. She take all the meat dead."

"I must emphasize again," Matt said, "that no one is to hear about this trip. It is completely private."

"Completely private," echoed the small vet and made a definitive, chopping gesture with his gloved hand.

They were climbing a steep hill. To their right the country they had just crossed stretched out in a great plain, all the way back to the sea. Petitjean indicated left. They drove for over a mile, down a potholed lane. Abruptly it ended in front of a blue metal gate.

"Crazy," Petitjean repeated.

The smell hit straightaway. It was the stench of putrefaction befouling the morning air that carried it. Frenzied barking came from behind the gate. To the left was a small house in considerable disrepair. Its front door opened and a stooped figure emerged. Matt could see an elderly woman wearing a scarf, a long, filthy overcoat, and black rubber boots. Her body was bent severely in the middle, causing her head to strain upward and her rheumy eyes to operate back and forth from the very top of their sockets. She used a stick for support.

"Madame la Baronne, *bonjour*," Petitjean greeted her.

The woman muttered to the vet and offered her hand, its purple knuckles swollen from arthritis. She surveyed Matt with suspicion. Petitjean spoke to her, occasionally turning to indicate Matt at the car. Madame la Baronne responded volubly. The conversation went on for over five minutes, Petitjean patiently explaining, the old woman occasionally stamping her stick on the ground for emphasis. The smell was nauseating.

"What's the problem?"

"Madame *a peur*, she is afraid you have come to close her place. She thinks you are from *le Ministère de la santé*, the health department."

"Haven't you explained to her?"

Petitjean shrugged hopelessly. The morning was defying his worst expectations. Matt stepped forward. He smiled at the old woman.

"Americano," he said tapping his chest.

This provoked a further lengthy exchange. All at once the old woman seemed to capitulate. She produced a bunch of keys from her pocket and shuffled to the metal door. The two men followed as it swung open.

Matt blinked. For a moment the scene presented to his eyes supplanted the sickening stink. They were at the back of the house in an enclosed area, surrounded by a high wall. In one corner a makeshift corral had been roughly fenced off with packing cases. But Matt's attention was riveted on the center of the enclosure. There lay an enormous brown and white cow, her eyes pathetic and staring toward the gate. She appeared to move, but the deception was caused by the half-dozen emaciated dogs who were rooting energetically in her belly.

"Jesus Christ," said Matt under his breath. From the other end of the yard a further pack of dogs rushed them, snapping and snarling.

"*Couchez-vous, couchez-vous, mes enfants!*" cried the old woman, wielding her stick. She shuffled across the yard toward the corner, kicking bones out of the way. On the wall ahead of them Matt could see pink and purple entrails waiting for the sun to bleach them and the skins of sheep and cattle hanging in a row like the day's washing.

"Where's the horse?" he asked, trying not to gag.

Monsieur Petitjean pointed ahead.

They had reached the corral.

Madame la Baronne untied a length of rope, which held a makeshift door in place. With surprising strength she lifted it and stepped hurriedly in, beckoning the men to follow. Twenty dogs scraped and barked at the closed door.

Inside was a scene straight from a nightmare. A pyramid of dead animals rose from the ground. They were mostly sheep, their stomachs swollen with fermentation, an ugly bubble of pink froth at their mouths. Many lacked eyes. A flock of birds rose into the air. Without preamble Madame la Baronne waded in and began to drag stiff carcasses from the pile. Two sheep flopped beside Matt, and then surprisingly, a goat. A good inch of slime and blood covered the ground. Abruptly the old woman stepped back, her work done.

"*Le voici!*" she said triumphantly.

The two men stared. There before them, his teeth grinning in awful, final agony, was the great victor of Longchamps, Cornucopia.

"Jesus," said Matt again.

Like the other animals, only raw sockets marked the eyes. Monsieur Petitjean moved in and, grasping the horse by its two ears, yanked hard. The corpse of the stallion slithered outward from the pile of decaying flesh and fell heavily onto the ground. In horror Matt saw the top of the dead animal's head open and then close again as if on a hinge. A rat leaped nimbly out and back into the pile.

"*Aeh! Sale bête!*" cried Madame la Baronne, lunging ineffectively with her stick.

Petitjean looked inquiringly at Matt.

"Just see if there's anything unusual," said Matt. He feared he would vomit. The animal lay before them, its head to the left. Petitjean removed his gloves, then bent and, catching the skin of the animal's belly, folded it back like someone opening an enormous suitcase. The stallion's white ribs stared at them. The little vet then began to bend back each rib until they all stood upright, an enormous bone rake over the rotting guts they had kept in place. Petitjean reached in and the guts slopped out, flowing toward the door like a fetid tide. A large, gaping hole was left, beginning at the horse's loins and running all the way to his chest cavity.

"Ah!" said Petitjean, shaking his head as if he had known all along. "*Voilà les tumeurs.*"

Matt peered at several knobs of red, swollen flesh, one as big as a man's head. Again Petitjean looked to his employer of the moment for instructions. His face did nothing to conceal his exasperation.

"What would you normally do?" Matt asked.

The vet made a face and shrugged. "Take a sample," he said.

"Well, take it," Matt ordered. The vet produced a small plastic box from his coat pocket and removed a scalpel from it. With precision he sliced a cut from the tumor and placed it carefully in a small bottle containing clear liquid.

"*Le pauvre,*" he said morosely. He looked at Matt accusingly before taking another section. Madame la Baronne stood watching patiently. Outside the small compound the dogs kept up their cry.

Petitjean appeared to have finished. His movements were quick and neat. Returning the box to his pocket, he stood up.

"The neck," said Matt tapping his own, "the neck."

Petitjean went to the head of the dead horse and ran his hand from its jaw down to its shoulder. Here too the skin was loose and could be folded back. Petitjean fingered it all the way down.

"This is the line," he said. "As you can see, there is nothing."

Matt bit his tongue. The man was right. The hair on the neck skin lay undisturbed. Yet Cathy had been so positive. Petitjean had confirmed that hair clipped in November might not have grown back by the early spring.

"What about the other side?" Matt asked, his heart sinking.

Petitjean shook his head wearily. He tapped the left side of his own neck. "Always here, this side," he said. "*Merci, madame,*" he was saying to the old woman as he made his way to the door.

"*Oh, je vous en prie,*" Madame la Baronne responded.

"Just a second."

They both stopped and looked around. Matt was lowering back the ribs. Then he stooped and lifted the horse's head. With difficulty he turned the body, its four heavy legs flailing the air without coordination before crashing over to lie on its other side. Matt could for the first time get some idea of what the horse must have looked like. He saw a deep chest behind withers which in their day had rippled with power. Even in death Cornucopia retained some of his beauty. Matt's head spun. He stepped over a sheep and went down on one knee, unmindful of the offal he knelt in.

"That's my girl!" he shouted. "*That's my girl!*"

Petitjean, fearing the worst, hurried over. Even the old woman shuffled in for a look. Matt's face was jubilant. There, nine inches below Cornucopia's jawbone, on the right-hand side of the stallion's neck was an area where the hairs fell unevenly, barely visible and no larger than a five-franc piece.

"How old?" he asked Petitjean.

The vet bent and his fingers examined the nearly invisible patch.

" 'ard to say," he said. "Old. *Peut-être trois ou quatre mois.* Four months maybe."

Matt ran his hand over the neck. Unless you were looking for it, the mark would not be seen.

"The pathologist did not even notice it," he said. "It's not in his report."

"It is nothing," said the vet standing up. "Nothing." He was looking at Matt in mystification.

"What could it be for?" Matt asked. Monsieur Petitjean blew air and allowed his regloved hands to flap by his sides.

" 'ow can I say?" he replied. "A hundred things: vitamin, antibiotic, 'ow can I tell?"

"But given four months ago, last November possibly?"

Petitjean nodded. "Yes," he said.

As they made their way out, Matt had a last look at the famous racehorse.

"You said the injection could only ever be on the left-hand side of the neck," Matt said. "How come this one's on the right-hand side?"

For a moment Monsieur Petitjean looked admonished.

"*De temps en temps,* occasionally," he said, "people inject in the right-hand side. For example, that is where a left-handed man might go. But usually . . ."

Outside, Madame la Baronne dispersed the pack of dogs that had gathered. A cold breeze blew across the macabre yard, causing the dead cow's hairs to stand upright. Matt saw a greyhound trot into the house, its mouth stuffed with entrails.

"Thank you very much, madame," Matt said, offering his hand. She caught it between her thumb and forefinger, then muttered something to the vet.

"Madame wonders," Petitjean began, "if for her trouble . . ."

"Of course, of course," said Matt. He produced two one-hundred-franc notes. "Thank you," he said again.

Two minutes later the money was still clutched in her distorted hands, as she watched them recede into the cold morning.

It was raining heavily as Matt pulled off the Autoroute de Normandie. Twenty minutes earlier he had dropped the disgruntled Monsieur

Petitjean back at his neat house in Caen, with its severely clipped line of standard roses and a polished yellow Volkswagen standing outside the door. Now, as Matt turned the BMW on to the open road for Deauville, a spray of water from a truck in front washed across the windshield; a wailing ambulance flashed by on the other side of the highway divider as Matt glanced at his watch. It was just after noon, seven A.M. Eastern Standard time; Jim Crabbe normally got in around eight.

Up the road to the hotel, water washed down its surface. He drove under a wooden footbridge; a party of golfers were inexplicably making their way cheerfully across it, water streaming from their bright clothes in the deluge.

In his bedroom Matt laid out all the papers on the bed. He felt the excitement pulse through him: he had been right.

He got through at once, dialing directly.

"Before you say a word," Jim Crabbe said, "let me first tell you that you have one hell of a lot of explaining to do. What in hell's name do you mean going off on a case like that and not letting me know where you can be reached? I've spent a fortune on transatlantic calls trying to find you. We've tried every goddam hotel in Deauville."

"I'm staying outside Deauville," Matt said.

"I want to know very clearly what it is you're up to over there," Crabbe rasped. "What the hell did you say to the Lloyd's man in Paris, and to the guy who runs the stud? Lloyd's have called here half a dozen times and they're mad as hell. So am I."

"I'm over here trying to find out if there's any way of getting you out of paying a million bucks on a dead horse," Matt said coolly.

"Well, as far as these guys are concerned Insurance Fidelity have their top, shit-ass investigator reopening the whole Cornucopia case, and they've been told by none other than Carlo Galatti."

Matt's heart thudded.

"Listen, Matt, this Galatti guy is heavy; when he starts throwing his weight around, little guys like me go and hide. That's what has started — he's threatening to sue Lloyd's for impunity of damages, you know what that means? That means he can collect up to three times the sum insured if he succeeds. Three times two hundred million is six hundred million, Matt. Three times one million is three million. I've made one mistake, I'm not now going to persist with another. I want you home."

"Come on, Jim," cried Matt. "This isn't Jim Crabbe. At least hear me out."

There was a long sigh on the other end of the phone. Matt spoke, and as he did so he found it difficult to keep the incredulity out of his own voice.

"So if I understand you correctly," said Jim Crabbe after five minutes, "this girl groom claims that last November Dijon gave the horse an injection while Galatti's wife was present."

"That's right."

"At midnight."

"Yes."

Matt could visualize Jim Crabbe's face.

"You're out of your mind, Matt," he said quietly.

"The neck patch is not noted in the pathologist's report," Matt said. "I checked before I went to see the animal. The mark is so faint that unless you were told it was there, you'd never find it. And it's on the wrong side of the neck."

"Wrong side?"

"Normally you inject a horse on the near side, the side closest to you if the horse is standing with his head to the left. It's the side you get up on a horse from. Nearly everything, including the postmortem, is done on that side. My vet says Cornucopia was probably injected on the other side by a left-hander. But Cambier is right-handed, I saw him write out the address of a restaurant for me yesterday. Besides, Cathy says he was away on vacation at that time. That only leaves Dijon."

"Jesus Christ, I don't know what to think," Crabbe said.

"I had to be sure Cathy was right," Matt said, "that's why I went to see for myself. Like I say: my vet says the mark probably dates from last November."

"Is there any other explanation? Is there any record of anyone treating him officially around that time?"

"Not that I can find. Both Dijon and Cambier say no treatment took place, that the horse never had a day's illness before January."

Four thousand miles away Matt could hear Jim Crabbe breathing heavily.

"Jim, the horse was sick back in November," Matt said, "just around the time of his insurance renewal. Galatti hid it from Lloyd's and was trying to treat the animal himself. He sent his wife over to supervise."

"If you can prove," Crabbe said slowly, "that the horse was sick in November but they didn't report it until January, then you may have something." He paused. "But it's still dynamite."

"Jim, the policy calls for immediate notification of any illness. Failure to do that — especially over three months ago — could make the whole policy null and void."

"We've still got to prove it," Crabbe said. "I'm not exaggerating when I tell you this guy Galatti is dynamite. He's really heavy. I just got a whole batch of stuff on him from our press-clipping agency in New York. The man is treated like royalty in the Middle East."

"The first step is to prove that his wife was in Normandy last November," Matt said.

"Prove that, and get your girlfriend to swear a statement," Crabbe said, "then maybe we've got something."

"Hold on," Matt said. "Cathy told me all this off the record."

"Off the record my ass," cried Crabbe. "In a two-hundred-million-dollar insurance claim, nothing's off the record."

"It's a difficult position, Jim," Matt said. "I need time."

"Jesus Christ," stormed Crabbe, "you either have a case or you haven't."

"I don't want her exposed, Jim. These people could be dangerous."

The snorting laugh echoed down the transatlantic line. "Dangerous? I'll tell you what's dangerous. Dangerous is Insurance Fidelity having the biggest insurance market in the world off-limits because we're fucking around with one of their biggest customers. That's dangerous."

"Look, Jim, I saw the horse, I saw the mark on his neck. This is Friday, it's no skin off anyone's nose if I go back to the stud and back to Cambier, the vet, on his own. He's sure to know about it. The whole thing stinks."

There was silence followed by a long sigh.

"Do it," Jim Crabbe said. "I don't like it, but do it."

Matt smiled.

"In the meantime I'll duck any further calls from Lloyd's; I'll see they're told I've gone away for the weekend." Jim paused. "Matt, if this turns out to be a load of shit, I won't like it one little bit."

"I'll keep you in touch, Jim."

Downstairs in the hotel bar Matt had a beer and two sandwiches. At two o'clock he drove past the long wall and crunched in over the gravel.

He looked around, hoping to see Cathy, but the gardens and front of the house seemed empty. Matt's face was grim as he thought of the part he hadn't told Jim, the suggestion he had made to Cathy that morning: that she leave Deauville with him, that the danger he had sensed was real, too real for her to stay. Now that her story had been backed up by physical evidence, it was all the more reason why she should.

Matt pulled an old bell-pull and could hear its chimes ringing inside the house.

After nearly a minute a woman with glasses and a tweed skirt answered the door.

"Ah," she said, "Monsieur Dijon is not here, monsieur. I think he has gone to Chantilly."

Matt looked at her face. It appeared white and drawn, her graying hair brought up and back severely. Matt could see the structure of what, not long ago, had been prettiness.

"Monsieur Cambier is here?"

"This is Monsieur Cambier's day off," the woman replied. "If you could leave a message . . ."

Matt smiled. "You are Monsieur Dijon's secretary?"

The woman nodded warily.

"I was here yesterday morning," Matt said and produced his card. "About Cornucopia."

The woman said, "Ah."

"Perhaps you can help me?" Matt asked pleasantly. "It's something a friend asked me, about Monsieur Dijon: what hand does he write with?"

The woman raised her eyebrows, then she laughed.

"Oh," she said, shaking her head, "*la main gauche,* his left hand. Now monsieur, if you will excuse me . . ."

Matt nodded. He heard wheels behind him and turned to see a blue Renault 4 with two policemen draw up to the door.

"*Oh, mon Dieu,*" sighed the woman.

Matt raised his eyebrows.

"I am sorry, monsieur, not to have more time," the woman said, "but as you can see . . ."

The policemen were making their way toward the house. One had a briefcase, the other a clipboard.

"You see, this morning there was an accident," the woman was saying.

"Accident?"

"Yes, one of the grooms this morning. She was kicked by a stallion."

"*She?*"

A lead weight hit Matt Blaney.

"Yes, Cathy, an American girl. She was found by the men early this morning, in the paddock." The woman made a face of pain. "She had let a horse out — and when she turned he must have kicked her." The woman tapped the side of her head. "She is unconscious in the hospital in Caen. It's very bad." She shook her head and grimaced. "She is a foreigner — the police must be told." She turned to the *gendarmes* who had been standing behind Matt. "*Bonjour, messieurs,*" she said and led them into the house.

In a daze Matt watched the two *gendarmes* take off their hats and enter the house. He stood staring at the closed door for fully a minute before he walked to his car and got in heavily. He saw a square face staring down at him from the upstairs window of the house; as Matt caught the stare the face withdrew, leaving only the moving curtain as evidence that it had been there.

Trembling, Matt brought the BMW to life.

Without knowing what he was doing he drove slowly down the avenue and out of the gates of Haras du Bois, a numbness spreading over him. One mile from the stud he pulled in and stared out at the countryside which still awaited the spring.

In the confines of the car the scent of her perfume was as real as the large splashes of rain which had begun to fall once again on the windscreen.

FRIDAY

19 SEYMOUR CROCKER BROUGHT HIS FINGERS TO HIS LIPS AND pondered the call he had just received. He was seated behind his desk on the forty-sixth floor, in his large office, prestigiously located at a corner of the building.

On the side was an arrangement of deep armchairs and a coffee table with a smoked-glass top. Behind was a drinks cabinet of inlaid walnut, walnut-fronted filing cabinets, a miniature maple tree in a heavy, terra-cotta pot and a coatstand on which the dark jacket of his suit was hung on a bright red hanger. Original oils and lithographs hung on the walls, part of his personal investment program — the identification of un-known artists at a point when their work was still cheap. Crocker pon-dered. The call had been from the securities section of the bank. He had asked them to keep him up to date on Galatti shares and they had just rung to say that the price had dropped three points.

The telephone rang again.

"Mr. Katz to see you," his secretary said.

Moments later a man entered.

"Come in," said Seymour Crocker.

Herman Katz was neat and compact. Aged fifty, he had light brown hair cut in what used to be called a crew-cut. His eyes were deep brown and restless, watchful keepers in a sallow face. The bank's comptrol-ler, and widely tipped heir apparent, had a mouth which was often composed in a smile, a sign which many people in First Transna-tional had learned to their cost had nothing whatsoever to do with happiness.

"Everything okay?" asked Crocker with an authority he did not feel in Katz's company.

"You could say," Katz responded. He had the unsettling habit of keeping his mouth open after he had spoken.

"I've been through the printout," Crocker said, "and there's nothing that I can see."

"The dollar's getting crucified," Katz said.

Crocker raised his eyebrows.

"We're okay," Katz said. "We've been short for a week."

"Have you seen the latest figures from our new branch in Panama?" Crocker asked. "They're stupendous. I've always said it — offshore is the way to go, it's where the real money is. When Hugh gets back I'm really going to push for the Channel Islands and Liberia. They're wait-ing to be taken."

Herman Katz's smile could have meant anything.

"I've been looking at the gap in our bond-trading desk," Crocker said. "Ever since Merrill hijacked Ross Murphy from us we've been weak there. I think it's time we gave Profita the top spot and got some new blood in underneath him."

"Hmm-hmm," agreed Katz.

"I'll tell Profita this evening."

"Hmm-hmm."

Crocker looked at the man who, he knew, would leapfrog over him. Catshit, he thought. What an appropriate name.

"How's our share price?" asked Seymour Crocker. Although he knew the answer.

"Steady, eighty-two a quarter," replied Katz.

"Hugh was right on when he said it would push higher. It will make Midwest Star all the easier to swallow."

Katz nodded his head and smiled tightly. "Hmm-hmm," he intoned.

"I've just been told that Galatti's down three points," Crocker went on. "In line with the fall in oil."

"I wanted you to know," responded the bank's comptroller slowly, "that five minutes ago I refused to renew Galatti's sixty-five-million-dollar revolving credit."

Crocker's intercom rang.

"Mr. Carlo Galatti is on the line, Mr. Crocker," said his secretary.

Herman Katz's smug smile was unruffled. "I suggest you call him back, Seymour," he said smoothly.

Crocker's hand trembled as he replaced the phone. He tried to control the blood he felt rushing to his head.

"Of course you've a good reason for this, Herman," he said.

"Of course I have," replied Katz. "They were due to bring in fifty million, latest this morning, from their big Gulf contract. It never got here. If they drew on the revolving loan, their outstandings to us would now be over three hundred and fifty million dollars."

Seymour Crocker's mind raced. "Their suppliers are going to hear," he said. "Unless Galatti has other funds, it could push them over the edge."

"Maybe that's why the shares dropped," Catshit said. His mouth remained open. Then: "We're covered, I checked."

Seymour Crocker's face was purple. "I resent this," he said. "I'm in possession of information about this account. I brought Galatti into this bank, we've made a fortune out of him. I resent your attempts to sabotage my client, as well as your usual efforts to wreck any innovative suggestion I've ever made. God help this bank if you ever get to be chairman — you've about the same vision as a dead whale."

"Banking is too staid for you, Seymour," said Katz, his composure intact. "You should have been a test pilot — it would have been ideal: hundred-million-dollar toys, built with other people's money for you to play with."

"I don't have to sit here —"

"The information, Seymour," said Katz smoothly, "you say you have information about Galatti."

Seymour Crocker took a deep breath. He was still trembling with rage. "This morning," he said, "I had a call from Galatti's chief financial guy. There's a big payment coming through from London next week to Galatti personally: two hundred million bucks. It's the insurance on some racehorse. Galatti intends to use the cash to fund his short-falls."

"A racehorse," said Katz in what he took to be an understanding tone.

"That's right."

"So you're proposing to fund it?"

Crocker met the disbelieving stare, then his eyes dropped. "I'm not saying that," he said. "All I do know is that cut off from cash, an outfit like Galatti will become crippled very, very quickly. I know Hugh's view on it, but if, for example, we were to have a cast-iron undertaking on a Lloyd's insurance payment, then I think it is possible that we might look at a proposal."

Herman Katz was looking out the window. He allowed Crocker to finish, then he turned, his open-mouthed smile a taunt.

"I've been studying Galatti, Seymour," he said, as if the whole matter had just come up. "They're owed an awful lot of money, nearly half a billion dollars, and most of it from guys who up to recently lived in goatskin tents." His face was smiling and frowning in a take-off of the village idiot. "I don't think we should loan Galatti any more money, do you?"

Crocker swallowed. "I wasn't suggesting it," he said quietly.

"Okay." Katz was drumming the steepled tips of his fingers together, his eyes large, his jaw in its hanging position.

"Have you decided whether you can manage to go down there to-morrow?" asked Crocker tersely.

"I'm going," Katz nodded.

"He's sending a plane," Crocker said.

The door opened after a soft knock and Crocker's secretary came in. She was a tall, very attractive girl with cascading black hair; Crocker noticed how Catshit's nostrils flared as she bent to place a file of papers on the bank president's desk.

"Mr. Galatti's office has called three times since, looking for you, sir," she said to Crocker before she left the room.

"What am I going to tell him?" Crocker asked. "That we've pulled the plug?"

Katz stood up. "Tell him nothing, Seymour," he said. "Get your girl to say you've gone out, but that you'll see him tomorrow in Barbados — when the banks are closed."

Crocker stood to see Katz to the door.

"I understand that he has quite a setup down there," Crocker ventured. "One of the best in the Caribbean."

Katz looked at him. "The guy is stretched on a rock," he said. "After what we've got to tell him, I would guess that we'll be coming home by commercial transport." He paused at the door. "I'll make the arrangements," he said.

Catshit, thought Crocker as the door closed. What a fucking appropriate name.

SATURDAY: A.M.

20 HE NEVER SLEPT THE NIGHT BEFORE A JOURNEY: NOT ON the night before he left Majdanek, nor in the filthy cabin which they slipped into in Theresienstadt in the confusion of the night before the convoy to Geneva, nor in Buenos Aires as a merchant seaman, on the eve of going to sea when shore leave was at an end.

He stretched his legs and turned his body in the big bed. Fifteen minutes before he had heard the door across the hall as Barbara had tried to slip quietly in. He grimaced. Everything had its use, but now that she was out most nights like a rabbit in heat he would have to be careful. He would take steps. When they came back he would take steps.

There are only so many things that a man can do, he thought in the dimly lighted room. A man sows the seeds, then the rest is up to time. Time was the commodity that he now simply had to have. If he had time, he would have cash in abundance, but a corporation like Galatti, if starved of cash for even a few short days, was like a brain denied its oxygen. An irreversible atrophy took place. Galatti regulated his breathing. Listening to the traffic noises of Manhattan's small hours, he breathed in and out, controlling the timing, until a kind of peace enveloped him.

Part of his mind listened, part of it slept.

The villa was pink. Perched high on a coastal promontory in a remote corner of the Persian Gulf, it was built in Italian marble and modeled on a similar but smaller residence owned by a Saudi prince who lived most of the year in Cap d'Antibes. Erected at a cost of three million dollars — about three hours' cash flow in the good days — it stood in four acres of gardens which cost a small fortune to maintain and was protected at all times by half a dozen members of the local territorial militia.

The sheikh was a fat man, repellent, but not without a certain reptilian charm. He sat beneath billowing silks and electric fans, gazing out across the heat-dancing water to the distant Strait of Hormuz.

The sheikh was a wildly ambitious man: for himself, for his small state, and for his part in the leadership of the Arab world. He had raised his country's spending from eight to thirty percent of the GNP and nearly bankrupted it. Now he spread his pudgy hands, his eyes drooped and hooded, his goateed mouth both mocking and mournful. He looked at Galatti.

"What more can I say, my good friend?" he asked in thick English. "We must reschedule our debts. It is not our fault that oil is where it is, but that of the Zionists who manipulate it to their own end."

"And I must have my money," Galatti said.

The sheikh's eyes were unhappy. "It is simple, my friend," he said.

"A man accumulates great wealth, many camels, gold. He indulges his favorite wives, his children, his friends. These are the happy times." The sheikh popped a sugarcoated truffle into his mouth. "But then come the bad times. Then comes the enemy who would destroy this man and all he loves and stands for. What does he do? His wealth must now go to paying his guards, his soldiers, to protecting those he loves. His wealth must run another course." The sheikh made a snaking motion with his paralleled hands, then shrugged, the parable at an end. "The Zionist enemy is on our very doorstep," said the sheikh. "We must defend."

"But then I suffer," Galatti said.

"Rid me of mine enemy," said the mournful sheikh, "and all our suffering will end."

He looked at the American to whom his country owed hundreds of millions of dollars. Galatti had suddenly gone pale.

"Are you not well, my old friend?" the sheikh inquired.

"What did you say?" whispered Carlo Galatti.

The sheikh frowned. "I said, 'Rid me of mine enemy,' " he said.

" 'And all our suffering will end,' " said Galatti, concluding the sentence in a shaking voice. He thought that his mind must explode, suddenly presented as it was with the incomparable vista of a new dimension.

The sheikh was on his feet, his eyes all at once clever and alert. "You have thoughts that might help, my friend?" he asked. "Great riches await he who can."

"How much is it worth?" Galatti asked, barely able to speak.

The sheikh was beside him. He could not arrest the trembling that had taken over his soft hands. "There is someone you must meet," he had said, his voice shaking with excitement. "There is someone you must meet."

In the dimly lighted room the bedside phone rang. Galatti picked it up.

"Yes?"

He listened, nodding, to what his caller had to say.

"You have done well," Galatti said eventually, "but not well enough. The American remains — he now knows."

"Yes," the caller said, "but he had returned home."

"He may have returned home," Galatti said, "but he now knows."

Down in the street the driver of the delivery van looked up at the lighted window, then reached for his notebook.

"Saturday, February eight, still lights at zero-two hundred," he logged in Hebrew.

SATURDAY: P.M.

21 MATT BLANEY DROVE SLOWLY DOWN THE RAMP INTO Insurance Fidelity's empty underground car park. It was two P.M., Saturday afternoon, but Matt's clock was still on European time. He turned off the ignition and sat for a moment, staring with unseeing eyes into the darkened, subterranean chamber whose low concrete ceilings and upright pillars made it look like a gigantic, empty morgue. A shape began to form in his midvision and then just at the threshold of its presentation it cut off, as if his mind was engaged in some autosubliminal process requiring continuous editing of a subject too painful to consider at length.

The head nurse in the Caen hospital had been a blocker's blocker. A formidable woman, nearly his own height, dressed in blue with a bust like a spinnaker and her badge of office pinned to it, she moved from one part of her meridian to another with the unquestionable omnipotence of a man o'war crossing a marina.

"*Non! ce n'est pas possible, monsieur!*" she said for the sixth time in over an hour and firmly escorted Matt back to the small waiting room, where at head height there was a ceiling of smoke caused by a man in the corner eating Gauloises. With a murderous glance the matron slammed the door. Matt walked to the double-glazed window; it refused to open. Outside there was a peaceful view over a park, with, in the distance, the sweeping, upward lines of Caen's Olympic-size municipal *piscine* thrusting over the tops of a band of conifers. He turned as the door opened again.

The woman with the hair drawn up and back frowned as she tried to reconcile his presence.

"Hello again," he said.

"I didn't know . . ." she began.

"I just met her two days ago," Matt said.

The stud secretary's mouth made an "ah," and then she smiled a fraction, as if the tall man's credentials had just improved in quality.

"I met her in Honfleur," Matt said.

They sat down. Once again Matt saw an ephemeral, softer face which in times past must have been there always.

"I can't make any headway," Matt said, indicating the door. "I've tried, but there's a lady out there and she missed her vocation — she should be commanding infantry."

The stud secretary smiled.

Matt said, "I've told her I'm a friend of Cathy's, but . . ."

"I'm sorry," said the woman, "today I was very busy — I hope you did not find me rude."

Matt shook his head. "Not at all, I understand," he said. "This is a shock for you. Did you contact her parents?"

The woman nodded. "Her father will come as soon as he can," she replied.

"What about Dijon?" Matt said. "Why isn't he here? A stud employee is in a coma having been kicked by one of his horses and he's in Chantilly?" He glanced at the man in the corner. "Do you know for sure it was a horse that did it? Did anyone see it happen?"

The woman looked at him. Her eyes examined his face, then suddenly lost their hardness. She fished in a large handbag and came out with cigarettes and a lighter.

"Did Cathy tell you about Dijon?" she asked, blowing smoke out of the side of her mouth and closing her bag.

Matt felt a jolt. The innate familiarity in her voice suddenly put them on the same side; it also exactly presupposed the correct nature of his relationship with Cathy Vandervater.

"Sort of," he said.

The woman crossed her legs and leaned forward, her elbows in her lap.

"Monsieur Dijon," she said, "he is like *le Mistral* — that is what we call the wind which blows in Marseilles. Some days it is warm, some days cold. Maybe you are lucky — you feel only the good wind, the warm. But then it comes cold . . ." she shrugged.

"I think I understand," said Matt gently.

The man in the corner had begun to cough.

"Cathy and Dijon," she said. "When she first came here, for Dijon there was no one else. I tried to tell her, but she thought she was in love." She inhaled deeply. "She is a young girl, very pretty. Then she was even younger, believing the best in everyone. Now . . ."

Her voice trailed off and they sat in silence. Outside the door they could hear the business of the hospital go on. The man in the corner lit up another cigarette.

"I saw her for a moment this morning," the secretary said. "Just when she came in." She looked kindly at Matt. "I had not seen her look so happy for many months."

Matt leaned his elbows on his knees and shook his head.

"*Enfin,*" said the woman, looking at her watch, "you have been here long?" She stubbed out her cigarette.

"Nearly an hour and a half," he replied.

"*Ah!*" she said impatiently and stood up. "Please wait a moment."

As she left the room, Matt walked to the window. A group of brightly uniformed schoolgirls had arrived in the park outside, led by their teacher. On some given signal they split into two sides and began to kick a football.

"Monsieur."

He turned. The stud secretary beckoned him from the door. In the background Matt could see the outline of the matron.

"We have just one minute," the secretary said softly as the stout nurse preceded them up a shining corridor. "It is hopeless," the woman was saying, "she is unconscious. If she does not *sort du coma,* wake up, today, then it is not good."

They went through doors and into a small office, where they wrote their names in a book. The nurse produced face masks, muzzled herself with one, then led them through further doors and down another long, polished passage. There was an air of controlled efficiency. Teams pushed green-smocked patients about on trolleys, nurses in clinging starch clipped in and out of wards, and a doctor, surrounded by a group of assistants, stood holding X rays up to a window.

They came to a door with a red sign over it. Inside there were a number of curtained cubicles. The lighting was subdued. Matt heard a soft moaning — he looked to the right. An old lady lay with her mouth open; as she breathed she moaned.

Three cubicles down the head nurse parted the curtains and stood back. Matt could hear the secretary suck in her breath. He stared. The face was the same but distorted by a translucent tube running from the nose to a bedside drip. She had the complexion of chalk and looked worried. The gaps between her breaths seemed unusually long, and just when one thought the worst, another breath came, causing the bed-clothes to jump. But it was her head that made Matt bite his lip: it was heavily bandaged all around, more on one side than the other and down over her left ear. On the right side of her head he could see the shining, honey-blond sheen of stubble. They had shaved her completely.

He bent forward and touched the waxen lips with the tips of his fingers. He heard the head nurse say something to the woman and the sound of the curtains being drawn.

They left the dim room and walked silently back down the bright passage. It was as if they had visited Limbo. In the brightness of the morning Matt had brought the tips of his fingers to his mouth and kissed them.

Matt inserted a precoded metallic card into a slot beside the basement elevator and stepped in as the chrome doors hummed open. He pressed the button for the tenth floor. The doors opened again directly into a carpeted reception area, now empty, with oak-paneled doors inset to one side, leading to the boardroom. He knocked once and entered. Jim Crabbe was at the far end of a long table surrounded by mounds of thick files.

"Ah, at last," he said, "the world traveler." He got up and sat on a chair with a clear space in front of it. He was wearing a three-piece suit of light gray flannel with a barely discernible pin-stripe. The vest containing his small chest had its buttons arranged in pairs rather than in a conventional line.

"So, how was the French cuisine?" he asked, then held up his two hands. "Okay, it's all my fault."

"Jim something bad has happened."

"Matt Blaney, I love you like a son. Let me tell you something —

something good for a change. You know my condominium development in Fort Lauderdale? The one I've been trying to unload for a year?"

Matt nodded wearily.

"Well yesterday, young man, I just rolled snake eyes. Twelve million bucks to a syndicate from Minneapolis — means I clear five. The sun has come out, the honey is flowing, and the bird is on the wing. Monday morning I send one million dollars to Lloyd's of London with a telex profusely regretting any misunderstanding. And the nearest I'll ever get to a horse again will be if I see John Wayne riding one on TV."

Matt thought that the tiredness would overwhelm him.

"Jim," he said in a flat voice, "I said something bad had happened. They tried to kill Cathy. She's in a coma in a French hospital."

Jim Crabbe blinked. "Okay," he said slowly, "let's hear it."

He tilted back his chair and put his short legs up on the table. As Matt spoke, Jim's face grew darker.

"Did anyone see this happen?" he asked in disbelief.

"No," Matt said, "but —"

"Then hold it!" Crabbe cried. "Let's not release all grips on reality. Did anyone say to you that the head injury was not consistent with being kicked by a goddamned horse?"

"No," Matt sighed.

Crabbe jumped to his feet. Standing, he was barely taller than sitting. "All right," he continued. "The woman at the stud, the secretary or whoever, did she suggest any funny stuff?"

"She implied Dijon was a complete bastard," Matt said.

"A complete bastard," Jim Crabbe echoed. "But not, perhaps, a completely murderous bastard." He shook his head. "Did you ask this woman if Cornucopia had been ill?"

"I did, and she said he hadn't."

"So that leaves the mark on the neck," Crabbe said. "I suppose you also asked her about that?"

"She said it was possibly an anti-influenza vaccine," Matt answered in a quiet voice.

Jim sat down. "No offense," he said, "I know you've been through a very rough experience, but thank God I wasn't specific with Lloyd's."

"What's their position?" Matt asked.

"It's back to normal, it'll blow over," Jim said. "But let me tell you when Carlo Galatti threatened them with impunity of damages three days ago, things were far from cozy between this office and Lloyd's of London."

Jim walked around the table and put his hand on Matt's shoulder.

"Let's forget it," he said quietly. "Thanks for trying. I should have known better than to get us into something we knew nothing about."

Matt looked square into the wizened face. "Jim," he said, "I believe Cathy. I came back here today because I believe her. Galatti's a crook. His horse was sick way back, yet he didn't tell Lloyd's and got his insurance renewed for the full value. He knew that Cathy knew, so he tried to put her away. The girl may die. I came back because this is where the power is. New York. This is where Galatti lives. This is where we can prove that this whole thing was a fraud."

"This is going off the wall," said Crabbe grimly.

"Jim," Matt said, "I'm going to find out who this guy Carlo Galatti really is. I'm going to find out who his wife is. I'm going to find out what is really going on." He set his jaw. "That's what I'm going to do."

Jim Crabbe shook his head. "Matt, Lloyd's is too important for me to be trailing my ass all over some dead horse. Impunity of damages? Jesus Christ, it terrifies me even to think of it. That's the final word. We're out. *Finito.* It's all over."

"Jim, I —"

"Matt, someone's got to call the shots. In this case I say no. I didn't realize what we were getting into. Sure it's rough on the girl if what you say is true, sure the whole thing may stink — but life stinks if you let it." He paused. "I think there's a strong possibility that your friend Cathy imagined everything."

Matt jumped hotly to his feet. "That I don't believe," he shouted.

"She'd had the hots for Dijon," rasped Crabbe. "She was out to get his guts. Goddammit, it's obvious!"

"You've never met the girl, for God's sake!"

Jim Crabbe's face was grim. He went down the table and took a blue manila file from the mound of papers. "You suggested the press-clipping agency," he said coolly.

Matt's heart sank; he knew Crabbe when he was holding a trump.

"When did your friend Cathy say she saw Mrs. Galatti?" Jim asked as he opened the file.

Matt felt suddenly dry. "November second of last year," he said.

Crabbe shook he head. He took out a photostat and threw it down on the table.

Matt's eyes refused to focus. "What is it?" he asked.

"It's a library photograph of Barbara Galatti," Crabbe snapped. "She's getting into a car in Amman on November third and she's been there for nearly a week."

Matt sat down, his head spinning. For some reason he began to see the nightmare image of the dead Cornucopia, guts slopping out. Matt felt as it he himself had just been disemboweled. Shakily, he stood up.

"Jim," he said, "I'm not sure I know my own name anymore."

Jim Crabbe came around the table. "Can I make a suggestion?" he asked.

Matt nodded.

"Do you still have that cabin in the country?" Jim asked.

"Sure," Matt answered.

"Then why don't you get your ass up there for a couple of days. Try and come off the boil. This thing has you seeing double."

Matt sighed. "There's a lot piled up in the week I've been away," he said.

"Screw it," Jim said. "I'll take care of it."

Matt smiled. "Thanks," he said, "but you've already got enough on your plate."

"Goddammit, I can handle it," Jim said. He saw the look on Matt's face. "All right," Jim said, "if it makes you feel any better, I'll damn well come up there and join you. We'll take it easy for the whole damn week."

"Now there's a good idea," Matt said.

"But not until Monday," Jim added. "I've got a meeting I can't break. You get up there now and on Monday night, eight o'clock, I'll join you."

"It's a deal," Matt said. "Where will I meet you? Do you think you can find your way to the cabin?"

"I doubt it," Jim said. "Best thing is I'll meet you at eight at the local bar."

"The bar at eight it is," Matt replied.

They walked to the elevator; Jim hit the button as Matt leaned against the wall and loosened his tie.

"Where as a matter of interest was she going?" Matt asked.

Jim looked at him blankly. "Was who going?" he asked.

"Barbara Galatti," Matt said. "You said the picture showed her getting into a car in Amman on November third. Did it say where she was going?"

"Oh," Jim screwed up his face in recall. "If I remember rightly," said Jim as the elevator's doors opened, "it said she was going on a sightseeing tour of Israel."

PART THREE

22 THE MUSIC FROM THE BRASS BAND WAS CARRIED BY THE breeze down the Sandy Lane beach and out over the craggy point of the lagoon. The tune was "Colonel Bogey," and its jaunty air crept faintly into the neighboring bay, up from the water and into the perfectly groomed grounds of the private estate whose gardens swept down to the lapping Caribbean.

Set back amid abundant shrubs and palms was a massive house, built of huge granite blocks in the Colossal order. Single stone columns rose from the ground of the façade through the building's two stories, while behind these great pillars hung two intricately ornate, wrought-iron gates, each nearly twenty feet high. Two wings, slightly recessed on either side of this colonnade, stretched out from it in perfect proportion, light streaming from their tall windows to the ocean.

To the left of the portico stood a man. Tall, his upright figure in a jacket of white sharkskin was pencil-slim. His head was domed and covered in white hair. Even in his own house he chose the shadow rather than the light. In the darkness the fingers of his right hand sought the gold band on his left and slowly revolved it as he stared out to sea.

Carlo Galatti listened to the abundant night sounds of the tropics, the distant music and the surge and ebb of the tide on the nearby beach. The heat of the soil rode the night air. He thought of the heat in another place.

The sheikh had been extremely apprehensive.
They had traveled in a small turboprop from Banghazi, across Khalij

Surt, the Gulf of Sitra, and southwest until they landed outside Zillah, a town in the foothills of Al-Harig Al-Aswad. The Leader, the sheikh kept saying, was a mercurial man, given to sudden rage, but a great king for his people.

A battered Peugeot brought them ten miles west until they reached the oasis, green trees and cool cut into the brown dust, an old fort, and a large, low building bristling with arials. Several dozen armed and bored-looking military hung around.

After half an hour they were admitted to a shaded enclave, via further guards who frisked Galatti. A man rose, touched cheeks with the sheikh, and nodded politely to the American. The Leader had an urgent, ageless face, sparkling teeth, olive skin, and a mass of black, curly hair. He was dressed in simply embroidered robes, his feet in sandals. Despite the sheikh's apprehension, the Leader was calm. He sat on a rug and invited his guests to join him.

The monologue ensued for almost an hour.

It was relayed to Galatti by a monotoned interpreter who sounded as if he had heard it all before. The Leader spoke in dimensions, he explained in parables; his world was not of the desert but of the universe of all living men. His eyes afire he spoke of his pact with God, with Muhammad, his battle against great Satans and his sacred duty to free Arabs from their scourge. He dismissed the value of his own life lightly: his apotheosis was assured. He invited them to pray silently with him.

Then it was over.

After ten minutes the sheikh joined Galatti outside.

"He is pleased," he said excitedly on their way back to Zillah. "He believes that your plan comes directly from God."

Galatti's face had been impassive.

"And what about the money?" he had asked.

The sheikh's eyes were bright.

"The money is arranged," he had answered.

His antennae twitched.

The music had stopped; the moon shone brightly making a path on the water and straight up the beach to the great house.

He smelled her before he heard her: not just the scent of her perfume but a tangible physical exhalation. Now she was close behind him and still he pretended, playing the game, staring out to sea. Her long, strong fingers covered his eyes and he felt her press him gently.

"Guess who?" she whispered.

Slowly he turned, and looked, and as he did so he felt anger rising.

Tonight Barbara Galatti had surpassed even her own standards of radiant beauty. Her long hair was piled high on her head. Her luscious figure was covered from throat to toe in a black, silk-and-lace meshed dress, which clung resolutely to her body in its undulating passage to the ground. The transparent black lace alternated evenly in horizontal turn with the silk, and into the lace had been sewn thousands of tiny, silver sequins that danced and twinkled in the reflection of the moon, cheating the eye in its endeavor to glimpse the proudly bare body underneath, which most men could only dream of possessing.

But Galatti felt only anger.

She kissed his cheek.

"What are you doing out here?" she asked him.

"Thinking," he replied. He looked at her anew. There was a freshness about her, a bloom that he could scarcely remember.

"You look well," he said.

"Thank you," she smiled. "I feel well."

"Naturally you do, my dear," he said shrewdly, then made her redden under his uncompromising, old man's eyes. He took in the swell of her breasts and idly wondered if she was pregnant. The anger in him screamed for vent. It was not that he had been cheated; he did not care, he was old.

It was with whom.

Galatti fought to control the poison that surged in him. He concentrated on the great strategic successes on which his life and his survival had been based.

Once he had used a boy.

Now he would use another boy. It was of no consequence to him that this boy was quite dead.

"Are they down?" Galatti asked.

"Just the usual one," Barbara answered. "He's on the other terrace, waiting."

"Give me time with him, alone," he said.

Then with his back as straight as a gun barrel he turned and walked into his house.

At the far side of the hall a room with tall french windows opened to a further terrace. Here white-jacketed servants were completing the arrangements to the linen and silver of an elegant dinner table. Tall candles, as yet unlit, stood in gleaming candelabra. Steps led from this terrace down to sweeping lawns, which in the lights of the house were as neat and crisp as new dollar bills. A man dressed in a dinner jacket stood looking out to sea.

"Seymour Crocker," said Galatti.

Seymour Crocker spun around and put down the tumbler he had been holding.

"Carlo," he beamed, grasping his host's hand.

"Are you being looked after?" asked Galatti.

Crocker smiled and nodded.

"This is an impressive place you've got, Carlo," he said, "really impressive."

Galatti inclined his head. A dark-suited butler had arrived at his elbow with a glass of frothing champagne. He raised it. "Your good health, Seymour," he said. "Did you have a good flight down?"

"So much more pleasant than the commercial airlines," said Crocker. "We left the office at three o'clock." He laughed. "We were here at eight."

Galatti nodded that he understood.

"You got the message that I wanted to bring Herman Katz along?" Crocker asked. He lowered his voice. "He's very much a numbers guy, but he's the bank's comptroller and it would be no harm at all to have him on your side."

"I did get the message about Mr. Katz," Galatti confirmed. "I have not met him before, but I have always been very happy for you to deal with the Galatti account, Seymour."

Crocker finished his drink in one clinking gulp and placed it on the tray which had materialized beside him.

"Thank you," he said, taking a fresh glass. "I still am dealing with your account, Carlo," he said, "it's still one million percent my responsibility. I just wanted Herman to see some action in the field — he's a young man and, after all, I won't be in this position forever."

Galatti nodded slowly. "How are your wife and daughter?" he inquired.

"Fine," replied Crocker beaming, "just fine, Carlo."

"Are you still sailing?"

"Whenever I get the weather — and the time."

"Time is the problem," said Galatti. He placed his glass on the low wall of the terrace and then turned to the banker. "I thought we might chat together before dinner, Seymour," he said. "There is something I wanted to raise with you."

"I'm glad," Crocker responded. "I wanted to see you as well; we're both probably thinking along the same lines."

"I do not have to tell you," Galatti continued, "about the basic soundness of Galatti. We're in the top five construction companies in the world — there's no one bigger in the area that all the big plays take place in: the Middle East."

Crocker nodded silently.

"As our bankers," Galatti said, "you know as much about our business as I do. You therefore know that we have very large amounts outstanding from Arab countries who are temporarily short of cash because of the falling price of oil. It's caused us to reschedule some of our repayments with you."

"That is something —" began Crocker.

"I say temporary" — the voice was steel — "because that is what I am completely certain the problem is." The smiling face belied the cold, piercing eyes swimming behind their thick lenses. "The world is greedy, an insatiable consumer of energy. The downward price in oil is false, probably manipulated. It is only a matter of time before that position changes and then the Arab cash will flow again."

"Oil is causing us as much trouble falling as it did rising," said Crocker.

"I have a proposal that I would like you to consider," Galatti said. "I understand you are the effective chairman of First Transnational, so it is therefore entirely appropriate that I should be putting the proposal directly to you."

Crocker put his scotch down and ran his tongue over his upper lip.

"First Transnational," Galatti was saying, "are secured over two to one on all Galatti borrowings. Correct?"

Crocker nodded.

"You may not be aware," Galatti was saying, "but a tragedy occurred over a week ago."

Seymour Crocker arched his eyebrows as Galatti nodded his domed head.

"You remember Cornucopia?" he asked.

"Of course," said the banker. "Your great horse."

"Well he's dead," Galatti said shortly. "Cancer. He died on my Normandy stud farm during an operation ten days ago."

"I'm very sorry, Carlo," Crocker said. "I had, of course, heard . . ."

"He was insured," said Galatti, "small compensation, but nonetheless . . ."

"Your financial man briefed me," Crocker said.

Galatti filled his lungs with air. "He was insured for two hundred million," he said. "Lloyd's have as good as agreed to pay, but it may be over a week before I get the money." He paused. "I need it right away, Seymour," he said, "I need it to survive. Our cash-flow situation is so critical that I do not expect our operations will be able to get beyond the middle of next week without a massive infusion of cash."

Crocker had paled. "I knew things were bad . . ." he began.

"You knew things were bad," snarled Galatti. "You are the bastard who bounced our paper yesterday. An hour later the news was all over Wall Street and out main suppliers were insisting on cash up front." He laughed, a short, sharp cough. "Don't try that shit with me, Seymour."

Crocker was shaking his head.

"Look," said Galatti, "bridge my Lloyd's payment and I'll make it." He caught Crocker's arm. "Two hundred million?" Galatti looked around him. "It's chicken feed." He lowered his voice. "There's something else happening," he said, "and even if you were God Almighty I couldn't tell you what it is, but believe me, in a few short weeks or less, I will have a multiple, yes, a multiple of all the money that I owe your bank." He strengthened his grip on the banker's arm. "You think I'm joking? Listen, within ten trading days Galatti stock will have at least doubled on Wall Street." His lips were drawn back, revealing ivory and pink dentures. "That's not a forecast, it's a promise. Seymour, why don't you get smart for once, smart for yourself. Look after me and you can take it I'll look after you. You want it in Switzerland, in the Bahamas? You just tell me."

Crocker took a deep breath and met the intense stare.

"Carlo," he said, "it's not on."

Galatti's face was a mask.

"Believe me," Crocker repeated, "it's not on."

"You could lend me the money and even without Lloyd's you'd be covered," Galatti hissed.

Seymour Crocker looked awkward. "Carlo," he said, "you remember when I said there was something I wanted to say to you?"

Galatti nodded.

"Well, Carlo, the whole reason for this trip, from the bank's point of view, is to explain our position." Crocker drained his glass and put it down. "If you want it straight" — Galatti nodded — "well, we're very unhappy."

"Why?"

In the great dome of the night the question was more like a sigh. A slight breeze had come off the sea to tease the edges of the linen tablecloth.

"Carlo," said Crocker, "the bank, up to recently, has been happy with Galatti. Then late last year we agreed a rescheduling of a major loan with you, over sixty-five million dollars. We understood your problems." He looked at the erect figure. "It hasn't happened, Carlo. You haven't met the new program. We're faced with making a possible provision for the debt if it goes much more overdue. Banks hate making provisions. We're getting spooked, Carlo, really spooked."

Carlo Galatti stared at Crocker like a father giving his third explanation to a child.

"Once oil has turned," he said to the banker, "such problems will automatically disappear. But the other matter which I mentioned will solve them much quicker — in a matter of two weeks at the most."

Crocker looked at him gravely.

"I've come down here to ask for an immediate reduction in Galatti's debt, Carlo," he said, "not to discuss increasing it by two hundred million."

Galatti shook his head in despair. "I've loyally used you as my bankers for years," he said. "Now at the very moment I need you most you're going to throw me to the wolves."

"Carlo," said Crocker, "let's be perfectly honest with each other. I may be acting bank chairman, but loans like these have to go through complex authorization procedures — not to mention the board of First Transnational. Even if I thought you had the keys to Fort Knox, I couldn't give you that kind of money on my own."

"Hugh Johnson could," said Galatti.

Crocker bit his lip in exasperation.

"Okay, Hugh could," he said, "but that's different. Even in his case he would come to the board for retroactive approval. But what are we talking about? There's no question of us loaning this account more money under the present circumstances. The bank comptroller is here, for Christ's sake. We're here to get our money back."

There was silence. Galatti turned away from the terrace and rested the tips of his fingers on its wall for what seemed a long time. In profile his face had the look of a wax model.

"This comptroller," he said at last, "this Katz. He could prevent you from making the loan?"

"It's not a question of his —"

"In a hypothetical situation?"

"You mean . . . ?"

"I mean if you were to approve the loan, any loan, as acting bank chairman, could Katz veto it?"

"That's very hypothetical."

"But?"

Seymour Crocker scratched his head.

"It's never arisen," he said. "My job is bank president. But even as acting chairman, if the comptroller frowned on a loan, that would make it very difficult for me to go through with. I'd have to have one hell of a reason."

Galatti's peculiar head was nodding up and down.

"But that's all hypothetical," Crocker was saying. "We really should be addressing the main issue, which is how and when you can give us a major and permanent reduction."

Galatti caught him lightly by the elbow. The bespectacled face had taken on an undefinable, different quality.

"We've been friends for some years," he said kindly.

The banker nodded.

"At least I've always tried to be your friend," Galatti said.

"Look," said Seymour Crocker, "I've no complaints. We've had some good times together." He laughed shortly.

"That's true," said Galatti, guiding the other man as they moved slowly toward the house. "I recall with particular pleasure the last time we met, two years ago in Bel Air."

Crocker chuckled sheepishly at the dim memory of the rather disgraceful house party. "That was one hell of a weekend," he said awkwardly.

They had arrived at a small recessed door and entered a book-lined study. Inside was a Reuters machine; a small television sat in the corner.

"You enjoyed it so much," Galatti was saying, "that I thought you might like to relive the fun."

A wedge of fright entered Crocker's belly.

"I don't . . ." he began.

Galatti went to a table and was loading a cassette into a VCR. He pressed a switch so that the lights went out and only the speckled TV screen illuminated the room. Suddenly a picture came flashing up. It showed Seymour Crocker, two years younger and naked as a baby, snorting deeply through a rolled dollar bill.

In terror Crocker stared at the screen as the events of the distant weekend came flooding back. Galatti had left on unexpected business, but had put his Bel Air mansion at Crocker's disposal for the weekend. It had been a debauch from the start, with a procession of young girls through the house, all of them supplied by Galatti and out of their minds on an endless supply of uncut Colombian. Seymour Crocker had abandoned himself for thirty-six straight hours, unable to believe how much his performance had improved with the mixture of cocaine and youth. It was a long remove from the intense weekend he had predicted to his wife, so tied up with financial negotiations that even a visit to their daughter in her first semester at Berkeley would be impossible.

Now he blinked as the film switched. The Seymour Crocker on the screen moved as if in a daze, into a dark bedroom where his progress was faithfully recorded by the lenses of an infrared camera. Two girls lay on the bed in shadow, their arms and legs entwined. Crocker could not remember them — he had been stoned to pulp.

"Jesus," he gasped in the small study.

With the dreamy motion of the heavily doped, one of the girls rolled over and was groping for him in the darkness. She found him as he bumped into the side of the bed and took him in her young mouth as he stood there swaying and grunting pleasurably. Crocker ran his hands over his head, hypnotized by the performance on the screen. Now he saw himself as he caught her head and lifted her off, then clambered up beside her. The other girl was smaller. He saw himself crawl across and cast for her like a great rutting boar. She moaned from her throat. He saw himself catch her by the hips and turn her around so that she knelt before him, her buttocks splayed. Then he was into her, the way he liked it, his hands groping for her tits. Despite himself he felt aroused. Then the cunning camera changed angle. Its magic lens took them both front on, just their faces at the moment of his roaring.

"Aaaaagh!"

In an uncontrollable spasm Seymour Crocker vomited on the rug of Carlo Galatti's study. He was kneeling in his own sick, his face as white as the now blank screen, trembling like a man with the palsy.

"It's all right," his concerned host murmured, "it's all right."

"She was only a child," choked the large banker.

"She never knew," the kindly Galatti assured him, resting a comforting hand on his shoulder. "She was stoned — she had no idea."

"Oh my God, my dear God, what have I done?" cried Crocker as he sat back in the chair, his shirt and suit front wet with the ugly, yellow stains. He began to weep.

For the next ten minutes no one could have been more solicitous than Carlo Galatti. It was kindness born of their friendship. Eventually the banker prepared to go upstairs to change.

"She's getting married in three weeks," Crocker whimpered to the white-haired man beside him.

"You'll have it all back by then," Galatti assured him as they left the small study.

For an instant a slight sea breeze bent the candle flames. From his position at the top of the table, Carlo Galatti's eyes rested on the short man. Two hours before, Galatti's flesh had actually crawled when they shook hands. Now Herman Katz was in deep conversation with a black girl whose hair was a fantastic halo of tiny, black curls, and whose amazing earrings fell in great concentric hoops to the ebony of her bare shoulders. She looked every inch the thousand-dollar-a-trick hooker that Galatti had flown in, as did the girl beside Crocker who had tousled, auburn hair, a face of open innocence and big, baby-blue eyes. Barbara Galatti met her husband's eye.

Herman Katz finished his drink and put his hand over it to prevent the attendant waiter from serving more. He touched the black girl lightly on the arm, then turned to Barbara Galatti at the far end of the table.

"An excellent meal," he said, bowing slightly, "in a beautiful setting."

She smiled at him warmly. Katz looked across at Seymour Crocker, whose food remained untouched in front of him, then turned to Galatti. "I would have liked," Katz said, "to have commenced discussions this evening, leaving tomorrow free to reach some positive conclusions." He looked again at the pale face of the acting chairman of his bank. "I can see, however, that this may not be possible."

"It is most unfortunate, Seymour," said Galatti with concern. "You must have picked up one of our island bugs." He smiled sympathetically, then turned back to Katz. "I am sure, however, Mr. Katz, that we will not need that much time for discussion. There is nothing we won't be able to resolve, nothing that should cause you to lose sleep."

Katz looked at him with a smile.

"My business, sir," he said, "is the husbanding of other people's money. If I give it out, I get it back. Losing sleep never bothers me."

"And you think you have a problem with Galatti Incorporated?" asked his host in jovial disbelief.

"That's what I wanted to discuss," Katz responded.

"You were saying you had just returned from South America, Mr. Katz," said Barbara Galatti. "I understand our banks have loaned them billions. Will they get it back?"

Katz considered the question.

"Like so many other things today, Mrs. Galatti," he said precisely, "it depends very much on the price of oil."

The statement hung over the terrace like a smog.

"What is your view on oil, Mr. Galatti?" Katz persisted. "You are someone, I am sure, who is following it closely."

Behind their thick lines the pale blue eyes surveyed the banker.

"The world is running out of oil," said Carlo Galatti. "This century has seen a quadrupling of the world's population, gigantic increases in industrialization, the invention of air travel. In less than one hundred years, in the year 2050 to be precise, the world's proven reserves of oil, gas, and coal will have run out."

"But the world has foreseen all that," said Katz dismissively. "People don't want oil anymore. Smart courtries like France now produce most of their electricity from the atom. Countries like India are following suit." He shook his head and laughed outright. "Oil is for suckers, Mr. Galatti. That's why it's on the way down."

In a masterly example of self-control, Galatti did not flinch.

"Then let's drink to the suckers, Mr. Katz," he said, raising his glass.

Katz raised his glass, but did not drink. "South America," he said. He left his mouth open and looked at Galatti. "Argentina, isn't that right, Mr. Galatti?"

Carlo Galatti's eyes met his.

"That's correct," he said evenly.

"What part?" Katz asked as his brain clicked into its selection process. "I worked for six years in Buenos Aires."

There was a complete silence. The black girl, Jane, looked toward the entrance. The butler had appeared and came over to whisper something in Galatti's ear.

"Tell him to come out," Galatti said.

The butler beckoned to the door and a squat, muscular Negro in shorts and a baseball cap came onto the terrace.

"Excuse me," Galatti said to the table. "This is Phillip, my boatman." He turned back. "Tomorrow night, Phillip," he said.

The boatman's face dropped. "Sure thing, boss," he said, turning to go.

"I'm sorry," Galatti said to his guests, "but I have this small indulgence. I like to dive at night. Phillip did not know I had guests."

"Dive at night? Out there?" Jane's eyes were wide as she looked from Galatti to his wife.

Barbara Galatti smiled. "Halfway between our beach and the point of the bay, the coral shelves very deeply, to over two hundred feet. Carlo's built this cage and we've stocked it with many different species of fish. Fish feed at night. It's a fascinating time to watch them."

"That sounds amazing," said Seymour Crocker's companion, Trudy. "But how do you see down there?"

"We've fitted out a special glass-bottomed boat," said Galatti. "Inside it we position lights that are run off the engines. We anchor over the cage and the coral is completely illuminated."

"I think it sounds fantastic," said the black girl, her eyes shining. "I've always wanted to dive at night." She caught Herman Katz's arm. "What d'you say?"

"I don't know," Katz said hesitating. He looked at Barbara Galatti, who smiled benevolently.

"There's no problem — have any of you dived before?" she asked.

Both girls' hands shot up like children in class.

"Mr. Katz?"

Jane was looking at him expectantly.

"It's been a long time . . ."

"Don't you fret," gushed Jane. "I'll look after you every second." She lowered her voice. "Help you get your gear on and everything."

The others laughed.

"Seymour?" asked Galatti.

Seymour Crocker's head shook wearily.

"No way," he said. He stood up. "If you will excuse me," he said to Barbara. Then he took his leave, walking slowly from the terrace, his shoulders hunched.

Galatti looked at a servant.

"Is Phillip still there?"

"Yessir, boss." The grinning boatman had been just inside the terrace door.

"Phillip — do you have equipment for my three guests?"

"No problem, Mr. Galatti, sir. Everything's in the locker room."

Jane and Trudy were excitedly discussing the proposed adventure.

"Will there be sharks, Mr. Galatti?" asked Trudy in a tiny voice.

"Of course, my dear," replied Galatti. "Shark, sting-ray, barracuda, you name it, all the great predators of the ocean are down there."

"Barracuda!" shrieked the girls.

Galatti beckoned to the boatman.

"Show my guests to the locker room," he ordered. He turned to the table and smiled. "I will join you shortly."

The boatman grinned and escorted the two girls and the banker down the steps from the terrace and through the scented garden, which was humming and clicking with the chorus of the night.

"I'll get changed," said Barbara Galatti and made her way into the house through the terrace doors.

At the head of the table Carlo Galatti sat silently, his right finger and thumb ceaselessly circling the gold ring on the ring finger of his left hand. His eyes were unseeing. There was a discreet cough. Galatti turned. The butler was holding a portable telephone.

"The line is bad, sir," he said.

Galatti took the instrument and the butler withdrew. Despite the static the voice on the other end was clear.

Galatti listened, the fingers of his free hand clenching until the knuckles stood out white.

"My instructions were specific," he rasped when his caller had finished. "This is a loose end which I do not wish. I had assumed that your call was to tell me that things were as I instructed."

"There is no need for you to worry," his caller said. "It has taken us over a day, but we have tracked him down."

"To where?" Galatti asked.

"Upstate New York," the caller answered. "A place called Rispey."

"Rispey," said Galatti, frowning at the unfamiliar name. "Call me with good news," he said and crashed down the telephone.

He sat at the table and gazed at the red candles, one of which had begun to smoke.

"Can I get you anything, sir?" The butler had reappeared. Galatti looked at him strangely. Then he stood up.

"I'm going to see some sharks," came his voice as his back was swallowed up in the darkness.

The front of the locker room opened onto a solid wooden jetty that ran for thirty yards out into the bay. A wide, twenty-foot, glass-bottomed boat was lying to, with the diving party sitting in two opposite rows, separated by a bank of chromed and cabled lights, their lenses pointing to the seabed.

"Okay, let's go!" cried Phillip, the boatman, expertly releasing ropes forward and aft and springing aboard. Another, older black, his assistant, was in charge of the throbbing motor. Phillip wore the briefest of swimwear, revealing a body that resembled the gnarled and knotted trunk of an ancient tree.

Barbara Galatti sat at the stern. Her glorious body radiated health in the warm night. Squat lead weights twined on a canvas belt sat on her hips, the belt fastened at her navel by a shining metal buckle. The black weights looked like toads clinging to her fresh skin. Galatti sat opposite. He was wearing the top of a black rubber wet suit; his bare legs had a hint of old-age gauntness about them. His eyes without their thick shields of glass looked for once normal. To his right Herman Katz was sitting contentedly beside Jane. The black girl was dressed in a plunging one-piece swimsuit: a single piece of thin, red toweling ran from her neck down her back and disappeared between the gleaming globes of her buttocks, emerging at the front to run upwards in a gradually widening fashion until it reached her small breasts and ended again at her neck. The result was to wildly exaggerate her endlessly long legs, one of which was being currently rubbed by Herman Katz's foot.

"You just follow me," the black girl said.

Herman Katz smiled.

The boat purred out on its short journey from the jetty and Phillip dropped an anchor overboard.

"Here we are," said Galatti, standing up. "Lights, Phillip," he commanded.

The boatman clicked a switch and all at once the scene below was starkly visible through the boat's glass bottom. Shoals of tiny, silver fish, millions of them, darted in and out of the area of the lights' influence. The water was a great, black, almost viscous mass, and far below, at about sixty feet, could be seen the first outcropping of coral, in sunlight a pink, living rockery, but now a dim shadow of brown. The boatman began to help the divers on with their air tanks, adjusting the webbing of the shoulder straps, and checking that the breathing regulator was correctly fitted to the top of the tank, its valve securely tight and open.

"How long are you going to be down there?" asked Herman Katz, his eyes drawn like magnets to the black girl's incredible, squirming posterior as she was helped into her straps.

"About twenty minutes," said Galatti. "Just a word to everybody. Our normal procedure is we meet below at the anchor. I suggest you stay behind either Barbara or myself as we make our way around the cage. Phillip stays back, just in case any barracuda try to sneak up from behind. Stay in the lights. If you have any problems, Toby will be up here." The old man at the helm grinned. "Remember," Galatti said, "when you come up, do so slowly, after your bubbles."

Then, pulling his face mask into position, he sat on the side of the boat and flipped over backward into the inky Caribbean.

Barbara Galatti went next. One by one the others followed, Katz going in last. Through the boat's glass bottom the illuminated, descending figures could be seen, the black girl getting the depth the quickest, like some fantastic, screwable black shark.

Sixty feet down on the coral, Carlo Galatti checked that the anchor had a secure hold, then turned to see the other divers. All five others were there, Barbara next to him, Phillip and Trudy together, and Katz who was following the black girl like a dog. Galatti gave them the circled thumb and finger okay sign and then pointed to the shadowy outline of the cage, which began just at the edge of the sphere of light. He finned toward it, followed by Barbara, then the others. Up on the surface, sixty or seventy feet away, Toby began to maneuver the boat, changing the direction of the lights.

All at once the divers could see the steel mesh of a cage. They glided up to it. Half a dozen sly barracuda came up to the wire from the back of their ocean prison for a look. Galatti took a knife from its sheath on his leg and, inserting it in a square of wire, rattled the cage vigorously. For an instant nothing happened. Then suddenly there was an explosion of activity and a fifteen-foot, six-hundred-pound hammerhead shark slammed into the mesh not a foot from Galatti's face.

The others fell back, including Katz, who now had his arm around Jane's lithe waist. The shark attack had dispersed the barracuda but the dark shape still lurked behind the wire, awaiting another provocation. Small silver sprats, butterfly-fish colored with bright red and yellow bands, and angel fish swam to and fro, in and out through the mesh without concern.

The cage at this point ran down the side of the coral reef to which it clung. Galatti finned down, the other divers on either side of him. To his right were Katz and the black girl, while to his left were Barbara, Trudy, and Phillip, in line with the cage.

Herman Katz checked his depth gauge. They were nearly at a hundred feet, the extremity and base of the fish cage. They began to round the corner, to make their way back up the other side of the reef. At this depth the illumination from the boat was at its weakest.

A marvelous black manta, nearly twenty feet from its head to the tip of its pointed tail, flapped lazily behind the wire. Katz scarcely noticed. He was now at the very edge of the light, farthest from the fish spectacle. His left hand was grasping that of the black girl and now he guided her down to grip the straining tumescence in his trunks. She turned and, despite the regulator in her mouth, smiled. Katz finned farther away from the main group, pulling her with him, so that he and Jane were outside the light, looking in at the others, as into a lighted goldfish bowl. The black girl was working him rhythmically as his legs wound around one of hers. Katz caught her waist. Suddenly, in the tar that was the tropical sea, he sensed rather than saw a dark shape above him, and then a gold flash that might have been a small fish. The other divers were still just in view and Katz's shrewd eyes automatically counted them. Realization took a second. Then it came to him.

In a frantic jerk Katz tried to adjust his body, tried to look upward, but at that instant the air supply to his mouth ceased. In horror he watched the others disappear around the far side of the bright cage. He spat the useless regulator from his mouth and lunged crazily at the black girl's face, tearing at her precious mouthpiece with the madness of the drowning. Her eyes wide, Jane hit back powerfully, causing Katz's face mask to flood with water, but somehow he had managed to grab hold of the pipe running from her regulator to the tank on her back. Holding the vital mouthpiece in place by sheer strength, Jane scored Katz's openmouthed face again and again with the long fingernails of her right hand as she kicked in frenzy for the distant surface. Now Katz blindly ripped at her face mask. It came off. In a final paroxysm of desperation he wrapped his two legs rigidly about her waist as he clawed for the air he needed to live.

As his efforts weakened and then stopped, their two entwined bodies shot upward toward the dark surface and broke it, inert.

It was dawn before Phillip found them.

MONDAY: P.M.

23

"BLUE LAGOON," CROONED THE SINGER AT THE WHITE piano, picked out by a single spot, beyond where the bar curved. Matt drained the glass and put it down.

"Same, Matt?"

He nodded. "Thanks, Paddy," he said, and looked around. The bar was virtually empty: a few couples sat in booths; two men who had been drinking quietly at the other end of the counter got up and left. There was a glass door to his right, and through it Matt could see the rain hammering down on the cars parked outside in Paddy's lot.

"Monday nights in Rispey," said Paddy shaking his head grimly. "It's hardly worth my while opening." He shrugged his shoulders as he poured out the beer into the tall glass. "It must cost me a hundred bucks to heat this place, light it, pay someone to come in and clear up later on. Liberace over there costs me fifty, cash." He placed the beer on a mat in front of Matt. "I've hardly taken that tonight."

Matt put a five-dollar bill on the counter.

"Ah, forget it," said Paddy. "I'm in a generous mood. This one's on me."

Matt smiled and raised the glass. "Cheers," he said. Paddy moved off down the bar to wash glasses. Matt looked at his watch: it was seven thirty. Earlier that day he had been at the small cabin in the trees that Delis had grudgingly agreed not to contest, and had telephoned the hospital in France. He had been put through to a man with a Brooklyn accent, who had found it difficult to keep his voice from choking.

"She's my little girl," Bill Vandervater kept saying. "I've two boys, but Cathy's my little girl."

"Hasn't there been any improvement?" Matt said.

"Nobody can tell me anything," the man had said. "She's just lying there as if she was asleep. I don't have much, but whatever I have I would give it right now to change places with my little girl."

Matt closed his eyes. He knew what he had to do, regardless of Jim Crabbe's agreement. In New York, in the lavish penthouse, Matt had seen Carlo Galatti's face: only once before had he seen a face like it: it had been in Vietnam, the day they had captured a small Cong patrol south of the Kontum Plateau. The Cong's officer had had the lower part of one arm blown away in the exchange, and as they awaited the choppers to take them out, Matt had moved to help tighten the man's bandages, which were oozing blood. The Vietnamese had drawn back like a wild animal, then spat, full into Matt's face. Matt remembered vividly first the shock of the hostile act, then, unforgettably, the man's face, rigid in its spasm of detestation, a face that would never compromise, regardless of any outcome including death.

So it was with Carlo Galatti. Compromise would not be a word in such a man's language. Anything that got in his way would be swept aside — as Cathy had been swept aside. Matt sipped his beer thoughtfully. He himself was probably in danger — but only if Galatti felt that Matt was still in pursuit. Matt brushed hair back from his forehead. He had never actually considered the implications for his own safety up to that point. He set his jaw: nor would he until he had proved to his own satisfaction that Cathy was right and Galatti's insurance claim on Cornucopia was a fraud. Matt balled his fist. The first thing Jim Crabbe would say when he arrived was that they had no proof. Matt shook his head. They had to get proof, evidence; that was the world they operated in. Otherwise Cathy would have suffered for nothing.

Paddy came up the bar with a cordless telephone. He put it on the counter.

"It's for you."

Matt raised his eyebrows but Paddy shrugged and returned to his glasses.

"Hullo?"

"Mr. Blaney?"

"Yes?"

"Are you enjoying your beer?"

Matt looked around him.

"Who is this?"

The voice was slightly nasal, the accent New York, Bronx.

"Miller's, off the shelf in a tall glass," said the voice. "It's your third. You're at the bar, on a stool. You've got a tartan shirt on, open at the neck." Matt felt his scalp tingle. "A brown jacket, cords, sneakers — should I go on?"

Matt looked through the glass door out into the wet night. He felt his mouth go dry.

"What is this?"

"Just someone who wants to trade," the voice said.

"Trade?"

"Information for money."

Matt's mind raced. "I don't know what you're talking about," he said, standing up and walking to the door with the phone. The parking lot held just four cars, including his own. They looked empty. Rain blew in squalls. "Is this a joke?"

He heard the other man breathe.

"This is no joke, my friend. Like I say, it's a trade. Let's call it a horse trade."

Matt's heart jumped; he sat down on a bar stool.

"Tell me more," he said.

"For five thousand cash I tell you more. Tonight."

Again Matt's eyes spun around. The voice seemed so near.

"That's impossible."

"Nothing's impossible. Bring the money to Jordan's Quarry in one hour."

"I tell you it's impossible."

"Come alone and don't even think of telling anyone."

"I need to know more. How do I know you're for real?" Matt said, every communications sense in his body rigid.

There was silence. Then:

"Pity about the girl — a good lay but now she'll never spread them again."

"*Who are you, you bastard?*"

Matt was on his feet, his face suffused. The line was dead. He threw down the phone and ran at the door, kicking it open. Out in the sheeting rain of the lot no vehicle had moved. To the right and high above Paddy's, cars moved back and forth on the main highway into Rispey. It was just possible that someone up there with a car phone and binoculars could see the bar door, but . . .

Matt walked back in. He was soaked. Slowly he sat down, trembling. His mind had completely reflooded with all its images of the previous five days: the white-faced Laurens, the set jaw of Dijon, the vets, Cambier and Petitjean, the distorted hands of Madame la Baronne as she stared at him kneeling in the offal of the dead racehorse, and the beautiful golden face on the pillow, sometimes the pillow of his own bed, sometimes of the hospital bed in Caen.

Matt looked at his watch. It was nearly eight and there was no sign of Jim Crabbe. With such weather the trip from New York would have taken longer than planned.

Taking a notebook from his pocket, Matt tore out a page and scribbled down a message. Then he signaled Paddy from down the bar.

"Anything wrong, Matt?"

'You know Jim Crabbe?" Matt asked.

"The guy you work with? Sure," Paddy said.

"Can you give him this note?" Matt asked. "And, Paddy?"

The bar owner looked at him.

"Do you by any chance keep any spare cash here?" Matt asked.

Jordan's Quarry is the name given to a group of disused sand and gravel pits cut out of the green rolling hills that run southeast from Bear Lake, a small town just over the state line in Pennsylvania. As the crow flies they're just twenty miles from Rispey but to drive it count on twice that as the road twists and turns around French Creek River, and meanders through the little communities that live within sight of the waters of Lake Erie.

Matt hit the long, narrow road running out over uncertain ground to the pits that earlier inhabitants of the area had quarried to build their homes. There were no houses on either side; no one had tried to farm the arid land. The rain had ceased ten miles out of Rispey and had been replaced by a lively wind. He passed a warning sign: some pits flooded in winter and the rock face was unsuitable for would-be mountaineers. The road came to a dead end and he turned up an even narrower road, peering ahead for a light or sign of another car.

It was more a track than a road; concreted in a former age, the remains of such surfacing now formed the contours of enormous potholes, their edges jagged and uncompromising. Matt swore as the Porsche's chassis scraped against the ground. He swerved from one side to the other. The track seemed endless, its quality relentlessly bad. Then just when he thought that he must have got it wrong, the lane opened out into a wide amphitheater. He stopped.

He was at the mouth of an old stone quarry. On all sides its sheer face rose in dark, jagged cliffs and at its center lay a rusting, yellow machine, its excavating days long over.

Very slowly Matt drove in over the gritty surface, turning left and right in an attempt to find his informant. Overhead, clouds were hurrying across the sky, making natural vision intermittent. Matt got out and slammed the door. He thrust his hands into his jacket pockets. The only sounds came from the wind as it shook the bare branches of a solitary tree, high on the quarry hill. There was a sudden creaking sound. He whirled. Speckled moonshadows played on the mechanical scoop, its engine fan revolving in response to the breeze.

Matt took a deep breath and looked around him. Any visitor would almost certainly have to enter the quarry using the same road he had: the cliffs behind were too steep. Matt returned to the car, then reversed it in an arc until it came to rest at the side of the quarry, its lights pointing out. It was fifteen minutes to 1 A.M. He killed the engine and opened the window, the better to hear an approaching car with its lights off. There was a thicker jacket on the back seat, which he drew around his shoulders. He scanned the desolate scene. The racing night sky played tricks with his eyes, causing shadows to take life on the black stone cliffs. On the horizon there was a warm glow from a sleeping Bear Lake.

Matt reclined his seat and sat perfectly still. Outside, he could hear the whine of the wind. He opened his window another inch. The wind was constant, almost reassuring. Matt stopped breathing. There had been another sound. He strained, his whole body an antenna, as he tried to place it, to separate what he had heard from the sound of the wind, and to dissect it. Then it came again and was suddenly, instantly recognizable. It was a footfall on gravel, close by.

At first Matt could see nothing. He concentrated on keeping his figure motionless in his reclined position. Then in the outside mirror mounted on the frame of the driving door he saw the twin black snouts of a shotgun being leveled at the back of his head.

In a reflex action Matt's hand snaked forward to the ignition keys and in a desperate wrench brought the car to sudden life. Simultaneously and still lying back, he pressed the accelerator to the floor and without recourse to the clutch slammed the gearshift into first. The car jumped forward with a screech of rubber, its lights ablaze.

Whatever instinct had persuaded him to remain supine now proved its worth. The ear-shattering explosions of a pump-action shotgun were followed by a rush of wind as fragmented glass from the back window showered the inside of the car over his head. He felt a searing pain in his scalp, then he was thrown forward as the front of the Porsche powered blindly into a solid object. Someone screamed. Matt sat up and stared out. Not two yards away a man wearing a knit cap stood riveted at his gut between the Porsche and the mechanical scoop.

Matt blinked in disbelief, then he felt a hot seeping down his ear. He heard shouting. Ramming the Porsche into reverse he locked the wheel hard left and lurched crazily away. His car's headlights were smashed but one remaining bulb illuminated the quarry. In horror, Matt saw two things: the victim of his hammer-charge into the scoop was still, inexplicably, fastened to the front of the Porsche, and another man, standing fifteen yards away, was leveling a heavy pistol, held in his two hands at the windshield. Matt's duck beneath the dashboard was totally instinctive. A series of deafening explosions was followed by fragmenting glass, which now showered the car in the opposite direction.

Matt stood on the accelerator. Still in first, the engine of the Porsche screamed. The sudden forward acceleration caused the victim on the hood to slide down and under the front wheels. Matt's head came back up in time to see the man with the pistol fumble for a reload. The car came straight at him. There was a rumbling thudding, then the Porsche caught him full on, his eyes staring out from his woollen ski mask. He sailed up in the air and then down, his neck catching heavily on the jagged rim of the broken windshield. Matt could hear a grunt as the inverted head and shoulders flopped in over the dashboard, the tongue protruding slyly from the side of the mouth.

There was some movement in the quarry behind. By some trick of the moonlight Matt's eye spotted a figure in the rearview mirror, a massive silhouette, someone square-headed and familiar. Matt saw the pump-action being raised. The Porsche shook as volleys caught its trunk and fenders. With a strength born of madness, Matt put his hand under the heavy lolling head and pushed mightily up and out. The dying or dead man's weight balance shifted outside and he slid off, his still-gripped pistol clanging on the quarry floor.

On pure adrenaline Matt flung the car down the pitted lane. The bitter wind sang through it like through a sieve. He glanced back but could see no sign of the remaining assailant. He crashed heavily from one concrete island to another as the exhaust began to sputter ominously. His eyes flooded with water. The wind stung his face and hands. Something reared out of the night. He braked desperately as the Porsche bounced from the depths of a venomous pothole onto grass.

A bank of headlights flashed on, blinding him. He wrenched into reverse and tried to crouch at dashboard level. The Porsche's wheel spun uselessly on the grass. Desperately he opened the door and rolled out, scrambling on his belly to find protection. He could see a flashlight joining the car lights and probing. Any moment he expected to feel the thump of a dumdum. The flashlight was coming around the back of the Porsche. Matt's hands clawed wildly and fastened on a rock. He stood up to hurl it. The light hit him straight on. He froze.

"It's me, you mad son-of-a-bitch," cried Jim Crabbe.

TUESDAY A.M.

THE JUDAEAN HILLS WERE ABLAZE WITH THE LIGHTS FROM a thousand homes; the only sounds were of dogs barking and the hum of traffic on the nearby motorway connecting Tel Aviv with Jerusalem.

Dr. Yoseph Shenlavi balanced a saucer in the palm of his left hand and raised the tiny cup of Turkish coffee to his lips. It had been a satisfactory day.

He had risen early and shaved, the first time in four days. He had completed his prayers, then breakfasted well on cheese, smoked fish, and coffee. He had taken the Volvo from the basement garage, having firstly removed the cylinder from the trunk. The morning had been warm, the air scented, the sky clear. At the base of the last hill before Jerusalem he had stopped to give a lone *sabra* a lift, a pretty girl with her brown hair in a short ponytail, her young figure proud in its military fatigues.

"Beautiful day," Dr. Shenlavi said.

The girl had smiled.

"Beautiful day — beautiful country," she replied.

She had not noticed the constant red battery light that shone steadily in the car's dashboard.

They climbed upward, through the rising ground covered in cypresses and pines. At the hilltop the morning sun was bathing the golden stone of Jerusalem in its light. The city sprawled out in a bowl below them, its noises wafting upward. He let the girl out at a bus terminal where dozens of young military sat around, their submachine guns and rifles propped in stacks. Levi would be older than them now, he thought, but Ruth and Rachel . . . Dr. Shenlavi frowned as if the question had just arisen. Why had Ruth and Rachel died? And who had killed them? His smiling mouth puckered. Then like someone who has just awoken from a nightmare, relief and peace flooded through him.

Levi would soon be home and justice was about to be done. For Levi, for Anna, for Ruth and Rachel and all the dead generations.

He drove the Volvo downhill, past manicured lawns and woodland on his right, and then sharply uphill until once again the shimmering city came into view.

He turned slowly into Eli'ezer Kaplan and pulled in at the curb. It was Tuesday and large numbers of tourist buses could be seen, their destinations the Israel Museum to his left, and to his right, on the highest point behind the tall wire fence, the Knesset.

Dr. Shenlavi switched off the ignition. Curiously the red dashboard light remained bright. He nodded confidently. The eighty-nine megahertz signal from the FM radio in his garage in Mevasseret had beamed steadily through to the car for the entire journey and was now as strong as ever. It had passed the test.

Dr. Shenlavi got out and put on a pair of Polaroids. He had not been up here for years. He squinted up at the squat building with its rows of Doric columns, the seat of all power for the Children of Israel.

A wide shrubbery separated the footpath from a low wall. Then came the fence, ten feet high and tilted outward, fully electrified. Behind the fence were impeding rolls of heavy barbed wire, staggered every few yards, and behind these a line of thick trip-wire, two feet off the ground and encircling the whole enclosure, which allowed the dogs attached to it to patrol each section of the boundary, the steel rings of their leads singing on the wire. It was security at its most obvious, and undoubtedly the open ground between the tethered dogs and the parliament building was crisscrossed with button-mines.

He approached the wall and one of the dogs dashed to the spot, snarling. Dr. Shenlavi stared at the parliament building. He had cal-

culated with precision and chosen the day with care. On the Sabbath
the Knesset and all the nearby government offices would be closed;
except for a few guards, they would be empty.

Dr. Shenlavi stared over the wall, oblivious to the barking dog, and
concentrated. If the plutonium yielded as he hoped, a massive but controlled explosion would occur. Heat equal to the sun's core would be
produced in the fraction of a millionth of a second needed to achieve
fission. Thus the Knesset would disappear as would most of the nearby
museum. But that was all.

He shrugged and sighed. Damage to bricks and mortar which could
be rebuilt; a few human casualties admittedly, but only a few: it was a
small price to pay.

He climbed into his car and drove slowly back toward Yafo. The only
remaining consideration was the damage that would be caused by the
limited fallout. This problem, too, caused him to smile. It was as if
God Himself had inspired the plan. With the prevailing winds coming from the west, most if not all of the radioactivity would be blown
east, across the Jordan and on into Syria, Iraq, and Saudi Arabia.
There was a good chance that the fertile land of Israel would escape
completely.

The sun was warm as he turned off the busy artery connecting the
two sides of the slim country. He rolled down the window and sniffed
the air. There was the smell of pines, of spring flowers, and of freshly
cut grass.

With a brief break for prayer he worked on the car through the
afternoon. It was a masterpiece, a booby trap of cataclysmic proportions.

The central concept was based on the rear window of the Volvo. Its
thin, embedded demisting strips were wired by a cable to the car's
battery. Midway down this cable, Dr. Shenlavi had incorporated a tiny
radio receiver, which was tuned to the FM radio transmitter farther
down the garage bench: the wires in the rear demister now worked as
an antenna. The FM signal could be used to keep the car battery live,
an essential condition, because the battery was itself connected to a
solenoid and onward to a detonator. As long as the battery remained
alive, the solenoid remained closed. But loss of power would open the
solenoid, create a magnetic field, and energize the detonator.

It was also of basic importance that the car should be impregnable.

An earth-loop linked pin-switches on the door locks, trunk lock, and

hood catch to the car battery. Inside the car, two Japanese-made ultra-
sonic sensors were finely tuned to pick up the slightest movement; if a
window was broken — or even struck hard — the sensors would acti-
vate and the circuits to the battery would be cut.

He had covered the trunk's four sides, floor, and lid minutely with
a fine web of tiny wires, their largest opening less than a square inch
and all connected back into the twelve-volt battery.

Under the hood, in the frame which normally held the windshield
sprayer, stood a shallow, concave glass dish with a lid, half filled with
mercury. Two-thirds of the way up the inside of the dish a band of
shining copper ran all the way around its circumference. A wire ran
from the copper to the nearby battery and on through the car, to the
trunk. A second wire ran the same route, through the center of the lid,
and now stood innocently in the mercury, which glinted in the garage
lights.

Any movement of the Volvo whatsoever, sideways, forward, or back,
would cause the active mercury to lap upward and touch the active
copper. The resulting contact was a perfect switch.

He had even anticipated that they might try to lift it away. This he
had foiled by incorporating a run of wires through the shock absorbers.
If the car was grabbed from the ground, the shocks would move as the
weight of the wheels hung down; if it was lifted, by forklift for example,
the reverse would happen. In each case the fragile wires in the shocks
would touch and cut the circuit.

The blue Volvo 340 family sedan now locked safely in the basement
garage was as lethal as a B-52 with a fully armed warhead.

Yoseph Shenlavi put down the cup and saucer and stared outward.

He had always been a brilliant student, right from the start.

The start had been the train journey from Geneva to Naples and then
the sea voyage to Palestine, lasting nearly two weeks. But before Geneva
what had there been? This was the question to which he frequently
returned. As soon as he concentrated on it his mind immediately
switched channels.

"And what is your name?"

The Red Cross worker, although it was nearly forty years ago and he
must now be well dead and buried, was as clear as the design on the
cup. The small becapped Jewish child with the purple cheek had not

replied. It was midwinter in Switzerland. Papa had taught him to say nothing.

"Did you like our nice train?" the kindly man asked with a smile. "It was crowded, I know, but at least it was clean."

The boy had watched as the man read some papers.

"Well, it's all over now," he was saying. He looked down a long list. "You're safe now, do you understand that?" The man shook his head grimly and put the list aside. Then he knelt beside the child. He had a salt-and-pepper beard and very clear green eyes.

"We know you're on your own now," he said gently. "Can you tell me what happened to your family in Theresienstadt?"

"Majdanek."

The man frowned, then he smiled again.

"You've just come from Theresienstadt," he said.

"Majdanek," cried the child, "Majdanek." He saw the papers in the Red Cross official's hands. It was on the tip of his tongue to say something else but then he again remembered Papa's advice.

The door opened and a woman came in. She was also kindly and smiling. She wore a tweed skirt, dark nylon stockings, and a tweed jacket. Spectacles hung around her neck on an elastic cord.

"Who have we here?" she asked.

"An unclaimed child," the man said. "By all accounts he was with an adult when they left Theresienstadt, but if he was, now he's been ditched."

The woman shook her head. Her brown hair was gathered behind in a bun and held with a crocheted net.

"We moved twelve hundred out," she said, "but quite a number have already gone their own way." She looked at the frightened child. "A child cannot identify himself," she said. "He could belong to anyone."

"I agree," said the man. He squatted down again.

"I'm your friend, okay?" he said.

The child nodded dumbly.

"Will you tell me your name?"

The child tried to smile, but large tears ran down his face.

"The poor darling," said the woman sadly. "There's no point, Karl-Heinz. He is no more than four. This is 1945. He was probably born in a camp."

She stooped down and mopped up the tears with a tiny embroidered handkerchief.

He could still smell the perfume.

"Everything will be fine, my little darling," the woman said, her arm around him. "We will find a family in the next convoy who are looking for a lovely boy."

"He tried to say something about Majdanek, just before you came in," said the man.

"Majdanek?" said the woman standing up. "Majdanek fell to the Russians ages ago. Last summer, if I remember." She looked pensively at the child. "Whoever he is, he is not from Majdanek. No one got out of there. They say over a quarter of a million were killed, mainly shot, and the figure may be higher."

"I know," said the man. "I read something in the newspaper last week, it was about a Russian who was one of the first in there. He was describing how efficiently the Germans had utilized everything — the clothes, the teeth, the hair. 'When a pig goes through a Moscow packing house,' he said, 'nothing is wasted but the squeal. So it was in Majdanek.'"

The two Red Cross workers had turned to look at the wide-eyed child.

"Come on little man," said the woman. "You look as if you could do with a hot meal."

Dr. Shenlavi rose stiffly from the chair and stretched.

Some lights in the surrounding hills had gone off. There were only three full days left before Saturday, and there was still much work to be done.

With the resolution born of duty he made his way slowly down the steps to the garage.

TUESDAY: A.M.

 THEY SAT IN JIM CRABBE'S APARTMENT, CRADLING MUGS of hot whiskey. Reluctantly, on the long drive back to Manhattan, Matt had agreed that it was too dangerous for him to go home.

"There's a very simple solution to this whole thing," Jim said.

Matt looked inquiringly at the small, wizened face behind the heat waves rising from the drink.

"Let me guess," Matt said. "Does it begin with the formula: 'First you write a check for one million dollars'?"

Jim got to his feet and began to pace the floor. "A million dollars is confetti compared to the cost of crossing these guys," he said. "I know what goes on, I've seen *The Godfather*. This guy Galatti will have you and me wasted while he sits picking his teeth." He shook his head. "Five minutes earlier this evening, and I would have been a dead man."

Matt closed his eyes. "You don't really mean to tell me, after all this," he said, "that you're going to let your payment to Lloyd's go through? Aren't you going to call them and tell them what we think is going on? That Carlo Galatti very probably suppressed information from them regarding his horse and very possibly even contrived the animal's death — although we have no idea how? You don't have to tell them that. But surely to Christ you're going to tell them your suspicions?"

"*Your* suspicions," Jim corrected him. He sat down and covered his face with his hands. Then he sat up. "I once worked for a very successful man," Jim said quietly. "He taught me one of the most important rules of life: Don't try to fart against thunder." He put up his hand to prevent Matt from speaking. "Just hear me out. I know all about principles and pretty women. I love them both. But when it comes right down to it, I prefer the breathing business." He looked at Matt straight in the eye. "I'm no hero, son," he said. "If you want to be a hero, go work for someone else."

Matt put down his mug and leaned forward.

"Jim."

Jim Crabbe looked away.

"Jim." Matt reached across and put his hand on the smaller man's arm. Jim looked down at the large hand with its black hairs at the wrist, then he looked up.

"I think you should know," Matt said softly, "that even if you pay up now, Carlo Galatti isn't going to forget that I exist."

Jim's eyes showed alarm. "You mean . . . ?"

"I mean," Matt said, "that regardless of what we do, I think there's a good chance that Galatti will try to finish me off. He realizes I know something I'm not meant to." Matt tightened his grip on Jim's arm. "Therefore, Jim, in a way we've got nothing to lose. You've got to hang in with me in this thing. It's our best chance."

Jim's head tossed around. "That doesn't answer how I'm going to deal with Galatti's bad-mouthing us around the market," he said. "I've already told you he's threatened to sue for three times the horse's insured value."

"All his threats will be meaningless if we can prove that he's been involved in a massive fraud," Matt said.

"But that's the key to the damn thing," Jim cried in despair. "Proof. And from what I can make out the only person who can even remotely testify is lying unconscious in France."

"There is someone else who can testify, Jim," Matt said.

Jim looked in bewilderment. "Who?" he asked.

"Barbara Galatti," Matt replied.

TUESDAY: P.M.

26 FAR BELOW THE CARS MOVED AND STOPPED. THE CABS were the most noticeable, their yellow roofs catching the sun's glare and bouncing it back up the forty-five floors.

Seymour Crocker stood, hands in pockets, looking out at the dim outline of Staten Island fading in the dying light. His phone rang.

"I've just concluded those arrangements, Mr. Crocker," came the voice of the bank's operations officer. "The local authorities should have completed their postmortem tomorrow. The body will be up here the day after tomorrow."

"All the next of kin have been notified?"

"Yes, sir."

"And what about Mr. Johnson?"

"No luck so far, sir," said the operations man. "It seems he and Mrs. Johnson have gone out on a deep-sea fishing trip. We're trying to find out the details and contact him by ship-to-shore radio."

"Keep trying," Crocker instructed.

He returned to the window. Any elation he might have felt by the sudden improvement in his own position was firmly counterbalanced by the fear that had entered his belly in Barbados and grown there ever since. For the first time he was truly, if briefly, in charge of First Transnational Bank. But Crocker felt no joy. On his return, his wife's concern had been not for the dead Herman Katz, but what effect his death would have on the society wedding of their daughter and on the three hundred guests expected in three weeks at their fine Connecticut home.

"I'm so glad Hugh and Mitzy Johnson are coming back for it," his wife had said. "It emphasizes your position in the bank."

Crocker had been unable to sleep for more than two hours and then only with the help of a lot of brandy.

Even sleep could not obliterate from his harried inner-eye the image that had settled there, like a hungry black crow on a carcass. It was with him all through the day no matter what he did; it leered at him from the dark windows of the train as he went home; it flapped like a bat in his troubled sleep, and when he awoke it was there in the cold light of the dawn: it was the sweet face of a child in her white veil on the day of her First Communion.

That morning he had called in the bank's chief legal officer to review the account.

"On paper at least we've an overlap of three hundred million," the lawyer said.

"We're completely secured?"

"We've the principal floating charge over everything," the lawyer replied. "Should anything happen, we're number one in line. But if anything does happen, a lot of those assets will shrink like hell — it's always that way."

"That's what Hugh said," Crocker replied.

"A caution, Seymour," the lawyer said. "One hundred and fifty mil-

lion of that collateral is Galatti's personal paper in his own corporation
— and that's off another five points already this morning: it's down to
thirty-eight."

The weight inside Seymour Crocker had hurt. "Thirty-eight?"

"That's right, Seymour," said the lawyer. "That's nearly a fifteen percent drop since last week. We should knock at least twenty-five million
off the value of his paper, to be on the safe side."

Crocker's brain raced. "But we've also got our hands on this Lloyd's
money, right?"

"Insofar as we can, Seymour," said the lawyer. "Mr. Galatti has
signed a lien to us, and instructed Lloyd's of its existence, telling them
to pay us direct. But that's assuming they will pay."

"Thank you," Crocker said.

"Glad to oblige, Seymour," said the lawyer.

Crocker was sure that he noticed a new note of respect in the man's
voice.

The call had come as he had known it would. It was the bank's chief
cashier. Mr. Galatti himself was on the line, insisting that Mr. Crocker
had personally cleared the borrowings.

"Two hundred million dollars is the request," said the cashier.

Crocker and his wife had once, many years before, pledged to each
other that there would be no secrets between them. Now, with Galatti's
face flickering in his vision, Crocker had actually reached for his private
phone. He would face the threat and tell his wife; she would understand. Then another image flickered into Crocker's mind: a tabloid
newspaper on the First Transnational boardroom table showing him naked. Crocker could see Hugh Johnson's slowly shaking head, and the
other directors, conservative men, disappointed in their delegation of
trust.

Crocker sat down heavily, his head buzzing.

"He's holding, sir."

The chief cashier's voice prodded with the inevitability of retribution.
Crocker's vision swam.

"Give it to him," he said.

He went to lunch with a long-standing client and after four martinis
and a bottle of Cabernet Sauvignon he began to improve. Hugh Johnson
made decisions of this nature every day of the week. Why should Seymour Crocker's brief tenure as acting chief executive of First Transna-

tional be distinguished by prevarication? And Galatti had said it was only for a couple of weeks.

After lunch, among the messages by his telephone was one from a government employee in Washington, a friend of Hugh Johnson's.

"Hugh asked me to keep you guys up to date," the man said, when Crocker got to him. "About this Galatti business."

The lead weight in Seymour Crocker's gut sank another fathom.

"The information I'm getting," the man said, "is that Justice have all but got their act together. They'll be ready to go after him, probably Friday of this week. It'll be all guns blazing, arrest, publicity, the works. He'll get bail, of course, but it's going to knock the shit out of his corporation."

"Thanks," Crocker had said.

Now the phone rang again.

"Seymour?"

It was the bank's legal officer.

"Have you seen the Galatti stock?" the lawyer asked.

Seymour Crocker thought he would vomit.

"It's been offered all over the Street at twenty-five," the lawyer said. "I've spoken with our dealing room: they say the selling could be overdone, but once something like this starts anything can happen."

"It's got to be a temporary problem," Crocker heard himself say.

"That paper collateral we discussed this morning," the lawyer was saying. "That should effectively now be discounted as an asset."

Crocker blinked.

"We're getting the preliminary paper work ready down here, just in case anything goes wrong," the man said. "But we're beginning to look a little exposed. We're near the bone."

"We've still got the Lloyd's money," said Crocker.

"Sure," said the lawyer, "but still, thank God Hugh drew the line on this one."

Crocker could not reply. The lawyer obviously had not yet seen the latest increase in Galatti's borrowing. Crocker found himself shaking uncontrollably as he replaced the phone.

"No more calls," he instructed his secretary through the intercom. Then he walked to the drinks cabinet and poured himself a generous measure of brandy, which he drank, neat, standing and in one gulp. As the warm liquid fired through him he replenished his glass and sat down shakily.

Dismissal from First Transnational would mean the loss of all pension benefits and the nightmarish prospect of being thrown on the Wall Street scrap-heap at the age of fifty-two. He had seen men in that position over the years, pathetic and redundant, trying to maintain the pretense that nothing had changed. Their eyes were the giveaway. Where before there had been confidence, humor, arrogance, now on the lip of old age without an income there was only fear.

The brandy was making him feel better. He finished the second glass and poured himself a third. Sorrow had begun to replace the fear. He blinked and then reached for a small notebook. Holding it open, he dialed a phone number on his private line.

An hour later, in a well-furnished, darkened apartment in the upper sixties, Trudy of the innocent face entwined her lithe, golden body around Crocker's white frame, her tousled hair falling in a cascade across his belly. At last she came up, her lips moist and shining.

"I dunno what's wrong with you," she said in exasperation.

He was lying in the crucifixion position, his eyes staring at the ceiling.

A half-empty bottle of brandy lay on the bed beside him.

"This is where you forget your problems, lover," said Trudy softly, working her long fingers down between his flabby legs. "I want a tiger," she growled. "Show me a tiger."

Crocker stretched up his hand, which felt like a ton weight, and rubbed the nape of her neck; then he worked it all the way down her supple back until he reached the tiny blond hairs at the base of her spine.

"That's nice," she murmured and wriggled appreciatively. "Now scratch me."

Crocker brought his hand in a claw from where her buttocks began up to the flatness between her shoulder blades.

"Again," she purred.

Crocker dug in more the next time, scoring the length of her and leaving two bright red marks.

"Nice!" cried Trudy from her throat.

"It's no good," he said, slumping back. He felt he would throw up.

"Come on," said Trudy, lying full length on top of him and slowly massaging his body with hers. "Come on, fuck me. I want to be fucked."

A great groaning sigh came from Seymour Crocker's chest. Trudy slid off him and reached for a cigarette beside the bed.

He looked at her. "I'm sorry about your friend," he said.

Trudy shrugged. "She was a hooker from Miami. I only met her an hour before you did." She shivered. "Still it was lousy luck. She was a good kid."

Idly she stroked his hairless chest and inhaled a deep lungful of smoke.

"What about your friend?" she asked. "Was he married?"

Crocker shook his head.

"He was sort of cute," Trudy said. "You want a joint?"

Crocker shook his head again on the white pillow.

"Come on, big boy," said Trudy, "I want to hear it. I'm your mom, okay? You can tell me."

She smiled and nestled into him. "It's money, isn't it?"

Seymour Crocker nodded.

"Have you gone and lost your ass?" asked the girl sweetly.

He nodded again.

"It's good to *talk*," said the girl, pressing him. "What are you, any-way? A trader or something?"

She looked at him. Crocker had slowly raised himself on his elbows and was staring at her as if her nose was missing.

"What is it, honey?" she asked him.

"What did you say just now?" he asked fiercely, catching her arm. "Repeat it!"

"Hey, you're hurting me, I was only trying to help, let go!"

"I'm sorry," he said, his breath heavy with brandy, "please just repeat what you said."

"You're all weird," said Trudy rubbing her red-blotched arm. "I just asked if you'd lost your ass."

"No. After that."

She frowned.

"I asked . . . if you were a trader."

"That's exactly it!"

In one leap he cleared the bed and began to dress hurriedly.

"You're a genius," he cried, kissing the girl's puzzled face, his own beaming in a huge smile of relief.

"A trader!" He laughed. "That's it. That's what's needed. A trader."

"Glad to be of help," said Trudy.

Seymour Crocker was wrestling into his coat, his shoelaces undone, his tie missing. All the passed-up breaks of his unfulfilled career suddenly converged in a glorious sunburst of opportunity as Carlo Galatti's words boomed in his ears: "Within ten trading days our stock will have doubled at least."

"It's been staring me in the face all day," Crocker shouted. "But it took you to make me see it."

"Hey, good," cried Trudy, "but what about my money?"

But Crocker was already down the steps of the brownstone and running up Fifth Avenue.

WEDNESDAY: A.M.

27 IT WAS ALREADY SEVENTY OUTSIDE THE TINTED GLASS OF the manager's office. Through the open door, the man in the white shirtsleeves could see the first customers lining up at the teller's windows; the business was mainly tourist currency in small amounts, traveler's checks, dollars, all changed into Bahamian dollars at lucrative spreads. This was the retail side; in two offices beside his, the business of First Transnational's offshore accounts was managed by a small team that he oversaw.

The manager was a native of Nassau, an ambitious young man of thirty who had trained for five years in the First Trans head office in New York, then as assistant manager in Fort Lauderdale. He was lean and alert and never forgot the fact that on the totem pole of First Transnational Banking Corporation he scored a very small notch, very far down.

His telephone rang. The manager raised his eyebrows, then said, "Of course, put him through." He cleared his throat. "Good morning, sir," he said, looking at his watch. It was nine thirty-five, the same time as in New York. "Pretty nice this morning," he said, answering the caller's question, "about seventy, rain last night." He paused, then said, "You should try to get away down here, sir, for a few days." Then: "Of course,

I understand." He frowned in concentration. "Yes, sir," he said and picked up a pen. He listened for five minutes, making notes, then he read back his instructions in detail to his caller.

"I completely understand, sir," he said. "No one will know; I will handle the order myself. Yes, I totally appreciate the delicacy."

He listened as his caller again emphasized the need for confidentiality. The manager recognized the voice well: after all, the man calling from New York had given him his present position.

The manager's brow deepened. "No cable confirmation to the head office," he repeated. He nodded cautiously. The First Trans internal audit manual was specific. "If you say so, sir." He nodded more vehemently. "Of course," he agreed. "Retroactively will be fine if you say so. Thank you. I'll call you to confirm."

Then without so much as a thought for the ethics of what he was about to do, or the audit manual, or his training in procedures, or indeed the prospects of his own career, he got an outside line and dialed the number he had been given in New York.

The trader at the dealing desk high in the World Trade Center had already made more money that morning for the securities firm he worked for than his father would earn in his entire lifetime. At twenty-two, while many of his high-school contemporaries were still laboring on college campuses all over America, he lived in an elegant studio near Battery Park, drove a vintage Aston Martin on weekends, and earned over four hundred thousand dollars a year.

He sat, his eyes scanning the screens in front of him: two of them gave up-to-the-minute values on the portfolio he was trading, one gave detailed information on all the stocks traded on the New York Stock Exchange, and the fourth was an electronic, touch-operated keyboard screen that plugged him into a vast communications network.

The morning had been quiet. The trader specialized in financial stocks, the corporate paper of the giants who ruled Wall Street. He could recall with precision the minutest detail of the balance sheet of up to thirty different banks and institutions. The portfolio on the screens in front of him showed an investment commitment, long and short, of fifty million dollars, although his discretion went to three times that.

His telephone rang. It was a contact from twenty floors below, a senior man in a highly respected brokerage firm.

"Right now?" asked the trader.

"Right now," said the broker.

Five minutes later they stood side by side at the urinals in the men's room of the broker's office.

"I thought you should know about a very peculiar order we've been working," the broker said.

The trader raised his eyebrows.

"It came in this morning, just after ten. It was a buy order for two million Galatti Incorporated at market."

"The construction outfit?"

The broker nodded.

"It's not my territory," the trader said, "but aren't they in some kind of trouble?"

His informant nodded again. "Their stock crapped out seriously last week," he said. "By over twenty points. The rumors have been flying, but one of them is that their bankers, First Transnational, are refusing to renew their loans."

The trader's interest quickened. First Trans was one of the stocks he favored, always trading it from the long side.

"First Trans have very adequate loan provisions," he said to the broker, his clear mind recalling the bank's balance sheet. "They're okay."

"Then why are they buying Galatti stock?" asked the broker.

The trader screwed up his face. Conversation was suspended as another man entered the washroom, used it, and left. The trader was washing his hands.

"Say that again," he said as the door closed.

"The order to buy Galatti stock," said the broker, "came from Credit Fidelity, acting for a client."

"Your old friends," said the trader.

"Right," the broker said. Up to a year before he had worked as an investment analyst at Credit Fidelity's Park Avenue headquarters.

"The account reference used," he said, "is one I remember well. It's a First Transnational nominee account, out of their Nassau branch in the Bahamas."

The trader's frown had deepened.

"The order has been repeated," said the broker. "That's when I called you."

"That's interesting," said the trader.

"Very interesting, " said the broker. "It represents nearly ten percent of Galatti Incorporated. The market's reacted favorably; Galatti's gone up seven, to thirty-one fifty."

"It's a bid," the trader said. "First Trans have got to be acting for someone."

"Bidding on someone else's behalf for their own customer?" asked the broker. "Most unlikely."

The trader bit his lip. Again they rewashed their hands as two men came in, then eventually left.

"They could be acting for Galatti himself," suggested the trader.

"I doubt it," the broker replied. "He's in a cash bind, he's owed millions from the Gulf. Why would he buy his own shares?"

"Thanks," said the trader. "This could be useful."

The broker winked at him. "Like I always say," he said with a smile, "there's enough in this business for everyone to get a slice."

Back at his desk the trader punched up Galatti Incorporated and confirmed what he had just been told. Then he hit the illuminated box on the communications screen with the back of his telephone for an outside line. It took three calls before he got the person he wanted. He spoke casually, his voice calm.

"Australia?" he said.

"He went a week ago," the girl on the other end said. "Great Barrier Reef. Why?"

"Just wondering. Say, how about dinner with me tonight?"

He sat back, cleared his mind of everything else, concentrated for two minutes, then made a decision. He touched the right-hand screen again, but his eyes were now glued to the screen in the middle.

In another building three blocks away, another trader with another firm answered.

"How are you this morning?" asked the World Trade Center man.

"Not too bad, all things considered," replied the other trader.

"I see you're a buyer of fifty thousand First Trans at eighty-three."

"That's right, if I can get them." The other man paused. "But I'm competing with you."

"Not anymore you're not," said the man in the World Trade Center. "You've just bought them."

"From you?"

"Fifty thousand First Trans at eighty-three, I sell to you, dealt."

"Whatever you say," the mystified trader agreed. "Now, would you like to tell me what's going —"

But the trader in the World Trade Center had already disconnected and was tapping the next box on his screen with his telephone.

WEDNESDAY: P.M.

"MRS. GALATTI, PLEASE."

"This is Mrs. Galatti."

"Mrs. Barbara Galatti?"

"Yes?"

"Barbara, this is Matt Blaney. We met in your husband's office."

Matt heard her intake of breath. "Who?"

"You heard me."

Large flakes of snow hit the glass wall of the pay phone and dissolved there before running downward in blotchy tracks.

"I'm sorry, but I don't believe I need . . ."

"Barbara, you are in a very dangerous position. What you have done probably makes you an accessory to a crime punishable by a long period in a federal penitentiary."

"Listen —"

"You listen, Barbara. You listen very carefully. Don't confirm or deny. Just listen."

Her breathing was broken.

"Early last November, Barbara, although it is thought that you were in the Middle East, you in fact were in France."

"This is ridiculous! Who —"

He could visualize the phone going down.

"Listen to me!" He had to let her hear it. "You were in France, in Normandy. On the night of November second you were in Haras du Bois when Dijon the stud manager administered an injection to Cornucopia."

He had worked hard on his own conviction; he had to get it across that there was no doubt.

"Dijon injected Cornucopia; you stood beside him."

He could hear breathing.

"Did you hear me, Barbara?"

"I heard you." The voice was small, flat.

He felt his heart jump.

"That injection, Barbara, has landed you in the mess you are now in."

Even her breathing was no longer audible.

"Do you understand?" Matt asked.

Despite the freezing cold he felt sweat breaking out all over him. He was losing her.

"A girl has probably been murdered, the girl who saw you there."

There was another sharp intake of breath.

"I say probably. She is in a coma in a French hospital; she was put there by your husband, Barbara. If she dies, then you will almost certainly be indicted as one of those responsible."

The snow had become heavier, practically obscuring vision.

"Barbara, are you there?"

"What do you want?"

"I saw you, Barbara. I saw you in his office. I saw your face where he hit you. You're trapped, Barbara. I'm offering you a way out."

He could sense rather than hear her.

"Barbara, this may be your last chance," he said urgently.

"Do you realize," she said in a strange, flat voice, "that right now you are as good as dead?"

"I'm talking about you, Barbara."

"Forget about me," Barbara said. "Think about yourself. Go away. Leave me alone."

"Is that what you really want, Barbara?" asked Matt. "A lifetime of terror with a monster who killed his horse, who has tried to kill a young girl, and who will certainly kill you if he thinks you will get in his way?"

"Go away!" She was sobbing, but she hadn't terminated the connection.

"Is that what you want, Barbara? Be honest with yourself. Is that the life you want, or do you want me to help you end the terror? I'm sure that I can."

Matt heard her try to compose herself. "Help me how?"

"Meet me. Tell me exactly what it was he made you do to Cornucopia. Save yourself; he's not going to get away with it, Barbara."

Matt could almost see the mind at work behind the beautiful face.

"I need time."

"Of course. I can call you back."

"Tomorrow."

"That's impossible, Barbara. Events are moving too fast. I need to see you today, in the next hour."

Now, rapid breaths.

"Two hours. Call me back."

"Okay, two hours,"agreed Matt, and put down the receiver.

He leaned against the wall of the glass booth, suddenly light-headed. It had been a straightforward gamble. But Cathy had been right. He stepped outside and, adjusting his collar against the driving snow, peered across at the house, its white door a hundred yards away. Matt's feet were almost detached and numb, but he was oblivious to them.

He stood in a doorway, hidden by its shadow and that of a delivery van parked at the curb.

The snow had for a moment lightened; streetlights had come on and glowed down yellow on encrusted ice and the small hillocks of drifts.

Matt settled down to wait.

WEDNESDAY: P.M.

29 IN THE UPPER SIXTIES, WITHIN VIEW OF CENTRAL PARK, two men sat in a parked delivery van. They were dressed in blue overalls and wore knitted woollen caps. It was seven P.M. Outside, it had been snowing. The back of the van was stacked with new Japanese TV sets, still in their cardboard boxes; if anyone asked, the man at the wheel could show a list of deliveries to be made in midtown Manhattan, correct import documentation made out to the Brooklyn firm they both worked for, and a clean driving license.

The street was quiet. It was a wealthy residential area: people here bought new TV sets the whole time.

The van driver, a Mossad officer who could scale a twelve-foot wall without grappling equipment, stretched and yawned. He was in his early twenties; his reclining body suggested physical competence: broad shoulders ran down to a slim waist, emphasized by the elastic tucks of his overalls. The wrists above his gloves were thick, their skin brown like that of his face.

The man next to him was smaller but equally fit. He had sallow skin. His dark eyes never left the street in front of them.

"What will your first step be, Yanni?" asked the driver, speaking in Hebrew.

His officer looked at him. "To verify beyond doubt that he is who he is," he said. "That is the overwhelming necessity. Relations between Washington and Jerusalem will be bad enough after this — to get the wrong man would be catastrophic for Israel."

"I suppose he will scream like a madman that he is someone else, that he has never even been to Europe," the driver said.

"Don't worry," Yanni said. "We know more about him than his mother ever did — that is, if he had one."

"The file grows?"

"Bit by bit it grows," Yanni replied. "Our friend in Vienna calls it his jigsaw. More people are coming forward, people who are prepared to give sworn evidence." He sighed. "Some of the testimonies I have read are so horrific that even Jerusalem will think twice before using them."

At the end of the street a patrol car from the New York Police Department appeared, cruising slowly toward them. Both men averted their faces. In his rearview mirror the driver could see it disappear toward Fifth Avenue.

"Can we link him right back to Majdanek?" the driver asked.

"The trail is slowly becoming clearer," Yanni replied. "Our friend tells me he is on the point of making a breakthrough that will answer the question that has always been asked."

"How he escaped Majdanek?"

Yanni nodded. "Our friend is here in the States," he said. "Two days ago he went to Florida to meet someone." He shrugged. "I know no more." He looked at his watch and put his feet up on the dashboard.

"Do you think our target suspects?" asked the driver after a few minutes.

His commanding officer considered the question. "Ask yourself," he replied. "What is the most shameful thing you ever did? Perhaps it is that you tied your little sister's knickers up so she peed in them; or maybe while your old *saba* slept you took money from his jamjar to buy yourself some candy? Each one of us, deep down, has something that we are still guilty of, that we expect to pay for. Now magnify that a million times."

The driver shook his head. "A million, million times," he said. Out of the corner of his eye he looked at the senior Israeli. To work with Yanni Israel on such an important mission was in itself a reward which few careers were crowned with. It was a rare chance to right a gargantuan wrong and at the same time to see a man in operation who was a living legend in their country.

"You enjoy these missions, Yanni?" he asked tentatively.

"I don't enjoy, or not enjoy," Yanni replied. "I am doing a job."

"You were undercover in Lebanon last year," said the other.

"Last August," Yanni nodded, "in the Maghdousheh hills."

"For long?"

"For six weeks."

"With success?"

Yanni curled his lip and shook his head. "We had information on the three Israelis who were captured near Sasa a month before that," he said. "But I could find nothing."

"They were only children," said the driver.

"The youngest was just seventeen," said Yanni.

"Has there been any further word?"

Again Yanni's head shook. "The faction that took them are Shi'ites reporting to no one," he said.

The cold had begun to conquer their body heat. Yanni stamped his feet.

"What will happen to his wife?" asked the driver suddenly. Although he was facing forward, his eyes locked on his superior's reaction.

Yanni said nothing for what seemed a long time. "I expect she will be looked after," he said at last. "Her husband's a millionaire."

"She's a real beauty," persisted the driver. "Is she as good in the flesh?"

Yanni's eyes strafed him. "This is a mission for your country," he said in an icy voice. "It is the highest honor you can be paid. What has to be done on the way to achieving success is nothing. You understand that? Nothing."

"I didn't mean . . ." said the other.

"This is not a game," said Yanni, his voice steel. "We are guardians of a sacred tradition. If in its defense certain things have to be done, then we do them, but they are meaningless."

The driver's mouth had grown dry as his mistake became clear.

"I am . . ." he began.

But Yanni's eyes were ahead.

A long limousine, its sidelights showing, pulled into the block and slowly approached. Twenty yards from the van it stopped. The chauffeur jumped out and opened the rear door. The men in the van stared intently. Carlo Galatti got out. He approached the steps of a house. A pedestrian paused, allowing Galatti to cross in, then walked on. He was a businessman, dressed in a dark coat and suit and carrying a briefcase. A wide-brimmed hat shaded most of his face. He walked straight past the van, on up the street. The chauffeur got back into the limousine and pulled away.

"*Bidiuk bazman,*" said Yanni. "Right on time."

"Amnon could have taken him at any time," the driver said, letting his breath out in a long hiss. Both men checked their watches.

"When?" asked the driver softly.

"Tomorrow," Yanni answered after a moment. "Thursday. It has got to be." He was nodding confidently to himself. "Amnon will take him from behind. At that point we will be level. I'll take the chauffeur — he's not armed as far as we can see. The Nurse will stay in the back of this van — he will help Amnon to load. The whole sequence should take no more than forty seconds."

The driver smiled at the mention of the six-and-a-half-foot Israeli paramedic who was known throughout the service as the Nurse.

"What if anything should go wrong?" he asked. "Local police, even FBI, for example?"

"In that case," Yanni replied quietly, "the Nurse has his instructions."

The driver nodded that he grasped the terminal implications of the Nurse's instructions.

"Three blocks east we change to a car," Yanni was saying. "By then he will be sedated. You will proceed back to Brooklyn with the van."

The driver shook his head and took a deep breath. "I just wish I could be there to hear the bastard admit," he said.

"Don't worry," said Yanni. "When the beast is chained in the deepest cell in Ayalon, your part will not be forgotten."

The driver smiled. "Thank you," he said. "And if earlier I over-stepped, than I'm sorry."

"Forget it," said Yanni. He clapped the man's broad shoulder. "What time are you being relieved?"

"In an hour," the driver said.

"I must go," Yanni said. "We will rendezvous tomorrow as ar-ranged."

The driver was about to reply. Yanni had not altered his position, but his entire body, like that of a wild animal, had turned rigid as his eyes locked on the van's curbside mirror.

"*Hara,*" whispered Yanni. "We've got company."

WEDNESDAY: P.M.

30 BARBARA GALATTI WALKED INTO HER BEDROOM AND turned the key in the lock. Only then, alone, did she allow her body to react.

She began to shake violently, uncontrollably, like a person with ague, groping her way to the bed, in the grip of a terror which she thought she had long left behind.

She sat hunched for several minutes, trying to bring the weight of her mind to control her condition, then having failed, she reached, jerking, to a bedside drawer from which she withdrew a small mirror. She put it down, then slid from her wrist the heavy gold charm-brace-let, observing the golden hairs on her arm as they stood upright on her shivering, porous flesh.

The bracelet was hung with half a dozen beautifully ornate trinkets. Barbara's fingers went to the miniature elephant, complete with his gilded howdah and saddlery of burnished gold. She grasped the tiny,

minaret-shaped cone which crowned his regalia and twisted it: the cap
on its microscopic hinges fell back.

Steadying the wrist of her pouring hand with the fingers of the other,
she turned the elephant upside-down and discharged two lines of white
powder onto the mirror. Snapping the cap shut, she took a slender silver
tube from the bedside, and then gratefully inhaled the powder.

Now calm and lucid she lay in the darkness, looking at the frame of
light of the curtained window, listening to the evening sounds, cars on
the snow in the street outside, the distant noise of traffic on Fifth Avenue.

She liked to rest naked. She liked the feel of clean, silk sheets pressing
both sides of her in the empty bed.

Her hands strayed involuntarily to her hips. At the start it had been
exciting: not only security, wealth, but also something more, relief, the
genuine deep-down relief that a person not born to poverty could never
understand. And, ultimately, escape. She had craved that escape since
she was a small girl in New Orleans: escape not only from the poverty,
but also from the terror, the terror of a drunken father whose frantic
libido had never discriminated among any of them, the terror of every
hateful night, of hunger, and of her mother's helpless, terrified eyes,
her belly always swollen with new life bursting to get out.

Barbara stoked her own belly.

God, she had worked. Her body, her face, her poise. In New York
she had carefully dissociated herself from any of her contacts from the
south. She had studied art at nights, held down a job at the gallery,
never turned a trick. She was not quite nineteen when she met Galatti.
On the third night he had proposed marriage; the following day they
had flown to Martinique.

She had escaped, triumphantly.

It was only twenty minutes ago, when the telephone had rung, that
she had finally realized she had not escaped at all.

She was married to a beast. Matt Blaney had been right. But the fact
that he had been right would not spare him. He had trespassed into a
forbidden area: like everyone else who had ever done so, he would be
eliminated.

But Matt Blaney had been right. Her life was one of terror. The man
she was married to — the monster — used people relentlessly, as if
they were toy soldiers, totally without regard to decency or feeling.

Barbara buried her head in her pillows. Soldiers! What about the boy soldier, the Israeli, whose tortured, almost demented father still believed him to be alive? Barbara shook. That Galatti could stoop so low . . . But worse! He had brought her down with him!

Barbara shivered as a fresh wave of nausea swept through her. She had read with fascination the graphic accounts of life in women's prisons. Suddenly she knew what she would do. She reached to a side-table for a telephone book. Flicking through it, her shaking finger eventually found the number of her lawyer. She tried to control her breathing as she was put through. "I'm sorry, but he's gone home for the day," the lawyer's secretary said.

Barbara lay back, tears running down her cheeks. Her options were running out. Matt Blaney worked for some insurance company: however, to see him meant no guarantee of reprieve.

But she had to escape. From them all.

Escape. Why had her whole life been a series of escapes? And to whom could she now run?

She felt a small glow.

She had become aroused within a minute of seeing him. In the middle of the great, buzzing hall the frankness of his eyes bespoke an understanding that had made her body feel on fire.

Her hands were more insistent, and in the dark room she became warm, her mouth open as her breathing shortened.

She began to move and kicked the sheets away. Her skin was moist. Her tongue came out. She had not cared if he knew how long it had been. She rocked. Like someone long deprived of water, on her knees she had drunk, abandoned to her senses. She panted and thrust. Upward to herself. With every ounce of her will she summoned his presence into the empty room. His deep brown eyes, his sallow skin, his body, strong and firm, his comforting man's smell. His need. Her body jumped. Hers.

Barbara Galatti sank back, her body glistening. Two tears of salt ran down her face and into the corners of her mouth. She licked them away. She brought her knees up and huddled as the coldness of fear and sorrow once more began to creep over her.

Suddenly a door closed across the hall and she sat bolt upright, the breath caught in her chest with fear.

Some crucial balance in her mind sprung. Her eyes wide, again she rolled onto her stomach and grabbed the telephone. Her finger was surprisingly steady as she pressed out the number on the illuminated face. It rang once.

"Yes?"

"Simon?" said Barbara Galatti. "Oh, Simon, thank God. I've got to see you."

Two floors below, in a darkened room beside a silently revolving tape-recorder, the Kaiser kept his hand over the mouthpiece as his listened, unemotionally, to the call.

WEDNESDAY: P.M.

31 MATT NARROWED HIS EYES; A BITTER WIND WAS WHIPPING in from New Jersey side to make them water. He was in a doorway, east of the house, near Madison Avenue, his hands in the pockets of his thick ski jacket. The snow had for the moment ceased and he had a view of the white doorway, around the back of the delivery van parked at the curb. But it was something else that was now riveting his attention: across Madison but on the same street a figure was walking briskly west.

Matt left the doorway. Traffic had stopped for the lights and he was able to get a view of the uncrowded sidewalk. Although no one had left by the main door of the house, Matt had gained a view, just for an instant, of a profile passing beneath a streetlight. She wore a jacket, a blue knitted cap, and blue jeans tucked into red leather boots. But it was the profile that he could never forget.

He began a crunching run. At Madison Avenue he swore as the traffic, streaming solidly northward, stopped him. He jumped to see better. She had vanished. There was a shriek of brakes and angry shouts as Matt weaved across, narrowly missed by an uptown bus; inside, its illuminated passengers stared out into the cold night at the tall man running toward Fifth Avenue.

The breath caught in his chest; she must be damn fast, he thought panting. On Fifth the traffic streamed downtown between himself and the shadow of Central Park. The streetlights threw yellow pools onto the snow-covered, empty sidewalks where mounds of garbage awaited collection, black plastic shining in the white snow. Matt scanned both ways furiously, then he slipped on snow and swore. He jumped on to the hood and then the roof of a parked car. The wind stung. A bolt transfixed him. Two hundred yards south along the wall by Central Park, a figure was running downtown.

"Hey, mister!"

Matt vaulted from the car, unmindful of its owner, who had just returned with dry-cleaning. On the west side of Fifth he ran flat out, downtown, separated from the evening traffic by a row of bare chestnut trees. Up ahead she had reached Fifty-ninth Street — Central Park South — and disappeared. Matt gritted his teeth as again he slipped on the compacted ice of the intersection. He could see the Plaza opposite, across from the chained-off statue of the mounted General Sherman; he saw a line of horsedrawn tourist buggies and smelled horse dung on the freezing breeze.

Sharp right the road cut back uptown through dark Central Park; no place to be on foot, thought Matt, and began to run across Fifty-ninth Street. The curb was empty. West and downtown, he thought, that's where she wants to go. But where was she?

He ran twenty yards west. Suddenly he felt a blast of warm air from the mouth of a subway entrance. Fumbling for a token he took the stone steps four at a time. He heard a train screech. Downtown. He scrambled through the barrier and hurled himself down further steps. Downtown. A line of upright girders made it impossible to see who was on the platform. He landed as the train doors hissed to close. He sprang, his arm outstretched. He felt the rubber guards squeeze him, then fly back. He fell in.

Matt held the overhead rail, his chest heaving. The car was packed. He glanced around: the other passengers, who seconds before had stared, had now lost interest.

At the next stop he stepped out to scrutinize the crowd. He made his way forward two cars, all packed, and got in as the doors closed.

At Forty-second Street a dense crowd waited to board. Matt got out. He had lost her. He swore to himself. He would take the local back uptown and decide what to do. He shouldered his way to the stairs that would take him up and over to the uptown platform; on the third step he stopped and stared: the blue cap was ascending a ramp, right at the other end of the platform. Matt turned, but the crowd held him. Swearing, he swung his leg over the iron rail and jumped.

People milled in both directions on the ramp as Matt weaved up it, barging, excusing himself, searching ahead. At the top, options arose: left for the 123 trains, or straight and up steps for the Seventh Avenue line. Matt sprang for the steps, elbowing through tired people going home. He made the top, the beginning of a long, teeming hall where the ceiling of mass concrete was no more than two inches above his head. He searched wildly. Fifty yards ahead, behind the table of a black vendor, he saw the familiar blue vanish to the left.

Matt sprinted, around men selling balloons and kids playing musical instruments. He leaped the open case of a double-bass, its bottom shining with coins, and swung left. He crashed down steps, on to a 123 platform. An uptown train was closing its doors. He nearly took it, then stopped as his eye sent a signal to his brain. Halfway down the next white-tiled, sloping walkway, something blue was jammed in the mouth of a trash can.

Desperately Matt dashed the length of the walkway, his fingers brushing the discarded, knitted blue cap as he rounded a smooth corner. More options: downtown. He sprinted up steps, then down again, on to a milling platform. Doors hissed. At the very last instant, four car lengths away, he saw the red hair board. Matt leaped on.

People stood chest to chest as they rocked downtown. Matt forced his way toward a connecting door. A black woman swore roundly at him. He reached the door and tugged. It was locked. Gritting his teeth he shouldered his way back.

"Here he comes again!" the black woman called out.

At each of the next two stops Matt tried to keep the forward car in sight. "World Trade Center," intoned the guard over the intercom. Just as the doors closed she got off; Matt had to jam them with his foot to stop being taken on to Brooklyn. She was walking fast, nearly a hundred yards ahead. She never looked back. Matt got a quick, distant glimpse of the face, cheeks flushed and lips full. In the cavernous vault of the station beneath the world's biggest business complex he stepped into the doorway of a boutique as seventy-five paces in front she rode an escalator to street level. He darted out and followed. There was a long and wide carpeted passageway: he was now in a hall of one of the Twin Towers. He scanned and cursed. To his right was a mezzanine the snow-covered, empty sidewalks where mounds of garbage awaited collection, black plastic shining in the white snow. Matt scanned both ways furiously, then he slipped on snow and swore. He jumped on to the hood and then the roof of a parked car. The wind stung. A bolt transfixed him. Two hundred yards south along the wall by Central Park, a figure was running downtown.

"Hey, mister!"

Matt vaulted from the car, unmindful of its owner, who had just returned with dry-cleaning. On the west side of Fifth he ran flat out, downtown, separated from the evening traffic by a row of bare chestnut trees. Up ahead she had reached Fifty-ninth Street — Central Park South — and disappeared. Matt gritted his teeth as again he slipped on the compacted ice of the intersection. He could see the Plaza opposite, across from the chained-off statue of the mounted General Sherman; he saw a line of horsedrawn tourist buggies and smelled horse dung on the freezing breeze.

Sharp right the road cut back uptown through dark Central Park; no place to be on foot, thought Matt, and began to run across Fifty-ninth Street. The curb was empty. West and downtown, he thought, that's where she wants to go. But where was she?

He ran twenty yards west. Suddenly he felt a blast of warm air from the mouth of a subway entrance. Fumbling for a token he took the stone steps four at a time. He heard a train screech. Downtown. He scrambled through the barrier and hurled himself down further steps. Downtown. A line of upright girders made it impossible to see who was on the platform. He landed as the train doors hissed to close. He sprang, his arm outstretched. He felt the rubber guards squeeze him, then fly back. He fell in.

Matt held the overhead rail, his chest heaving. The car was packed. He glanced around: the other passengers, who seconds before had stared, had now lost interest.

At the next stop he stepped out to scrutinize the crowd. He made his way forward two cars, all packed, and got in as the doors closed.

At Forty-second Street a dense crowd waited to board. Matt got out. He had lost her. He swore to himself. He would take the local back uptown and decide what to do. He shouldered his way to the stairs that would take him up and over to the uptown platform; on the third step he stopped and stared: the blue cap was ascending a ramp, right at the other end of the platform. Matt turned, but the crowd held him. Swearing, he swung his leg over the iron rail and jumped.

People milled in both directions on the ramp as Matt weaved up it, barging, excusing himself, searching ahead. At the top, options arose: left for the 123 trains, or straight and up steps for the Seventh Avenue line. Matt sprang for the steps, elbowing through tired people going home. He made the top, the beginning of a long, teeming hall where the ceiling of mass concrete was no more than two inches above his head. He searched wildly. Fifty yards ahead, behind the table of a black vendor, he saw the familiar blue vanish to the left.

Matt sprinted, around men selling balloons and kids playing musical instruments. He leaped the open case of a double-bass, its bottom shining with coins, and swung left. He crashed down steps, on to a 123 platform. An uptown train was closing its doors. He nearly took it, then stopped as his eye sent a signal to his brain. Halfway down the next white-tiled, sloping walkway, something blue was jammed in the mouth of a trash can.

Desperately Matt dashed the length of the walkway, his fingers brushing the discarded, knitted blue cap as he rounded a smooth corner. More options: downtown. He sprinted up steps, then down again, on to a milling platform. Doors hissed. At the very last instant, four car lengths away, he saw the red hair board. Matt leaped on.

People stood chest to chest as they rocked downtown. Matt forced his way toward a connecting door. A black woman swore roundly at him. He reached the door and tugged. It was locked. Gritting his teeth he shouldered his way back.

"Here he comes again!" the black woman called out.

At each of the next two stops Matt tried to keep the forward car in sight. "World Trade Center," intoned the guard over the intercom. Just as the doors closed she got off; Matt had to jam them with his foot to stop being taken on to Brooklyn. She was walking fast, nearly a hundred yards ahead. She never looked back. Matt got a quick, distant glimpse of the face, cheeks flushed and lips full. In the cavernous vault of the station beneath the world's biggest business complex he stepped into the doorway of a boutique as seventy-five paces in front she rode an escalator to street level. He darted out and followed. There was a long and wide carpeted passageway: he was now in a hall of one of the Twin Towers. He scanned and cursed. To his right was a mezzanine level. He saw red hair. He took the steps of the up-escalator in threes. On the mezzanine was a long, curling line waiting at a theater-ticket office. He again saw the red hair flash. He stared. A girl in a black fur coat laughed and shook her red hair out as she talked to the man next to her.

Matt ground his teeth. The vastness of the place did not permit mistakes. He walked to the parapet of the mezzanine and looked down. It swarmed with people. He shook his head and walked to its other side, where massive windows gave on to a wide plaza. He blinked. Down on a white Cortland Street, thirty-five feet below and fifty yards away, he saw blue jeans and red boots climbing into the back of a yellow cab.

Matt crashed down the escalator. Out on the plaza he could just see the cab pulling slowly up Church Street in the slush. Matt ran flat out. Another cab was turning into Trinity. He wrenched its back door open.

"Hey, I'm off-duty," shouted the driver.

A fifty-dollar bill appeared over the back seat.

"I'm back on duty," said the driver and swung uptown.

They followed half a block behind all the way up Broadway.

"How we doin'?" asked the cabbie.

"Just fine," Matt murmured. "Just keep this far back."

They kept uptown, through Union Square Park, through Times Square and Columbus Circle. At Seventy-second Street the cab ahead caught a light and Matt's driver pulled up to the curb like a professional. They crossed 110th Street, then Columbia on the right.

"Hold it."

The cab swung in. Matt remained motionless. Almost a block away, at 120th Street, the woman had got out. They sat and watched. She had crossed Broadway and was walking uptown.

"Thanks, pal," said the driver quietly as Matt slipped out.

Matt trailed her, a block behind, under the shadows of the university. At 122nd Street the gradient rose sharply. Nearby church bells rang, their tone tossed by a sudden wind. At the very hilltop he saw her disappear to the right. Matt sprinted it, head down. On the steep hill his feet slipped twice on compacted ice. He paused at the top and peered around the corner. It was a quiet, badly lighted avenue. She was walk-

188 / ALL RISKS MORTALITY

ing downhill, the urgency gone from her movements. Using cars for protection he followed. He saw her climb steps and go through a doorway.

As he entered the lobby, Matt could hear her feet on the stairs above him.

WEDNESDAY: P.M.

32

IT WAS SNOWING AGAIN OVER MIDTOWN. THE SNOW COVered Central Park in a fine coating and the residential streets nearby, where there was no activity and the only sound to be heard was of cars moving along the great avenues into the city, like the hum of a never-sleeping machine.

On one such street, at a curtained first-floor window, stood the solitary figure of a man. He had stood there for nearly three hours, his face closed like a sea anemone as his mind worked. He parted the curtains a fraction, surveyed the street below, then allowed the heavy drape to fall back, a movement he had made twenty times in the hour before.

The van was in position again. It could be coincidence, but in the world that had become his life, coincidences were as welcome as a loaded Mauser at your temple.

They were closing in.

As clear as the Russian guns in the eastern sky, the signs were there. Like swill eased from the belly of the devil, their soil was seeping out to blemish everything he had worked for.

The signs were there. In the falling price of oil, in the crazy gyrations of his stock, in the information he had received about the Justice Department's intentions, and in the presence of the van.

He had seen them earlier as he had come in. Darting eyes in dark faces. He knew such faces as he knew his own. Scarcely a night went by without a parade of them through his internal vision. And he had spotted them again, by chance, one afternoon, behind the long lens of a camera in a car, quickly withdrawn when he had unexpectedly turned.

Die Jauche. Now the swill had come to claim him. He shook himself. He had seen Eichmann, an easy target, going in the end like a lamb to a slaughterhouse. He snarled in the silence of the room. Terrorists! He had heard that before poor Eichmann's lungs had at last filled with their filthy gas, he had received a beating which few men could endure.

Schwein. Soon they would again be devouring their favorite dish, the anal exudate of sows.

But the banks were closing in, looking for their hunk of flesh. And the American, the insurance man who surely knew about Cornucopia, had, despite his every effort, disappeared.

If he could have just a few more days!

Galatti remembered the radiant look on the Arab's face, almost a month before. They had been in the suite overlooking New York Harbor. The Arab was swarthy and thick-lipped; soft, black hair marked a line beneath his nose. He was an unattractive man, endlessly promiscuous with both sexes, but he was the sheikh's emissary.

"It will happen on their Sabbath," Galatti repeated, and gave the date.

The Arab's head went up and down. "My master says that the Leader will be ready," he said. "A great blow will be struck for freedom."

"And the money?"

The Arab smiled. "It has been assembled," he said.

"How much?"

"As agreed. One billion U.S. dollars."

Galatti grunted his satisfaction.

"It is assembled in an account in Zurich," the Arab said. "I have the teller's receipt."

Galatti bent forward and saw the slip; the Arab covered half of it. "It is a numbered account," the Arab said. "As soon as . . . it happens, I shall telephone you."

"I shall call you," Galatti said. "Shortly after noon on the day in question."

The Arab made to take his leave.

"One final thing," Galatti said. "Our other project; what result of your inquiries in Beirut?"

"The boy?"

Galatti nodded.

Slowly the Arab shook his head from side to side. Then he drew his finger in a line across his gullet.

"I see," Galatti had said.

*   *   *

Now he ground his jaws. The mistake had been to go to Europe to watch the horse. He would remember forever the expression on the old hag's face, just at the moment of his greatest triumph. She was hunched like a barren sow but when she saw him she had straightened and gasped as if all the air had been punched from her lungs. *Abfall!* He had seen eyes like hers a million times, close eyes either side of a curving snout. She had stood there as he had walked away, her mouth open, her hand straight out, pointing as if she had just seen a dead man walk.

He ground his jaws. It had been Barbara who had persuaded him to go.

Barbara. He had seen her leave, running toward Fifth Avenue like a rabbit in heat. He grimaced. He looked to a table and to the tape-recorder on it. Once a whore, always.

Galatti pressed a bell. Everything had its use. But what she now knew was too dangerous.

The door opened and the Kaiser entered. For some moments he and Galatti spoke. Then, nodding his unquestioning understanding, the Kaiser left the room.

Galatti walked once more to the window and looked out. Now that he had given the order, he felt oddly empty, not emotionally drained, just empty. He tried to analyze his feelings. Despite himself, he came to the conclusion that now, here and now, on the brink of his greatest triumph, he was totally alone. He realized that he had always been alone, but at this vital moment, it struck him with force. What he needed was someone to talk to, reassurance for the righteous nature of what was about to happen.

Galatti walked to a telephone and punched out the transatlantic number with the thick index finger of his right hand.

"*Oui?*"

The voice which answered was as melodious as ever. Galatti went over his position, meticulously explaining everything.

"Everything you have done, are doing," the person on the other end said, "one day will all be vindicated by history."

Nodding with satisfaction, Galatti put down the phone.

It was time.

The snow was falling heavily. On the other side of the block, in a yard strewn with boxes and cartons, the egress of a small supermarket, a gate only rarely used opened stiffly. The bent figure of an old man came through it, shuffling as though motion was painful. He wore a long black coat and rough shoes. In his gloved hand was a tattered suitcase. He paused for a moment. His head was encased in a fur hat showing just wrinkled skin and a mottled, dripping nose. Easing open the door to the supermarket, he slipped through it, unnoticed, and then exited from its brightly lighted main entrance. He walked west to the end of the block in a peculiar rolling walk, laboriously, like a wounded cockroach. On Fifth Avenue he turned downtown, pausing at the lights to look once into the street to his left where parked vehicles, including a delivery van, were receiving a good covering of snow. His face screwed up in hatred and he spat on the ground. Then he carried on. A block later he hailed a cab: shoving the suitcase in along the back seat, he painfully clambered after it and slammed the door.

"Kennedy," he grunted to the driver.

"Kennedy it is," said the driver as he flipped his meter and swung east, his first fare of the evening a good one.

As they headed toward the East River, the snow had become really thick, big floating blobs of white, so large you could catch them in your hands.

WEDNESDAY: P.M.

 MATT PRESSED HIMSELF BETWEEN A LINE OF MAILBOXES and the stairwell, which had a bicycle chained to it. He could look up and see the red boots as they ascended to the very top of the five-story building. Then he took the stairs himself.

On the first landing a door opened a crack on its chain; he saw eyes and a snarling dog. He moved up. He could hear music and then a disc-jockey's voice giving an update on the snow over Manhattan. He got to the fourth floor. Boards were missing underfoot. He heard a woman shrieking at someone volubly in Spanish.

The very top floor was reached more by a ladder than stairs. It was pitch dark. Matt went silently to the door and listened, but the thick door allowed no eavesdropping. His eyes adjusted to the darkness and he inspected the small landing. The door to the top apartment was the only one at this level. He looked up and saw the white rectangular shape of a wooden trapdoor, recessed in the ceiling. Standing on the banisters he was able to grasp and push the trapdoor upward and in; then he jumped and caught its tip. He hauled, his arms aching. The wooden frame held and he levered himself in.

The transverse beams were narrow, cutting into his knees. Matt could hear hissing and saw that the noise came from a water tank immediately in his path. He crawled around it. His head cracked painfully against an angled rafter. He lit a match; he was nearly at the gable end of the house. His hand felt something wide and smooth. He squatted. The trapdoor was flush with its frame; it was designed to be pushed up from underneath, like the one by which he had entered. There was a rustling to his left. He concentrated. With the nails of his fingers he raised the trapdoor a fraction, then tried to jump his fingertips in. The heavy wooden panel fell back snug. Three times he tried, the nerve-ends of his fingers screaming. The fourth time he caught it. It took an infinite number of tiny movements, his entire body strength concentrated on his finger extremities, to work it upward. Eventually he slid it aside and peered down.

The trapdoor was near the end of the ceiling in a long studio running nearly the length of the narrow house. Immediately underneath there was darkness, but by lying down Matt could see a warm glow at the other end; he saw bare, polished boards, rough, whitewashed walls with some rug hangings, and at the extremity of his vision a small kerosene stove, its heat radiating out on the mattress laid before it.

Cross-legged on the mattress, her red hair flowing out like a cloak, sat Barbara Galatti.

Matt stared. A man knelt behind her, steadying her shoulders as her body shuddered with sobs. He was dressed in jeans and an open-necked checked shirt; he had olive skin and dark hair.

"Just relax," he was saying to Barbara Galatti, "just try to relax."

Gradually she regained control of herself, dabbing at her eyes, biting her lip.

"You have no idea who he was?" the man asked her.

Barbara shook her head. "I'm in big trouble," she whispered. "I need help." Her voice broke again.

"But you lost him?"

She nodded.

"Just take it easy," her companion said. "Everything's going to be fine."

"Oh, Simon," she cried.

"Why don't you tell me," he said, "from the beginning."

She twisted her handkerchief, then took a deep breath.

"My husband knows a man in Israel," she began. "He's a nuclear physicist and he gave me radioactive material in liquid form to bring to France."

For fifteen minutes in the blackness of the attic space, Matt sat listening in growing astonishment to what the woman beneath him was saying. She huddled like a child by her confidant, who stroked her and encouraged her as she went along. He rose and poured them two mugs of steaming coffee.

"There," she said at last. "I've said it."

The explosion underneath threw Matt. Askew, he stared. Barbara Galatti stood on the mattress, one hand near her mouth, as unmoving as a window mannequin in Saks. Her companion had crash-dived, left.

"Get down!"

Then once more there was thunder.

The shell caught Barbara somewhere in midchest and lifted her up and back, slamming her against the wall behind the stove. Another ripped indiscriminately across her throat and severed her head. Matt stared: what had seconds before been a creation of incomparable beauty now slid twitching to the floor.

The pump-action spoke again. The man in the checked shirt had up-ended the heavy wooden table and Matt could see shot pattern spatter over its surface. Then there was another noise, two solid-sounding thuds. A man staggered into Matt's vision, his hands at his head. There was a further thud. The figure kept going, kicking over things in his path, going for the table. The check-shirted man got to his feet. He had a gun in his hand, but his eyes were calmly assessing the scene even as Barbara Galatti's executioner collapsed beside him. Then he reached for his jacket and, looking down once at each of the figures, Barbara Galatti's grotesque and lying in a lake of her own blood, he pocketed the gun and left.

Matt was not conscious of the fact that he had scarcely breathed in the minutes before. Now he felt a hammering, which he dully realized was his heart panicking for air. His ears humming, he lowered himself into the room, thick with the stench of cordite. He saw warm blood, still brimming. At his feet a man lay face down, a gleaming shotgun across his neck. Matt removed it and turned the head. He stared. Almost without surprise he saw his assailant from Jordan's Quarry, the man who had held the stallion in Haras du Bois, the Kaiser.

For minutes Matt stood. There was now no sound, no cries, no sound of voices, nothing. He stood, barely comprehending the mutilation. He wondered, oddly, if he was awake.

He began to retrace his steps, first slowly, then with more urgency as he reached the stairs.

In the street the cold hit him like a bat in the face.

He started to run.

THURSDAY: A.M.

34 SLEEP WAS A LUXURY DR. SHENLAVI HAD NEARLY FORGOTten. He had tossed for over an hour before he gave up, pulling on a pair of old trousers and padding in his bare feet into the kitchen. He considered going down to the garage to check his work but then decided against it.

Opening the back door, Dr. Shenlavi walked, still barefoot, across the patio and up the steep lawn toward the fig tree. Reaching it he sat down and stared toward the Jerusalem plateau, just becoming visible in the first light of dawn. There had been rain earlier and now a light westerly breeze blew the sweet scent of pine over the Judaean Hills. He sat still as a pillar of salt. The fragrance unlocked a memory, embalmed for nearly a lifetime in a crypt of his mind. His mouth puckered.

The stench had ceased for two days. A westerly wind blew sweet pine fragrance through the wire and into the bitter-cold huts. Papa was distraught — he had been told that Mama had been gone from her hut for over an hour, taken by two armed guards. The soldiers had found the *lehem,* the bread which she had smuggled out of the commandant's kitchen and secreted beneath her bunk. But this time she had been seen: they followed her back and then dragged her away. It was dusk.

Papa could not contain himself. He crept from the hut, telling him to remain there — but he had disobeyed, silently opening the door and following the tall figure down to the end of the block. He peeped between Papa's long legs.

A group of officers stood in a circle. At their center knelt the naked figure of an emaciated woman, her shanks raw from the flogging being dealt to her by a sturdy young SS officer, sweating in his rolled shirt-sleeves despite the coldness of the evening. The woman clutched her shaved head. All at once she lost control of her bowels. The officers laughed. Then one of them, taller than the others, his figure erect and pencil-slim, his blond hair curling at the neck, stepped forward. He was so like Papa. He stretched out a highly polished boot and nudged the woman.

"*Wisch es auf du Sau!*" he commanded. "Clean it up!"

The other officers laughed with glee as the woman tried to scrape up the mess with her hands.

There was a deep, hecking noise overhead. Papa had covered his face with his hands and was sobbing. They stumbled back up the block. Papa clutched him tight. "If only I had the courage," he wept over and over again, "if only . . ."

The boy, now the man, had felt shame as well, but for another reason. In the garden in Mevasseret he tried for the millionth time to comprehend it: it was that he had wished his father was the German officer and not the weeping Jew.

Dr. Shenlavi's hand strayed up to the bough of the generous fig and his fingers felt for the indentations that he knew were there. He had had three fathers in his life and the handsome German officer had been one of them. In Dr. Shenlavi's mind's eye he would always be the one he remembered best: tall, strong, young, and endlessly courageous. A curious beast had come right up to them one night as they had snatched an hour's sleep in a hole, hollowed from the snow where dead fern lay warmly beneath. He awoke screaming, a waking nightmare, jaws of a beast at his face. But his papa had kicked the animal in the mouth with the full force of his foot and sent it yelping back into the night.

"Back to sleep, little one," said his father, and drew him in and under the coat that wrapped them both in the bracken. He huddled his colored face close to the larger body. Then Papa had sung from deep in his throat so that both their bodies vibrated with the familiar words, and there was warm breath on his face. "Rosamunde, where are you now?"

At nights he had whispered endlessly to him, the child a wide-eyed, mute audience, of a land of golden warriors where shields and swords sparkled with the light from a sun that never set, of beautiful maidens who rode snow-white horses, and of great kings who were wise and just and ever-powerful.

"You will be a great man," his father had said. "Always remember."

Dr. Shenlavi shivered. The wind had freshened and he was barefoot. Climbing stiffly down between high rows of raspberries, he returned to the house. He was indescribably tired, weary, spent. He sighed. It was irrelevant.

Soon Levi would be home.

THURSDAY: A.M.

35 THROUGH THE WINDOW THE HUDSON COULD BE SEEN, gray and cold in the morning light. Matt looked at the telephone and, shaking his head, began to pace.

"What in hell's name is keeping him?" he said.

Jim Crabbe drained his cup of coffee and poured himself another. Both men were unshaven and looked exhausted.

It had been after midnight the night before when Jim had opened the door to Matt's knock.

The chairman of Insurance Fidelity's shrewd eyes took in Matt's face. "Are you okay?" he asked.

"I'm okay," said Matt.

Jim sat back. Five minutes later he was on the edge of his chair, his eyes wide.

"I don't believe this," he kept saying.

"It's got be all over the papers tomorrow morning," Matt said. "I've been checking the news bulletins, but there's nothing yet. Even by New York standards it's big stuff."

"Jesus Christ," said Jim Crabbe. "And who was the guy she was with — the guy who killed the Kaiser? I mean he's got to be Cosa Nostra. Was his name on the apartment?"

Matt shook his head.

"Jesus Christ," said Crabbe again.

"You brought the file?" asked Matt.

His boss nodded.

"The name of the pathologist, the guy who did the autopsy on Cornucopia," Matt said. "It's on the telex that Lloyd's sent."

It was nearly three in the morning New York time, eight in London, when they got through. Despite the early intrusion, the English veterinarian was mild-mannered and helpful.

"I'm very sorry," he said, "but it's not one of the tests that we do."

"You took tumor sections," said Matt, his heart sinking. "Have you kept them?"

"Good Lord, no," laughed the eminent pathologist. "If we kept every sample we test, we couldn't get in or out of the place. When the report's finished, out they go."

"Sorry to bother you," said Matt quietly, and replaced the phone.

Jim Crabbe was eyeing him with apprehension.

"So it's down to one last chance," said Matt.

The transatlantic connection was loud and clear.

"*Oui?*"

"Monsieur Petitjean?"

There was a hesitation.

"*Oui?*"

"This is Matt Blaney, Insurance Fidelity in New York? How are you?"

Matt could hear a sigh.

"Yes, Mr. Blaney?"

"Monsieur Petitjean, you remember our trip last week to see the dead horse, Cornucopia?"

"Yes."

Matt closed his eyes. "Do you still have the tumor sections you took, the ones that you put in the bottle?"

"I think so, yes."

Matt stabbed his upright thumb at Jim Crabbe.

"Monsieur Petitjean," Matt said, dry-mouthed, "this is very important, do you understand? Very important. This is what I want you to do."

For five minutes Matt relayed the instructions to the vet four thousand miles away. In the end it was only the promise of an exorbitant fee that had won Petitjean's agreement.

They had drunk so much coffee that sleep was difficult. Now at 8 A.M. the waiting was almost too much.

"He's a nervy little son-of-a-bitch," Matt said, still pacing. "He's just as likely to . . ."

They both froze as the telephone rang. Matt grabbed it.

"Yes? Monsieur Petitjean, yes, it's me. What have you got?"

Jim Crabbe felt his excitement mount as he looked at Matt: the younger man was standing, holding the telephone in one hand, the receiver to his ear. As he listened, his face brightened as if some inner light was coming on. And then he began to dance, jumping lightly from one foot to the other in front of the window.

"How about that," he cried. *"How about that!"*

Crabbe was on his feet, his eyes inquiring. Matt was still jumping around. "Monsieur Petitjean, that's amazing. You agree? Very good. Now, Monsieur Petitjean, I want you to do the following. I want you to write out a certificate on your notepaper, testifying all this. I'm going to have someone call up to you this morning — sorry, this afternoon — to collect the certificate plus part of that tumor section. You understand? You've done a great job."

He put down the phone and punched the air.

"Bull's-eye!" he cried.

"C'mon, for Christ's sake," said Crabbe, "what did he find?"

"Radioactive phosphorus," said Matt beaming. "The tumor shows traces of radioactive phosphorus. It's a substance with a short half-life, but it's still present in the tumor. The reason for the delay was that Caen University — that's where Petitjean brought it — put it through their lab twice to make sure. There's no doubt. The thing's emitting gamma rays as we speak."

"That bastard, Galatti," said Jim, sitting down. "He gave the poor horse cancer."

"I couldn't believe it when Barbara Galatti began to tell her friend, whoever he was," Matt said. "She described the whole thing, how they'd been in the Middle East, how Galatti had her go to Jordan, how he'd arranged for her to be photographed and then had the local press agency fix the dates. She then met this Dr. Shenlavi in Jerusalem, he gave her the dose, she went to France, and they injected Cornucopia. Galatti insisted she be present. It's the last thing anyone would look for — they'd have to run a Geiger counter over every dead animal."

"Did she say anything else?" asked Jim.

"She didn't have time to," Matt replied.

"If they still have guillotines in France," said Jim grimly, "they should try one out on this guy Galatti." He looked at Matt. "What are we going to do?" he asked. "You're now the witness to a double murder."

"I'm going to get Carlo Galatti," said Matt evenly. "What I witnessed doesn't directly incriminate him, even though I know he set it up — just like I know he sent the Kaiser to kill me two nights ago. And Cathy." He gritted his teeth. "Galatti's the man I'm going to get."

"This is a police matter," said Jim.

"So what do I tell them?" Matt asked. "That I called up Galatti's wife, spooked her with information the police should probably know anyway, and then followed her to a house where I broke in and observed two people being murdered? Come on, Jim, my prints are on that shotgun."

"The cops are going to be involved," Jim said.

"But not with us as yet," said Matt. "Involve them in what we know now and their footprints will be over everything within hours. We can't take the risk of alerting Dijon, for example, before our evidence is safely in place."

"And then?"

"Then we have a case bursting with evidence," replied Matt.

"Mostly circumstantial," Jim said.

"Not as it relates to Cornucopia," Matt said. "There we have an open-and-shut case — a radioactive tumor. Lloyd's policy excludes payment where death occurs due to radiation."

"Okay," said Jim Crabbe cautiously.

"What we then have," Matt continued, "is a large volume of admittedly circumstantial evidence. But Galatti's wife is dead, his horse is dead, Cathy is in a coma; the cops will at least arrest him on suspicion. And when they do, the people all around Galatti, they'll begin to feel the pressure, they may easily crack." Matt looked at Crabbe. "Then we'll be on the attack," he said.

"All right," said Jim. "I agree we leave the cops out of it until our evidence is safely in Lloyd's hands. You told your friend Petitjean that someone would collect the evidence from him. Who did you have in mind?"

"Laurens," said Matt, "the adjuster in Paris. He knows the case."

"Is he reliable?"

"I think so," Matt said. "He had a good grasp of the facts."

"You think you should tell him the whole story?"

"Most of it," Matt said. "Otherwise he won't know what he's being asked to do, or why he's doing it."

Jim nodded. "Okay," he said. "I'm going to call Lloyd's and prepare them for what's about to happen." He paused. "I can't wait for their reaction," he said.

"Of course, Jim," said Matt, a smile tugging his mouth, "you'll also be saving yourself a million bucks."

"I hadn't overlooked that," said Jim Crabbe dryly.

THURSDAY: A.M.

36 THE DIN ON THE FLOOR HAD REACHED ITS USUAL PITCH even though the market had been open for only thirty seconds. It was Thursday morning, ten o'clock. Bill Kennedy, forty-six years old and a specialist on the New York Stock Exchange for twenty of them, leaned against the small ledge that was his pitch and scanned the corner, illuminated ticker. Kennedy was a round, rumpled man with a happy face and eyes that twinkled behind his glasses. Now he bit his lip and pondered the business he had just concluded.

It had been with a dealer. Kennedy had just purchased twenty-five thousand First Transnational Bank from the dealer at seventy-eight and a half dollars each. Two things bothered Bill about the trade: one, the firm in question for which the dealer worked had recently put out a buy recommendation for First Trans; and two, Bill's bid of seventy-eight and a half had been snapped up without even so much as a token haggle.

Now Kennedy narrowed his eyes as the trade came up on the ticker. He noted the other Wall Street banks: like First Trans they were all steady on their last night's close. Again he saw First Trans marked, this time at seventy-eight and five-eighths, up a further twelve and a half cents.

Bill Kennedy went to the small screen beside his cluster of telephones. He tapped up the page devoted exclusively to financial news and quickly read it. There was nothing on any bank, never mind First Trans. He brought up foreign exchange: the dollar was steady after a good day in Europe. He went to general news: two people had been victims of a grisly murder in New York's Morningside Heights the night before. Bill Kennedy shook his head and turned back to the floor.

The minute the same dealer approached, Bill knew what it would be.

"First Trans?" Kennedy said. "Eight and a quarter, nine."

"What's this, Bill Kennedy benevolent day?" asked the broker. "I know you guys earn your money easy, but this is ridiculous."

"That's my market," Kennedy said. "Do you have much to do?"

"Oh, maybe fifty thousand," said the dealer.

"Buyer or seller?"

"Seller."

"Seventy-eight and a quarter bucks I pay."

"It's just traded seventy-eight and five-eighths, Bill, what's wrong? Am I suddenly a leper?"

"I got a wife and kids," said Kennedy.

"So have I, Bill, give me a break."

"I'll pay you three-eighths top, just because I love you. Otherwise forget it."

"You're an old shit."

"Fill or kill."

"Dealt," said the dealer.

Bill Kennedy wrote a chit for fifty thousand shares of First Transnational Bank, then instantly walked around to another dealer and unloaded them back into the market at breakeven, plus the twenty-five thousand he had bought earlier, plus another hundred thousand which he did not have.

For the next two hours, like a surfer who has caught the crest of a once-in-a-lifetime dream roller, Bill Kennedy sold the stock of First

Transnational Bank, as first it edged, then slipped, and finally plummeted downward, breaking the seventy-dollar-a-share marker without a pause and finally ending the session offered all over Wall Street at sixty-six.

Bill Kennedy made his triumphant way to his local watering-hole, together with a floor broker who had been following the trades.

"You old fox," the broker said. "You must be keeping something up your sleeve."

"I swear to God I'm not," Kennedy protested. "But you don't have to be an infant prodigy to know that something must be wrong."

"Cheers," said the broker. "I'm happy for you."

Bill Kennedy looked down at his beer. "Why the hell are we drinking this piss?" he cried, summoning the waiter. "My man, let me have some of your best champagne!"

THURSDAY: P.M.

37 SOUTH OF CAEN, IN THE ROLLING COUNTRYSIDE OF CALvados, the pink tips of the apple tree had just begun to bud. It is a landscape of fragrant country lanes, high hedges, and rippling streams that flow into the River Orne. Dairy cows in small pastures produce thick, rich milk, bacon is cured in eighteenth-century smokehouses, and in villages such as Thury-Harcourt on market day the merchants' tables groan under the weight of fresh vegetables.

Gendarme Gaston Bouffechoux yawned as his Peugeot 304 breasted a hill outside Thury-Harcourt and plunged down into one of the undulations that marked the path of the road into Caen. Bouffechoux was working a relief posting in the town of Fleurs; he lived in Villars-Bocage and each morning and evening made the thirty-mile commute. Now he was on his way home. The day had been uneventful, routine work, keeping the paper moving for the man who was ill; Bouffechoux was tired and hungry. He began to address his mind to the likely menu his excellent wife might have prepared.

At first he thought it was a bonfire. The flames leaped so high, bursting in vivid tongues skyward, that he felt it was a farmer burning hedge cuttings before the spring grass came. Then he looked again. The shape of the yellow Volkswagen was unmistakable in the roaring flames. Bouffechoux swung off the road and down a bumpy track, which ended in an acre of wasteland containing wrecks of a dozen cars. Bouffechoux got out and peered at the inferno from a distance of twenty yards. Even at that distance the heat was so intense that it had buckled the chassis of the Volkswagen and twisted it into a slowly inverting "U".

Bouffechoux looked around to see who might have caused the fire. There was no one. Thick smoke was billowing dangerously out and toward the main road; all at once the wind changed and flattened the direction of the flames. Bouffechoux then saw the figure. He thought that the heat might be playing tricks with his eyes and peered intently. There was no trick: a human shape was sitting upright in the driver's seat of the Volkswagen, ablaze like a torch. The hair and head were on fire, the flames licking upward giving the appearance of hair standing on end. The mouth was soundlessly open as fire licked from it.

Gaston Bouffechoux could get no closer. His eyes steaming, his face and clothes blackened with soot, he ran all the way back to the main road, to the pay telephone on the hilltop.

THURSDAY: P.M.

38 MATT BLANEY CLENCHED HIS TEETH.

"Thank you," he said quietly. "I appreciate it. Please keep trying and keep us informed." Slowly he replaced the telephone and looked across the room at Jim Crabbe.

"Nothing?" said Crabbe. The chairman of Insurance Fidelity was dressed in an immaculate three-piece tweed suit. He wore a tie with a fox-hunting motif, impaled at its center by a fox's head of solid gold, its two shining eyes a pair of rubies.

Matt shook his head. He put the shoe of his right foot on his left knee and rubbed the stubble of his chin.

"There's not a sign of him," he said. "Laurens has looked everywhere. No one has seen Petitjean since this morning. Now it's nearly midnight over there. The last person to see him was the physics lab technician at Caen University. I guess the last person to speak to him was me."

"Shit," said Crabbe. "What do you think has happened?"

204 / ALL RISKS MORTALITY

"I don't know, Jim. Either Dijon has got to him like he got to Cathy — if that's what happened — or else they've bought him off, sent him on a trip around the world, all expenses paid. That's most likely. Petitjean responded to money."

"Has Laurens been able to find anything to help us — samples from the horse, for example?"

Matt shook his head. "He's been very good, he really wants to help in any way he can. He says he's tried to get into the house, but Petitjean's wife is in hysterics. She's informed the police."

"Shit," said Crabbe again. "Just when we thought we had it cold. Christ, am I going to look stupid in London. Lloyd's will think I've lost my marbles."

"What did you tell Lloyd's?"

"The whole story," Jim said. "Just like you told me, except that I omitted any reference to your adventures last night."

"But they've obviously heard what happened?" Matt said.

"Of course," said Jim. "It's the lead item on every news bulletin. The latest is that Galatti's nowhere to be found and his company is going down the tubes. They've just filed for protection from their creditors."

"What was Lloyd's reaction to what you told them?" Matt asked.

"After their initial astonishment, they were okay," Jim said. "But they need to have the evidence in hand, hard and fast. Galatti's other misfortunes have nothing to do with his claim on Cornucopia — his lawyers are still screaming for payment to be made to a bank account here in New York. And they've made it clear that their action for impunity of damages — that's for three times the sum insured — is going ahead."

"So what will Lloyd's do?"

"They've agreed to stall until Monday, based on what I've told them." Jim ran his hands through the white, wiry stubble of his hair. "Christ, if Lloyd's get sued because of information I've given them, and they lose, my name will be shit in the insurance business forevermore — that's if it's not already."

Matt's hand went to the phone first.

"Yes?" he said.

Jim saw him shake his head and briefly close his eyes.

"I'm pretty good, Delis," Matt said with masterful control. "How in God's name did you find me here?"

"Well, when I kept getting no answer from your apartment, I asked myself where else might you be," Delis said. "You hadn't said you were going away. Have you moved in with him?"

"No, Delis, I haven't moved in with him," Matt said.

"I just wanted to say I'm leaving for Venezuela in the morning," Delis said.

Matt looked at his watch and gritted his teeth. "I hope you have a good time," he replied. "Delis, I'm sorry if this sounds short, but I'm expecting a very important long-distance call at this number."

"So what's new?" Delis said sharply. "Either no answer or you're too busy."

"I'm sorry," Matt said, "but . . ."

"Forget it," she said. Then she gave a laugh. "By the way, thanks for the check," she said, and hung up.

Matt took a deep breath and replaced the telephone.

"Delis?" Jim said.

"Who else?" said Matt.

Suddenly the telephone rang and Matt snatched it.

Crabbe saw his mouth open a few times as he listened. Then Matt sat down heavily.

"I see," he said eventually. "Of course. I really don't know," he said. "Can you call this number back in an hour? Thank you Monsieur Laurens."

He looked heavily at Jim Crabbe as he hung up. "They found Petitjean," he said. He drew his index finger across his Adam's apple. "He totaled himself in his Volkswagen. They only identified him an hour ago, but Laurens doesn't think there was any foul play involved."

Jim Crabbe closed his eyes. "And no . . ." he said.

"Nothing," said Matt. "No certificate, no piece of the horse, nothing."

For a moment Jim Crabbe sat as if in meditation. Then he took out a notebook, sprang to his feet, and picked up the phone.

"What are you doing?" asked Matt.

"I'm ringing my Lloyd's man at his home to say it's all been a big mistake," he said punching out the numbers.

Matt stood up. "Jim, after what's happened we can't let them pay Galatti now," he said.

"No?" said Crabbe. "If we don't forget this whole fucking business

I'm going to end up being sued for slander, libel, false accusations, and probably child molesting. Shit!" he said as the transatlantic line sounded the busy signal. He dialed again.

"Jim," said Matt, "just hold it a minute. Just listen to me."

"Matt, you're a friend as well as an employee, but don't push it. We've gotten into the middle of something way over our heads. I'm out, as of now."

"Jim, please, listen to me."

"My ass, Matt. We're into big Mafiosa stuff here. Jesus Christ, I read the papers, you know, I know what goes on. This guy killed his own wife, blew her away." He held up his hand for silence. "Chris Downs, please."

"Goddammit, you little bastard, hear me out!" With a crash Matt Blaney brought his fist down and disconnected the call. Crabbe was left holding the receiver, his face rapidly turning the color of his white silk shirt.

"What the . . . ?"

"Jim," said Matt catching the small man gently and easing him onto a chair, "just sit down and listen. There's another way here."

Warily Crabbe sat down, his eyes still wide and riveted to Matt.

"Look," said Matt, "I'm sorry about what happened just now but there is one final person who can help us."

Jim Crabbe shook his head in mystification.

"This Dr. Shenlavi, Jim," said Matt gently. "He gave the phosphorus to Barbara Galatti in Jerusalem. He's our man."

"Dr. Shenlavi," repeated Crabbe.

"Exactly," said Matt. "The Israeli scientist. I'm going to Israel, Jim, and see him. This is Thursday evening. Lloyd's have already told you they won't pay Galatti until Monday. What have we to lose?"

"Apart from my money, just our lives," said Crabbe, regaining his composure. He got up and walked to the window. Light caught the fox's eyes and made them flash. "What's the latest news from France?" he asked.

"No change," Matt replied. "I spoke with her father. He's just got back. He's pretty cut up."

Crabbe shook his head.

"Its all very rough," he said. He took off his glasses and rubbed his eyes, then he fitted them back on and looked at Matt. "So what exactly are you proposing now?" he asked.

Matt's face was urgent. "The only person who can say for sure if Barbara Galatti was telling the truth is in Israel," he said, "this Dr. Shenlavi. Chances are, I realize, that he will deny everything — but we don't know. He may just say, yes, I gave Mrs. Galatti radioactive phosphorus because her husband asked me how much of it it would take to kill his horse. I don't know what he'll say, Jim, until I ask him."

"I've paid my money over, Matt," Jim said wearily, "I've written it off."

"But we can't write off what Galatti did to Cathy," Matt said quietly. "If there's the remotest chance that by going to Israel I can build a case against Galatti that will put him behind bars for the rest of his life, then that is what I want to do."

Jim Crabbe looked spent. "The police . . ." he began.

"They'd start an investigation that would go on for months," Matt said. "It's almost certain they would arrest me at the outset. In the meantime Lloyd's might be pressured into paying over the money."

Crabbe was shaking his head.

"We've come such a long way already," Matt said. "It's Thursday. I'll be back in two days." He met the small man's eye. "I owe it to Cathy, Jim," he said softly. "So do you."

Jim Crabbe looked toward the window. The curtains had not been drawn and the cold, dark night shivered outside the double-glazing.

"Okay," he said, turning slowly. "Okay. Go. But this makes us even."

Matt nodded.

"By Sunday," Crabbe was saying, "this man Shenlavi is either prepared to testify or we forget the whole business, is that clearly agreed?" He shook himself. "I just hope that Lloyd's don't lose a bundle of money because of all this," he said. "They could take me for every cent."

"Don't fret," Matt said.

"What do I tell Laurens when he calls back?" Jim said. "He sounded pretty steamed up about the whole thing."

"Tell him there's just one last possibility," Matt said. "Tell him it involves my going to the Middle East, but that we'll let him know the outcome as soon as I get back." He looked at his watch. "Speaking of which," he said, "I'd better get going. There's a flight tonight, out of Kennedy at ten, which goes to Tel Aviv through Paris."

"I'll get you booked on it," said Crabbe, reaching for the phone.

Matt was at the door.

"I, ah, I already took that precaution, Jim," he said.

"Get out of here!" cried the chairman of Insurance Fidelity. "Hey, Matt!" Matt turned. The small wizened face was serious. "Listen, you big mother, you be careful out there. That's a dangerous place you're going to."

Matt nodded once, then he was gone.

"And keep in touch, you hear?" shouted Jim to the closed door. He sighed; then he sat and resumed his view over the city, which looked as stark and as deserted as a moonscape.

THURSDAY: P.M.

 THE ISRAELI AND THE BULKY VIENNESE SAT FACING EACH other in the small apartment. Located on the Upper West Side, in the daytime its view took in the Hudson and the snow-covered Palisades.

Yanni Israel looked at the older man and spread his hands.

"So," he said, "for the moment it is over."

The big head nodded in resignation. "Escape was always his strength," he said. "From Majdanek, from Europe, and now from New York."

"We went in this afternoon," said the Mossad agent. "The two houses interconnect at basement level — like a fox he had to have another way out. He had foreseen all this from a long, long way back."

"So clever," said the older man, "so fiendishly clever."

The Israeli struck his palm with his fist. "To think," he said grimly, "that he deceived us with a disguise that a child should have seen through." He shook his head. "It's very disappointing for you," he said.

"What's disappointment?" The older man smiled bravely. "To be thwarted by one day in something that God has an eternity to put right?" He leaned forward in a fatherly way. "Jerusalem has been told?"

The Israeli nodded. "They're wailing so loud," he said, "you can hear them behind the closed doors of the temple. I have just transmitted a full report. The first feedback is bad."

"How bad?"

"Bad. Following the scene last night and the news which it is generating, we only went in on my insistence. Now we find Galatti's gone. It's bad."

"Jerusalem cannot blame you," said the older man.

Yanni's lip curled in a sneer. "It was my project, it is my disaster," he said. "Over two and a half months of time and effort have been wasted. The possibility that I might have been under observation the whole time really blew their minds."

"Who was the man?" asked the Viennese.

"CIA or FBI," Yanni said, "must be. One of my men tailed him as far as the World Trade Center, lost him, then picked him up again — coming out of the studio."

"He saw . . . ?"

"I don't know," Yanni said. "We're still with him." He checked his watch. "My man is due to call in shortly. When he does, I've been told to pull him off." Yanni sighed and looked over at the old face. "Another dimension has arisen to this whole thing," he said quietly, "an Israeli dimension. Barbara Galatti told me about it before she was killed. Jerusalem has not cleared me to brief you about it, but it is extremely perplexing." Yanni rubbed his hand across the light stubble of his jaw. "Even so, Jerusalem is not interested in anything at this stage except damage limitation. I am not to move a muscle without specific orders — regardless of what I think I may have found. We are all to disband. I am to return to Jerusalem within two days to face the music."

"O Lord, Thou hast strange ways," said the older man clasping his hands across his midriff in a gesture of resignation.

A man in excess of six and a half feet tall and aged about thirty came silently in from the back room. He placed a tray with a jug of coffee and cups on the table before withdrawing.

"*Toda Ahot*," said Yanni. "Thank you, Nurse."

The Viennese leaned forward to pour.

"You remember my jigsaw?" he asked quietly, sitting back with his cup.

Yanni looked at him. The narrow eyes were again bright.

"It may now be too late, but nearly all the pieces have found their place."

The big head checked around; he sat slightly slumped in his chair, his head forward, both large hands around the coffee cup.

"I am hearing about a family. A Polish family named Dofinzinsky. And a man, Jacob Dofinzinsky, born in Bialystok, northeastern Poland, in 1904."

Yanni Israel listened.

"Jacob Dofinzinsky was unusual for a Jew; he had blond hair and bright blue eyes, the very essence of Aryan perfection in a Jewish suit." He drank coffee and licked his lips. "In 1932 the Dofinzinskys moved to Paris where Jacob set up a small watch-repair shop. In 1940 the Nazis arrested the whole family and interned them in Drancy. In 1942 they were deported by rail back to Poland, to Majdanek, then nominally a labor camp. The camp commandant was Reto Deutsch, the Beast of Majdanek, who used newborn babies for target practice and later had them flushed down latrines." He looked at Yanni without emotion. "The Dofinzinskys were all murdered, of course, the whole family gassed or shot, including the father, Jacob, the least Semitic-looking of them all."

Yanni stared at the crooked mouth speaking its halting Hebrew.

"The records for Majdanek are largely intact," the Viennese was saying. "I've checked with Yad Vashem. Three entire Dofinzinsky families, all from the same area of Poland, were exterminated there in 'forty-three and 'forty-four. All their papers were preserved." He paused and looked shrewdly at the Israeli. "Except Jacob Dofinzinsky's."

He put his empty cup on the table and leaned forward. "I have already mentioned the father and son who made it on foot from Majdanek to Theresienstadt in the winter of 'forty-four?"

Yanni nodded.

"It was a heroic journey," said the Viennese. "They first went south, toward Krakow, then had to cross the Carpathian mountains before turning north again for Prague. They arrived in Theresienstadt literally the night before the convoy to Geneva, more dead than alive. In the confusion they were shipped."

Yanni saw the old eyes ablaze.

"I told you about my contact in Florida," the Viennese said. "Abraham Seidmann was taken in Kristallnacht, spent two years in Dachau before being shipped to Shanghai."

In the back room the two other agents could be heard talking quietly.

"When I heard about Theresienstadt," said the old man, "I remembered Abraham. He married a Swiss girl from Zurich after the war, a Jew. From 'forty-three to 'forty-seven she worked with the Red Cross in Geneva, I remembered."

The big head was almost touching that of the Mossad man.

"Three days ago I went to Florida. Abraham's wife told me that when the convoys came from Theresienstadt they were split into groups. I asked her about a father and son. She remembers a father and son, Yanni, particularly because the child had a distinguishing face disfiguration, a hemangioma, and because the father abandoned the child almost immediately."

He sighed deeply.

"I showed her all our Galatti photographs; she is positive that he is the father."

The Israeli let out his breath. "And the child?"

"Abraham's wife is also quite clear about what happened to him," the old man said. "He was noted on arrival from his father's papers as being a Pole, Dofinzinsky. The Red Cross fostered him to another couple, Austrians, who had spent the war in Theresienstadt and lost their children there." The Viennese shook his head. "They're both dead now, but they called the child Yoseph, smuggled their way into Israel in 'forty-seven and settled in Bat Yam." The old man licked his upper lip. "Yoseph was a brilliant student. He left school and majored in physics, then he joined the Weizmann. His speciality is the atom."

The Israeli agent's eyes narrowed.

The Viennese continued: "In 1963 he married Anna Dreyfus, a lab technician in Rehovot. They first had one child, a son, Levi. Then they had two more children, two girls, Ruth and Rachel."

The old man sighed.

"A year ago in Haifa, both children and their mother were killed in the shopping precinct bomb explosion."

Yanni looked like a cat about to spring.

"Last summer," the Viennese was saying, "Levi, his son, was one of those captured near Sasa. He's never been heard of since. Abraham's wife has followed the whole, sad life."

"His name," Yanni said, "his name."

"Dr. Yoseph Shenlavi," the old man answered, taking two photographs from his briefcase. "He's a possible nominee for the Nobel Prize."

Yanni's face had gone white. His fists were clenched. The old Viennese looked at him with concern, as Yanni studied the unhappy face in the print.

"The boy in the Maghdousheh hill," Yanni whispered. "Somehow all these things are connected, but how I don't know. Barbara Galatti knew only one part of it, now here is another."

The older man's eyes were shrewd. "The Israeli dimension?" he asked softly.

There was a knock on the door and the Nurse entered. He beckoned Yanni, then spoke quietly to him at the door. The Viennese could see Yanni shake his head in bewilderment.

"Does Jerusalem know this?" he heard him ask.

The Nurse shook his head. "We're due to transmit again in fifteen minutes," he replied.

Yanni Israel shoved his hands into his pockets and walked alone to the window of the small room. Outside the curtains everything was black. He turned around.

"Tell him to stand by," he instructed. "Tell him to set up a seat — I'm on my way." He looked at the big figure. "And *Ahot* . . ."

The Nurse stopped at the door.

"As far as the transmission is concerned, we have aborted and are about to disband."

The Nurse nodded his understanding and disappeared. Slowly the Israeli returned to the older man.

"It seems I'm going to *Ha'aretz* sooner than I thought," he said, his face set.

"To Israel?" asked his companion.

"That was my man who has been trailing the U.S. agent since yesterday," the Israeli said. He paused. "They are now in the TWA terminal at Kennedy. The man has just checked in on a flight to Tel Aviv."

He sat down and looked into the middle distance.

"I'm going to follow him," he said. "I'm not going to request clearance from Jerusalem. They would not give it — they would simply pick him up themselves when he arrived. We would be out in the cold, especially after what has happened over here." He clenched his teeth. "There is something at work here that we are very close to," he said, "something involving Galatti." He looked at the Viennese. "You know the feeling when someone has just walked over your grave?"

The inclination of the big head was barely perceptible.

"Well," said Yanni softly, "whoever it is, right now they are standing on mine."

For a moment the two men held each other's eyes in an understanding that made words unnecessary. It was the Viennese who bent down to the floor.

"Take this with you," he said, handing Yanni a file and putting one of Shenlavi's photographs into it. "Maybe you can finish my jigsaw for me."

The Israeli stood up and, touching the broad shoulder briefly, left the room.

The Viennese sat back. As in the hundreds of other cases he had spent his lifetime investigating, there came a point when the sheer magnitude of human misery threatened to overwhelm him. He picked up the remaining photograph and stared intently at it.

"Who art thou, wandering in the sands of the desert?" he whispered to the smiling, unhappy face. "O children of Israel, I have not forsaken you."

The departure lounge was crowded. Bearded Orthodox Jews in stern black clothes and hats, some with long side curls, sat reading, while Jews wearing the *kipa* on their heads settled tired children on their knees. A row of seats with built-in, coin-slot TVs was fully occupied; dark-suited businessmen with briefcases looked in annoyance at their watches, which showed the flight to be fifty minutes late.

"TWA announces the delayed departure of Flight 803 to Paris and Tel Aviv."

As one, the people in the departure lounge rose and made for the gate. At the very back Yanni Israel kept the tall figure in sight. Once on board he could relax and catch up on some sleep.

It had taken a frantic hour, first to delay the flight and then to arrange, via El Al, that he could board without going through the stringent security process. Now reflexively he checked the snug feel of the Beretta 84, loaded with its full complement of thirteen cartridges.

Slowly the boarding line moved forward and Israel fingered his pass. The big man ahead had checked in all the way to Tel Aviv. Yanni passed a small TV screen still broadcasting to its empty chair. It was newstime and the newscaster's voice blared out to the emptying departure lounge. "On Wall Street tonight," he was saying, "a major crisis is developing in one of the country's most respected banks."

Yanni Israel was the last passenger to hand his boarding pass to the steward and board the flight to the land after which he had been named.

FRIDAY: A.M.

40 IT WAS 5 A.M. FRIDAY MORNING AND SEYMOUR CROCKER had been waiting for over ten minutes. He again got up from the deep couch and walked around a clump of plants; the trickling of the waterfall continued incessantly. The blond receptionist glanced up at him, her shining hair down around her shoulders. She looked tired and pale.

Crocker walked back around the greenery and leaned his weight against the floor-to ceiling glass, pressing his forehead against its tinted surface. For an instant merciful cool shafted through his headache. He opened his eyes and looked down on Wall Street, fifty-three stories below and still in darkness.

When he had spoken to the bank's Nassau office on Wednesday morning, Crocker had thought that his head would actually burst with the pressure. An hour later he was silently congratulating himself: Galatti's stock had leaped to thirty-two; Crocker could sell and make the bank a profit. Instead he had sat back and watched it rise to thirty-five, where he had doubled the entire position. First Transnational now owned, for its own book, four million Galatti at an average price of thirty, an investment of one hundred and twenty million dollars. But it was a short-term investment: each dollar rise would further erode any exposure the bank might have on the additional Galatti loan.

Crocker had felt his blood quicken. This was what he had been born to do.

At nine yesterday, the phones had started to ring. The first to get through was the head of the stockbroking firm that looked after First Transnational.

"Seymour, where's Hugh?"

Seymour Crocker explained.

"There are some pretty hairy rumors making the rounds," the broker said. "Have you guys got problems over there?"

"No more than anyone else," Crocker said. "What are you hearing?"

"That you've got a major bad loan," the broker said. "Haven't you heard? Carlo Galatti's wife's been murdered; the cops are looking for Galatti, but he's disappeared. Word is that his stock will be suspended."

At that moment Crocker's secretary came in and placed a piece of paper in front of the banker. It read: "Galatti opening: $13.00 offered."

"Did you hear me, Seymour?" asked the broker.

"Yes," said Crocker, who felt light-headed.

"We may need to hold the First Trans stock," the broker was saying. "Do I have your permission to —"

"Do what you have to," said Crocker and hung up.

He spent the morning avoiding calls from board members, fending off the bank's legal officer, and presiding over the debacle for which he was responsible. When Galatti hit eleven dollars he had picked up the phone like a man in a trance and called Nassau.

"Again?" exclaimed the branch manager. "Aren't we breaching SEC regulations?"

"I'll worry about regulations," Crocker snarled. "Do it. Use a different nominee account."

"You're the boss," said the man down in the Caribbean. "Another twelve million on the way."

At three the New York stockbroker had called again.

"Jesus," he said, "have you seen your stock?"

Crocker felt acute chest pains.

"No," he replied.

"Fell like a stone in the last fifteen minutes," the broker said. "It happened so fast, we couldn't hold it. It's gone from seventy-six bid to sixty-five offered. . . . Seymour, are you there?"

"I'm here." The reply was a whisper. He prayed that if the heart attack came it would be quick and terminal.

"It's now being offered all over the Street, at sixty bucks," the broker was saying. "What the hell's going on, Seymour?"

"Nothing," said Crocker. His tongue adhered to the roof of his mouth. "Absolutely nothing."

"I have Midwest Star's bankers holding for me, right now," the broker said. "You can imagine their reaction to something like this. They may want to pull out, Seymour."

The image of Hugh Johnson's blue eyes floated into Crocker's vision.

"The SEC has been on as well," the broker said. "I didn't speak to them, but they'll need a hell of a good explanation in the next hour if First Trans is to be listed tomorrow. This thing is blowing up into a major storm." Seymour Crocker was not really listening.

"People are comparing it to Continental Illinois, Seymour, you hear me? You've got to put out a statement saying this Galatti business doesn't affect First Trans."

Crocker allowed the receiver to fall back onto the telephone as he stood up and went to the walnut cabinet. The amber liquid was no longer an option. It scorched on its way down — dimly he wondered if it was causing the pain in his chest. His wet hand lifted the phone and he made the call.

"I'll have to cancel someone else," the girl's voice said. "It'll cost you two big ones."

A man who caused a billion-dollar run on a bank did not haggle with a hooker.

"You got it," he said. The next call was automatic.

"You sound exhausted," his wife said.

"I am," Crocker replied. "We've got problems. I'm in charge. I'm staying here for the night."

"Poor Seymour," his wife said warmly. "Find a minute to call, won't you?"

He went straight to Trudy's apartment.

For an hour the girl had worked on him. At last even Trudy was exhausted. They got in the Jacuzzi together, the girl's golden body luxuriating over the jets of water. Then they dressed and went out, to Lutèce, where they ate a dinner fit for a prince followed by goblets of rare Armagnac at fifty dollars a shot. It had been nearly two — just over three hours ago — when they returned to her apartment. Still in a party mood, Trudy peeled off her clinging gown and went to the refrigerator, where she found a bottle of New York State champagne.

Crocker followed suit and held the glasses as Trudy solemnly opened the bottle.

"To us," she whispered, brushing his skin with hers and raising her glass. It was at that point that he remembered.

"What is it?"

His mouth sagged a bit.

"I've got to make a call," he said. Trudy shrugged.

"There's the phone."

Crocker placed his glass of champagne on the table and picked up the extension. As he stood there dialing, Trudy turned her back to him and then slowly began to revolve her buttocks. Instantly he was up, hard. He could hear the phone ringing in Connecticut. He licked his lips. She was only an inch from him. Then she reached back her hand and, taking him, guided him in. There was a click as the phone was answered.

"Hello?" said a sleepy voice.

"Pam?"

"Seymour?"

He felt he would explode — she was so warm. He felt his knees crumble. He had never been so deep.

"Pam. I'm sorry, it's late." His voice was thick.

"Don't worry, darling, I'm so glad you called."

She cupped him.

"Are you all right?" He was dizzy and barely able to get the question out.

"I'm fine," came the reply, "but the phone's been going here all evening. Where are you? Hugh Johnson has been on three times, calling from the bank. I said I thought you were there, but he says not. Where are you, love?"

As if a freight-train had run over him, he had died. Trudy replaced the receiver as he stumbled, first into her bedroom and then her bathroom where he knelt for an hour, bellowing into her toilet bowl of vitreous china.

Now Crocker stood staring dumbly out at the city towering all around him. Abruptly a door to the left opened; a smallish man with the midnight version of five o'clock shadow stood looking for an instant at Crocker, then turned and walked back in, leaving the door ajar.

Crocker recognized him as George Hogg, the chief executive of Hogg Aerospace and a key board member of the bank.

The room was enormous, almost half the width of the building. To one side sat the bank's principal legal officer with a senior vice-president. They looked grim. At the center of the room stood a huge oval table surrounded by leather chairs and strewn with newspapers. Five of the chairs near the head were occupied, four by board members, including Hogg, the fifth by the very tanned but unshaven Hugh Johnson. Startlingly, he was dressed in a bright, floral-patterned shirt. His clenched fists lay on the white pad in front of him. All the men's eyes surveyed the figure of the bank's president as he shuffled into the room and stood before them.

"What the fuck's going on?" asked Hugh Johnson.

Crocker tried to meet the light blue eyes; in the tanned face they shone like lights in a Chinese lantern.

"Morning, gentlemen," Crocker said, gulping air. "Did you have a good trip, Hugh?"

"The answer is 'yes' until I happened to listen to a news broadcast on the radio of the boat I was fishing off." He sat coiled like a cornered beast. "Now we need some explanations, fast!"

Seymour Crocker spread his hands helplessly.

"If you're talking about the bank stock," he said, "I've spoken with our brokers. No one seems to know what's happening."

"Listen, you simpleton," Johnson snarled, "Salomon Brothers have just been on here. Midwest Star has pulled out of the deal. They're being taken over by CitiCorp."

Crocker opened his mouth and closed it. Terror was spreading through him. He felt as if he was going to puke again.

"I've been looking for you since midnight," Johnson was saying. "Here's a list of our major outstanding loans. It shows Galatti as having jumped over two hundred million. How in the name of all that's holy could that have happened?"

Seymour Crocker swayed slightly. "I was acting chairman, Hugh," he croaked. "I authorized it."

With an enraged roar Hugh Johnson sprang to his feet, causing his chair to crash backward. In two strides he was on Crocker, his powerful hands grabbing the bank president's shirt and coat.

"You fucking bastard!" he bellowed as Crocker went down like a slaughtered bullock. Johnson was on top of him, one knee on his chest, his thumbs on the windpipe. There was pandemonium. The four other men all jumped to their feet and began to tear Hugh Johnson off. One of them, an ex-naval officer and currently head of a pet-food conglomerate, pinned back the powerful arms, while the aerospace chief prised the strong fingers off Crocker's larynx. Three directors pushed Hugh Johnson to the far end of the room while the chief executive of the country's biggest department store helped Seymour Crocker to a chair.

"Gentlemen," said George Hogg when he had got back his breath, "we are not going to save First Trans by adding murder to our problems. Please sit down and be reasonable."

Hugh Johnson's breath was coming in shaky bursts.

"The first time I've taken a break in six years," he said, his eyes on the floor. "I come back and find Herman Katz is dead and this bank facing suspension on the NYSE." He buried his head in his hands. "You shouldn't have pulled me off him," he said. "I would gladly do life to rid the world of such an idiot."

"Hugh, gentlemen," said George Hogg. "We must get to the bottom of this, urgently. Even another two hundred million added to Galatti doesn't mean the end of the world. We're still covered beyond his total borrowings, am I not right?"

The board directors all turned to look again at Crocker, who sat slumped, his face ashen.

"That's correct," he whispered. "I checked every aspect of the collateral before I let him have the money. I even got a lien on the insurance coming in from his dead horse."

Hugh Johnson's voice was guttural. "Have you seen this morning's papers?" he asked. "Galatti's shares have been suspended. They've filed for protection from their creditors. The outfit is bust, defunct. They think he may have even murdered his wife. Look!"

Seymour Crocker's jaw dropped as he looked down at early editions of the newspapers strewn across the boardroom table. He began to tremble.

"Galatti's wife left a document with her lawyers," Johnson was saying. "It tells everything. The guy even poisoned his horse, for Christ's sake, Lloyd's in London aren't going to pay a cent."

"Poisoned," Crocker managed to say.

The bank chairman looked at him pityingly. Crocker heard Johnson's voice like the echo in a tomb. "Is there anything, anything at all, which has registered in your brain which could explain this run?" he asked.

"Have there been any unusual movements of cash in our offshore branches, for example, any significant withdrawal of funds or account closures?"

Seymour Crocker shook his head hopelessly. Terror had taken resolute hold of his system.

"It's a classic run," Johnson was saying. "Our stock is plummeting; when we open — if we open — for business today, we'll be stripped of cash within hours." For nearly a minute he said nothing, then he stood up and began pacing behind his chair.

"I don't know what's going on," he said, "but I've been on Wall Street nearly forty years and the one thing I've learned is that you can't stop rumors." He glared at Crocker. "Your decision to directly countermand my instructions is going to cost you dearly, believe me," he said. "I just hope you have some cash put away someplace, because I promise you, you'll never work another hour on Wall Street."

Johnson's face swam in and out of Crocker's focus.

Hugh Johnson faced his board members. "Like it or not, we have a crisis," he said grimly. "Our stock is plunging, the SEC will be in here in hours, as will the Fed." He laughed. "Who said that all our castles are built on sand?" he murmured. There was silence in the huge room. Johnson walked back to the head of the board table and leaned on it, the sinews in his arms rigid, his jaw set.

"We're going to get to the bottom of what's going on," he said in a whisper, "and we're going to ride it out."

The heads on either side of him nodded vigorously.

"You," he said to Crocker, "are relieved of any executive function in First Trans, effective now."

A steel knife entered Seymour Crocker's belly.

"But," Johnson continued, "you are to remain nominally as bank president until such time as things are sorted out. Any high-level personnel moves could create added lack of confidence, which is the last thing we want."

Seymour Crocker wanted to scream.

"You won't have much to do," Johnson was saying. "I'm putting a corporate-finance vice-president in your office straightaway." He brought his tightly clenched fist down silently on the shiny waxed surface of the table. "This bank is solid," he said. "I've built it, I know. Galatti could go down the tubes twice over and we would still have half a billion in reserve." He clenched his fist. "I'm going to call the chief executive of every bank on Wall Street just as soon as we're through."

There was a murmur of assent around the table.

"I've brought this bank to where it is," Hugh Johnson said, his hands defiantly on his hips, "and I'm damned if she's going to go under like this."

As one, the dark-suited, unshaven men on either side of him rose to their feet and applauded. Hugh Johnson nodded confidently. He turned to George Hogg. "George, you heard me speak an hour ago to Jay Russell of Archibald Tree? They can have forty top auditors in here at a few hours' notice." He punched the air with his fist as his adrenaline began to flow. "Get him, George, get him now. I want them here this morning." Hogg wrote busily. "We're going to copper-fasten every single area of this bank in the next forty-eight hours," Johnson said. "Every loan, no matter how small, every movement of cash in the last six months, every cent." He paused. "We're going to tear this place asunder," he said to the seated men, his voice now fighting. "We're going to go through every department, offshore branches included, like shit through a cat. We're going to square up to this thing right away." He turned at the end of the room, his capable hands balled fists before him. "We're going to square up to it," he said, the vigor pulsing out from him, "and when we're a million percent sure of our facts, then we're going to tell Wall Street to go fuck themselves."

Seymour Crocker walked straight past his secretary into his office and locked the door. Later the girl would report that the president of First Transnational Trust had seemed like a man in a daze. He stumbled to the inlaid corner cabinet and took out a bottle of brandy and a glass. Then, returning to his desk, he slopped out the amber liquid, spilling several ounces of it on his office carpet. He almost retched in his effort to swallow the first mouthful. Then the burning comfort began to spread, first just a tiny flame of warmth cutting through the great chill of his fear, but by the fourth glass an explosion of heat that had ignited fires all over his body.

Crocker sat there staring into the middle distance, a dark dribble now running from his mouth and down his clean shirt. Massive sorrow replaced the terror. He began to cry, hecking like a child as tears ran down his jowls to join the brandy on his shirt. He drained the glass and then in a gesture of impotent fury threw it across the room, where it shattered against a wood-grained filing cabinet. Just as surely as he had broken the glass, so he had in all probability destroyed the bank as well. Anger was futile; now all that was left was remorse, and ruin. He slugged heavily from the neck of the bottle. All at once his wife's face floated into his harried vision. He reached for his direct phone and punched the number.

"Hello?"

He stared at the instrument, his whole body shaking with sobs.

"Hello, yes?"

Crocker replaced the receiver and stood up, draining the remains of the bottle as he did so. Behind his desk the morning was now clear, the sky blue, the vista over New York Harbor and out to Staten Island memorable. Still holding the bottle, Seymour Crocker launched it with all his strength at the large window. There was a deep cracking noise like ice thawing, and a fungus of tiny lines appeared all over the un-openable glass.

Dimly, Crocker was aware of a knocking on his door, and voices. In desperation he looked around him for a heavier object. His eyes rested on the rounded, terra-cotta plant pot with the miniature maple tree. He seized the trunk of the small tree and the base of the bowl, and with difficulty lifted it.

There were several voices now outside the locked door, calling for his attention. Someone had decided to put his shoulder to it. Both tele-phones on his desk were ringing. As the door strained to the weight of the people outside, Seymour Crocker staggered toward the window. He stood up on his chair and, with a strength he never knew he had, brought the heavy pot up behind him. Then with a great cry he launched it at the fractured window.

There was a deafening explosion. Ice-cold air flooded inward and a vicious wind whipped all the papers on his desk into a snowstorm.

Crocker was aware of nothing except the overpowering need to terminate the agony. He was oblivious to the traffic noises, suddenly audible, or the heavy crashing at his own door. He stepped onto the sill and looked at the amazing view.

It was going to be a lovely day.

FRIDAY: A.M.

41 MATT BLANEY SPLASHED HANDFUL AFTER HANDFUL OF cold water on his face and then dried it gratefully with a towel. A dour-looking Frenchwoman glared at him as he left a franc on her saucer and walked out into the bright transit lounge of Charles de Gaulle Airport. Everywhere praying Jews wrapped in their *talit* swayed silently at *tephillot*. A fresh group of passengers were being admitted to the lounge for the Paris–Tel Aviv leg of the journey.

Matt went to a wall phone and dialed the number that he had called at least once every day for the last six days. Nearly two hundred and fifty miles northwest of Roissy the duty nurse in a ward of the large hospital answered the call.

"Say that again?"

Matt's voice bellowed around the tiled lounge. Someone was droning over the public announcement system and he clapped a hand over his ear.

"It is really too soon to be certain, Mr. Blaney," the nurse said. "But she did open her eyes briefly this morning and tried to speak. She is sleeping again, but not nearly so deeply."

"That's the best news I've ever heard," said Matt as he hung up. In a spontaneous burst of exultation he turned away from the phone and jumped into the air with a loud whoop. Several Jews turned in mid-*tephillot* and a few cool French officials laughed among themselves. The public address system droned on.

At the back of the transit lounge Yanni Israel glanced fractionally over the paper he was reading. As the flight was called, he folded the paper, then waited until the tall man with the mustache had boarded. As in New York, Yanni was last on, one behind another passenger, a distinguished, well-built man with wavy, snow-white hair who had just joined the flight. The Mossad man barely noticed him as he resumed his seat.

"*Monsieur Blenne, téléphone,*" droned the public address system, "*Monsieur Blenne.*"

FRIDAY: P.M.

42 WITH A HAND THAT WAS ALMOST ROCK-STEADY HE WITHdrew the tongs, then allowed his breath to escape in a long hiss. The sixth crystalline lump of plutonium slipped snugly into the wax nest, a slight glint from its innocent surface reflecting the garage lights. Dr. Shenlavi replaced the tongs on the wooden work bench and wiped sweat from his forehead. The tension was almost too much. He reached for the wads of gray plastic explosive and very gingerly packed them on and around the central nucleus of the upright cylinder. Soon the lethal putty was up to the rim, completing the explosive cocoon.

From the workbench he took the detonator and nudged it so that it was recessed dead center in the plastic, two wires running out from it and down the side of the cylinder. He stood up and took down a heavy, circular steel plate with bolt holes drilled into its circumference. With minute care he lifted the heavy lid into place. He blinked. Like a distant train the noise began to fill his ears. He shook his head as his vision began to go.

"Not now," he muttered, "not now."

Every movement he made was a roar, every scrape and rustle in the closeness of the basement garage a scream to his tortured ears. He sat gripping himself, his knees brought up as the climax came. It always lasted for several minutes and took different forms. Sometimes his vision went and everything appeared in miniature; this time the roaring was accompanied by towering images, giants looming upward and over him, successions of them, graduating like enormous forest trees toward the sky. The noise was at once terrifying and pitiful, a stern roar and a helpless wailing against a background of tinny music.

Dr. Yoseph Shenlavi's eyes were closed tight but still the tears came. For twenty years he had known the nightly, soft embrace of a beautiful wife who had painstakingly reached into the very depths of his soul to cure him. Since her death, a dramatic regression had taken place. Dr. Shenlavi shook as he tried desperately to recall her, but in her place another face appeared, older, different, but still familiar. It was kindly and had the doctor's smiling mouth. Her hair was prematurely gray. In shame he averted his eyes from her startlingly white flesh. The looming men were gone but before his eyes as he walked away was a seething pit. He stared: the pit was boiling full with white fish, their mouths uniformly open. And the farther he went the less the wailing from their open mouths. He was naked and the snow had just started, allowing him to weep. And he wept, as he sat, for himself and for Eretz Israel.

"*Baruch Shemo,*" he intoned, "blessed be the name . . . This is the day which the Lord hath made to show His awful fury."

Matt Blaney sat back and looked around the small dining room of the kibbutz. The tables were full, mainly with American Jews who had arrived late in a gleaming bus and were now discussing their arrangements for the next day, the *Shabbat.* There was a long table running along one wall of the clean room carrying cheeses, fruits, and smoked fish. The dusk had come early to the Judaean Hills and a sturdy, middle-aged woman wearing jeans and an apron came out of the kitchen and walked to the end window where she drew its curtains.

The *kibbutzniks* had built the guest house in the center of their property, reached by a winding road and fenced off from the village of Abu Ghosh. The land was rolling hills and scrub running down to a fertile valley whose river gave life to the lowlands, turned by the industrious Jews into a patchwork of dark greens. Directed by the Ben Gurion Airport reservations office, Matt had earlier come up the steep road, a series of hairpins cut into the arid hill, climbing through terraces of olives and vines where the white, stony earth peeped through at every opportunity.

The *kibbutzniks* lived in clusters of houses built in the shelter of pines. There were minor tracks bordered by beds of roses, and a pungent dairy, home to a herd of dappled cows whose pink, bulging udders rolled gently against their hocks as they ambled into the relief of their milking parlors.

Matt strolled from the dining area to the lounge, which opened onto a garden. His room was one in a row of six cottages built a little distance from the guest house, down steps and under an arch of clematis. The flight from Paris had been on time, but there had been delays during the customs formalities at the airport and in hiring a car — Matt was now resigned to tracking down Yoseph Shenlavi the next day.

He passed the door of his cottage and began climbing a long row of stone steps bordered by thick bushes and illuminated by the lights of the guest house on his right. Everywhere there had been soldiers dressed in green fatigues and carrying rifles; he had given two of them a lift right to the gates of Jerusalem before turning back to find the kibbutz. The youthful soldiers on their way home for the *Shabbat* had reminded him of another war on a different continent. Soldiers were the same everywhere. The boys he had driven to Jerusalem were no more than twenty. They smelled of the healthy scent of sweat on khaki, their faces grimy and lightly stubbled, their brown hands resting lightly on the barrels of their Galils. They had looked forward to being at home, to washing, shaving, and changing.

Matt reached the top of the steps and turned right. He breathed in deeply as pine, its fragrance released by recent rain, rode the night air. Up here there was little light. Since he had heard the news in Charles de Gaulle that morning, life had taken on an altogether more cheerful complexion; hopefully the visit to Shenlavi the next morning could be concluded quickly and Matt could go back to France. He would not call Jim Crabbe until there were positive results.

He was on a path high above the hotel and looking down over the sleeping village at the other side of the valley. The road ran downhill and sharply to the right, becoming progressively darker the farther it went from the guest house. He inhaled the scents again as he descended. In the last fraction of a second he heard the footfall. Out of the corner of his eye he saw the blur, then there was only red-hot pain as his neck snapped backward and a powerful knee thrust savagely into him. Just at the moment of impact he had brought his right hand reflexively up; now his thumb was crushed agonizingly into his neck. He had no control over what was happening. There was no air. In almost detached horror he realized he was dying. His legs began to kick. Blood filled the dark sky. He vaguely heard a soft, popping noise like a paper bag being burst. Matt's knees gave and he collapsed back on the dark road. Shock took over.

Matt lay there, sucking air, his whole body shaking. He had the overpowering notion that there was something vital in which he had failed: his whole being screamed with impotence: he had failed.

"Shenlavi," he gasped.

Gradually he became aware that his face and neck were covered with something wet and sticky. There was a weight across his chest. He felt it being lifted, then he saw the outline of a man's head looking at him.

"Sit up."

The accent was foreign, Americanized. Matt allowed himself to be helped. Blood gushed from the deep weal in his thumb. His helper wrapped a handkerchief around it.

"Can you hear me?"

Still shaking, Matt nodded.

"Piano wire," the dark man said. "He very nearly had you."

Matt's breath was coming in gasps. Dimly he looked at the man's silhouette against the night sky. The way he moved was familiar.

Matt spat something out. Blood was welling into the groove around his neck. He was shaking uncontrollably, his mouth a rictus. His helper flicked a cigarette lighter and held it down near the road. Slowly Matt's eyes followed the flame. Lying on the path beside him was a corpse; a hole the size of a small bowl occupied the area where one normally expected to find a forehead, eyes, and a nose.

"Recognize him?" the man asked.

Matt shook his head dumbly.

"Look again."

Matt looked at his questioner and then back at the body. Something triggered a signal in his agony-swamped brain. Shakily, he put his hand at the corpse's ear and pushed the head to one side. His fingers touched white wavy hair.

"Laurens," he gasped.

"Laurens," the other repeated and gave a short laugh.

Matt's head swam.

"Who are you?" he managed to ask.

"You spoke a name just now — Shenlavi." Matt felt his arm gripped. "What do you know of Shenlavi?"

Matt shook his head.

"What do you know of Shenlavi?" the voice was urgent; the man moved to crouch beside Matt. "What is he to Galatti?"

Matt used all his strength to prop himself up on one knee; with the other man's sudden, lithe movement, recognition became complete. "I've got to get to a phone," Matt said.

"Why are you in Israel? What do you know of Yoseph Shenlavi? You must answer."

Matt sucked air. His thumb throbbed agonizingly.

"Answer me!" said his questioner, catching his shoulder.

"Go to hell," said Matt as a massive shaking spasm racked him. On his face and chest, his own blood and that of Laurens had already caked.

The other man rose.

"Stand up," he said. "Now."

As he tottered upright Matt felt a strong arm steady him; there was also the unmistakable feel of a gun through his helper's jacket.

"I must make a call," Matt said again.

The dark man had caught the corpse by its two legs and was pulling it beneath a bush. Then Matt felt himself being guided back up the hill — he was ridiculously weak; without the smaller man's support he would have been unable to walk.

They paused at the top of the hill as Matt retched for three minutes into a patch of the Judaean hills. Then, like a large rag doll, he allowed himself to be half-carried down the steep steps to the tiny bedroom.

At the door to the cottage the other man stood back to let him in. He reached the bed, then crashed, flat out, his face the color of its starched covers. The other man piled blankets over his prostrate figure.

Ten minutes later, but only when he was sure that the breathing was regular, did Yanni Israel leave the room.

SATURDAY: A.M.

 IN THE DARKENED TWO-BED COTTAGE, THE ISRAELI handed two small white tablets and a glass of water to the American.

"Take these," he said.

Matt winced as he swallowed; he still felt light-headed, but the worst of the nausea had passed. A bandage like a dog collar ran around his neck; he brought his fingers up to feel it; his thumb was also bandaged, and it throbbed. He had been awakened five minutes before. Outside it was still pitch dark. All at once the eerie wailing of a Moslem prayer broadcast over a loudspeaker in the nearby village could be heard.

"All right," the Israeli said. "You've had it all your way for three days. You are at least partly responsible for sabotaging an extremely important mission and, in the process, you have made me look a fool. Now, you are in my country. I want you to talk."

Matt looked at the sallow features, the brown eyes, and the compact figure leaning over him like a judge on his bench. Matt moved his head painfully. On the other bed he could see his own passport and plane ticket laid out. There was a loaded shoulder holster, its straps wound neatly around it, within easy reach of the man; undoubtedly it was the same caliber that had been used so effectively in New York against Barbara Galatti's murderer.

Matt felt himself being lightly pushed.

"Who are you? CIA?"

"You've been through my papers," Matt answered, "you should know."

"Ah yes, of course, Mr. Blaney, the insurance investigator." Matt could see the jawbones working in the face, which now came a fraction nearer his own. "I want answers," said the hard voice. "I do not have much time, so do not play games with me."

"You would seem to have the answers," Matt said. "Maybe you can explain why Laurens, a Parisian insurance adjuster, tried to strangle me here a few hours ago."

"Laurens," said Matt's questionner, repeating the name for the second time that evening. "You were lucky. If you hadn't got your thumb in, you would be dead."

Matt sized the man up. In a normal one-on-one he judged he could take him. Again Matt's eyes took in the gun on the bed.

"Why did you stop him?" Matt asked.

"For two reasons," said the other slowly. "One, his name is not Laurens, it is Herman Kindler. He was an officer in the Austrian SS and one of the senior personnel in the Nazi internment camp at Drancy." The Israeli's lips curled. "He was a pig of the first order; however, I expect that he's now accounting for his sins. Two, I require to know why you have been staking out Carlo Galatti's house in New York, what you know about me and the people I work for, and now, what it is you know about Yoseph Shenlavi." He paused. "I must tell you, despite what you may believe, that your life to me is irrelevant. Now talk."

Matt's eyes flickered briefly to the bed. "The man I work for," he said carefully, "insured part of a very expensive horse called Cornucopia." He saw the eyes opposite him narrow. "I think Barbara Galatti already told you a little about the animal in question."

The Israeli sat motionless for over thirty seconds, then he let his breath out in a long hiss.

"So. You did see," he said simply.

The two men looked at each other in silence.

"She was a beautiful woman," Matt said eventually.

"She was nothing," came the reply.

There was something startling about the callousness of the other man's tone. In the dim light Matt could see the lips curl, almost distort, as his questioner's mind came to grips with the latest information. Alarm bells went off all over Matt's body; his head screamed. At the same instant both men understood the decision that had to be made. Matt sprang first.

He landed perfectly between the seated man and the far bed, blocking the Israeli's reach for his gun. His bandaged right hand went to the Beretta, while with his left arm he struck powerfully downward. He felt the edge of his flattened hand strike something hard, but now he was rolling, his right shoulder leading, across the second bed, the leather holster beneath him. The Israeli's reflexes were lightning. The blow had caught his shoulder and felled him. But as he hit the floor he kept going, out into the far side of the room, to the base of a wardrobe near the outside door. Matt tugged the squat revolver from its leather holster and brought it up, just as the other man leaped. In a quick sidestep he brought up his angled left knee, hard. The Israeli went down, gasping. Slowly Matt circled him, the gun readied, his eyes riveted to the figure on the floor.

He caught an upright chair, pulled it toward the door, then, turning it around, sat, the pistol steadied on its back. It seemed that the adrenaline had opened every valve in his body, for he now felt no pain.

"Up," Matt ordered.

Slowly the Israeli rose, then sat on the side of the bed. He laughed shortly. "Whoever you are, you are good, I will give you that," he said. "No one but me has ever held that gun before. However, I should not have underestimated the CIA."

"I am not CIA," Matt said, his teeth clenched.

"Oh, I see," the Israeli said, "I suppose you learned the little trick you've just played behind the desk of your insurance company, or from a correspondence course, maybe?"

"You will now listen," Matt said, both hands on the gun. "You saved my life last night, so maybe I do owe you something. The fact that I was present for the bloodbath in New York doesn't mean that we can't both be on the same side."

The Israeli was motionless.

"I'm not the only one who knows what happened in New York," Matt continued. "If anything happens to me, I can assure you it will only make things a lot worse. But we can still help each other. For a start, who are you? Simon?"

The Israeli shrugged and smiled coldly. "If you must give me a label, call me Yanni," he said. "I'm a senior field agent in a special service of the Israeli government. The gun you are pointing at me will get you nowhere. The people I work with, who back me up, will be here within minutes — they are already overdue."

He sat perfectly still. Matt's mind was racing. Suddenly he felt he understood. "Very well," he said slowly. He motioned with the muzzle of the Beretta. "There's the telephone. Call them; call whomever you like."

In the confines of the small room the two men's erratic breathing was loud.

"What do you want?" asked Yanni after what seemed a very long time.

"I want to make a deal," Matt said. "In exchange for your help, you have my word that what I saw in New York will be forgotten." He paused. "We're both in the same boat," he said gently, "I don't think the people you work for are interested in Carlo Galatti anymore."

He looked at the dark face. "I'm right, am I not?"

The Israeli may or may not have inclined his head a fraction. His eyes were on the gun.

"But you are," Matt said. "And so am I." He adjusted the gun. "This is what is going to happen," Matt said. "I am going to tell you exactly why I am here. You are going to listen. If at any point you try anything, I'm going to shoot you — I know how: I was a soldier." He took a breath. "And when I'm finished, you can then decide if I'm telling the truth, and whether we have a deal."

Matt began to speak. He began with his meeting ten days before with Jim Crabbe. He described in detail what had happened in France, his meeting with Cathy, and the neck-mark on the dead horse. When he recounted what had then happened to Cathy, he saw the Israeli catch his breath.

"*Hara,*" he whispered, almost to himself.

"I have come here to see this Dr. Shenlavi," Matt concluded. "I don't know why he did it, but it seems he can ultimately implicate Carlo Galatti. That would be justice, and you can help me to do it."

Suddenly Matt felt drained. It was now an effort to keep the gun steady.

"And if I do not help you? If in fact I try to prevent you?" The Israeli's voice was quiet.

"I won't be prevented," said Matt, his mouth dry.

Yanni nodded his head a number of times. He closed his eyes, then seemed to make a decision. "Perhaps you are right," he said at last.

He adjusted his position minutely on the bed, then sighed deeply. "You see, there is something happening that neither of us is aware of. It concerns Dr. Shenlavi, it concerns Carlo Galatti, and, even though my country for me comes before everything, it concerns me." He closed his eyes.

"May I tell you a story?"

Matt nodded.

"Many years ago," Yanni said, "over forty years ago, Carlo Galatti had another name and another career." He looked at the dark-haired man behind the gun. "Then, Mr. Blaney, Galatti's name was Reto Deutsch and he was the commandant of a Nazi extermination camp in a place in Poland called Majdanek."

"Galatti is Argentinian," Matt said.

Yanni smiled. "I won't bore you with all the details," he said, "but I can assure you, Mr. Blaney, that we don't make mistakes in matters like this." He set his face. "Majdanek was the model of efficiency," he continued. "It was a green-field site, nearly seven hundred acres with plans to extend to over two thousand, beautifully designed, as good as any modern industrial or factory complex. There were rows and rows of sleeping-blocks, each one identical, forty yards long, nine yards wide, constructed of native pine, each one with two hundred and fifty bunks — although the guests who used them normally averaged twice that number. Everything had been masterfully designed, in Berlin, Mr. Blaney, including the sparkling new crematorium used to dispose of the bodies." He paused. "Deutsch was particularly proud of his crematorium," the Israeli went on. "It was said to be the newest of its kind, rivaling even the ovens at Auschwitz, which were reputed to handle record numbers of bodies an hour."

Outside the window, the texture of the darkness had subtly changed.

"One day," Yanni said, "sometime in March 1943, Reto Deutsch heard that he would be honored the following week by a visit from no less a personage than Himmler himself. Deutsch was ecstatic. Such a visit would put the highest seal of approval on his already dazzling career. But how could he possibly honor the great man, how could he, Reto Deutsch, mark the occasion in a manner fitting to the man, who next to the Führer himself was the most important in all of Germany?" The Israeli leaned forward. "The night of Himmler's visit, Mr. Blaney," he said, "was a night Majdanek would never forget. A great banquet was prepared for the Reichsführer and attended by all the high-ranking Nazi personnel from Lublin. There was good food, wine, and music. Deutsch was in heaven, seated at the head of the table beside arguably the most powerful man in the world. The feast was over. Himmler sat back, his face glowing with pride. What further treat would this talented young camp commandant, Deutsch, have for him?

"There was silence. Reto Deutsch barked an order. The doors into the wooden dining room opened and a group of young women, fifteen of them, were ushered in by storm troopers." Yanni took a deep breath. "They were the prime selection of all the Jewish women in Majdanek," he said quietly. "None of them was over eighteen, all of them were beautiful, attractive, in most cases just recently arrived in the camp, for none of them yet bore the ravages of starvation."

Matt realized that he was pointing the gun toward the floor. He brought it back up.

"For the occasion," Yanni was saying, "these girls wore their very best clothes, specially retrieved for the occasion, But they were shivering, as they had been waiting outside the banquet hall in the freezing cold for over an hour for the command to enter. None of them spoke.

"Deutsch issued another order and the girls were marched back out. Aides ran to help Himmler into his greatcoat as the dining party followed. A path from the dining hall into the camp proper had been illuminated with hundreds of storm lamps, and this odd little procession of beautiful Jewish girls, storm troopers, and greatcoated Nazis wound their way in the clear night, down the lighted path until eventually they came to a halt before the new crematorium."

Matt's mouth had gone dry.

"It was a treat for Himmler, Mr. Blaney. There was no protest, no wailing. They stood there clutching each other." His voice dropped. "They were all burned alive, in pairs, strapped to iron stretchers. The only sound they made was when their hair caught fire. Then they screamed — once. And after each performance Himmler clapped enthusiastically — and when he did all the other dinner guests followed suit, like people at the royal premiere of an opera who are waiting for the sovereign's reaction before they dare to applaud."

Dawn was creeping into the valley. The Israeli rose. "When it was over," he said, "they returned to the dining hall to drink wine and to listen to Wagner for the remainder of the evening."

Matt shook his head.

"I have two corroborating sources for that story, Mr. Blaney," Yanni said quietly. "One from statements made by German soldiers to the Russians who took Majdanek in 'forty-four. The other," he said sitting again, "the other is my own father. He was a Majdanek internee who survived." His voice was a whisper. "I was not yet born. But my eldest sister was. She was very beautiful." He put his head in his hands. "At fourteen she was the youngest murdered that night for Himmler."

Cocks began to crow in Abu Ghosh.

"Galatti is Deutsch?" Matt asked.

Yanni nodded. "There's no doubt," he answered. "We have checked exhaustively. Had we caught him, we had further evidence, definitive proof."

"You were going to . . . ?"

"Yes," Yanni said. "To face the justice of the people he desecrated. That is until you turned up — and he gave us the slip. Now the operation is officially aborted. I am disobeying orders being here — that is why I was so anxious to know your part." He looked at the broad frame on the chair, now silhouetted against the brightening door. "You will understand it when I say that this matter for me now goes beyond the simple obeying of orders."

"And Galatti knew Laurens?" Matt asked.

Yanni's head nodded. "As I said, his name is, or was, Herman Kindler," he replied quietly. "We got on to him about the same time Galatti was spotted. Kindler was in the Austrian SS; he was a brother officer of Deutsch's or Galatti's in Berlin. He was in Paris in 'forty-four; in the confusion following the liberation he fled to Rome, where we think we met up with Galatti, perhaps even introduced him to a contact in the Vatican. Kindler resurfaced back in Paris in 'forty-eight or 'forty-nine as Laurens. We believe he and Galatti kept in touch."

Matt rubbed a hand to his neck. "Galatti's web reaches everywhere," he said. "For example, who exactly is Yoseph Shenlavi?"

Yanni met his eyes. "He's a brilliant man," he replied, "one of our top nuclear scientists, a very much respected Israeli."

"So how does he get to be used by Carlo Galatti?"

"To answer your question," said Yanni slowly, "you have to go back to 1944 and begin with an inmate of Majdanek called Dofinzinsky."

Ten minutes later Matt shook his head. "It seems that Shenlavi has lost everything," he said, "his parents in Majdanek, his wife and daughters a year ago, and then his son. Is there any chance his son could still be alive?"

Yanni's face was grim. "He is not," he said. "Our latest intelligence reports say that all three kids were shot in the head within a week of their capture. That's now confirmed — in Lebanon it's very difficult to confirm anything, but that's confirmed."

Slowly Matt nodded.

"I won't screw things up for you," he said quietly. "He has visited far the greater crime on your house."

He looked into the brown eyes, then down at the gun. "What I saw in New York," he said, "is forgotten."

"I believe you," the other man said.

Slowly Matt turned the gun in his hand, then he handed it butt first to the Israeli. Yanni took it, then slotted it into its holster. They shook hands.

"It has been a long night," the Israeli said. "I need to sleep for a short time." He lay down on the narrow bed. "I suggest you do the same," he murmured, flocking a blanket over himself. "It may be a long day."

With one hand on his Beretta, he was immediately asleep.

SATURDAY (SHABBAT)

44 SLOWLY THE FIREBALL CREPT OUT OF JORDAN. IT FLOATED up over the earth's spiky rim where everything below was still in deep shadow, flinging its first shafts of heat westward, over the dead waters of Yam-Ha-Melah, and onward over the endless bare hills whose white, Arab townships cling to them like dentures. The heat from the fireball caressed the sleeping golden city, at rest on its *Shabbat,* making the reddish stone of its clustered buildings sparkle. As the giant orb climbed, it leaped across the Valley of Kidron to flash brilliantly on the golden Dome of the Rock from where the prophet Muhammad finally ascended to take his place with God. Its rays bounced on the church dome where God's son himself was crucified and threw brief light into the winding Via Dolorosa. But in the Jewish quarter, the western wall, the last remaining edifice of the Temple of David, lay in deep shadow.

Less than two miles west, in Qiryat Ben Gurion, the guard at the entrance of the Knesset rose and stretched. He glanced at his watch. It was 5:50 A.M. In just over an hour his replacement would come on and allow him to go home for a well-earned sleep. He walked out to the middle of a wide road; six days a week it was filled with tour buses, as people from the world over swarmed in to gaze at the tapestries designed by Chagall and at the seat of government of the nation they said could never be.

The guard waved downhill to two of his colleagues in the blockhouse, manning the traffic barrier from Eli'ezer Kaplan up to James de Rothschild. Opposite was a wooden seat, an extensive rose garden, and, in bronze, an enormous, traditional candelabrum.

The guard sat down; he took off his blue cap and ran his fingers through his greasy hair. The day was warming up quickly. Everything from where he sat was downhill. To his right he could see the white

stone of the seven-story building that housed the office of the Israeli
prime minister. Down to his left was the squat outline of the Israel
Museum. He could see a caretaker unlock the entrance door and go in:
the museum was one of the few public buildings in Jerusalem that
would open on the Sabbath. And on out westward over Giv'at Ram,
the Hebrew University, he could just about make out the large modern
sculpture that marked the road intersection leading to Yad Vashem, the
memorial to the Holocaust, the never-ending nightmare of the Jewish
people.

The guard sighed. He was one of the lucky ones. His parents had
got out of Germany in '35.

He got up again and patted the Beretta on his hip. The scent of roses
and geraniums followed him back across the road. Below him, a
hundred yards away, cars were moving on Eli'ezer Kaplan. The guard
yawned as he walked toward his blockhouse. Jerusalem was waking.

Traffic began to hum in the eastern city. At Damascus Gate where
Arab pop music blared from cassette players, a black-market money
changer was already open for business. Stallholders prepared for their
busiest day, when tourists from a silent Jerusalem would flood into the
Moslem quarter of the Old City. Arab vendors hung bags and shirts,
rugs, silks, and miles of necklaces from their doorframes; they feather-
dusted shelves filled with bronze and wooden statuary; a boy balancing
a platter of freshly baked bread on his head weaved down a dark alley;
tables were dragged outside and laden with brimming baskets of the
house speciality: nuts, spices, corn, figs, sweetmeats, cheeses, pastries,
or fresh, green vegetables brought through the night from the Judaean
hills on the back of an ass. Arabs greeted each other for the new day,
kissing lightly on the cheek. Old men sat outside their houses smoking
water-pipes; younger men sat in groups, discoursing, drinking coffee,
or reading the paper, ready as spiders to pounce on any early tourist
who descended the long, winding street from Yafo Gate to rattle their
web. Two dogs chased each other into a house; a child began to cry.
Jerusalem was awakening.

Within a stone's throw of Damascus Gate is Migrash Harussim, a
walled, five-acre enclosure also known as the Russian compound. Here
a sprawling, three-story colonial building, surrounded by an eight-foot-

high wire fence is constantly protected by armed guards with trained dogs. It is the headquarters of the Jerusalem police.

In a bright office on the first floor, Chief Superintendent Uzi Yadin smiled up as his secretary placed a cup of coffee, the second in thirty minutes, in front of him. As she turned, Yadin looked at her legs, long and brown and well shaped beneath her colorful skirt. She had been with him a week, transferred from national police headquarters in Derech Shechem. Yadin snorted deeply and selected a plastic-tipped, miniature cigar from the pack on his desk. He was a well-built man, still slim, with close-cropped graying hair and a salt-and-pepper beard. He had quick, deep blue eyes, a sensuous mouth, and a nose like the beak of a Caspian eagle. Like most people in Israel over forty Uzi Yadin had a story.

In 1944, aged sixteen, he had joined the Soviet partisans in his hometown of Korno near the Baltic. After the liberation of Vilna in the early days of 1945, he had embarked alone on a remarkable journey. Begging lifts on haycarts and the odd truck, but mainly walking, he had made his way down the length of Poland and into Rumania. When he reached Bucharest in May, he learned that the war was over. He then walked through Hungary, into Yugoslavia, across the Julian Alps, and down into Italy, where he arrived in Bologna in September. On the first day of November 1945, Uzi Yadin and twelve other Jewish youngsters sailed for Palestine out of the Italian port of Bari. After two weeks they disembarked in Haifa at the dead of night, avoiding British land and sea patrols. Eight years later Yadin joined the tiny, newly formed police force.

Now in Jerusalem Yadin was the man responsible for the city's security. As the chief superintendent of police, he had under his command four hundred policemen, including Mahleket-Hachhabala, the Jerusalem bomb squad. Uzi Yadin had another role: he was the chief of Jerusalem's volunteer civil guard. Of his six desk telephones, two were direct links to a network which, within thirty minutes, could mobilize four thousand armed men and women.

Yadin chewed the tip of his cigar. Middle age had not slowed him up; he still played football with the police 'D' team and swam regularly with his grandchildren when they camped together in the Galilee or Eilat. He liked to come in early on the *Shabbat,* to catch up on some of the paperwork. His office was quiet — its two large windows looked out on to a sunny courtyard now full of blue-and-white police cars and vans. Shelves behind Yadin's desk were crammed with trophies, cups, and medals; there was a board mounted with the insignia of visiting police chiefs and a signed photograph from the president of Israel. Maps on the walls showed the city of Jerusalem, its environs, and the famous straggling "green line," which prior to 1967 had been the country's border with Jordan.

Uzi Yadin finished his coffee and stubbed out the cigar. He was dressed in light green khaki trousers and shirt and a blue woollen pullover with the green epaulets and pips of a chief superintendent. He picked up a file from his in-tray. It was the report of an Arab gasoline bomb attack two days ago on a bus in a northern suburb of Jerusalem. Ten people had been badly burned in the incident. Yadin shook his head: the *fedayeen* made sure that Israeli vigilance in Jerusalem was never relaxed. A Molotov cocktail or incendiary in the ancient city of David guaranteed the terrorists instant publicity around the world. He flicked through the file, making notes. The door opened and his new secretary reappeared with a sheet of paper. She colored slightly under his appreciative gaze, then placed the document before him before retreating, her hips swinging. Yadin took a deep breath. The kind of girls they were recruiting nowadays were a lot different from what they used to be. He reached into a drawer for a package of cigarettes and sliced them open across the top with his thumbnail. He took the smoke gratefully into his lungs. It was difficult enough to work on the *Shabbat* without added distractions. He smiled to himself. In spring it was always the same, always had been, even all those years ago in Korno. He forced himself to study the memo. It was a current position update, produced by a unit along the corridor.

The night before two Arabs had knifed each other to death on Salah Ed Din, beside Herod's Gate; there had been a pile-up involving six vehicles on Yafo, near the Energy Ministry: traffic had been blocked for three hours but was now free. A group called Independent Children of Israel were planning a march in three hours through the center of Jerusalem to the Knesset to protest against Israeli concessions to the Syrians. Yadin sighed. There would be the usual TV coverage, press photographers, and fringe politicians. As a policeman he had never held

political views beyond the obvious one, which was Israel's right to exist
— and that was not so much political as divine. The organizers had
chosen the *Shabbat* as their day to emphasize the sacrilege they now
insisted their government was performing. Traffic on the Sabbath would
be light, disturbance minimal, the key people on the ground in control.

Yadin sucked the very last bit of smoke from his cigarette before
grinding it out in the ashtray. He reached to his tray for the next file
and glanced at the wall clock. He wanted to be home by midday —
his eldest son, a captain in the army, and his wife and children were
coming from Ashdod for the day.

As he scrutinized the contents of the file the second-hand of the clock
swept through 7:00.

They drove down the narrow, twisting road, past the dairy, through
high cypresses. Some children in a playground climbed in and out of
the painted shell of an old car.

"Tell me," said Matt. "A man like Galatti or Deutsch. He's an old
man now — many people would say that he's had to live with himself
for forty years, that that is punishment enough. Are you not risking
being guilty of revenge?"

"I live with the old-fashioned notion of justice and retribution,"
Yanni replied. "You could leave any criminal at large and say that he
has to live with himself as punishment."

They drove down another hill.

"Yes, but normally we jail people, even kill them as a deterrent, as
an example to others," Matt said. "In this case, surely the crimes, hideous though they are, are unlikely to be repeated?"

"My friend," said Yanni, "I am a Jew. In the last century, my ancestors, merchants near Kiev, came to believe that anti-Semitism was an
incurable disease. That is why they and countless thousands of others
began a move to come to this country, Eretz Israel." They had swung
on to the highway. "Today you only have to look at a map or read a
paper to realize that anti-Semitism, or more particularly anti-Jewism,
is flourishing," Yanni said. "Deutsch became Galatti by courtesy of the
Roman Catholic Church, who shipped him through Naples to Buenos
Aires. You might say, 'Ah, but that was a long time ago, there were
special circumstances and times have changed.' Have they? Have they
changed at all?" He laughed bitterly. "Even today the Vatican State does

not recognize the existence of the State of Israel," he said. "We must continue to bring animals like Deutsch to trial in Israel, publicly enumerating their terrible crimes, making sure the world never forgets: it is the only effective countermeasure to the anti-Semitism that is always there, bubbling away just beneath the surface. That, my friend, is my belief."

Matt looked at the face, hard in profile. Yanni lifted a finger from the wheel and pointed.

"Mevasseret," he said.

He wanted to look his best. Meticulously he had shaved and then dressed in the clothes he had so carefully kept: a brightly patterned shirt with short sleeves, light gray slacks with a sharp crease, and a pair of open-toed, brown leather sandals. The significance of the clothes could be known only to him: the last time he had worn them was exactly this day, a year ago, when he had rushed northward to the hospital in Haifa like a crazy man.

Placing the *kipa* on his crown he walked into the garden. The sun's heat on his face was good. He had brought his prayer shawl and the Talmud with him. For ten minutes Dr. Shenlavi prayed intently, not just for himself but for all men. Then he returned indoors and made his way down the wooden steps.

Dr. Shenlavi opened the trunk of the Volvo and looked at the squat, yellow cylinder sitting there harmlessly. He licked his lips as he threaded out the bolts with his fingers, then lifted the flat lid. The small detonator lay in its bed of explosives, connected to the solenoid. A further wire ran up to its antenna, the heater in the car's rear window. Beside the yellow cylinder a small nine-volt battery sat in a clip.

It took ten minutes to insert and lock home the eight bolts that kept the tamper lid tightly in place. Dr. Shenlavi put down the shining vise grips and checked the left-hand side of the trunk; there a small black box was firmly taped to the chassis. A thin wire ran from it and neatly joined the wire that connected the radio receiver to the Volvo's back window. The black box contained a conventional multiplexer, a further radio device, tuned to respond to a hand-held transmitter with a range of four miles. The multiplexer's signal was arranged, when decoded, to cut across the FM wave radio signal and disrupt it. Such disruption would open the solenoid immediately. When that occurred, the tiny nine-volt battery would energize the detonator and explosion would be achieved.

He narrowed his eyes as he opened the garage door. Far below Mevasseret the traffic hummed on the four-lane highway. He walked six paces to the edge of the garden and breathed in deeply the sweet scent of coriander wafting down the hill and into the valley.

For some moments he stood looking into the middle distance, then with a sigh he got into the Volvo. He looked at his watch; it was nearly eight-thirty. Normally the drive to Jerusalem would take less than fifteen minutes, but today he would drive with exceptional care. He locked the garage door and drove down from the modest, split-level house.

Keeping in to the extreme right-hand side, he descended the hill from Mevasseret and joined the motorway to Jerusalem. Crawling at no more than twenty, the green Volvo made its way down into the valley, then up the final, winding hill to the gates of the ancient, hilltop city.

He stopped at lights. There was a gas station to the left, closed for the *Shabbat*. The peace radiating from him was almost palpable. His smiling face glowed with a happiness he had nearly forgotten, a veil of serenity enveloping him. He wanted to shout for joy. Levi was coming home!

The lights changed and he drove straight on. At the next intersection he swung right; a taxi caught behind him honked impatiently, then pulled out and screeched past. He was now sweeping downhill past a public park with well-trimmed lawns and shrubbery rising back and up the high mount behind. The road climbed again. He kept to the right. At the junction of Ruppin and Eli'ezer Kaplan the lights were red once more. He began to frown. Tour buses were pulled in beside the Israel Museum. The light changed and he turned.

The Knesset, squat and imposing, appeared a hundred yards to his right. Dr. Shenlavi pulled the Volvo up to the curb behind another car. Leaning forward, he found two wires beneath the dashboard; he first crossed them, then twisted them around each other. He got out of the car, closed the door gently, and then locked it. The guard dogs inside the perimeter fence snarled and barked as they had done a week before. His face creased in concern, Dr. Shenlavi walked quickly uphill and into James de Rothschild. A guard stepped out of the blockhouse.

"*Shalom*," said Dr. Shenlavi.

"*Boker tov.*"

The guard wore a white belt; his hand rested lightly on his gun holster.

"*Sliha*," said Dr. Shenlavi, "but the Knesset — it is open today?"

The guard shook his head.

"Today is the *Shabbat,* my friend," he said patiently. He looked at the worried face. "Nothing is open today."

"But the museum is open," said the slight man, looking downhill as another busload of tourists arrived.

The guard exchanged glances with his colleague in the blockhouse.

"So the museum is open." He shrugged. "Go see the museum. To-morrow come back and see the Knesset." He walked back into the guard post. "That's a clever one!" he said to the other guard. "Look at his face — if you shook his head it would sound like shekels in an empty tin."

The two guards laughed outright. The man outside opened his mouth to say something, then he turned and slowly made his way back down the hill. The shrubbery on the grounds of the parliament building concealed his further progress from the guards in their hut.

Without breaking his stride he kept walking, downhill. The sun was gaining heat with every minute.

At the intersection of Ramban and Ibn Shaprut streets he hailed a taxi. Within ten minutes he was back in the garage at Mevasseret.

His heart thudding, he stood on a chair and checked the dials of the FM radio transmitter. Biting his lip, he turned it on. Its dials quivered as the frequency beamed out through the rooftop aerial into the atmosphere and found its receiver seven miles away. Trembling, he got down. The nuclear device was armed. Between it and detonation there was now only the constant signal from the shortwave radio transmitter keeping the solonoid closed.

He picked up a briefcase and left by the back door, locking it with shaking hands. Down on the road the taxi stood waiting.

"*Shalom, Doktor!*"

Dr. Shenlavi blinked.

"*Shalom, Doktor!*"

Dr. Shenlavi focused on where the voice came from. Beside the taxi a young Arab sat astride a donkey. He waved up, his teeth sparkling in his dark face. Dr. Shenlavi smiled slightly and raised his hand. It was the boy from the village who did his garden. The boy kicked the donkey with his bare heels and they trotted uphill.

Like someone in a dream, Dr. Shenlavi walked down the path. At the gate he paused. For a long moment he looked back at the tidy dwelling with its neat garden of flowers and vegetables, its lawn, and its spreading fig tree. The sun was hot now; its heat bounced from the two solar panels on the roof and on the slim, silver radio aerial.

"*Yerushalyim?*" queried the driver.

"*Yerushalyim,*" replied Dr. Shenlavi.

The blue-and-white Ford Sierra sat patiently behind the bus. At the wheel police sergeant Abraham Lipstein drummed his fingers on the outside of the door while beside him Chaim Kessler, also a sergeant, leaned back in his seat and stretched. Lipstein glanced at his gold watch. Their tour of area number five, which included all the government buildings and the Knesset itself, would be routine for at least another hour. Some fringe group were marching through Jerusalem and up to the Knesset around ten. Lipstein yawned. With luck they would disperse after about an hour, the time it usually took for the speeches. He slowed down a bit to allow the exhaust from the bus to miss him. It was a glorious day; the flowerbeds and lawns had a freshness about them which in Israel lasted only for a few weeks. Soon the same sun that parched the Negev would turn the clay into a hard caked slab. People were strolling in the park, enjoying the day of rest, women pushed baby carriages, children kicked a ball with their father.

As the bus turned left for the museum, Lipstein swung the patrol car to the right. Chaim Kessler's eyes took in groups of children lined up for admittance, two men and a woman jogging toward the Knesset, and three or four cars parked outside its perimeter fence. From habit, the fingers of his left hand went underneath his seat, where they felt the cold steel of the Uzi.

Now they were at the blockhouse on James de Rothschild.

"Everything okay?" Lipstein asked the guards.

"*Beseder,*" they called back, "okay."

The barrier went up and Lipstein took the car up to the hilltop, empty of cars. There was a high steel gate on electronic rollers, which allowed civil servants and MPs into the Knesset parking lot. The two policemen could see half a dozen cars inside despite its being Saturday morning.

"Someone else has to work today as well," said Lipstein as they drove downhill, past the blockhouse. Kessler unhooked the hand microphone of their Motorola radio unit.

"Car eleven to base, over," he said.

A mile and a half to the east, in the basement of the Russian compound, Golda Levy, a girl of twenty, her hair in a ponytail, punched the illuminated key to take the call.

"*Shalom,* car eleven," she said.

Golda Levy was one of eighteen telephone operators who, on a shift system, maintain the communications center of the Jerusalem police force around the clock.

"We're just leaving the Knesset," came Kessler's voice. "Everything is A-okay."

"*Toda raba,* car eleven," said Golda Levy. "Thank you."

She took her pen and logged the call. It was two minutes before nine o'clock.

Up the steeply winding hill and into the township of Mevasseret, the Tel Aviv–Jerusalem highway was far below them, undulating through the Judaean foothills like a black adder weaving over rocks.

Matt looked at houses, tastefully built of Jerusalem stone, some with wooden beams, all of them with cheerful gardens; the Israeli looked at the Hebrew street names. They climbed higher. Eventually they stopped outside a split-level house, its low gates partially open. Matt saw a short driveway, neat lawns, and a garden devoted to vegetables and fruit trees rising behind the house.

The two men got out and walked toward the front door. Matt saw the Mossad agent transfer his Beretta from its holster to the small of his back.

"*Shalom!*"

They whirled.

A smiling face was looking out at them from a row of raspberries.

"*Shalom,*" replied Yanni Israel, cautiously bringing his hand away from the gun. "This is Dr. Shenlavi's house?"

The Arab boy nodded vigorously, his teeth sparkling in the sunshine.

There was another movement and the two men spun again as a white-faced donkey poked his head through the bushes. He saw the two men and began to bray loudly.

"*Ikhras ya abba!*" cried the boy, laughing, and he slapped the animal on the neck. "Shut up, you old fool!"

Matt let out a long breath. The Israeli was questioning the boy, who pointed down the road into the valley, the way they had just come.

"It seems we have just missed him," Yanni said eventually. "He left less than thirty minutes ago in a taxi; the boy thinks they drove toward Jerusalem."

He turned again to the young Arab.

"He says he doesn't know when he'll be back," explained Yanni. "He says the *doktor* works far away and often does not come home for weeks. However, before he goes away like that he normally pays him *kesef*, money to look after the garden. This time he paid nothing, so the boy thinks that he'll be back."

Matt scratched his head.

"So what do we do? Wait?" he asked.

Yanni was looking up at the house.

"Perhaps as we wait," he said, "we can also learn."

He took out his wallet and gave the boy some money, patting him on the back. Delighted, the young Arab grabbed his donkey and was soon kicking him down the road.

"I've just given him the day off," Yanni said.

The front door of the house was locked, as was the garage. They tried all the front downstairs windows without success. They made their way up smooth paving stones and around the back. There was a glass-fronted door leading to a kitchen. It was locked. Matt peered in and saw a tidy table with a single vase of flowers at its center. There was a small refrigerator, chairs neatly in their place, a bare red-and-white checked tablecloth.

"Locked," murmured Israel as he pressed the door.

They moved farther along the patio, hidden from the road. The sun beat down warmly. In the hillside garden there were well-tended rows of cucumbers, tomatoes, and peppers; there were pomegranates, some vines, and a prosperous fig tree with thick boughs and large green, glossy leaves. A white bench sat beneath it. They came to a small window of frosted glass; its upper part was open an inch for ventilation, held in place by a thin, rigid arm with holes that slotted onto an upright steel pin. Matt took out a pen and poked it up into the arm. He shoved, and the tiny window opened outward. Even so the opening was barely nine inches by eight.

"Do you have a knife?" he asked.

The Israeli handed him an open penknife. There were two small top hinges, each held in place by three countersunk screws. By brute force Matt loosened them until at last he was able to lift the small window out. He jumped up and knelt on the ledge. He was looking into a toilet. Getting one arm and most of one shoulder in, he could lean down and open the catch of the larger window below.

"Be my guest," he said, standing back.

The smaller man eased himself through without difficulty. A minute later they were both standing in the kitchen.

"What are we looking for?" Matt asked.

"I'm not sure," Yanni replied. "There's a radio antenna on the roof — I saw it when we came in. It's not what you see on every house. Let's find it — maybe Dr. Shenlavi is in radio contact."

Matt went to the first door. It was a child's bedroom, a girl's. There were two unmade beds on which a number of dresses were laid out. Numerous stuffed animals, games, and other toys littered the floor. On the walls were pictures of pop stars and a king-size Snoopy poster saying "I love you so much, it hurts." Dust covered everything and could be seen thick in the air in the bright shafts of sunlight beaming through.

"Have a look at this," Matt said.

The Mossad man came, then took a deep breath.

"They've been dead a year," he said grimly. "He's left their room untouched."

The next bedroom was larger. At its center was a large double bed with items of women's clothing, blouses, some underwear, a handbag. There was an open wardrobe, crammed full of dresses. Beside the bed lay an opened book and next to it a vase of withered stems that had once been flowers. As in the room next door, dust covered everything. To one side was a busy dressing-table, the face of its mirror obscured by dust. There were silver brushes, an open jewelry box, a variety of bottles and jars, and a large color photograph in a silver frame which showed a happy family picnic underneath the fig-tree outside.

"It's all preserved," said Yanni.

"The man's living in the past," said Matt.

The final bedroom was different: it was ordered, the narrow bed carefully made. On the walls hung some pop posters, a framed photograph of a group of uniformed youngsters, and a miniature regimental flag. The surface tops were clean; fresh flowers stood in a vase. Matt opened a wardrobe: some drip-dry shirts hung beside a light khaki uniform.

"The son?" asked Matt.

Yanni inclined his head once.

The rest of the house yielded nothing. Back in the kitchen the remaining inside door was locked.

"It must lead down to the garage," Matt said trying the handle. Unlike the other lightly paneled doors of the house, this was made of heavy wood. There was a chrome knob and an inset, mortised lock. Yanni put his weight to it.

"We need a lever," he said.

They both searched the kitchen. Yanni found a long metal skewer and worked it in between the door rim and frame. He leaned on it and the light utensil bent like plastic.

"Just a minute."

Matt went outside and shortly returned with a thin-bladed garden spade.

"It's going to make one hell of a mess," he said.

"Go ahead," said the Israeli.

There was a loud splintering of wood as Matt leaned on the spade, up near its head, then with a crack the lock burst from its keeper in the doorframe.

The two men looked at the almost vertical wooden steps. Reaching for his Beretta and holding it in his right hand, Yanni led the way down into Dr. Shenlavi's garage.

The sun on his bare head was intense. He had paid off the taxi at the gates of Jerusalem. Now he plodded eastward on Ramban, a wide, tree-lined avenue, the briefcase clutched tightly under his arm. He had an all-consuming desire to be reunited with the last remaining person that he loved. What better day to achieve everything that he could wish?

There was little traffic on the lovely *Shabbat* morning — a few tourists on the move, police patrol cars on their routine rounds. The Sabbath begins at sunset on Friday and ends with darkness on Saturday. In east Jerusalem there would be more activity as the largely Arab population ignored the holy day of the Yehuda.

He only gradually became aware of the commotion up ahead — it was the noise that eventually forced him to focus. He was nearly at the intersection of Ramban with Ha Melech George and Karen HaYessod. Bright sunlight danced from the roofs of the police Sierras and the helmets of the motorcycle outriders who were slowly turning into Ramban at the head of a noisy, swelling crowd. Between the police and the march he could see two open-topped jeeps filled with photographers and TV cameramen. Dr. Shenlavi stood staring as the first of the police escort went by. Then he saw the marchers. The ones in front held a long red banner, which spanned the road. It was in English and read: "Independent Children of Israel say No to Sellout."

Numerous other placards denounced the government. But it was the marchers themselves that he was staring at. Age-wise there was a complete cross-section, from white-haired grandmothers to babies in strollers. There was a pulsing, carnival atmosphere and much laughter; many of the crowd waved to the lone roadside spectator.

"*Tarvitanu!*" a man cried. "Come and join us! We are marching to the Knesset." The marching man held two little boys, one by each hand. The children wore small white *kipot* and smiled at Dr. Shenlavi, their dark eyes big and round.

"*Tarvitanu!*" they chorused, looking back.

As the last of the crowd passed by, Dr. Shenlavi could hear the spirited music of a pipe band striking up in their midst. With a sigh he looked at his watch — in five minutes it would be ten o'clock. Crossing the wide intersection he continued east on Gershun Agrun.

In ten minutes he would reach the ancient walled city.

As the fluorescent lights snapped on, Matt's eyes took in the low, cluttered garage. To the right was the space for a car and double doors out. A car wheel lay propped beside an oxyacetylene metal-cutting device. There were two cylindrical gas tubes to fuel the metal cutter, an open cardboard box containing what looked like half a dozen large Thermos flasks, and three twelve-volt car batteries, stacked one on top of the other. To the left, right along the back wall, was a tidy wooden workbench with a shelf above it. There were two wooden stools and a small electric heater. Matt's eye went to a second, higher shelf, built in the left-hand, near corner. He peered closer.

"Here's your radio," he said to the Israeli.

A square, black radio transmitter, a red light beaming from it, sat on the shelf; it had two front white dials with needles that quivered vertically upright and a row of switches, the first of them marked "Off/On."

"If it's a house-to-car radio," Matt said, "where's the mike?"

His hand went to the first switch.

"Better not," Yanni said. He looked down the workbench. "Do you smell something?" he asked.

On the wall behind the bench and under the upper shelf were neat rows of instruments ranging from surgical stainless steel to heavy mechanical. There was a row of clean glass beakers and pipettes, a measuring scales, a microscope, a powerful lamp, and, at the very end, a heavy lead-lined apron. A small tin contained scraps of recently clipped copper wire ends. Matt sat on a stool and ran his hands underneath the bench; the small drawers slid smoothly out. The Israeli was bending down to a small cubby hole, beneath the bench at the far end. He took a screwdriver from the wall rack and prised it open. He removed a large tin to the bench and opened it. There was an inch of greasy paraffin wax on its bottom. A second, smaller tin contained white powder. He frowned, wet his finger, and dipped it in the tin, then dabbed his tongue.

"Picric acid," he said.

At the base of the cubby hole, right at its back, was a small, cardboard box. Yanni reached and took it out. The scraps of plastic explosive lay there like strips of glazier's putty.

"Le'azazel!" swore Yanni. "I knew I'd smelled it!"

"Plastic explosive?" asked Matt.

The Israeli nodded grimly.

"There's a tin full of fresh wire cuttings on the bench," Matt said.

The two men's eyes met.

"Christ," said Matt softly.

Yanni Israel took the wooden steps in two strides. From the silence of the garage Matt could hear him dialing.

*   *   *

begins at sunset on Friday and ends with darkness on Saturday. In east Jerusalem there would be more activity as the largely Arab population ignored the holy day of the Yehuda.

He only gradually became aware of the commotion up ahead — it was the noise that eventually forced him to focus. He was nearly at the intersection of Ramban with Ha Melech George and Karen HaYessod. Bright sunlight danced from the roofs of the police Sierras and the helmets of the motorcycle outriders who were slowly turning into Ramban at the head of a noisy, swelling crowd. Between the police and the march he could see two open-topped jeeps filled with photographers and TV cameramen. Dr. Shenlavi stood staring as the first of the police escort went by. Then he saw the marchers. The ones in front held a long red banner, which spanned the road. It was in English and read: "Independent Children of Israel say No to Sellout."

Numerous other placards denounced the government. But it was the marchers themselves that he was staring at. Age-wise there was a complete cross-section, from white-haired grandmothers to babies in strollers. There was a pulsing, carnival atmosphere and much laughter; many of the crowd waved to the lone roadside spectator.

"Tarvitanu!" a man cried. "Come and join us! We are marching to the Knesset." The marching man held two little boys, one by each hand. The children wore small white *kipot* and smiled at Dr. Shenlavi, their dark eyes big and round.

"Tarvitanu!" they chorused, looking back.

As the last of the crowd passed by, Dr. Shenlavi could hear the spirited music of a pipe band striking up in their midst. With a sigh he looked at his watch — in five minutes it would be ten o'clock. Crossing the wide intersection he continued east on Gershun Agrun.

In ten minutes he would reach the ancient walled city.

As the fluorescent lights snapped on, Matt's eyes took in the low, cluttered garage. To the right was the space for a car and double doors out. A car wheel lay propped beside an oxyacetylene metal-cutting device. There were two cylindrical gas tubes to fuel the metal cutter, an open cardboard box containing what looked like half a dozen large Thermos flasks, and three twelve-volt car batteries, stacked one on top of the other. To the left, right along the back wall, was a tidy wooden workbench with a shelf above it. There were two wooden stools and a small electric heater. Matt's eye went to a second, higher shelf, built in the left-hand, near corner. He peered closer.

"Here's your radio," he said to the Israeli.

A square, black radio transmitter, a red light beaming from it, sat on the shelf; it had two front white dials with needles that quivered vertically upright and a row of switches, the first of them marked "Off/ On."

"If it's a house-to-car radio," Matt said, "where's the mike?"

His hand went to the first switch.

"Better not," Yanni said. He looked down the workbench. "Do you smell something?" he asked.

On the wall behind the bench and under the upper shelf were neat rows of instruments ranging from surgical stainless steel to heavy mechanical. There was a row of clean glass beakers and pipettes, a measuring scales, a microscope, a powerful lamp, and, at the very end, a heavy lead-lined apron. A small tin contained scraps of recently clipped copper wire ends. Matt sat on a stool and ran his hands underneath the bench; the small drawers slid smoothly out. The Israeli was bending down to a small cubby hole, beneath the bench at the far end. He took a screwdriver from the wall rack and prised it open. He removed a large tin to the bench and opened it. There was an inch of greasy paraffin wax on its bottom. A second, smaller tin contained white powder. He frowned, wet his finger, and dipped it in the tin, then dabbed his tongue.

"Picric acid," he said.

At the base of the cubby hole, right at its back, was a small, cardboard box. Yanni reached and took it out. The scraps of plastic explosive lay there like strips of glazier's putty.

"*Le'azazel!*" swore Yanni. "I knew I'd smelled it!"

"Plastic explosive?" asked Matt.

The Israeli nodded grimly.

"There's a tin full of fresh wire cuttings on the bench," Matt said.

The two men's eyes met.

"Christ," said Matt softly.

Yanni Israel took the wooden steps in two strides. From the silence of the garage Matt could hear him dialing.

*   *   *

In the basement of the Russian compound, Golda Levy hit the button to take the call.

"Jerusalem police, *shalom,*" she said. She listened to the caller, then said, "Just a minute," as she put him on hold. She logged the call at ten twenty-five, then punched out an internal number. Two floors above her, Inspector Yoram Tamir, an undercover policeman specializing in security, put down the magazine he had been reading, swung his feet off the desk, and picked up his phone.

"*Beseder,*" he said, "put him through."

For thirty seconds Tamir listened to the man on the other end, then he grabbed a pen and began writing. A colleague on the same duty roster wandered into the office and began to joke about something; Tamir waved him away. "I'm putting you on hold," he said; "don't go," then he pressed out another number.

Uzi Yadin had just finished his third coffee of the morning when the phone rang. He thought it might be his wife.

"Yes, Tamir?" he said.

As the police inspector spoke, Yadin sat upright, his body suddenly on alert.

"All right," he said. "Just give me the names again." He tore a fresh page from a pad and wrote Yanni Israel's name on it, then Yoseph Shenlavi's. "Okay," he said to Tamir, "keep him on hold, then get on to Mahleket-Hachabala. Tell them we think we have a car bomb, maybe a big one; get a team in if they're not already here and tell them to stand by. See if the Signal Corps can't find that radio frequency. I want someone from Forensic and a patrol car out in Mevasseret immediately. Are you tracing the car? Good."

Cutting off Tamir, Uzi Yadin picked up another phone, a direct outside line, and dialed a number.

Beside the basement communication center in the Russian compound, Wolf Bernstein, a police trainee in jeans and a T-shirt, tapped the information into the on-line computer. He watched the screen flash as it accessed the IBM mainframe, two miles away in national police headquarters on Derech Shechem. Stored in the memory of the giant computer are the personal details of every man, woman, and child who are citizens of Israel, cross-referenced where appropriate to each and every motor vehicle licensed by the state.

It took less than a minute to acquire the information requested by Inspector Tamir.

Wolf Bernstein picked up his phone.

"Its a Volvo 340 D," said Inspector Tamir, "color green. We've put out a general alert on all wavelengths."

Uzi Yadin nodded. The Jerusalem police headquarters had the capacity to broadcast simultaneously on a number of frequencies, right across the country. Within five minutes, every on-duty police officer in Israel would be on the lookout for the green Volvo.

"Is your caller still there?" asked Yadin.

"Yes," confirmed Tamir.

"Put him through," the chief superintendent said. A minute earlier his private line had rung back with the information on Yanni Israel.

"*Shalom*," said Yadin as the call was transferred.

"*Shalom, boker tov.*"

"It looks as if we have a problem," Yadin said.

"It looks that way," Yanni agreed. "There are also other aspects to this which are worrying."

"I see," Yadin said. The presence of the Mossad agent in Mevasseret could mean anything. "We know the car is a Volvo 340 D," Yadin said. "Do you have any way of confirming that it's the car he's using?"

The chief superintendent heard Yanni speak to someone else.

"Yes, we think it is a Volvo," said Yanni, returning to the phone; "we've got the spare wheel here."

"Good," Yadin said. "Can you stay out there for the moment? Our forensic team is on its way."

"*Beseder,*" said Yanni.

Uzi Yadin reached again for his private line. His next call was to his wife, explaining why he might be late for their *Shabbat* lunch.

Along the corridor from the communications center in the Jerusalem police headquarters is a steel door with two mortise locks. The keys to this room are carried only by members of Mahleket-Hachabala, the Jerusalem bomb squad. Inside, the room is split into two by free-standing shelves that display with grim pertinence the reason for Mahleket-Hachabala's existence. Here are all the devices the bomb squad got to and defused: cans, bottles, T-end steel pipes, transistor radios, all wired and primed in their day to cause devastation; there are children's toys, a smiling miniature Buddha, even a full-size Katushkah rocket.

Now a copper shell casing held the door open as two members of the bomb squad sat back in easy chairs and drank Coke from cans.

"*Hara,*" said one of them, "and I had hoped we might have a quiet day." He was blond with blue eyes, slightly but competently built; he wore blue denim jeans, sneakers, and a white T-shirt.

His companion, who was dark, sallow, and had an ample paunch, shrugged. "That's life," he said. His name was Amos Suchovolsky and his parents had come to the new land from a dark and wet village in Poland where his ancestors had lived on and off in terror for two hundred years. The other man's name was Ben Joel. His parents had come from England in 1952.

Ben Joel drained his Coke and tossed the empty can accurately into a bin at the other side of the room.

"Has there been a telephoned warning?" he asked.

Suchovolosky shrugged again. "I expect we'll hear shortly," he said. "Uzi has taken charge."

Joel made a face that showed he was impressed. The chief superintendent had come up through the ranks and had himself once been with Mahleket-Hachabala.

"Forensic left in a cloud of dust for Mevasseret just two minutes ago," Suchovolsky said. "And there's a rumor that Shin Beth are involved."

Joel stretched in his chair, relaxing every muscle, dispersing the inevitable tension. It was the waiting that was always the worst, the waiting for the warning, the waiting until the bomb had been found, for the area to be evacuated. Then all the nerve ends in the body started a slow adrenaline charge, which would bring them to peak when they were needed.

They had skills enjoyed by few men — skill, and pure, ice cool. When it came down to the line, one of them would be out there, dead center, totally alone in a helmet of reinforced steel, softly speaking into the microphone incorporated within the helmet, describing to his distant colleagues each minute step as the secrets of the terrorists' explosive device were agonizingly dissected. It was the ultimate test of raw nerve. No actor, no athlete, no philosopher could quite know the unique experience in the solitary handling of the dividing line between one's own vigorous, healthy life and a bottomless eternity. It was a high. Afterward it was all downhill: a limp anticlimax and the dull realization that there would be a next time, and a next.

Ben Joel twisted his neck around and let his shoulders sag. By unspoken agreement, it was his turn next. He held his hand out flat in front of him. It was rock steady.

With a screech of rubber the Sierra pulled up in front of the split-level house in Mevasseret and a man with very black hair, a voluminous black beard, and very white skin jumped out. Jean-Claude Perin had been brought up on the family vineyard that swept down from the chalky hills of Loupiac to the sandy banks of the Garonne. From the Perin family château you could, on a good day, see across Sauternes to the modest rise which is Château d'Yquem. One Saturday, when he was twenty-two, Jean-Claude Perin had walked out of the house and gone to Israel. He had never returned. Now head of the Forensic Department of the Jerusalem police, his office was located in a long, low building, one of twelve, in the courtyard behind the main building in Migrash Harussim.

Perin ran up the path of the Mevasseret house, followed by his assistant, carrying a large box, and the police driver. The front door opened and Perin was ushered in by a man in an open-necked shirt.

"*Shalom,*" said Yanni, "you didn't waste any time."

"Where do we start?" asked Perin. He spoke very rapidly. "Who's he?"

"He is okay," Yanni said as Matt nodded to the bearded man.

Perin shrugged and followed the two men down the steps to the garage. His assistant brought the large box. It contained state-of-the-art equipment for the primary analysis and identification of almost any substance. There was also a portable keyboard and modem to feed the on-site information back into the mainframe computer in national police headquarters.

"What does this guy do?" said Perin as his eyes took in the workbench.

"He's a nuclear physicist," Yanni replied.

"*Oh là là,*" said Perin as he began to set up his equipment.

For the second time that morning police sergeants Kessler and Lipstein drove up the hill toward Qiryat Ben Gurion, the mountaintop plateau that is the home of the Knesset. Unlike their first tour, however, this time the policemen sat upright, their intelligent eyes scanning every parked or moving car. They had already examined two parked Volvos and stopped a third: the Arab who was making his way from Shoresh to Jericho had been highly indignant.

Abraham Lipstein now approached the Knesset from the west on Wolfsohn Avenue; the eastern side of the hill was blocked solid with the marchers who would shortly converge on the road leading to the parliament building. Lipstein swung onto Eli'ezer Kaplan. At the entrance to James de Rothschild, extra police had erected crowd barriers to prevent the march from getting anywhere near the Knesset. A mobile TV unit was in place and technicians prepared to take footage of the march, which had not yet come into view.

"Damned journalists," said Lipstein. "They make a mountain out of a pimple on your ass."

His companion, Sergeant Kessler, nodded and smiled. They were stopped at the entrance to James de Rothschild up which they had earlier driven. A uniformed policeman came over.

"You want to go up?" he asked. "We can take down the barriers."

Lipstein looked at Kessler. They shook their heads.

Although procedure dictated that they should go up to the very gates of the Knesset, there was hardly much point as they had done so just over an hour before.

"*Toda raba,*" Lipstein said, "it's not necessary." He moved the car away. "Enjoy the speeches," he said to the policeman.

"Ten fifty-two," said Kessler, reaching for the mike of the radio. "*Shalom,* base, over."

They were driving downhill, the Knesset on their left, toward the junction of Kaplan and Ruppin. The marchers were still not in sight. There was a line of parked cars. They approached the busy Israel Museum.

"*Shalom,*" came Gold Levy's voice in the Russian compound.

"We're leaving the Knesset," Kessler said. "Everything is A——"

He put out his hand to save himself as the Sierra stopped dead. He looked at Lipstein, who was pointing. A green Volvo 340 stood at the curb, one in a line of cars. Two fair-haired, sunburned girls in shorts were standing beside the car — one was leaning against it. The policemen jumped out; Lipstein held a notebook into which he had written the registration number that had been broadcast all over Israel. They both unholstered their Berettas. Lipstein's mouth went dry as he read the yellow rear license plate. The girl who was leaning against the Volvo clapped her hand over her mouth and grabbed her friend as the two policemen approached, guns at the ready.

"Put your hands slowly in the air," Lipstein ordered.

The other girl began to scream. Lipstein glanced across at Kessler and nodded. Kessler ran back to the car. The girl was still screaming.

"I'm still here, car eleven," came the voice of Golda Levy over the radio. "Who's screaming?"

"Golda," said Kessler breathlessly, "tell the boss we've found it."

Uzi Yadin took the stone steps six at a time. Out in the sunny court-yard a large blue-and-white Ford Thames van with a specially incorpo-rated bubble roof was waiting, its engine running.

"*Aharai!*" cried Yadin, and the heavy van lurched out under the cen-tral stone arch, past the manned guardpost and onto Yafo Road, which runs west. Yadin glanced around him. The van was being driven by a sergeant who doubled as an assistant in the basement armory. In the back, running the full length of one side of the van, were six intercon-necting switchboards, fully compatible and interchangeable with the communications center at police headquarters. Run from powerful bat-teries and a special generator, the entire telecommunications network of the Jerusalem police, including telex, radio, and computer links, could be transferred within minutes to the back of this van. In this instance just one switchboard was manned by a girl, her hair gathered in a brown ponytail. She had just been transferred to the van by Inspector Yoram Tamir, who now sat between Uzi Yadin and the driver. Yadin grinned at her.

"*Shalom,* Golda," he said.

"*Shalom,*" said Golda Levy with a smile.

The driver put on the siren as they drove up the middle of Yafo.

"Fill me in," Yadin ordered.

"We've told the prime minister's office," Tamir said. "The man him-self is working there right now and has asked to be kept informed. There's obviously no danger at that range, but just in case . . ."

Yadin nodded his understanding.

"The bomb squad is on its way; they're probably there by now."

"Who'll be handling it?"

"Joel and Sucholovsky."

Yadin nodded again, this time his approval.

"There's a fucking march up there," he said, "and I suppose crews from every TV station in the Middle East. What are we doing?"

"The marchers have been stopped at Ruppin, beside the museum," Tamir said. "They think it's a ruse to keep them away from the Knesset. We've explained that we'll let them through when the car is safe."

Uzi Yadin shook his head. Whoever had planted the bomb, if bomb it was, clearly knew about the march and the publicity it would draw. Jerusalem would once again be world news; that night the *fedayeen* would be rubbing their hands in glee.

"Perin is out in Mevasseret right now," Tamir continued. "He is to come through here directly if he finds anything."

"Who is this Shenlavi?" Yadin asked.

The van had careered onto Herzel Avenue, its rubber mudguard scraping the road.

"I have two men digging for every piece of information that can be found," said Tamir. "We know that he's a famous nuclear scientist, he's worked in the Weizmann most of his life, and he's been mentioned as a possible Nobel Prize candidate. We should have more on him within minutes. I've told them to call us immediately."

"There must be something going on," Yadin said. "A security leak most likely; otherwise why are the Mossad out in his house?"

"I thought you might have found out more," said Tamir, looking at him.

Yadin shook his head. "You know those boys," he said. He held on to the dashboard. "Get everything you can on Shenlavi," Yadin said, "background, where he comes from. If we're dealing with a nut, we may have to involve his family. Get a description of him. He's got to be somewhere in Jerusalem — he only parked the car within the last two hours. Get his description out to the civil guard as well. We want to talk to Dr. Shenlavi without delay."

The driver made a left turn onto Wolfsohn.

"Yadin."

Uzi Yadin turned around. Golda Levy was holding up a phone with a long extension. She raised her eyebrows.

"Hello," said Yadin taking the instrument. As the van roared uphill, past a white building on the right, the chief superintendent's back stiffened. *"Shalom, hamefaked,"* he said. "Good morning, sir."

Amos Suchovolsky parked the white Escort at the far curb. A police tow truck was removing the last of the other parked cars, leaving the green Volvo alone, its polished paintwork gleaming in the hot midmorning sun. At the bottom of the road a large silent crowd stood behind police barriers; uphill, there were TV crews, police cars, and additional barriers. Ben Joel got out and saw the unmistakable shape of the mobile HQ van pull to a stop.

"Yadin's here," he said.

Suchovolsky nodded as they walked across the road to the parked car. Like prizefighters sizing up the opposition, the two policemen slowly circled the green Volvo, their trained eyes examining each lock, each window, scrutinizing their adversary as it sat quietly *in situ*, trying to garner any scrap of information that might tilt the balance in their favor and better their chances of going home to their families that night.

Amos Suchovolsky took out a small flashlight, then went down on his knees and, rolling onto his back, carefully levered himself underneath the chassis.

Ben Joel's eyes went to the car's interior. It was well kept and empty of any personal items. The dark fabric of the upholstery was clean; a few dead flies lay on the rear shelf, under the electrically heated back window. His eyes went to the dashboard.

"Amos," he called softly, and pointed. Sucholovsky got to his feet. On the long indication strip, running above the rev-counter and speedometer, a red light shone brightly.

There were steps on the road behind them and the two men turned. *"Shalom."*

Uzi Yadin smiled briefly and patted each man lightly on the back.

"There's a light shining on the dash," Joel said. "Could be a radio of some sort."

"Not could be, it is," Yadin replied. "There's an FM transmitter out in his house in Mevasseret and it's beaming right to this car. We've just been told."

Ben Joel licked his lips and reappraised the four-door car.

"Where's the antenna?" he asked. "How is the signal received?"

The two men from Mahleket-Hachabala and their chief superintendent began a fresh scrutiny of the Volvo. As one, they all stopped at the back window.

"It has to be," said Uzi Yadin. "There's no other possibility."

"What are we dealing with here, chief?" asked Suchovolsky. "Is this a hoax, is this guy a nut, or what?"

"We'll know shortly, I hope," Yadin replied. "We're pulling out all the stops to evaluate the car owner, his possible motives — and we're trying to find him. He only parked here in the last couple of hours."

"Why the radio beam?" Joel asked. "If the bomb is radio-controlled, it would be detonated by turning on the frequency. The frequency is already on."

"It could be a hoax," Suchovolsky suggested. "'Red light in parked car beside Knesset.' That's sure to cause a scare and is worth a bit of coverage."

"But that would invariably be accompanied by a terrorist warning," Yadin said. "Besides, this is not a terrorist, at least as far as we know — this is an Israeli nuclear physicist."

He scratched his head as Yoran Tamir came down the hill from the mobile HQ.

"That was Derech Shechem again," he said having greeted the two bomb-squad men. Derech Shechem contained the office of the inspector general of the Israeli police. "This thing is going out on nationwide TV. The old man is having a fit. He wants to know why we can't neutralize the car and get it the fuck out of here."

The three men looked uphill at the TV cameras that were bearing their faces across Israel.

"Those marchers are also making demands," Tamir said. "They're saying any unnecessary delay is being fabricated to screw up their plans. Some of them are even alleging that we've instigated this whole thing."

Ben Joel took a deep breath and shook his head. Uzi Yadin looked at him. "It's up to you," he said quietly, "you're in charge."

Joel nodded. "Okay," he said. He looked at the car. "Whatever it is, it's probably in the trunk. The inside looks clean. I know those cars; there's not enough room up front, under the hood. The body is clean, the chassis is clean . . ." Suchovolsky nodded. ". . . it's got to be in the trunk." He took another deep breath. "It could well be booby-trapped; there's no point in fiddling around with keys." He looked at the other men. "We'll blow the trunk," he said.

"Okay," said Yadin, nodding.

"And Uzi," said Joel, "see if you can get those TV guys back down the other side of the hill. It's bad enough on your own out there, but TV coverage . . ."

"*Beseder,*" Yadin said, "consider it done." He turned to Tamir. "And get those marchers back another five hundred yards," he snapped. "I don't care what they say. Get them down below the museum."

"What about the museum itself?" Tamir asked. "Do you want it evacuated?"

Yadin looked at Joel, who shook his head.

"No need," Yadin replied. "Even if it's a real biggie, it won't go that far. Just keep crowds from coming up, that's all." He looked Ben Joel straight in the eye. "Good luck!" he said. "I'll be in the van listening. See you later."

Ben Joel smiled briefly, then he walked back to the car and began to assemble his equipment.

In the kitchen in Mevasseret, Matt Blaney wiped coffee from his mustache. In front of him the TV screen showed a newsflash from the scene at the Knesset. It was 11:06.

"How long do you think he'll be downstairs?" Matt asked. Perin, the forensic chief, had asked that he and his assistant be allowed to work alone in the garage. Yanni Israel shrugged.

"I wonder where our friend Shenlavi is?" Matt said.

"There are four hundred men in the Jerusalem police force," Yanni replied, "and a reserve civil guard of eight thousand. He only left home this morning." He smiled wryly. "They should be able to find him."

There was the sound of feet on the wooden steps from the garage. The fractured door flew open and the black-bearded figure of Jean-Claude Perin burst into the room. His eyes were wild; his face, normally pale, was the color of chalk.

"Out of my way!" he cried as he snatched up the phone.

Matt was on his feet. He could see the policeman had to steady his finger before he found each number.

"Yadin! Yadin!" shouted Perin into the receiver as the call was answered. There was a pause as the Frenchman was put through. There followed an excited babble in Hebrew, incomprehensible to the American. Matt saw Yanni's eyes widen. With a final cry Perin threw down the phone and, without pausing, ran back down the steep steps.

"What the hell was all that about?" Matt asked. Yanni was looking at him, a strange expression on his face.

"It's what Perin has found downstairs," he said, speaking as if he did not believe what he said. "He thinks it's in the car." He looked at Matt and shook his head. "He's found traces of plutonium."

Ben Joel inspected the small circle of plastic explosive around the trunk lock and the tiny detonator that he had positioned in it. He was wearing a large silver helmet with an adjustable visor. He ran back to a distance of fifty yards, following the line of gray wire that snaked along the road and ended behind the Escort in a six-volt battery wired to a switch. When he turned the switch, the positive and negative poles of the battery would unite and voltage would shoot to the detonator, causing the plastic chemical to explode. Positioned as it was on the outside of the trunk lid, the object was to dismantle the lock without touching the bomb inside. If it was booby-trapped, however, the result might be quite different.

It was eerily quiet on Eli'ezer Kaplan. The police had brought the crowd down below the Israel Museum, out of sight. Uphill, the massed police cars, patrols, armed guards, and the mobile HQ could be seen. Yadin had sent the TV crews back out of range. Besides the Escort, the only other vehicle in this part of the wide street was the statutory red-and-white ambulance, which followed the bomb squad everywhere.

Ben Joel reached the Escort and crouched down behind it. He picked up the switch and looked at Amos Suchovolsky, who was kneeling beside him.

"On the count of zero?" he said.

Suchovolsky nodded.

"Three, two, one . . ."

"*Ben!*"

Ben Joel's eardrums vibrated in the heavy helmet that he still wore. His hand had half-turned the black, detonating switch.

"Ben." It was Yadin's voice from the uphill HQ bellowing directly into the receiver within the helmet. "Ben, don't blow it! Don't blow it! Do you understand?"

The voice was raw with urgency.

"*Hevanti,*" Joel said. "Understood." He looked across at Suchovolsky, who had heard nothing and was frowning. "Why, Uzi?" Joel asked. "What's the matter?"

There was no reply and he looked uphill. Suchovolsky followed his gaze. The lone figure of Uzi Yadin was running down the empty street toward them.

At Damascus Gate he could hear the Moslem prayers, which had just begun. The wide footpath and steps down to the entrance of the ancient city teemed with people: Arabs mingled with tourists, who stepped around reclining camels and asses tethered to the railings. Women with timeless faces sat on the ground, propped against the rock of the walls, their greens sprawled out on sheets set before them. He passed two old Arabs crouched over a checkerboard, using pencil sharpeners for counters.

The traffic in east Jerusalem was unmindful of the Jewish *Shabbat.* As the sun approached its zenith in the clear sky there was a swell of noise, which contrasted sharply with the quiet city he had just come through. He continued east on Sultan Sulieman Street. The cars on the road beside him were jammed tight — up front, two Arab boys pushing high trolleys of bread had collided and were frantically gathering up their scattered loaves. To his right the walls rose massively, built at this point on the huge rock outcroppings of Jerusalem itself. He passed a group of four civil guards in green battle fatigues, who had paused for a smoke, their M-1 carbines stacked at their feet. A blind Arab with a white stick like a shepherd's crook attempted to cross the busy road; one of the guards took him over. Sun danced on the face of a sign for the Rockefeller Museum. A bus honked impatiently.

It had been the same a year ago to the day. The scant cortège had taken almost thirty minutes to get through. There were three caskets: one, full-size brown oak, and two shorter white ones. He insisted they all travel together, the two children on either side of their mother. There were some flowers; he and Levi rode in the car behind, Levi simultaneously proud and bewildered in his crisp uniform. In Mevasseret later that evening the inexplicable speed of events had left Dr. Shenlavi totally confused. Forty-eight hours earlier he had piggy-backed Rachel down the high lawn, and when he had slipped, the seat of his trousers became bright green from the sweet grass. They had lain there overcome with laughter.

"*Yoseph!*" Her voice, even when attempting to be stern, still sounded like tinkling spring water over the stones of the Galilee. "Do you know the time?"

"Again, Papa, again!" the child squealed.

"Come on, little one," he said, "you have an early start in the morning. You are going all the way to Haifa. Your big sister is already in bed."

"No she isn't!" the child cried.

At the door in her nightdress stood an older girl with long blond hair. She had his father's hair. And his looks — tall, fine cut, most unlike a Jew. His father . . . Dr. Shenlavi frowned.

"Won't you come too, Papa?" she asked, coming over and gathering his funny face in her hands.

"The next time, my love," he said, still sitting on the grass.

"Papa must work, Ruth," her mother said. "He must work for Eretz Israel."

A little wind blew a breath of chill over Mevasseret.

At that moment the children put their arms around his neck. "Come on, you two," their mother said. "Kiss Papa goodnight."

It was then that he caught her eye. It was the instant of total understanding, the second in time when no further mysteries existed, when the whole complex circuitry of life was at long last dazzlingly comprehensible. For a few brief hours the fire had kindled; then it had forever died.

Dr. Shenlavi passed Herod's Gate, at the very northerly point of ancient Jerusalem. He clutched the briefcase and began to smile. When Levi got home they would begin a new life together. He was looking into a sweeping valley, the last vestige of vegetation before he reached the desert. On the upward-sloping hill were clusters of houses and sparkling new hotels; but to the right and toward the highest point, the sun danced on the polished white stone of a hundred thousand tombs. Midday was approaching. A light wind blew the wailing prayers of Islam in little gusts over the towering walls and up toward the sleeping Jewish cemetery.

Unmindful of the blaring traffic, Dr. Shenlavi stepped off the curb and made his way into the Valley of Kidron.

Golda Levy leaned forward and tapped Yadin on the shoulder.

"Derech Shechem again," she said.

"Yes, sir," Yadin responded, taking the phone. He was sitting at a round table in the van; Yanni Israel sat opposite him, Tamir to one side. They had been joined by an Israeli radionics expert from the Signal Corps and a dumpy white-haired man of about seventy who looked strangely out of place in the company. On the table lay several open files, photographs, and a detailed wiring diagram of a Volvo 340 D. On the other end of the line the Mafkal, the inspector general of the Israeli's police, was speaking in a low, controlled voice.

"I have been on to the prime minister's office, Yadin," he said quietly. "Checks are being made in Dimona as we speak, and we should know their outcome within minutes. What is the up-to-date situation on the ground?"

Downhill, Yadin could see Ben Joel positioning a portable X-ray machine like a forklift truck beside the green Volvo.

"We're about to have a look inside, sir," he said. "We'll know more shortly."

"What about the civil guard?" asked the inspector general.

"They are mobilizing at this moment," Yadin replied.

Special call-up codes had been broadcast over Jerusalem radio and TV for the past thirty minutes. Now groups of armed men and women were assembling at prearranged points around the city.

"You're going to evacuate the city?" asked the Mafkal.

"Not immediately," replied Yadin. "Not until first we know exactly what we're faced with — and second, not until everyone is in place. We're keeping a very tight lid on it for obvious reasons — we don't want a full-scale panic on our hands." Despite the fan in the ceiling of the van, Yadin was sweating freely. "There is a comprehensive procedure for our civilian population in the event of a nuclear attack," he said. "It pivots on the civil guard and so, on a nationwide basis. I suggest you put phase one of it into effect, on a red-alert basis, within the next ten minutes."

"Agreed," said the Mafkal. "I'll give the order. In the meantime, what are you doing?"

"Trying to come to grips with what we might have," Yadin said. "This is a first for all of us. It is of the most extreme importance that Shenlavi himself is found." He paused. "What are your impressions, sir?"

"It bears all the signs of an unbalanced mind," the Mafkal said quietly. "And in the hands of a psychopath a nuclear device, however crude, could be a source of ineffable tragedy."

Yadin's mouth went dry. Even in the '67 war he had never heard his superior worried.

"I'll keep in touch," Yadin said and handed back the telephone. He turned to the table.

"Well," he said grimly, "what have we got?"

"A very disturbed man, a nut," said Yanni. "I've been going over his personal history — it looks as if his mind has been blown."

The white-haired man nodded his agreement.

"This American, who is he?" Yadin asked.

Yanni had left Matt Blaney sitting in the car, on the other side of the police barriers.

"It seems he's an insurance investigator," Yanni replied. "It's too detailed to get into it now, but he stumbled onto our Dr. Shenlavi from a completely different direction."

The door to the mobile HQ opened and Ben Joel stepped in. His face looked drawn. He was carrying a number of small X-ray prints. The men looked at him as he sat down.

"It's a bomb all right," he said simply, putting the prints on the table. "It's a steel container of some sort, very professionally secured and tamped. Amos is X-raying the rest of the car right now, but if the trunk is anything to go by, we're in a lot of trouble."

He pointed to a print that showed a maze of tiny lines representing steel wires. "Everything is wired into this main cable here," he indicated, "which is itself connected to the lid of the metal container. If there's plutonium in there and we had blown the lock five minutes ago, we'd be in orbit by now."

"Can we not ascertain whether there is plutonium in there or not?" Yadin asked.

"From the little I know," Ben Joel replied, "one of the characteristics of plutonium is that its presence is very difficult to detect."

Again there was nodded agreement from the small, dumpy man.

They all looked downhill again to the parked green car. Yadin clenched his teeth to contain the primeval urge to stand up and get as far away from where he now was, as quickly as possible.

"Yadin."

Golda Levy was holding the telephone again.

"Mafkal," she mouthed.

Yadin took the receiver and listened in silence. the other men in the cramped van stared at his face; beneath the tan and the leathery texture a pallor of whitish gray had crept in.

"*Beseder,*" he said and handed back the phone. He looked around the table. "That was the Mafkal," he said. "The people from Dimona have come through. They've checked their production records against their holding tanks." It was totally quiet. Outside a bird sang. "They're missing an unspecified quantity of plutonium nitrate."

They all looked at each other. Even the pretty telephone operator was staring, her big eyes wide.

"Good God," said Ben Joel. "We're sitting on a nuke."

Yadin closed his eyes to concentrate, then opened them again.

"Dr. Wucher," he said to the small man, "there is probably a plutonium bomb in the car. Please outline what can happen."

Dr. Wucher, a distinguished elder member of the Israeli scientific community, bowed his head slightly. If he felt any annoyance at having been interrupted from his weekly family meal in his apartment in the Old City, he did not show it. He spread his hands.

"The first problem for the bomb maker is to achieve fission," he began. "However, if we assume that in this case the maker is extremely capable — which he is: I taught him many years ago — let us assume there is at least a ten percent chance that fission will occur."

He paused, a reasonable smile on his pale lips. "You could expect, for example," he said, "in twenty to twenty-five pounds of plutonium, which would be the amount I would use, just above critical mass, an explosion equivalent to a hundred thousand tons of TNT." He shrugged unworriedly, as if the matter was still firmly in the academic realm. "In such a case the surface burst would vaporize anything within a square mile of the center as heat equal to that at the sun's core is produced in the fraction of a millionth of a second needed to achieve fission." He looked calmly around at the rigid faces. "Everybody, everything made up of biological components within the immediate blast area will be instantly destroyed. In addition there will be extensive damage for up to three miles, caused by flash burns, radiation, and the simple, mechanical hazards created by buildings falling on people. The blast wave — a moving wall of highly compressed air — will move away from ground zero — that is, from here — and through all of Jerusalem, much faster than the speed of sound." The scientist shook his head sadly. "The damage to the environment, the ecology, the earth for hundreds of miles around will be inestimable," he said. He looked at Yadin. "There is an expression to describe the situation, Superintendent," he said. "It is Armageddon."

Yadin had difficulty in drawing his breath. His hands were in fists.

"Thank you, Doctor," he said. He turned to the Signal Corps officer. "Hartal," he said, "we have a nuclear bomb in a car." He swallowed. "How does he detonate it?"

Shimnel Hartal was no more than thirty-five. He had longish, thick, deep brown hair and a flourishing handlebar mustache. He was bronzed and fit and wore an open-necked khaki shirt with the single oak-leaf shoulder epaulet of *rav-seren,* a major in the army of Israel. He picked up a pen.

"Normally," he said, "the terrorist gets himself a small radio transmitter and receiver. In countries like Germany, you can buy equipment off the shelf, even in toy shops, for example — model boats, model airplanes all work on a transmitter/receiver principle. Your terrorist simply wires up the receiver to a solenoid, an elementary electrical circuit. It's wired in turn to a battery and the battery to some sort of firing device, lead azide perhaps, which is implanted in high explosive. The terrorist just turns on the frequency and initiates the chain. Bang!"

The men at the table all looked at him.

"In the event of finding such a device in time," Hartal continued, "then the options are pretty numerous. Essentially you can disarm the device by preventing the signal from getting to it: put the bomb in a steel container; if it's a car drive it into a tunnel or throw a wire-mesh Faraday cage around it — any of them will stop the frequency."

The Signal Corps major allowed his forefinger and thumb to stroke the spikes of his mustache.

"This one, however, looks particularly ingenious," he said. "We have a car, a bomb, and an FM radio signal beaming into the car on a constant basis. The only logic is that he's done it in reverse. He's wired the solenoid so that the radio signal is keeping it closed — there's therefore no way I can think of to disarm it without having access to the car itself." He picked up an X-ray print. "You see this little fellow here?" He was pointing with his pen to a rectangular black object on the left-hand side of the trunk. "You asked how he was going to detonate — well, here's how. My money says that what you see here is a conventional switching device called a multiplexer. It's actually a small radio receiver itself. You see this wire running from it to the bomb?"

The men stared, transfixed.

"He'll send a separate signal to the multiplexer, probably from a hand-held transmitter. The multiplexer is probably set up to block the main FM frequency coming from Mevasseret. The solenoid will open and . . ."

For a long moment no one said a word.

"We'll have to move it," Ben Joel said, "out into the desert someplace."

Yanni shook his head. "You think this guy is going to hang around while you move his car into the desert?" he asked. "This thing could go up literally any second." He ran his hand through his hair. "Our only hope is to find the man."

Major Hartal cleared his throat. "We could try grabbing it with a claw slung underneath a chopper," he said. "We could have it out of the area in fifteen minutes."

"He's thought of that as well."

They all turned at the voice. Amos Suchovolsky was standing at the van door. He was breathing hard, having run uphill, and was holding a fresh batch of X-ray prints. "The car is wired like a piano," he said. "Its got internal sensors, some sort of antitilt bowl under the lid, even wires running through the shock absorbers. You lift that car and she'll go off."

All the men looked at Uzi Yadin.

"We need more information," he said in a quiet voice. "We have no response to this." He looked to Dr. Wucher. "We've heard your explanation, but can you put a nuclear bomb in the trunk of a car like this and make it go off?"

The aging doctor smiled and nodded.

"First he has to achieve fission," he said. "But even if he doesn't and there's plutonium involved, he'll send enough poison up into the atmosphere to kill everyone in Jerusalem anyway."

"There are some senior military people on their way here from the Negev," Yadin said. He looked around him. "I understand they've recommended that we evacuate the city immediately."

Yoram Tamir, who had been speaking quietly into a telephone at the rear of the van, cleared his throat. His face was gray. "That was headquarters," he said. "The military is about to broadcast a full mobilization call — war footing. The PM has evacuated his office and is in emergency session with the cabinet." He paused. "They're pretty sure that if there is a nuclear explosion in Jerusalem, that Syria and probably Egypt will use the opportunity, within ten minutes, to try to finish us off."

Yadin slammed his fist into his palm. "Shenlavi must be found," he said. He stared out the window and down Eli'ezer Kaplan Street at the innocent family car. "This city hasn't been evacuated since the time of David," he said to no one in particular.

On the wall of the van the clock showed eleven-thirty.

At the northerly end of Eli'ezer Kaplan, Matt Blaney sat in the passenger seat of the car. On the dashboard in front of him was a brown folder containing photographs of Yoseph Shenlavi and a three-page report handwritten in Hebrew. Yanni's car was parked inside the police cordon; TV crews and spectators had been pushed even farther back. Now Matt looked out and saw small groups of blue-capped policemen standing around, chatting quietly. There was a nervousness, a noticeable edginess about their manner: the magnitude of what was happening three hundred yards up the road was beginning to get through.

Suddenly Yanni's face appeared at the window.

"What's happening up there?" asked Matt. Israel shook his head. He glanced quickly around.

"It's not too good," he said quietly. "They're pretty sure our friend here has assembled some sort of nuclear bomb in the back of his car."

"Christ," Matt said as Yanni leaned in and took the file. "Can they defuse it?"

"That's what they are working on," Yanni said. "However, its a state-of-the art booby trap; they can't touch it or it will blow. It's been assembled by a genius." He tapped the file. "They need the same genius to make it safe."

"No one has found him?"

Yanni shook his head grimly.

"No," he said. "We've got a lunatic walking around Jerusalem about to blow us into orbit and there's nothing we can do to stop it." He bit his lip. "This won't stop here, you know," he said. "It's just the sort of excuse our military needs to take things into their own hands." He looked at Matt. "Look, my friend," he said, "there is no reason for you to be here." He reached into a pocket and handed Matt the car keys. "Confidentially," he said, "the police chief is just about to issue orders for the evacuation of Jerusalem. In an hour — if we last that long — there's going to be panic like you've never seen. There is no need for you to be here. Take the car. Drive west toward Tel Aviv as fast as you can. The prevailing wind is west to east. There's a good chance you'll escape any fallout if you go now. There is a shelter in a place called Shefayim, half an hour north of Tel Aviv, on the coast. Go there and stay there until this thing is over." He put out his hand. "Good luck," he said. He straightened up and turned to walk back up the hill.

"Yanni."

Yanni stopped. Matt had got out. He was holding the brown folder.

"Yanni, when you were up at the command post, I read this file on Shenlavi," Matt said. "It's in Hebrew, I could only make out the dates."

Yanni nodded slowly. "So . . ." he said.

"This date here," Matt said, opening the file and pointing, "it's to-day's date, but a year ago." He could see the Israeli's eyes narrow. "What happened a year ago on this date, Yanni?" asked Matt. "What does the file say?"

Yanni took the folder. He read it, then looked at Matt.

"This day one year ago," he said haltingly, "Shenlavi's wife and chil-dren were buried together."

"Where?" Matt asked, shaking his head.

"In Har-Ha-Zetim," Yanni whispered, "the ancient Jewish burial ground on the Mount of Olives."

Matt did not want to believe what he was hearing. "When, Yanni?" he cried. "What time?"

The Israeli went back to the file. "At twelve noon," he said, his eyes wide.

Matt looked at his watch.

"That's in fifteen minutes' time," he said. "This cemetery, where is it?"

"Get in!" shouted Yanni, wrenching the car door open.

The nearby policemen turned as the car's engine screamed into life. Yanni reversed in a sweeping arc and then crashed it into first as they tore down the street, away from the Knesset. They passed the white building on the left, which housed the office of Israel's prime minister.

"The Mount of Olives!" cried Yanni. "It's in east Jerusalem, one of the highest points of the city. It overlooks everything."

They ran the lights at Herzel and took the intersection into Zalman on two wheels. A green-uniformed group of the civil guard were gathered at the corner. They saw the small white Fiat careering toward them. Their leader, a man with a long beard, put up his hand and stepped out. Yanni missed him by all of six inches and weaved speedily downhill and then to the right.

They were now screaming east on Yafo, a one-way street whose traffic runs west, out of Jerusalem to Tel Aviv. Mercifully, the traffic was still light, since it was the *Shabbat.* Yanni kept to the right-hand side and flew across half a dozen intersections. Somewhere behind them a police siren could be heard.

"Watch out!"

A taxi pulled slowly from a road to the right and turned toward them. Yanni lurched left, around its front. Another car coming up Yafo screeched onto the sidewalk and straight into the window of a shop. The siren was getting closer.

"*Hara!*" cried the Mossad agent. He gunned on, oblivious to the horns and flashing lights of the few cars coming toward him. They were approaching a major intersection. The traffic was thickening. Matt could see the high walls of Old Jerusalem. A line of cars, waiting at a red light to come up Yafo, was blocking them. Yanni threw the small car up on the left-hand curb — there was a scraping sound as the back axle caught the stone lip — and they squeezed between an upright pole carrying overhead wires and the front of a house.

"Time?" shouted Yanni as they bounced down again and hurtled downhill, ancient Jerusalem to their right.

"Nine minutes," Matt replied. He had opened a map and had found the Mount of Olives. "Where are we now?" he called.

"Damascus Gate," cried Yanni, "but look behind. Fools!"

A hundred yards behind a blue-and-white Sierra, its light flashing, was closing. Matt could see the passenger-side policeman lean out, a firearm in his hand. The lights at Damascus Gate were red. Waiting cars were three deep. A camel led by an Arab was making its stately crossing of the road, which traditionally led to Syria. Yanni put his hand on the horn and yanked the steering wheel left. The Fiat crashed up onto the narrow sidewalk. Arabs threw themselves into doorways. Women screamed. Matt ducked as they plowed into a tall, stainless-steel trolley carrying shelves of bread. The trolley leaped up and hit the windshield hard before skidding off again. There was a dull cracking, and a spreading web of ruptured glass began to slowly grow outward from the point of impact.

"Shit!" cried Yanni again as they hit the road proper. Matt looked back and saw the patrol car blaring its way through the traffic. He looked at his watch. There remained seven minutes before noon. He was vaguely aware of blaring Islamic prayers, broadcast behind the thick city wall to their right.

They ran another set of lights and passed a sign for the Rockefeller Museum. They came to a major intersection, the northern corner of the old city. A long tour bus ground uphill ahead of them. Slamming the aching car into second, Yanni drove straight across the road, clipping the front fender of the bus as he did so. It lurched to a standstill. Matt could hear the police car closing in again.

Now they were scorching almost vertically downhill. In a station to their left, red fire engines were mobilizing. The Fiat charged on. Across the bed of the valley, they were now climbing the uphill east-side gradient. The windshield's disintegration was nearly complete and Yanni was peering through an unaffected area, the size of a handkerchief.

"Mount of Olives!" he yelled, pointing up and to their right.

In the middle distance Matt could see the far shoulder of the mountain; at first sight it looked like a mountain of chalk — but on closer inspection the chalk turned into numerous white blocks as the outline of a hundred thousand Jewish tombs came into view, shimmering in the noonday heat-haze of the lovely day.

Two more tour buses crawled the steep hill in front of them, out of the Valley of Kidron, up to the mount. Yanni tried to pull out. He swore viciously. A long line of cars bedecked with bunting and streamers was descending. Behind and downhill the police car had crossed the valley. Matt saw the policemen leaning out again. A black Mercedes passed them, then a car containing an Arab girl in a white dress, smiling radiantly out at the world, her family packed around her and in the procession behind.

Halfway up the narrow hill Yanni decided to go for it. He swung the Fiat out and roared up beside the bus in a space too small for a bicycle. There was a hideous scraping. The bus stopped and the black Mercedes on the other side swung right and smashed into the back of the car carrying the bride. Somehow they got through. Matt heard a hiss — they had punctured the Fiat's radiator. The top of the road was a T-junction. Yanni rolled right. Matt looked back and saw that the patrol car was through. The passenger cop was now leaning out and readying something at them. There was a clatter as he squeezed off half a dozen rounds from the Uzi, but the Fiat was around the bend and the shells hit the road behind them, flicking its dusty surface like tracers. Arabs were sitting in groups on the right-hand curb. Some of them got to their feet at the sound of the gun and stared as the battered white Fiat screamed on up the mount. Clouds of steam now gushed from the car's radiator. Yanni had opened his window and was forced to lean out in order to see. At the top of the road there were shops with cars and buses parked around. There were the usual groups of curious Arabs. By Matt's watch it was three minutes to noon. He heard the Uzi speak again, and simultaneously Yanni cried out.

They were past the shops and at a winding, narrow part of the road. The Fiat lurched first to one side and then to the other. They were now very definitely out of control. Matt tried to grab the wheel. He was conscious of blood. They caught the fender of a parked car and dragged it with them before they powered into a wall, the two cars sprawled across the road. Yanni was grimacing in pain.

"Go on!" he gasped. "There's very little time!"

Behind them the patrol car had drawn up and was being besieged by an angry Arab crowd who had identified with the Fiat. Matt kicked his door open. Yanni had been hit across his left shoulder and down the back of his left arm. With his good hand he pointed forward and again winced.

Matt Blaney began to run.

He was standing on the parapet of a high wall overlooking his city. On the mountainside sweeping below him were the final homes of the kindly couple who had brought him to Eretz Israel and made him their son; of his daughters, who had been taken in innocence and would never feel the sun's heat on their faces again; and of his wife, who had reached into the cavern of his soul and touched the wound that had coldly lain there for so long. The white tombs, fashioned by masons out of the very stone of Yerushalyim, swept to the base of the hill and all along it. Across the valley he was looking directly down on the golden Dome of the Rock, the El Aqsa Mosque, over the Temple Pinnacle and on outward over the the monotheistic capital of the world. On the horizon he could make out the outline of Qiryat Ben Gurion, which he had left two hours before.

Dr. Shenlavi's sore face was set in its smile. He had prayed, and his prayers had at last been answered for Levi. He zipped open the briefcase and took out the small, black plastic transmitter with its silver switch. He put the briefcase at his feet, then held the box in both his hands. He looked at his watch. It was a minute to noon. He could hear police sirens and shouting in the background.

It would happen in less than a minute. "*O Lord,*" he began, "*Thou hast taken us from the desert. Thou has marked us out as Thy special people. Thine anger and fury is most terrible.*"

His hand went to the switch.

Matt was forty yards ahead of the pursuing policeman. The other one had stayed with Yanni. Matt rounded the downhill corner, his breath caught in his chest. Before him the road forked: to the left there was an observation area for tourists, to the right and below it there was another deck, with a stone-walled parapet built around the steep mountain. Matt took the left. There were buses and cars parked there, and camels lay on the footpath. Arabs touted postcards and souvenirs. Matt looked frantically around, his chest heaving. The policeman was shouting something. The crowd began to turn. On Matt's watch the second hand swept toward twelve.

Then he saw him.

On the parapet of the wall at the next level, a slightly built man was standing alone, up on the wall, holding something in front of him.

"*Shenlavi!*"

At the sound of Matt's bellowing voice, it seemed the whole hillside froze. The tourists, the policemen, even the sharp-eyed Arabs all stared. Then slowly their gaze went downhill. The man on the wall slowly turned. Deep lines of worry and bewilderment were creased into his brow. His mouth both smiled and puckered. The sun picked up the water welling into his eyes. Matt scrambled over the higher wall ledge and jumped. The rocks beneath were uneven, and as he landed his ankle turned under his weight. He cried out. He saw the weeping man begin to turn back toward the city.

All at once the deep bells of a Christian church began to toll over the valley.

"*Shenlavi, don't do it!*" roared Matt.

He jumped again. He was on the lower parapet. He saw the man hold the box out in front of him, like an offering. He saw the mouth twisting as it repeated its words over and over.

"Levi," he heard, "Levi, Levi." The sinews in the thin arms stiffened.

With a great cry Matt leaped. The two bodies hurtled into space.

Then there was only darkness.

WEDNESDAY: P.M.

45 HE COULD FEEL THE HEAT ON HIS FACE. SLOWLY HE opened one eye, then the other. The scene presented to them was breathtaking: an endless vista of parched hills, miles of them folded one upon the other to infinity, with the air above bent and dancing in the shimmering heat, and at the very limit of vision the outline of blue mountains that might have been a thousand miles away. A shaft of pain split his head, causing him to close his eyes. Slowly he eased them open again.

"Are you awake?"

There was no mistaking the voice.

"What time is it?"

"It's three, Wednesday afternoon," said Jim Crabbe.

Matt tried to move; he winced in pain.

"You're in plaster, you stupid mother," said Crabbe. "Lie still."

The door opened and a plump nurse came in. She inspected Matt and adjusted the pillows behind his head. Then she helped him to a sip from a water glass.

"The doctor will be here shortly," she said, smiling.

"What happened?" asked Matt, sinking back. His face was as pale as the turbanlike head bandage. He rubbed his face and gasped.

Jim Crabbe laughed. "It'll grow again," he said. "Up to this morning you had a tube up your nose. Besides, it makes you look at least a year younger."

Matt rubbed his naked upper lip. He looked at Crabbe. "What happened?" he asked again, weakly.

Jim Crabbe drew a chair along the shiny linoleum floor to the bedside and sat down so that Matt could see him. His wizened face floated in and out of focus. "In a nutshell," Jim said, "you probably averted the incineration of Jerusalem. That guy Shenlavi was crazy: he had a trunkful of plutonium in his car ready to blow up the Knesset. They eventually defused it by using liquid nitrogen."

"Liquid nitrogen?" Matt managed to ask.

"That's right," said Crabbe. "They froze the car at something like minus two hundred. A battery isn't viable at that level — it can't produce any energizing voltage. The bomb couldn't detonate."

Crabbe looked out the window. "The Israelis are playing down the whole incident. They're now saying the bomb was too crude to go off, but from what I hear, if it had detonated there was a very good chance of its achieving fission."

Matt licked his dry lips and Crabbe helped him to water. He felt an irresistible need to sleep.

"Shenlavi . . . ?"

"He's dead," Jim said. "You and he fell twenty-five feet onto solid concrete. He broke his neck under you and somehow cushioned your fall. You've badly cracked your skull and smashed three vertebrae." He grinned. "Otherwise you're fine." He looked at the bandaged figure, the eyes closed. "The miracle is that Shenlavi didn't detonate the bomb when you took him. The radio transmitter flew out of his hand and landed the right way up — in a pile of builder's sand in the cemetery."

Matt heard Jim's voice as if from a great distance. A weight descended on him; he opened his eyes again after what could have been a minute or an hour. Crabbe still sat there. Outside the whole landscape seemed to move.

"Galatti," Matt said, as Jim returned the water glass to the bedside table.

"Galatti?" responded Crabbe. "He's gone, disappeared, they think to his island retreat down in the Caribbean. His corporation has gone down the tubes and nearly taken a big Wall Street bank, First Transnational, with it. It's been the lead news story for the past four days. Both the Justice Department and the New York police are trying to extradite the bastard, but it looks as if they may have their work cut out."

"And the insurance money?"

Jim Crabbe spread his hands. "Lloyd's isn't going to pay a cent. I tried to catch you at the Paris airport to tell you. Barbara Galatti left a description with her lawyers of exactly how they had killed the horse. They told Dijon, the stud manager, for example, that it was some sort of a hormone shot that they wanted kept quiet about — he didn't know a thing. And the only reason that Galatti kept delaying his permission to operate on the poor animal was that he was afraid surgery might save it." Jim gave a big smile.

"Cathy was right," he said, "and I saved myself one big one."

Matt tried to prop on an elbow. "How is Cathy?"

"She's in great shape," said Crabbe, glancing at his watch. "Now you just lie back or I'll go get that very fat nurse to come sit on you."

Jim's smiling face swam in and out of Matt's vision. He raised his right hand, a ton weight, to scratch his nose; he felt the fabric of the bandage on his thumb. He put his elbow beneath him again.

"What about Laurens?" he asked, his pulse suddenly quickening.

Crabbe stood up and went to rest himself against the window ledge. "That's one of the damnedest things," he said. "When you spoke to him from New York, did he mention anything about coming out here on vacation?"

Matt blinked to concentrate. "Vacation?"

Crabbe's white head was nodding. "That's right. Last Saturday when you were having your fun and games in Jerusalem, there was a pile-up near the Dead Sea. It's in the papers. A truck, full of heavy rocks, ran over a car being driven by a French tourist. It killed him outright, took his head off. He was your Mr. Laurens."

Matt was aware that his mouth was hanging open.

"I swear I'll call her if you don't lie back," Jim said.

"Jim," said Matt, his chest heaving, "Laurens was a Nazi. He tried to strangle me last night, but the Mossad agent got to him first."

Jim's face was understanding, smiling. "Last night?" he said gently. "A Nazi?"

Matt shook his head in agitation. "Galatti's a Nazi as well, a war criminal," he said. "He escaped capture after the war by using Shenlavi as his cover. Jim, the Israelis were on the point of lifting him from New York."

"Matt, Galatti's an Argentinian," Crabbe said benevolently. "Now lie back, goddammit."

Matt's breaths came in gasps as his head went back on the pillows.

"Explain, then, the Galatti–Shenlavi relationship," he panted. "How, for example, did Shenlavi come to give Galatti the phosphorus?"

"The authorities here have found letters, correspondence, in Shenlavi's house," Jim replied patiently. "They're not saying too much about it obviously, because it's such an embarrassment to them, but Shenlavi was evidently in financial difficulties. His sale of phosphorus to Galatti was only one of a number of transactions to different people and organizations. Evidently they now think he was trying to sell plutonium to the Syrians before he went off his head and decided to nuke the Knesset."

Matt was gulping for air. "Jim," he said, "I don't know what they're telling you here, but nuking the Knesset was probably Galatti's idea, not Shenlavi's. Why don't you go talk to Yanni, the Mossad guy who shot Laurens, the guy who was Barbara Galatti's lover in New York? He'll confirm what I'm saying. I'm sure it was all Galatti's idea."

The sun was now in decline and the landscape behind Jim Crabbe had begun to creep with gray. Matt was dizzy.

"Take it easy, okay?" Crabbe was saying with one of his better fatherly smiles.

Matt came up on both elbows. "Jim," he said in exasperation, "who do you think drove the car that got me up to the Mount of Olives? It was Yanni. They shot him right across the back. He's got to be in some hospital."

Jim Crabbe stood up. "Now I am going to call the nurse," he said. He bent over the figure in the bed. "Look," he said, "you're hallucinating, for Christ's sake, relax, you're in shock." He shook his head. "They said this might happen."

"I'm not in shock."

"Matt Blaney, I love you like a son," Jim said. "Would I tell you a lie? You're a hero, goddammit, but you drove the car up the Mount of Olives your goddamn self. There are several hundred witnesses."

At that moment the door opened and the nurse came in followed by a man in uniform; his hair and beard were gray-flecked and he had a magnificent, curving nose.

"This is Chief Superintendent Yadin," the nurse said to Crabbe. Matt closed his eyes and lay back. The effort to fight was too much. "He's in quite severe shock," came Crabbe's voice. "He doesn't seem to know what happened."

"We all owe him a lot." The voice was deep, the English broken. "We will do anything we possibly can."

Matt suddenly sat up in the bed. He raised a hand to fend off the nurse. "Just a minute!" he cried. He looked at the policeman. "My friend here thinks I'm making it up," he said. "Would you please tell him that a man exists called Yanni, who is an Israeli agent, and that Carlo Galatti is a war criminal wanted by your country."

The policeman came to the bed. A smile played on his lips, but his dark eyes could have signified anything. He put his hand lightly on Matt's shoulder. "For the man who may have saved my city," he said, "my friend, I will tell anyone anything you want."

Matt's eyes were wide. He barely felt the nurse slip the hypodermic into his arm.

He opened his eyes a fraction. It was dark outside. In the lights of the room he cold see Jim Crabbe look at his watch and walk to the door. There were footsteps. It was the same nurse, followed by someone taller. Matt could not keep his eyes open. He felt the nurse's hand behind his head.

"Come on," she whispered, "it's someone very special."

Her voice floated down to Matt like the echo in a dream. She propped him under her strong arm. His head swam luxuriously.

"Come on," she urged him.

With the effort of a lifetime he made himself focus. Fireworks went off all over his constellation.

"Matt?" The voice was strong, her hand firm. "It's me." She bent over him. Matt felt her lips on his. "Cathy," he murmured, as Jim Crabbe tiptoed from the room.

EPILOGUE

THE SAND WAS STILL WARM BENEATH HIS FEET AS HE HUGGED THE shadow of the beachhead. Left and inland were bedroom blocks of a hotel; as the night before, their windows were dark, their occupants retired.

He followed the contour, feeling his way along the headland with a sure touch. The equipment on his back caused him no problem: two small twin-tanks, harnessed with canvas straps that partly concealed the fresh, livid scar across his left shoulder blade and down the back of that arm.

There was a noise five yards dead ahead. He froze. Reflexively his hand went to the knife on his bare leg. He saw one figure get up, then another. Laughing quietly, the couple walked arm in arm, back to the hotel through the towering coconut trees.

He moved on, the land's sweep bringing him to the ocean. He could hear the slap of water on the wet sand, then its sucking ebb as it swept away.

The fence was of small mesh, nine feet high, sloping inward at its top and finished with a double strand of barbed wire. He felt it lightly, then used it to guide himself to the water. For an instant the moon peeped; he could see the fence line, straight as a rifle's barrel, running into the water.

Noiselessly he put down the dark bag and opened its neck. Taking out a jar, he smeared the grease all over his body. Then he stepped into the tide and, bending, wetted the rubber fins before he slipped them over his feet. Next was the face mask. He spat on it, inside, rubbed his saliva all around, rinsed it off, then fitted the black straps over his dark-brown hair. He took a short snorkel and shoved it up beside his ear, under the strap. Last came a pair of heavy pliers fitted in a holder, which he strapped to the calf of his other leg. Bending, he poked the bag through the wire, tying it once around. Reaching back for the regulator, the diver blew through it once to test; then he turned, and walking backward, his right hand on the fence, he slowly disappeared into the water. As the Caribbean came to the level of his chin, the moon again darted out for an instant and caught the reflection of his dark brown eyes through the glass of the face mask.

The fence ended at two fathoms. Using a pencil flashlight, the diver finned over, scanning the seabed; an abundance of colored fish darted to the light's edge then banked away in shadowy shoals. He turned inshore. He had come to coral where, as he glided over, nests of sea urchins braced and quivered.

The diver was in the private bay. Quenching the light he rose silently to the dark surface and broke it with no more ripple than an inshore grouper rising. He checked his watch, the phosphorescent digital gleaming green.

It was time.

As if reacting to a signal, a boat came to life and hummed slowly out into the bay. The diver could hear voices and the engine as it skimmed the water within thirty yards of him. There was the sound of an anchor splashing and more voices, then suddenly two great beams of light shafted down into the depths.

Tucking his chin into his chest, the diver vanished.

The beams were to the diver's right, playing on the sleeping coral. He could make out the anchor line curling upward in the lights and the bottom of the boat tossing overhead in the light swell. Keeping well outside the pool of brightness, he finned left, not daring to use his light. For the second time in minutes his left hand touched wire. He guided himself, following the descent of the cage on its reef, his hand probing and searching, half his attention on the powerful lights in case they should swivel and hit him.

He felt, stopped, and turned fully to check. He ran both his hands up and found the hinges; he ran his fingers over and found the three bolts, fastened by short padlocks, firmly locked. Reaching down his leg, the diver took the pliers and went to work.

The descending figure was visible from the moment it broke the surface. The diver leaned with all his strength on the final padlock and it snapped, sending a sharp sting up his arm; he hung the padlock loosely back, then, his eyes on the figure high above, he darted behind a craggy outcropping that in the daytime would reflect a hundred colors.

The figure was alone, coming down slowly, long legs first, like a tadpole in a bottle. He glided unhurriedly down until he reached the anchor; checking it, he made his way to the cage. He remained at all times in the center of the two beams of converging light, finning with the light glued to him, so that it seemed to the diver as if the beam did not follow him but was actually the force that made him move. Droves of little fish swam beside the figure as if with familiarity. A silent silver barracuda swam into the beam for a look, then backed away. He crossed a magnificent turtle, some yellow trumpet-fish, and brightly colored red and white mollusks before reaching the cage. The diver behind the outcropping stared. The body was still thin but fit. A gaunt hand was unstrapping a knife from its leg holster. The white hair, once blond, streamed out behind the head. Suddenly light pierced the cage. He rattled the wire mesh loudly.

From the depths of the wire prison a black shape charged. With all the force of its powerful body the hammerhead struck the wire. The white haired man stood his ground and rattled again. He failed to notice that the impact had caused the nearby gate to fall ajar. Such an opportunity was not missed by the shark. With a lithe flick of its supple tail, it was through. The tormentor stared, unable to immediately comprehend the dramatically altered odds. He kicked as he tried to rise. He was alone in the light beam. He had made ten feet when the hammerhead caught him. There was an explosion of blood. His right hand flailed uselessly with the knife. The shark was tossing it head back and forth like a cat with a rat. Blood and gristle in suspension filled the beams of light. Then they were gone.

Silently the diver made his way back across the bay, gliding along just above the bed of the ocean. It was not until he had rounded the point and made his way up to his beach that he broke the surface.

Stripping off his face mask, he took the regulator from his mouth and sat waist deep in the warm tide. The moon still flitted in and out of cloud. He breathed in deeply the sweet fragrance of the night.

"*Zedek*," he said to the sky. "*Zedek*."

It was the Hebrew word for justice.